# WILD HORSES
# &
# 10lb PENALTY

## Also by Dick Francis in Pan Books

THE SPORT OF QUEENS
(autobiography)

LESTER: The Official Biography

DEAD CERT
NERVE
FOR KICKS
ODDS AGAINST
FLYING FINISH
BLOOD SPORT
FORFEIT
ENQUIRY
RAT RACE
BONECRACK
SMOKESCREEN
SLAY-RIDE
KNOCK DOWN
HIGH STAKES
IN THE FRAME
RISK
TRIAL RUN
WHIP HAND
REFLEX
TWICE SHY
BANKER
THE DANGER
PROOF
BREAK IN
BOLT
HOT MONEY

THE EDGE
STRAIGHT
LONGSHOT
COMEBACK
DRIVING FORCE
DECIDER
COME TO GRIEF
TO THE HILT
FIELD OF 13
SECOND WIND
SHATTERED

DICK FRANCIS
OMNIBUS ONE:
Long Shot, Straight,
High Stakes

DICK FRANCIS
OMNIBUS TWO:
Forfeit, Risk, Reflex

DICK FRANCIS
OMNIBUS THREE:
Slay-Ride, Banker, Proof

DICK FRANCIS
OMNIBUS FOUR:
Enquiry, Rat Race, Smokescreen

SID HALLEY OMNIBUS:
Odds Against, Whip Hand,
Come to Grief

Dick Francis has written over forty-one international best-sellers and is widely acclaimed as one of the world's finest thriller writers. His awards include the Crime Writers' Association's Cartier Diamond Dagger for his outstanding contribution to the crime genre, and an honorary Doctorate of Humane Letters from Tufts University of Boston. In 1996 Dick Francis was made a Mystery Writers of America Grand Master for a lifetime's achievement and in 2000 he received a CBE in the Queen's Birthday Honours list.

# Dick Francis

# WILD HORSES
# &
# 10lb PENALTY

PAN BOOKS

*Wild Horses* first published 1994 by Michael Joseph.
First published by Pan Books 1995
*10lb Penalty* first published 1997 by Michael Joseph.
First published by Pan Books 1998

This omnibus edition published 2005 by Pan Books
an imprint of Pan Macmillan Ltd
Pan Macmillan, 20 New Wharf Road, London N1 9RR
Basingstoke and Oxford
Associated companies throughout the world
www.panmacmillan.com

ISBN 0 330 44092 6

1 3 5 7 9 8 6 4 2

A CIP catalogue record for this book is available from
the British Library.

Printed and bound in Great Britain by
Mackays of Chatham plc, Chatham, Kent

# WILD HORSES

We are spirits clad in veils;
Man by man was never seen;
All our deep communing fails
To remove the shadowy screen.

*Christopher Pearse Cranch*
*(1813–1893)*

# CHAPTER ONE

Dying slowly of bone cancer, the old man, shrivelled now, sat as ever in his great armchair, tears of lonely pain sliding down crepuscular cheeks.

That Tuesday, his last, his stringy grip on my wrist tightened convulsively in a long silence while I watched his mouth tremble and move in abortive struggles to speak.

'Father.' The words finally wavered out; a whisper, desperate, driven by ultimate need. 'Father, I must make my confession. I must ask . . . absolution.'

In great surprise and with compassion I said, 'But . . . I'm not a priest.'

He paid no attention. The feeble voice, a truer measure of affairs than the fiercely clutching hand, simply repeated, 'Father . . . forgive me.'

'Valentine,' I said reasonably, 'I'm Thomas. Thomas Lyon. Don't you remember? I've come to read to you.'

He could no longer see newsprint or anything straight ahead, though peripheral vision partly remained. I called in more or less every week, both to keep him up to date with the racing columns in the newspapers and also to let his beleaguered and chronically tired old sister go out for shopping and gossip.

I hadn't actually read to him on that day. When I arrived he'd been suffering badly from one of his intermittent bouts of agony, with Dorothea, his sister, feeding him a teaspoon of liquid morphine and giving him whisky and water to help the numbness work faster.

He hadn't felt well enough for the racing papers.

'Just sit with him,' Dorothea begged. 'How long can you stay?'

'Two hours.'

She'd kissed me gratefully on the cheek, stretching on tiptoes, and had hurried away, plump in her late seventies, forthright in mind.

I sat as usual on a tapestry stool right beside the old man, as he liked the physical contact, as if to make up for sight.

The fluttery voice persisted, creeping effortfully into the quiet room, determined and intimate. 'I confess to God Almighty and to Thee, my Father, that I have sinned exceedingly ... and I must confess ... before ... before ...'

'Valentine,' I repeated more sharply, 'I'm not a priest.'

It was as if he hadn't heard. He seemed to be focusing all the energy left in him into one extraordinary spiritual gamble, a last throw of hell-defeating dice on the brink of the abyss.

'I ask pardon for my mortal sin ... I ask peace with God ...'

I protested no more. The old man knew he was dying; knew death was near. In earlier weeks he had

2

discussed with equanimity, and even with humour, his lack of a future. He had reminisced about his long life. He'd told me he had left me all his books in his will. Never had he made any mention of even the most rudimentary religious belief, except to remark once that the idea of life after death was a load of superstitious twaddle.

I hadn't known he was a Roman Catholic.

'I confess,' he said, '. . . that I killed him . . . God, forgive me. I humbly ask pardon . . . I pray to God Almighty to have mercy on me . . .'

'Valentine . . .'

'I left the knife with Derry and I killed the Cornish boy and I've never said a word about that week and I accuse myself . . . and I lied about everything . . . *mea culpa* . . . I've done such harm . . . I destroyed their lives . . . and they didn't know, they went on liking me . . . I despise myself . . . all this time. Father, give me a penance . . . and say the words . . . say them . . . *ego te absolvo* . . . I forgive your sins in the name of the Father . . . I beg you . . . I beg you . . .'

I had never heard of the sins he was talking about. His words tumbled out as if on the edge of delirium, making no cohesive sense. I thought it most likely that his sins were dreams; that he was confused, imagining great guilt where none lay.

There was no mistaking, however, the frantic nature of his repeated plea.

'Father, absolve me. Father, say the words . . . say them, I beg you.'

I couldn't see what harm it would do. He was desperate to die in peace. Any priest would have given

3

him absolution: who was I cruelly to withhold it? I was not of his faith. I would square it later, I thought, with my own immortal soul.

So I said what he wanted. Said the words, dredging them from memory. Said them in Latin, as he would clearly understand them, because they seemed less of a lie that way than in bald English.

'*Ego te absolvo*,' I said.

I felt a shiver through my body. Superstition, I thought.

I remembered more words. They floated on my tongue. '*Ego te absolvo a peccatis tuis, In nomine Patris et Filii et Spiritus Sancti. Amen.*'

I absolve you from your sins in the name of the Father and of the Son and of the Holy Ghost. Amen.

The greatest blasphemy of my life to date. God forgive me my sin, I thought.

The dreadful tension subsided in the old man. The rheumy near-blind eyes closed. The grip on my wrist loosened: the old hand fell away. His face relaxed. He faintly smiled, and then grew still.

Alarmed, I felt for a pulse under his jaw and was relieved to feel the threadlike beat. He didn't move under my touch. I shook him a little, but he didn't wake. After five minutes I shook him again, more strongly, without results. Indecisively then I got up from my seat beside him and, crossing to the telephone, dialled the number prominently written on a notepad nearby, to get through to his doctor.

The medicine man was less than pleased.

'I've told the old fool he should be in hospital,' he

said. 'I can't keep running out to hold his hand. Who are you, anyway? And where's Mrs Pannier?'

'I'm a visitor,' I said. 'Mrs Pannier is out shopping.'

'Is he groaning?' demanded the doctor.

'He was, earlier. Mrs Pannier gave him some pain-killer before she went out. Then he was talking. Now he's in a sort of sleep from which I can't seem to wake him.'

The doctor growled a smothered curse and crashed his receiver into its cradle, leaving me to guess his intentions.

I hoped that he wouldn't send a wailing ambulance with busy figures and stretchers and all the rough paraphernalia of making the terminally ill feel worse. Old Valentine had wanted to die quietly in his own bed. Waiting there, I regretted my call to the doctor, thinking that I'd probably set in motion, in my anxiety, precisely what Valentine had most wanted to avoid.

Feeling stupid and remorseful, I sat opposite the steadily sleeping man, no longer on a stool beside him but in a more comfortable armchair.

The room was warm. He wore blue cotton pyjamas, with a rug over his knees. He sat near the window, bare branched trees outside giving promise of a spring he wouldn't know.

The study-like room, intensely his own, charted an unusual journey through time that had begun in heavy manual labour and ended in journalism. Born the son of a farrier, he'd been apprenticed to the forge in childhood, working the bellows for his father, skinny arms straining, young eyes excited by the noise and the

5

fire. There had never been any question that he would follow in the trade, nor had he in fact veered towards anything else until his working pattern had long been settled.

Framed fading photographs on his walls showed a young Valentine with the biceps and pectorals of a giant, a prizewinning wielder of brute power with the wide happy grin of an innocent. But the idyll of the village smithy under the chestnut tree had already long gone. Valentine in his maturity had driven from job to job with his tools and portable brazier in a mobile working van.

He had for years shod a stableful of racehorses trained by my grandfather. He'd looked after the feet of the ponies I'd been given to ride. He had seemed to me to be already a wise man of incredible age, though I knew now he'd been barely sixty-five when I was ten.

His education had consisted of reading (the racing newspapers), writing (bills for his customers) and arithmetic (costing the work and materials so that he made a profit). Not until his forties had his mental capacity expanded to match his muscles. Not until, he'd told me during the past debilitated weeks, not decisively until in his job he was no longer expected to make individual shoes to fit the hooves of horses, but to trim the hooves to fit mass-produced uniform shoes. No longer was he expected to hammer white-hot iron bars into shape, but to tap softer metals cold.

He had begun to read history and biography, at first all to do with racing but later with wider horizons. He had begun in shy anonymity to submit observations and anecdotes to the newspapers he daily studied. He wrote about horses, people, events, opinions. One of the papers had given him a regular column with a regular salary and room to grow a reputation. While still plying his original trade, Valentine had become an honoured institution in print, truly admired and enjoyed for his insights and his wit.

As physical strength waned, his journalistic prowess had grown. He'd written on into his eighties, written into semi-blindness, written indeed until four weeks earlier, when the cancer battle had entered the stage of defeat.

And this was the old man, amusing, wise and revered, who had poured out in panic an apparently unbearable secret.

'I killed the Cornish boy . . .'

He must have meant, I thought, that he was blaming himself for an error in his shoeing, that by some mischance a lost nail in a race had caused a fatal accident to a jockey.

Not for nothing had Valentine adopted often enough the doctrine of doing things thoroughly, quoting now and then the fable of the horseshoe nail. For want of a nail the kingdom was lost . . . little oversights led to great disasters.

A dying mind, I thought again, was scrambling old small guilts into mountainous terrors. Poor old Valentine. I watched him sleep, the white hair scanty on his scalp, big blotchy freckles brown in his skin.

For a long time, no one came. Valentine's breathing grew heavier, but not to the point of snoring. I looked round the familiar room, at the horses' photographs I'd come to know well in the past few months, at the framed awards on the dark green wall, the flower-printed curtains, the worn brown carpet, the studded leather chairs, the basic portable typewriter on an unfussy desk, the struggling potted plant.

Nothing had changed from week to week: only the old man's tenure there was slipping away.

One wall, shelved from floor to ceiling, held the books that I supposed would soon be mine. There were years and years of form books listing thousands upon thousands of bygone races, with a small red dot inked in beside the name of every horse Valentine had fitted with racing shoes for the test.

Winners, hundreds of them, had been accorded an exclamation mark.

Below the form books there were many volumes of an ancient encyclopaedia and rows of glossily jacketed life stories of recently dead racing titans, their bustling, swearing vigour reduced to pale paper memories. I'd met many of those people. My grandfather was among them. Their world, their passions, their achievements were passing into oblivion and already the young jockeys I'd star-gazed at ten were grandfathers.

I wondered who would write Valentine's life story, a worthy subject if ever there was one. He had steadfastly refused to write it himself, despite heavy prompting from all around. Too boring, he'd said. Tomorrow's world, that was where interest lay.

Dorothea came back apologetically half an hour late and tried without success to rouse her brother. I told her I'd phoned the doctor fruitlessly, which didn't surprise her.

'He says Valentine should be in hospital,' she said.

'Valentine refuses to go. He and the doctor swear at each other.' She shrugged resignedly. 'I expect the doctor will come in time. He usually does.'

'I'll have to leave you,' I said regretfully. 'I'm already overdue at a meeting.' I hesitated. 'Are you by any chance Roman Catholic?' I asked. 'I mean ... Valentine said something about wanting a priest.'

'A priest?' She looked astounded. 'He was rambling on all morning ... his mind is going ... but the old bugger would never ask for a *priest*.'

'I just thought ... perhaps ... last rites?'

Dorothea gave me a look of sweet sisterly exasperation.

'Our mother was Roman Catholic, but not Dad. Lot of nonsense, he used to say. Valentine and I grew up outside the Church and were never the worse for it. Our mother died when he was sixteen and I was eleven. A mass was said for her. Dad took us to that but it made him sweat, he said. Anyway, Valentine's not much of a sinner except for swearing and such, and I know that being so weak as he is he wouldn't want to be bothered by a *priest*.'

'I just thought I'd tell you,' I said.

'You're a dear to come here, Thomas, but I know you're mistaken.' She paused. 'My poor dear boy is very ill now, isn't he?' She looked down at him in concern. 'Much worse?'

'I'm afraid so.'

'Going.' She nodded, and tears came into her eyes. 'We've known it would come, but when it happens ... oh, dear.'

'He's had a good life.'

9

She disregarded the inadequate words and said forlornly, 'I'll be so *alone*.'

'Couldn't you live with your son?'

'No!' She straightened herself scornfully. 'Paul is forty-five and pompous and domineering, though I hate to say it, and I don't get on with his wife. They have three obnoxious teenagers who switch on deafening radios all the time until the walls vibrate.' She broke off and smoothed her brother's unresponsive head fondly. 'No. Me and Valentine, we set up home here together when his Cathy died and my Bill passed on. Well, you know all that ... and we always liked each other, Valentine and me, and I'll miss him. I'll miss him something awful, but I'll stay here.' She swallowed. 'I'll get used to being alone, same as I did after Bill went.'

Dorothea, like many elderly women, it seemed to me, had a resolute independence that survived where youth quaked. With help once daily from the district nurse, she'd cared for her failing brother, taking on ever more personal tasks for him, exhausting herself to give him comfort and painkillers when he lay awake in the night. She might mourn him when he'd gone, but her dark-rimmed eyes showed she was much overdue on rest.

She sat down tiredly on the tapestry stool and held her brother's hand. He breathed slowly, shallowly, the sound rasping. Fading daylight from the window beside Valentine fell softly on the aged couple, light and shadow emphasising the rounded commitment of the one and the skeletal dependence of the other, the hovering imminence of death as plain as if the scythe had hung above their heads.

I wished I had a camera. Wished indeed for a whole camera crew. My normal day-to-day life involved the catching of emotion on the wing, the recording of ephemeral images to illumine a bedrock of truth. I dealt with unreality to give illusion the insight of revelation.

I directed films.

Knowing that one day I would use and re-create the quiet drama before me, I looked at my watch and asked Dorothea if I might use her telephone.

'Of course, dear. On the desk.'

I reached Ed, my earnest assistant, who as usual sounded flustered in my absence.

'It can't be helped,' I said. 'I'm running late. Is everyone there? Well, get some drinks sent over. Keep them happy, but don't let Jimmy have more than two G and Ts, and make sure we have enough copies of the script alterations. Right? Good. See you.'

I regretted having to leave Dorothea at such a time, but in fact I'd squeezed my visit into a day's schedule that had made no provision for it, keeping the promise I'd given week after week.

Three months back, in the preliminary pre-production stage of the film I was currently engaged on, I'd called to see Valentine as a brief matter of courtesy, a gesture to tell him I remembered him in the old days in my grandfather's time, and had always admired, even if from a distance, his emergence as a sage.

'Sage my foot!' He'd disclaimed the flattery but enjoyed it all the same. 'I can't see very well these days, boy. How about reading to me for a bit?'

He lived on the outer edge of Newmarket, the town long held to be the home and heart of the horseracing industry worldwide. 'Headquarters', the racing press called it. Fifteen hundred of the thoroughbred élite rocketed there over the windswept training gallops and over the wide difficult tracks, throwing up occasional prodigies that passed their glorious genes to flying generations of the future. An ancient wealth-producing business, the breeding of fast horses.

I was on the point of leaving when the front doorbell rang, and to save Dorothea's tired feet I went to answer it.

A short thirtyish man stood there looking at his watch, impatient.

'Can I help you?' I asked.

He gave me a brief glance and called past me, 'Dorothea?'

Regardless of fatigue, she appeared from Valentine's room and said miserably, 'He's . . . in a coma, I think. Come in. This is Thomas Lyon who's been reading to Valentine, like I told you.'

As if on an afterthought, she finished the introduction, flapping a hand and saying, 'Robbie Gill, our doctor.'

Robbie Gill had red hair, a Scots accent, no small-talk and a poor bedside manner. He carried a medical bag into Valentine's room and snapped it open. He rolled up the ill man's eyelids with his thumb and pensively held one of the fragile wrists. Then he silently busied himself with stethoscope, syringes and swabs.

'We'd better get him to bed,' he said finally. No mention, I was glad to notice, of transportation to hospital.

12

'Is he – ?' Dorothea asked anxiously, leaving the question hovering, not wanting an affirmative answer.

'Dying?' Robbie Gill said it kindly enough in his brusque way. 'In a day or two, I'd say. Can't tell. His old heart's still fairly strong. I don't really think he'll wake again, but he might. It partly depends on what he wants.'

'How do you mean, what he wants?' I asked, surprised.

He spent time answering me, chiefly, I thought, for Dorothea's sake, but also from a teacher's pleasure in imparting technical information.

'Old people,' he said, 'very often stay alive if there's something they particularly want to do, and then after they've done it they die quite quickly. This week I've lost a patient who wanted to see her grandson married. She went to the wedding and enjoyed it, and was dead two days later. Common occurrence. If Valentine has no unfinished business, he may slip away very soon. If he were looking forward to receiving another award, something like that, it might be different. He's a strong-willed man, and amazing things can happen even with cancer as advanced as this.'

Dorothea shook her head sadly. 'No awards.'

'Then let's get him settled. I've arranged for Nurse Davies to pop in late this evening. She'll give him another injection, which will keep him free from any pain he might feel in the night, and I'll come back first thing in the morning. The old codger's beaten me, dammit. He's got his way. I'll not move him now. He can die here at home.'

13

Dorothea's tears thanked him.

'It's lucky he has you,' the doctor told her, 'and don't make yourself ill.' He looked from her to my height assessingly, and said, 'You look bigger than both of us. Can you carry him? Nurse Davies would help Dorothea move him, as she always does, but usually he's conscious and doing his best to walk. Can you manage him on your own?'

I nodded. He weighed pathetically little for a man once as strong as horses. I lifted the tall sleeping figure in my arms and carried him from his armchair, through the small hallway and into his bedroom, putting him down gently on the white sheet, revealed by Dorothea peeling back the bed covers. Her brother's breathing rasped. I straightened his pyjamas and helped Dorothea cover him. He didn't wake. He had died inside, I thought, from the moment he'd believed in his absolution.

I didn't bring up the subject of a priest again with Dorothea, nor mention it to the doctor. I was convinced they would both disapprove of what I'd done, even though Valentine was now dying in peace because of it. Leave things as they are, I decided. Don't add to Dorothea's distress.

I kissed the old lady, shook hands with the doctor and, offering vague but willing future help, drove back to my job.

Life, both real and imaginary, was loud and vigorous along in Newmarket, where the company I was working for had rented an empty racing stable for three months,

14

paying the bankrupt owner-trainer enough to keep him in multiple child-support for ever.

Although a good hour late for the script conference I'd called for five-thirty, I did not apologise, having found that the bunch I was working with took regrets for weakness, chiefly because of their own personal insecurities. It was essential, I understood, for them to regard me as rock, even if to myself sometimes the rock was no more durable than compressed sand.

They were gathered in what had earlier been the dining-room of the trainer's cavernous house (all the furniture having passed under the bankruptcy hammer, satiny green and gold striped paper still adhering richly to the walls) and were variously draped round a basic trestle table, sitting on collapsible white plastic garden chairs on the bare boards of the floor. The drinks provided by the catering unit had barely lasted the hour: no one on the production was wasting money on excess comfort.

'Right,' I said, ousting Ed from the seat I wanted, halfway along one side of the table, 'have you all read the alterations and additions?'

They had. Three were character actors, one a cinematographer, one a production manager, one a note-taker, one an assistant director – Ed – and one a scriptwriter that I would like to have done without. He had made the current changes at my reasonable insistence, but felt aggrieved. He believed I was intent on giving a slant to the story that departed at ninety degrees from his original vision.

He was right.

It was disastrously easy to make bad horseracing

pictures and only possible to do it at bankable level, in my view, if racing became the framing background to human drama. I'd been given the present job for three reasons that I knew of, the third being that I'd previously stood two animal stories on their heads with profitable results, the second being that I'd been trained in my work in Hollywood, the source of finance for the present epic, and – first – that I'd spent my childhood and teens in racing stables and might be considered to know the industrial terrain.

We were ten days into production: that is to say we had shot about one-sixth of the picture, or, putting it another way, roughly twenty minutes a day of usable footage, whole cloth from which the final film would be cut. We'd been scheduled to finish in sixty working days; a span of under ten weeks, as rest days were precious and rare. I, as director, decided which scenes would actually be shot on which days, though I'd made and distributed in advance a programme to which we mostly adhered.

'As you've seen,' I said generally, 'these changes mean that tomorrow we'll be shooting on the railed forecourt in front of the Jockey Club's headquarters in the High Street. Cars arrive and leave through the gates. The local police will help with the town's regular traffic from eleven to twelve only, so all of our arrivals and departures will be condensed into that time. The Jockey Club has agreed to our using their front door for entering and leaving shots. The internal sets have, of course, been built here in this house. You three ...' I said to the actors, '... can put some useful poison into your various encounters. George, be sly. Iago stuff. You are now secretly engineering Cibber's downfall.'

The script-writer moaned, 'That's not the right interpretation. I don't like what you've made me do. Those two are very good friends.'

'Only up to the point of opportunist betrayal,' I said.

Howard Tyler, the writer, had already complained about small earlier changes to the producer, to the accountant and to the film company's top brass, all without getting me fired. I could put up with his animosity in the same way as I stifled irritation at his round granny glasses, his relentlessly prim little mouth and his determination to insert long pointless silences where only movement and action would fill cinema seats. He adored convoluted unspoken subtleties that were beyond most actors' powers. He should have stuck to the voluminous moody novels whence he came.

His book that he'd adapted for the present film was loosely based on a real-life story, a twenty-six-year-old Newmarket racing scandal very successfully hushed up. Howard's fictional version purported to be the truth, but almost certainly wasn't, as none of the still living real participants had shown the slightest sign of indignant rebuttal.

'You'll find you each have a plan of the Jockey Club forecourt,' I said to the meeting. They nodded, flicking over pages. 'Also,' I went on, 'you've a list of the order of shooting, with approximate times. The three cars involved will be driven to the forecourt first thing in the morning. Get all the crews alerted so that lights and cameras can be set up where shown on the plan. If everyone's willing and ready, we should finish well before the daylight yellows. Any questions?'

There were always questions. To ask a question meant attention had been paid and, as often happened, it was actors with the smallest parts who asked most. George, in this case, wanted to know how his character would develop from the extra scene. Only, I enlightened him, as just one more factor in Cibber's troubles. Cibber, eventually, would crack. Bang. Fireworks. Cibber said 'Hallelujah' gratefully. George compressed his mouth.

'But they were friends,' Howard repeated stubbornly.

'As we discussed,' I said mildly, 'if Cibber cracks, your motivation makes better sense.'

He opened his little mouth, saw everyone else nodding, folded his lips and began to act as if Cibber's cracking was all his own idea.

'If it rains tomorrow,' I said, 'we'll shoot the internal Jockey Club scenes instead and trust it will be fine on Thursday. We are due to complete the first Newmarket segment on Saturday. On Sunday, as I think you know, we're shifting the horses forty miles west to Huntingdon racecourse, to the stable block there. Actors and technicians will travel early on Monday morning. Rehearsals, Monday, from noon onwards. Shooting Tuesday to Friday, return here the following weekend. Ed will distribute times and running order to everyone concerned. OK? Oh, and by the way, the rushes from yesterday are fine. Thought you'd like to know. It was a lot of hard work, but worth it.'

The resulting sighs round the table came from relief. We'd spent the whole day in the stable yard, the human action in the foreground taking place against a background of routine equine life. Never could rows of horses have been mucked out, fed, watered and groomed more times in any twelve hours before: but we had enough shots in the can to give the fictional stable unending life.

The script meeting over, everyone dispersed except a tall thin, disjointed-looking man in an untidy beard and unkempt clothes whose unimpressive appearance hid an artistic confidence as unassailable as granite. He raised his eyebrows. I nodded. He slouched in his seat and waited until all backs but our own had passed through the door.

'You wanted me to stay?' he asked. 'Ed said.'

'Yes.'

Every film with any hope of acclaimed success needed an eye that saw all life as through a camera lens. Someone to whom focus and light intensities were extrasensory dimensions taken for granted. His title on the credits might variously be 'cinematographer' or 'director of photography'. I'd had a mathematical friend once who said he thought in algebra: Moncrieff, director of photography, thought in moving light and shadows.

We were used to each other. This was our third film together. I'd been disconcerted the first time by his surrealist sense of humour, then seen that it was the aquifer of his geysers of visual genius, then felt that to work without him would leave me nakedly exposed in the realm of translating my own perceptions into revelations on the screen. When I told Moncrieff what I wanted an audience to understand, he could instinctively slant a lens to achieve it.

We had once staged a 'last rites' scene for a man about to be murdered by terrorists: the ultimate cruelty of that wicked blasphemy had been underscored by Moncrieff's lighting of the faces; the petrified victim, the sweating priest and the hard men's absence of mercy. *Ego te absolvo* ... it had brought me death threats by post.

On that Tuesday in Newmarket I asked Moncrieff, 'Have you seen the railings outside the Jockey Club? The ones enclosing the private parking forecourt?'

'Tall and black? Yes.'

'I want a shot that emphasises the barrier qualities. I want to establish the way the railings shut out everyone but the élite. Inside can be mandarins of racing. Outside, *hoi polloi.*'

Moncrieff nodded.

I said, 'I also want to give an impression that the people inside, Cibber and George, the Jockey Club members, are themselves prisoners in their own conventions. Behind bars, one might say.'

Moncrieff nodded.

'And,' I said, 'take a five-second shot of the hinges of the gates as they open, also as they close.'

'Right.'

'The scene between Cibber and George is shot to begin with from outside the bars. I'd like the zoo aspect made clear. Then track the lens forward between the railings to establish where they're standing. The rest of that conversation is in close-ups.'

Moncrieff nodded. He seldom made notes while we talked, but he would write a meticulous worksheet before bedtime.

'We're not being judgmental,' I said. 'Not heavy handed. No great social stance. Just a fleeting impression.'

'A feather touch,' Moncrieff said. 'Got you.'

'Contributing to Cibber's crack-up,' I said.

He nodded.

'I'll get Howard to write that crack-up tomorrow,' I said. 'It's mainly a matter of a shift in intensity from the calm scene already in the script. Howard just needs to put some juice into it.'

'Howard's juice is watered cranberry.' Moncrieff picked up a vodka bottle from among the drinks clutter, and squinted at it against the light. 'Empty,' he commented morosely. 'Have you tried vodka and cranberry juice? It's disgusting.'

Howard drank it all the time.

'Howard,' Moncrieff said, 'is radioactive waste. You can't get rid of it safely.'

He knew as well as I did that Howard Tyler's name on the billboards would bring to the film both the lending library audience and attention from upmarket critics. Howard Tyler won prestigious prizes and had received honorary doctorates on both sides of the Atlantic. Moncrieff and I were considered lucky to be working with such a luminous figure.

Few authors could, or even wanted to, write screenplays of their own novels: Howard Tyler had been nominated for an Oscar at his first attempt and subsequently refused to sell his film rights unless the

21

package included himself. Moncrieff and I were stuck with Howard, to put it briefly, as fast as it seemed he was stuck with me.

Our producer, bald, sixty, a heavily-framed American, had put a canny deal together for the company. Big-name author (Howard), proven camera wizard (Moncrieff), vastly successful producer (himself) and young but experienced director (T. Lyon), all allied to one mega-star (male) and one deliciously pretty new actress; money spent on the big names and saved on the actress and me. He, producer O'Hara, had told me once that in the matter of acting talent it was a waste of resources employing five big stars in any one picture. One great star would bring in the customers and maybe two could be afforded. Get more and the costs would run away with the gross.

O'Hara had taught me a lot about finance and Moncrieff a lot about illusion. I'd begun to feel recently that I finally understood my trade – but was realistic enough to know that at any minute I could judge everything wrong and come an artistic cropper. If public reaction could be reliably foretold, there would be no flops. No one could ever be sure about public taste: it was as fickle as horseracing luck.

O'Hara, that Tuesday, was already in the Bedford Lodge Hotel dining-room when I joined him for dinner. The studio bosses liked him to keep an eye on what I was doing, and report back. He marched into operations accordingly week by week, sometimes from London, sometimes from California, spending a couple of days watching the shooting and an evening with me going over the state of the budget and the time schedule.

Owing to his sensible planning in the first place, I hoped we would come in under budget and with a couple of days to spare, which would encourage any future employers to believe I had organisational talents.

'Yesterday's rushes were good, and this morning went well,' O'Hara said objectively. 'Where did you get to this afternoon? Ed couldn't find you.'

I paused with a glass of studio-impressing Perrier halfway to my mouth, remembering vividly the rasping of Valentine's breath.

'I was here in Newmarket,' I said, putting down the water. 'I've a friend who's dying. I called to see him.'

'Oh.' O'Hara showed no censure, registering the explanation as a reason, not an excuse. He knew anyway – and took it for granted – that I'd started work at six that morning and would put in eighteen hours most days until we'd completed the shooting.

'Is he a film man?' O'Hara asked.

'No. Racing . . . a racing writer.'

'Oh. Nothing to do with us, then.'

'No,' I said.

Ah, well. One can get things wrong.

23

# CHAPTER TWO

Fortunately, Wednesday morning dawned bright and clear, and Moncrieff, his camera crew and I attended sunrise beside the Jockey Club's railings, filming atmospheric barred shadows without interruption.

Rehearsals with Cibber and George went fine later on the forecourt, with Moncrieff opening his floods easily to supplement the sun, and with me peering through the camera eyepiece to be sure the angles brought out the spite developing in the erstwhile 'best friends'. By eleven we were ready for the cars-inward, cars-outward sequences, the police cooperating efficiently in the spirit of things.

Our male mega-star, laconic as always, patiently made three arrivals behind the wheel of a car, and four times uncomplainingly repeated a marching-to-execution type entrance through the hallowed front door, switching his fictional persona on and off with the confidence and expertise of a consummate pro. As if absentmindedly, he finally gave me an encouraging pat on the shoulder and left in his personal Rolls-Royce for the rest of the day.

At midday we broke for a well-earned hour for lunch.

O'Hara came in the afternoon to watch George's Iago touch (which basically needed only an inoffensive 'cool it just a bit' comment from myself) and sat smiling in a director's chair for most of the afternoon. O'Hara's hovering smile, though I was never sure he knew it, acted like oil on the actors and technical crews, getting things smoothly done: under his occasional slit-eyed disapproval, problems geometrically increased.

After wrapping things up on the forecourt O'Hara and I went together to Bedford Lodge for an early beverage (light on alcohol, following the film company's overall puritanical ethos), discussing progress and plans before he left fantasy land en route for marketing and advertisement in offices in London. Making the film was never enough; one had to sell the product as well.

'I see you've booked our chief stuntman for Monday,' he said casually, standing to leave. 'What do you have in mind?'

'Untamed horses on a beach.'

I answered him lightly, giving him the option of believing me or not.

'Do you mean it?' he asked. 'It's not in the script.'

I said, 'I can fit in the beach reconnaissance with the stuntman very early on Monday morning. Dawn, in fact. I'll be back in good time for rehearsals. But . . .' I paused indecisively.

'But what?'

'In the past you've given me an extra day here or there,' I said. 'What if I could use one this time? What if I get an idea?'

Twice in the past, granted latitude, I'd slanted his productions into a dimension the public had liked. Without demanding to know details in advance of a process I found came only from spur-of-the-moment inspiration in myself, he gave me merely a five-second considering stare, then a brief nod, and then a virtual carte blanche.

'Three days,' he said. 'OK.'

Time was very expensive. Three days equalled trust. I said, '*Great*.'

'If you hadn't asked,' he said reflectively, 'we'd be in trouble.'

'Don't you think it's going well?' I had anxieties always.

'It's going professionally,' he said. 'But I hired you for something more.'

I didn't feel flattered so much as increasingly pressured. The days when not much had been expected had been relatively restful: success had brought an upward spiral of awaited miracles, and one of these days, I thought, I would fly off the top of the unsteady tower and crash down in Pisa, and no sane finance department would consider my name again.

On the doorstep of the hotel, with his chauffeured car waiting, O'Hara said, 'You very well know that in the matter of film making there's power and there's money. On big budget productions the money men dictate what the directors may do. On medium budget productions, like this one, the power lies in the director. So use your power. *Use* it.'

I gazed at him dumbly. I saw him as the mover behind this film, saw *him* as the power. He, after all, had made the whole project possible. I saw that chiefly I had been trying to please *him*, more than myself; and he was telling me that that wasn't what he wanted.

'Stand or fall,' he said, 'it's your picture.'

I thought that if I were shooting this scene, it would be clear, whatever he said, that the real power lay in the older, craggily self-assured, lived-in face atop a wide-shouldered gone-to-overweight but comfortable body, and not in the unremarkable thirty-year-old easily mistaken for an extra.

'The power is yours,' he said again. 'Believe it.'

He gave me an uncompromising nod, allowing me no excuses, and went onwards to his car, being driven away without a farewell glance.

I walked thoughtfully across the drive to my own car and set off along the road to Valentine's house, aware of being at the same time powerful and obscure, an odd mixture. I couldn't deny to myself that I did quite often feel a spurting ability to produce the goods, a soaring satisfaction that could nosedive the next minute into doubt. I needed confidence if I were to give life to anything worthwhile, yet I dreaded arrogance, which could at once mislead into sterile *folie de grandeur*. Why, I often wondered, hadn't I settled for a useful occupation that didn't regularly lay itself open to public evaluation, like, say, delivering the mail?

Valentine and Dorothea had bought a four-roomed single-storey house, taking two rooms each as bedroom and sitting-room, constructing an extra bathroom so that they had their privacy, and sharing one large kitchen furnished with a dining table. Living that way had, they had both told me, been an ideal solution to their widowed state, a separate togetherness that gave them both company and retreat.

Everything looked quiet there when I parked outside on the road and walked up the concrete path to the front door. Dorothea opened it before I could ring the bell, and she'd been crying.

I said awkwardly, 'Valentine . . .?'

She shook her head miserably. 'He's still alive, the poor poor old love. Come in, dear. He won't know you, but come and see him.'

I followed her into Valentine's bedroom, where she said she had been sitting in a wing-chair near the window so that she could see the road and visitors arriving.

Valentine, yellowly pale, lay unmoving on the bed, his heavy slow breath noisy, regular and implacably terminal.

'He hasn't woken or said anything since you went yesterday,' Dorothea said. 'We don't need to whisper in here, you know, we're not disturbing him. Robbie Gill came at lunchtime, not that I had any lunch, can't eat, somehow. Anyway, Robbie says Valentine is breathing with difficulty because fluid is collecting in his lungs, and he's slipping away now and will go either tonight or tomorrow, and to be ready. How can I be ready?'

'What does he mean by ready?'

'Oh, just in my feelings, I think. He said to let him know tomorrow morning how things are. He more or less asked me not to phone him in the middle of the night. He said if Valentine dies, just to phone him at home at seven. He isn't really heartless, you know. He

28

still thinks it would be easier on me if Valentine were in hospital, but I know the old boy's happier here. He's peaceful, you can see it. I just know he is.'

'Yes,' I said.

She insisted on making me a cup of tea and I didn't dissuade her because I thought she needed one herself. I followed her into the brightly painted blue and yellow kitchen and sat at the table while she set out pretty china cups and a sugar bowl. We could hear Valentine breathing, the slow rasping almost a groan, though Nurse Davies, Dorothea said, had been an absolute brick, injecting painkiller so that her brother couldn't possibly suffer, not even in some deep brain recess below the coma.

'Kind,' I said.

'She's fond of Valentine.'

I drank the hot weak liquid, not liking it much.

'It's an extraordinary thing,' Dorothea said, sitting opposite me and sipping, 'you know what you said about Valentine wanting a priest?'

I nodded.

'Well, I told you he couldn't have meant it, but then, I would never have believed it, this morning a neighbour of ours – Betty from across the road, you've met her, dear – she came to see how he was and she said, did he get his priest all right? Well! I just stared at her, and she said, didn't I know that Valentine had been rambling on about some priest our mother had had to give her absolution before she died, and she said he'd asked her to fetch that priest. She said, what priest? I mean, she told me she never knew either of us ever saw a priest and I told her of course we hadn't, hardly even

29

with our mother, but she said Valentine was talking as if he were very young indeed and he was saying he liked to listen to bells in church. Delirious, she said he was. She couldn't make sense of it. What do you think?'

I said slowly, 'People often go back to their child-hood, don't they, when they're very old.'

'I mean, do you think I should get Valentine a priest? I don't know any. What should I do?'

I looked at her tired lined face, at the worry and the grief. I felt the exhaustion that had brought her to this indecision as if it had been my own.

I said, 'The doctor will know of a priest, if you want one.'

'But it wouldn't be any good! Valentine wouldn't know. He can't hear anything.'

'I don't think it matters that Valentine can't hear. I think that if you don't get a priest you'll wonder for the rest of your life whether you should have done. So yes, either the doctor or I will find one for you at once, if you like.'

Tears ran weakly down her cheeks as she nodded agreement. She was clearly grateful not to have had to make the decision herself. I went into Valentine's sitting-room and used the phone there, and went back to report to Dorothea that a man from a local church would arrive quite soon.

'Stay with me?' she begged. 'I mean ... he may not be pleased to be called out by a lapsed non-practising Catholic.'

He hadn't been, as it happened. I'd exhorted him as persuasively as I knew how; so without hesitation I agreed to stay with Dorothea, if only to see properly done what I'd done improperly.

We waited barely half an hour, long enough only for evening to draw in, with Dorothea switching on the lights. Then the real priest, a tubby, slightly grubby-looking middle-aged man hopelessly lacking in charisma, parked his car behind my own and walked up the concrete path unenthusiastically.

Dorothea let him in and brought him into Valentine's bedroom where he wasted little time or emotion. From a bag reminiscent of the doctor's he produced a purple stole which he hung round his neck, a rich colour against the faded black of his coat and the white band round his throat. He produced a small container, opened it, dipped in his thumb and then made a small cross on Valentine's forehead, saying, 'By this holy anointing oil . . .'

'Oh!' Dorothea protested impulsively, as he began. 'Can you say it in Latin? I mean, with our mother it was always in Latin. Valentine would want it in Latin.'

He looked as if he might refuse, but instead shrugged his shoulders, found a small book in his bag and read from that instead.

'*Misereatur tui omnipotens Deus, et dimissis peccatis tuis, perducat te ad vitam aeternam. Amen.*'

May almighty God have mercy upon you, forgive you your sins, and bring you to everlasting life.

'*Dominus noster Jesus Christus te absolvat . . .*'

Our Lord Jesus Christ absolves you . . .

He said the words without passion, a task undertaken for strangers, giving blanket absolution for he knew not

31

what sins. He droned on and on, finally repeating, more or less, the words I'd used, the real thing now but without the commitment I'd felt.

'*Ego te absolvo ab omnibus censuris, et peccatis tuis, in nomine Patris et Filii et Spiritus Sancti. Amen.*'

He made the sign of the cross over Valentine, who went on breathing without tremor, then he paused briefly before removing the purple stole and replacing it, with the book and the oil, in his bag.

'Is that all?' asked Dorothea blankly.

The priest said, 'My daughter, in the authority vested in me I have absolved him from all blame, from all his sins. He has received absolution. I can do no more.'

I went with him to the front door and gave him a generous donation for his church funds. He thanked me tiredly, and he'd gone before I thought of asking him about a funeral service – a requiem mass – within a week.

Dorothea had found no comfort in his visit.

'He didn't *care* about Valentine,' she said.

'He doesn't know him.'

'I wish he hadn't come.'

'Don't feel like that,' I said. 'Valentine has truly received what he wanted.'

'But he doesn't *know*.'

'I'm absolutely certain,' I told her with conviction, 'that Valentine is at peace.'

She nodded relievedly. She thought so herself, with or without benefit of religion. I gave her the phone number of the Bedford Lodge Hotel, and my room number, and told her I would return at any time if she couldn't cope.

She smiled ruefully. 'Valentine says you were a real little devil when you were a boy. He said you ran wild.'

'Only sometimes.'

She stretched up to kiss my cheek in farewell, and I gave her a sympathetic hug. She hadn't lived in New-market when I'd been young and I hadn't known her before coming back for the film, but she seemed already like a cosy old aunt I'd had for ever.

'I'm always awake by six,' I said.

She sighed. 'I'll let you know.'

I nodded and drove away, waving to her as she stood in Valentine's window, watching forlornly in her sor-rowful vigil.

I drove to the stable yard we were using in the film and stood in the dark there, deeply breathing cool March evening air and looking up at the night sky. The bright clear day had carried into darkness, the stars now in such brilliant 3D that one could actually perceive the infinite depths and distances of space.

Making a film about muddy passions on earth seemed frivolous in eternity's context, yet, as we were bodies, not spirits, we could do no more than reveal our souls to ourselves.

*Spiritus sanctus. Spiritus* meant 'breath' in Latin. Holy breath. *In nomine Spiritus Sancti.* In the name of the Holy Spirit, the Holy Breath, the Holy Ghost. As a schoolboy I'd liked the logic and discipline of Latin. As a man, I found in it mystery and majesty. As a film director I'd used it to instil terror. For Valentine, I'd usurped its power. God forgive me, I thought ... if there is a God.

The mega-star's Roller whispered gently into the

yard and out he popped, door opened for him as always by his attentive chauffeur. Male mega-stars came equipped normally with a driver, a valet, a secretary/assistant and occasionally a bodyguard, a masseur or a butler. For female mega-stars, add a hairdresser. Either could require a personal make-up artist. These retinues all had to be housed, fed and provided with rented transport, which was one reason why wasted days painfully escalated the costs.

'Thomas?' he asked, catching sight of me in the shadows. 'I suppose I'm late.'

'No,' I assured him. Mega-stars were *never* late, however overdue. Mega-stars were walking green lights, the term that in the film world denoted the capacity to bring finance and credence to a project, allied with the inability to do wrong. What green lights desired, they got.

This particular green light had so far belied his pernickety reputation and had delivered such goods that he'd been asked for in good humour and with sufficient panache to please his fans.

He was fifty, looked forty, and stood eye to eye with me at a shade over six feet. Though his features off-screen were good but unremarkable, he had the priceless ability of being able to switch on inside and act with his eyes. With tiny shifts of muscle he achieved huge messages in close-up, and the smile he constructed with his lower eyelids had earned him the tag of 'the sexiest man in films', though to my mind that smile was simply where his talents began.

I'd never before been appointed to direct such an actor, which he knew and made allowances for: yet he'd told me, much as O'Hara had, to get on with things and use my authority.

The mega-star, Nash Rourke, had himself asked for this night's meeting.

'A bit of quiet, Thomas, that's what I want. And I need to get the feel of the Jockey Club room you've had built in the trainer's house.'

Accordingly we walked together to the house's rear entrance, where the night-watchman let us in and logged our arrival.

'All quiet, Mr Lyon,' he reported.

'Good.'

Within the barn of a house the production manager, with my and O'Hara's approval and input, had reconstructed a fictional drawing-room within the original drawing-room space, and also re-created the former trainer's office as it had been, looking out to the stable yard.

Upstairs, removing a wall or two and using old photographs as well as a sight of the real thing, we had built a reproduction of the imposing room still to be found within the Jockey Club headquarters in the High Street, the room where, in the historic past, enquiries had been held, with reputations and livelihoods at stake.

Real official enquiries had for forty years or more been conducted in the racing industry's main offices in London, but in Howard Tyler's book, and in our film, a kangaroo court, an unofficial and totally dramatic and damning enquiry, was taking place within the old forbidding ambiance.

I switched on the few available lights, which gave only a deadened view of a richly-polished wood floor,

Stubbs and Herring on the walls and luxurious studded leather armchairs ranged round the outer side of a large horseshoe-shaped table.

The constructed replica room, to allow space for cameras, was a good deal larger than the real thing. Also, complete with cornices and paintings, the solid-seeming walls could obligingly roll aside. Bulbs on ceiling tracks, dark now, waited with a tangle of floods, spots and cables for the life to come in the morning.

Nash Rourke crossed to one side of the table, pulled out a green leather armchair and sat on it, and I joined him. He had brought with him several pages of newly rewritten script which he slapped down on the polished wood, saying, 'This scene we're doing tomorrow is the big one, right?'

'One of them,' I nodded.

'The man is accused, baffled, angry and innocent.'

'Yes.'

'Yeah. Well, our friend, Howard Tyler, is driving me crazy.'

Nash Rourke's accent, educated American, Boston overtones, didn't sit exactly with the British upper-class racehorse trainer he was purporting to be, a minor detail in almost everyone's eyes, including my own but excluding (unsurprisingly) Howard's.

'Howard wants to change the way I say things, and for me to play the whole scene in a throttled whisper.'

'Is that what he said?' I asked.

Nash shrugged a partial negative. 'He wants what he called "a stiff upper lip".'

'And you?'

'This guy would *yell*, for Christ's sake. He's a big powerful man accused of murdering his wife, right?'

'Right.'

'Which he didn't do. And he's faced with a lot of stick-in-the-muds bent on ruining him one way or the other, right?'

'Right.'

'And the chairman is married to his dead wife's sister, right?'

I nodded. 'The chairman, Cibber, eventually goes to pieces. We established that today.'

'Which Howard is spitting blue murder about.'

'Tomorrow, here,' I waved a hand around the make-believe courtroom, 'you yell.'

Nash smiled.

'Also you put a great deal of menace into the way you talk back to Chairman Cibber. You convince the Jockey Club members, *and* the audience, that you do have enough force of personality to kill. Sow a seed or two. Don't be long-suffering and passive.'

Nash leaned back in his chair, relaxing. 'Howard will bust a gut. He's mad as hell with what you're doing.'

'I'll soothe him.'

Nash wore, as I did, unpressed trousers, an open-necked shirt and a thick loose sweater. He picked up the sheets of script, shuffled them a bit, and asked a question.

'How different is the whole script than the one I saw originally?'

'There's more action, more bitterness and a lot more suspense.'

37

'But my character – this guy – he still doesn't kill his wife, does he?'

'No. But there's doubt about it right to the end, now.'

Nash looked philosophical. 'O'Hara sweet-talked me into this,' he said. 'I had three months free between projects. Fill them, he said. Nice little movie about horseracing. O'Hara knows I'm a sucker for the horses. An old real-life scandal, he tells me, written by our world-famous Howard, who of course I've heard of. Prestige movie, not a sink-without-trace, O'Hara says. Director? I ask. He's young, O'Hara says. You won't have worked with him before. Too damn right, I haven't. Trust me, O'Hara says.'

'Trust me,' I said.

Nash gave me one of the smiles an alligator would be proud of, the sort that in his Westerns had the baddies flinging themselves sideways in shoot-outs.

'Tomorrow,' I said, 'is the opening day of the main Flat racing season in England.'

'I know it.'

'They run the Lincoln Handicap on Saturday.'

Nash nodded. 'At Doncaster. Where's Doncaster?'

'Seventy miles north of here. Less than an hour by helicopter. Do you want to go?'

Nash stared. 'You're bribing me!'

'Sure.'

'What about insurance?'

'I cleared it with O'Hara.'

'Be damned!' he said.

He stood up abruptly in amused good humour and began measuring his distances in paces round the set.

'It says in the script,' he said, 'that I stand on the mat. Is this the mat, this thing across the open end of the table?'

'Yes. It's actually a bit of carpet. Historically the person accused at a Newmarket horseracing enquiry had to stand there, on the carpet, and that's the origin of the phrase, to be carpeted.'

'Poor bastards.'

He stood on the carpet and quietly said his lines, repeating and memorising them, putting in pauses and gestures, shifting his weight as if in frustration and finally marching the inside distance of the horseshoe to lean menacingly over the top chair, which would contain Cibber, the inquisitor.

'And I yell,' he said.

'Yes,' I agreed.

With the fury at that point silent, he murmured the shout of protest, and in time returned to his former seat beside me.

'What happened to those people in real life?' he asked. 'Howard swears what he's written are the true events. O'Hara tells me you're sure they're not, because no one's screaming foul. So what really did happen?'

I sighed. 'Howard's guessing. Also he's playing safe. For a start, none of the people who were really involved are called by their real names in his book. And I don't honestly know more than anyone else, because it all happened in this town twenty-six years ago, when I was only four. I can't remember even hearing about it then, and in any case the whole thing fizzled out. The trainer you're playing was a man called Jackson Wells. His wife was found hanged in one of the boxes in his stable yard,

39

and a lot of people thought he'd done it. His wife had had a lover. His wife's sister was married to a member of the Jockey Club. That's about as far as the known facts go. No one could ever prove Jackson Wells had hanged his wife and he swore he hadn't.'

'Howard says he's still alive.'

I nodded. 'The scandal finished him in racing. He could never prove he *hadn't* hanged his wife and although the Jockey Club didn't actually take away his licence, people stopped sending him horses. He sold his place and bought a farm in Oxfordshire, I think, and got married again. He must be nearly sixty now, I suppose. There apparently hasn't been any reaction at all from him, and Howard's book's been out over a year.'

'So he won't come bursting onto the set here swinging a noose to lynch me.'

'Believe in his innocence,' I said.

'Oh, I do.'

'Our film is fiction,' I said. 'The real Jackson Wells was a middle-ability man with a middle-sized training stable and no outstanding personality. He wasn't the upper-class powerful figure in Howard's book, still less was he the tough, wronged, resourceful conqueror we'll make of you before we're done.'

'O'Hara promised an up-beat ending.'

'He'll get it.'

'But the script doesn't say who *did* hang the wife, only who didn't.'

I said, 'That's because Howard doesn't know and can't make up his mind what to invent. Haven't you read Howard's book?'

'I never read the books scripts are written from. I find it's too often confusing and contradictory.'

'Just as well,' I said, smiling. 'In Howard's book your character is not having an affair with his wife's sister.'

'Not?' He was astonished. He'd spent a whole busy day tumbling about in bedclothes half naked with the actress playing his wife's sister. 'However did Howard agree to *that*?'

I said, 'Howard also agreed that Cibber, the sister-in-law's husband, should find out about the affair so that Cibber could have an overpowering reason for his persecution of your character; in fact, for the scene you're playing here tomorrow.'

Nash said disbelievingly, 'And *none* of that was in Howard's book?'

I shook my head. O'Hara had leaned on Howard from the beginning to spice up the story, in essence warning him 'No changes, no movie.' The shifts of mood and plotline that I'd recently introduced were as nothing compared with O'Hara's earlier manipulations. With me, Howard was fighting a rearguard action, and with luck he would lose that too.

Nash said bemusedly, 'Is the real Cibber still alive as well? And how about the wife's sister?'

'About her, I don't know. The real Cibber died three or so years ago. Apparently someone dug up this old story about him, which is what gave Howard the idea for his book. But the real Cibber didn't persecute Jackson Wells as relentlessly as he does in the film. The real Cibber had little power. It was all a pretty low-key story, in reality. Nothing like O'Hara's version.'

'Or yours.'

'Or mine.'

Nash gave me a straight look verging on the suspicious and said, 'What are you not telling me about more script changes?'

I liked him. I might even trust him. But I'd learned the hard way once that nothing was ever off the record. The urge to confide *had* to be resisted. Even with O'Hara, I'd been reticent.

'Devious,' O'Hara had called me. 'An illusionist.'

'It's what's needed.'

'I'll not deny it. But get the conjuring right.'

Conjurors never explained their tricks. The gasp of surprise was their best reward.

'I'll always tell you,' I said to Nash, 'what your character would be feeling in any given scene.'

He perceived the evasion. He thought things over in silence for a long full minute while he decided whether or not to demand details I might not give. In the end, what he said was, 'Trust is a lot to ask.'

I didn't deny it. After a pause he sighed deeply as if in acceptance, and I supposed he'd embraced blind faith as a way out if the whole enterprise should fail. 'One *should* never trust a director . . .'

In any case he bent his head to his script, reading it again swiftly, then he stood up, left the pages on the table and repeated the whole scene, speaking the lines carefully, forgetting them only once, putting in the pauses, the gestures, the changes of physical balance, the pouncing advance down the horseshoe and the over-towering anger at the end.

Then, without comment, he went through the whole thing again. Even without much sound, the emotion stunned: and he'd put into the last walk-through even the suggestion that he could be a killer, a murderer of wives, however passionately he denied it.

This quiet, concentrated mental vigour, I saw, was what had turned a good actor into a mega-star.

I hadn't been going to shoot the scene in one long take, but his performance changed my mind. He'd given it a rhythm and intensity one couldn't get from cutting. The close shot of Cibber's malevolence could come after.

'Thanks for this,' Nash said, breaking off.

'Anything.'

His smile was ironic. 'I hear I'm the green light around here.'

'I ride on your coat tails.'

'You,' he said, 'do not need to grovel.'

We left the set and the house and signed ourselves out with the night-watchman. Nash was driven away in the Roller by his chauffeur, and I returned to Bedford Lodge for a final long session with Moncrieff, discussing the visual impacts and camera angles of tomorrow's scene.

I was in bed by midnight. At five, the telephone rang beside my head.

'Thomas?'

Dorothea's wavery voice, apologetic.

'I'm on my way,' I said.

# CHAPTER THREE

Valentine was dead.

When I arrived at his house I found not the muted private grief I expected, but a showy car, not the doctor's or the priest's, parked at the kerbside, and bright lights behind the curtains in every window.

I walked up the concrete path to the closed front door and rang the bell.

After a long pause the door was opened, but not by Dorothea. The man filling the entry was large, soft and unwelcoming. He looked me up and down with a practised superciliousness and said, almost insultingly, 'Are you the doctor?'

'Er . . . no.'

'Then what do you want so early?'

A minor civil servant, I diagnosed: one of those who enjoyed saying no. His accent was distantly Norfolk, prominently London-suburban and careful.

'Mrs Pannier asked me to come,' I said without provocation. 'She telephoned.'

'At this hour? She can't have done.'

'I'd like to speak to her,' I said.

'I'll tell her someone called.'

Down in the hall behind him, Dorothea appeared from her bathroom and, seeing me, hurried towards the front door.

'Thomas! Come in, dear.' She beckoned me to sidle past the blockage. 'This is my son, Paul,' she explained to me. 'And Paul, this is Valentine's friend Thomas, that I told you about.'

'How is he?' I asked. 'Valentine?'

Her face told me.

'He's slipped away, dear. Come in, do. I need your help.' She was flustered by this son whom she'd described as pompous and domineering; and nowhere had she exaggerated. Apart from his hard bossy stare he sported a thin dark moustache and a fleshy upturned nose with the nostrils showing from in front. The thrust-forward chin was intended to intimidate, and he wore a three-piece important dark blue suit with a striped tie even at that hour in the morning. Standing about five feet ten, he must have weighed well over fourteen stone.

'Mother,' he said repressively, 'I'm all the help you need. I can cope perfectly well by myself.' He gestured to me to leave, a motion I pleasantly ignored, edging past him, kissing Dorothea's sad cheek and suggesting a cup of tea.

'Of course, dear. What am I thinking of? Come into the kitchen.'

She herself was dressed in yesterday's green skirt and jumper and I guessed she hadn't been to bed. The dark rings of tiredness had deepened round her eyes and her plump body looked shakily weak.

'I phoned Paul later, long after you'd gone, dear,'

she said almost apologetically, running water into an electric kettle. 'I felt so lonely, you see. I thought I would just warn him that his uncle's end was near . . .'

'So, of course, although it was already late, I set off at once,' Paul said expansively. 'It was only right. My duty. You should never have been here alone with a dying man, mother. He should have been in hospital.'

I lifted the kettle from Dorothea's hands and begged her to sit down, telling her I would assemble the cups and saucers and everything else. Gratefully she let me take over while the universal coper continued to rock on his heels and expound his own virtues.

'Valentine had already died when I got here.' He sounded aggrieved. 'Of course I insisted on telephoning the doctor at once, though Mother ridiculously wanted to let him sleep! I ask you! What are doctors for?'

Dorothea raised her eyes in a sort of despair.

'The damned man was *rude* to me,' Paul complained. 'He should be struck off. He said Valentine should have been in hospital and he would be here at seven, not before.'

'He couldn't *do* anything by coming,' Dorothea said miserably. 'Dying here was what Valentine wanted. It was *all right.*'

Paul mulishly repeated his contrary opinions. Deeply bored with him, I asked Dorothea if I could pay my respects to Valentine.

'Just go in, dear,' she said, nodding. 'He's very peaceful.'

I left her listening dutifully to her offspring and went into Valentine's bedroom which was brightly and brutally lit by a centre bulb hanging from the ceiling in an inadequate lampshade. A kinder lamp stood unlit on a bedside table, and I crossed to it and switched it on.

Valentine's old face was pale and smoothed by death, his forehead already cooler to the touch than in life. The laboured breathing had given way to eternal silence. His eyes were fully closed. His mouth, half open, had been covered, by Dorothea, I supposed, with a flap of sheet. He did indeed look remarkably at peace.

I crossed to the doorway and switched off the cold overhead light. Dorothea was coming towards me from the kitchen, entering Valentine's room past me to look down fondly at her dead brother.

'He died in the dark,' she said, distressed.

'He wouldn't mind that.'

'No . . . but . . . I switched off his bedside light so that people wouldn't see in, and I was sitting in that chair looking out of the window waiting for Paul to come, listening to Valentine breathing, and I went to sleep. I just drifted off.' Tears filled her eyes. 'I didn't know . . . I mean, I couldn't help it.'

'You've been very tired.'

'Yes, but when I woke up it was so dark . . . and absolutely quiet, and I realised . . . it was *awful*, dear. I realised Valentine had stopped breathing . . . and he'd died while I was *asleep*, and I hadn't been there beside him to hold his hand or anything . . .' Her voice wavered into a sob and she wiped her eyes with her fist.

I put an arm round her shoulders as we stood beside Valentine's bed. I thought it lucky on the whole that she hadn't seen the jolt of her brother's heart stopping, nor heard the last rattle of his breath. I'd watched my own mother die, and would never forget it.

'What time did your son get here?'

'Oh, it must have been getting on for three. He lives in Surrey, you see, dear. It's quite a long drive, and he'd been ready for bed, he said. I told him not to come ... I only wanted someone to talk to, really, when I rang him, but he insisted on coming ... very good of him, dear, really.'

'Yes,' I said.

'He closed the curtains, of course, and switched on all the lights. He was quite cross with me for sitting in the dark, and for not getting Robbie Gill out. I mean, Robbie could only say officially that Valentine was dead. Paul didn't understand that I *wanted* just to be in the dark with Valentine. It was a sort of *comfort*, you see, dear. A sort of goodbye. Just the two of us, like when we were children.'

'Yes,' I said.

'Paul means well,' she insisted, 'but I do find him tiring. I'm sorry to wake you up so early. But Paul was so cross with me ... so I phoned you when he went to the bathroom because he might have stopped me, otherwise. I'm not myself somehow, I feel so weak.'

'I'm happy to be here,' I assured her. 'What you need is to go to bed.'

'Oh, I couldn't. I'll have to be awake for Robbie. I'm so afraid Paul will be rude to him.'

A certainty, I thought.

The great Paul himself came into the room, switching on the overhead light again.

'What are you two doing in here?' he demanded. 'Mother, do come away and stop distressing yourself.

48

The old man's had a merciful release, as we all know. What we've got to talk about now is your future, and I've got plans made for that.'

Dorothea's frame stiffened under my embracing arm. I let it fall away from her shoulders and went with her out of Valentine's room and back to the kitchen, flicking the harsh light off again as I went and looking back to the quiet old face in its semi-shadow. Permanent timeless shadow.

'Of *course*, you must leave here,' Paul was saying to his mother in the kitchen. 'You're almost eighty. I can't look after you properly when you live so far away from me. I've already arranged with a retirement home that when Valentine died you would rent a room there. I'll tell them you'll be coming within a week. It's less than a mile from my house so Janet will be able to drop in every day.'

Dorothea looked almost frightened. 'I'm not going, Paul,' she contradicted. 'I'm staying here.'

Ignoring her, Paul said, 'You may as well start packing your things at once. Why waste time? I'll put this house on the market tomorrow and I'll move you immediately after the funeral.'

'No,' Dorothea said.

'I'll help you while I'm here,' her son said grandly. 'All Valentine's things will need sorting and disposing of, of course. In fact, I may as well clear some of the books away at once. I brought two or three empty boxes.'

'Not the books,' I said positively. 'He left his books to me.'

'*What?*' Paul's mouth unattractively dropped open. 'He can't have done,' he said fiercely. 'He left everything to Mother. We all know that.'

'Everything to your mother except his books.'

Dorothea nodded. 'Valentine added a codicil to his will about two months ago, leaving his books to Thomas.'

'The old man was ga-ga. I'll contest it.'

'You can't contest it,' I pointed out reasonably. 'Valentine left everything but the books to your mother, not to you.'

'Then Mother will contest it!'

'No, I won't, dear,' Dorothea said gently. 'When Valentine asked me what I thought about him leaving his books and papers to Thomas, I told him it was a very nice idea. I would never read them or ever look at them much, and Valentine knew Thomas would treasure them, so he got a solicitor to draw up the codicil, and Betty, a friend of mine, and Robbie Gill, our doctor, witnessed his signature with the solicitor watching. He signed it here in his own sitting-room, and there was no question of Valentine being ga-ga, which both the solicitor and the doctor will agree on. And I can't see what you're so bothered about, there's just a lot of old form books and scrap books and books about racing.'

Paul was, it seemed to me, a great deal more disconcerted than seemed natural. He seemed also to become aware of my surprise, because he groped and produced a specious explanation, hating me while he delivered it.

'Valentine once told me there might be some value

in his collection,' he said. 'I intend to get them valued and sold . . . for Mother's benefit, naturally.'

'The books are for Thomas,' Dorothea repeated doughtily, 'and I never heard Valentine suggest they were valuable. He wanted Thomas to have them for old times' sake, and for being so kind, coming to read to him.'

'*Ah-hah!*' Paul almost shouted in triumph. 'Valentine's codicil will be invalid because he *couldn't see* what he was signing!'

Dorothea protested, 'But he *knew* what he was signing.'

'*How* did he know? Tell me that.'

'Excuse me,' I said, halting the brewing bad temper. 'If Valentine's codicil is judged invalid, which I think unlikely if his solicitor drew it up and witnessed its signing, then the books belong to Dorothea, who alone can decide what to do with them.'

'Oh, *thank you*, dear,' she said, her expression relaxing, 'then if they are mine, I will give them to you, Thomas, because I know that's what Valentine intended.'

Paul looked aghast. 'But you *can't.*'

'Why not, dear?'

'They . . . they may be *valuable.*'

'I'll get them valued,' I said, 'and if they really are worth an appreciable amount, I'll give that much to Dorothea.'

'No, dear,' she vehemently shook her head.

'Hush,' I said to her. 'Let it lie for now.'

Paul paced up and down the kitchen in a fury and came to a halt on the far side of the table from where I

51

sat with Dorothea beside me, demanding forcefully, 'Just who are you, anyway, apart from ingratiating yourself with a helpless, dying old man? I mean, it's *criminal*.'

I saw no need to explain myself to him, but Dorothea wearily informed him, 'Thomas's grandfather trained horses that Valentine shod. Valentine's known Thomas for more than twenty years, and he's always liked him, he told me so.'

As if unable to stop himself, Paul marched his bulk away from this unwelcome news, abruptly leaving the kitchen and disappearing down the hall. One might have written him off as a pompous ass were it not for the fugitive impression of an underlying, heavy, half-glimpsed predator in the undergrowth. I wouldn't want to be at a disadvantage with him, I thought.

Dorothea said despairingly, 'I don't *want* to live near Paul. I couldn't bear to have Janet coming to see me every day. I don't get on with her, dear. She bosses me about.'

'You don't have to go,' I said. 'Paul can't put this house up for sale, because it isn't his. But, dearest Dorothea . . .' I paused, hesitating.

'But what, dear?'

'Well, don't *sign* anything.'

'How do you mean?'

'I mean, don't sign *anything*. Ask your solicitor friend first.'

She gazed at me earnestly. 'I may *have* to sign things, now Valentine's gone.'

'Yes, but . . . don't sign any paper just because Paul wants you to.'

'All right,' she said doubtfully.

I asked her, 'Do you know what a power of attorney is?'

'Doesn't it give people permission to do things on your behalf?'

I nodded.

She thought briefly and said, 'You're telling me not to sign a paper giving Paul permission to sell this house. Is that it?'

'It sure is.'

She patted my hand. 'Thank you, Thomas. I promise not to sign anything like that. I'll read everything carefully. I hate to say it, but Paul does try too hard sometimes to get his own way.'

Paul, to my mind, had been quiet for a suspiciously long time. I stood up and left the kitchen, going in search of him, and I found him in Valentine's sitting-room taking books off the shelves and setting them in stacks on the floor.

'What are you doing?' I asked. 'Please leave those alone.'

Paul said, 'I'm looking for a book I loaned Valentine. I want it back.'

'What's it called?'

Paul's spur-of-the-occasion lie hadn't got as far as a title. 'I'll know it when I see it,' he said.

'If any book has your name in it,' I said politely, 'I'll make sure that you get it back.'

'That's not good enough.'

Dorothea appeared in the doorway, saw the books piled on the floor and looked aghast and annoyed at the same time.

'Paul! Stop that! Those books are Thomas's. If you take them you'll be *stealing*.'

Paul showed no sign of caring about such a minor accusation.

'He won't take them,' I told her reassuringly.

Paul curled his lip at me, shouldered his way past and opened the front door.

'What is he doing, dear?' Dorothea asked, perplexed, watching her son's back go purposefully down the path.

'It seems,' I said, 'that he's fetching one of his boxes to pack the books in.' I closed the front door and shot its bolts, top and bottom. Then I hurried through into the kitchen and secured its outside door in the same way, and made a quick trip through all the rooms, and both bathrooms, to make sure the windows were shut and locked.

'But Paul's my son,' Dorothea protested.

'And he's trying to steal Valentine's books.'

'Oh, *dear*.'

Paul began hammering on the front door. 'Mother, let me in *at once*.'

'Perhaps I *should*,' Dorothea worried.

'He'll come to no harm out there. It's nowhere near freezing and he can sit in his car. Or go home, of course.'

'Sometimes Paul isn't *likeable*,' Dorothea said sadly.

I put the stacks of books back on Valentine's shelves. The ones that Paul had chosen to steal first were those with the glossiest covers, the recently published racing biographies, which were, in commercial resale terms, almost worthless. I guessed that chiefly it was Paul's vanity that was reacting against being thwarted by his mother and by me.

I had never underestimated the virulence of outraged vanity since directing a disturbing film about a real-life fanatical body-builder who'd killed his girl-friend because she'd left him for a wimp. I'd had to understand him, to crawl into his mind, and I'd hated it.

Paul's heavy hand banged repeatedly on the door and he pressed unremittingly on the doorbell. This last resulted not in a shrill nerve-shredding single note, but in a less insupportable non-stop quiet ding-dong; quiet because Dorothea had turned down the volume to avoid disturbing Valentine as he'd grown weaker.

I looked at my watch: five minutes to six. Perhaps an hour before we could expect the doctor but only thirty minutes before I should start my own workday.

'Oh, dear,' Dorothea said for about the tenth time, 'I do wish he'd stop.'

'Tell him you'll let him in if he promises to leave the books alone.'

'Do you think he'll agree?' she asked dubiously.

'A good chance,' I said.

He wouldn't want to lose too much face with the awakening neighbours, I reckoned: only a fool would allow himself to be seen to be shut out like a naughty boy by his aged mother.

With evident relief she relayed the terms, to which her son with bad grace agreed. She unbolted the door and let him in, an entrance I carefully didn't watch, as the slightest smile on my face would be interpreted by him as a jeer which would set him off again. Motorists had been shot for cutting in.

I stayed for a while in Valentine's sitting-room with the door shut while mother and son sorted themselves out in the kitchen. I sat in the armchair opposite the one no longer occupied by the old man, and thought how easy it was to get embroiled in a senseless fracas. Without expecting it, I'd made an enemy of Paul Pannier: and I surmised that what he really wanted was not so much the books themselves, but to get me and my influence out of his mother's life, so that he could control and order her future as best suited his beneficent view of himself.

At least, I *hoped* that was the case. Anything worse was more than I felt like dealing with in the middle of making a film.

I stared vacantly at the wall of books, wondering if after all there were anything there of value. If so, I was sure Valentine had been unaware of it. When I'd mentioned the possibility of an autobiography and he'd vetoed the idea, he hadn't referred to any diaries or other raw material that could be used as sources by anyone else but, sitting there, I wondered if by any chance Paul had made some sort of deal with a writer or publisher, to trade Valentine's papers for a share of the profits. No biography of Valentine's would make a fortune, but Paul, I guessed, would be content with modest pickings. Anything was better than nothing, one might hear him say.

Howard Tyler's book was not on the shelves.

Valentine had asked me, the first time I'd called on him, what had brought me back to Newmarket, and when I'd explained about Howard's book – *Unstable Times* – and the film we were to make of it, he'd said he'd heard of the book but he hadn't bought it, since at the time of its publication his eyesight had been fast deteriorating.

'I hear it's a load of rubbish,' he said.

'Is it?'

'I knew Jacksy Wells. I often shod his horses. He never murdered that mousey wife of his, he hadn't got the guts.'

'The book doesn't say he did,' I assured him.

'And I hear it doesn't say he didn't, neither.'

'Well, no.'

'It wasn't worth writing a book about it. Waste of time making a film.'

I'd smiled. Film-makers notoriously and wilfully distorted historical facts. Films knowingly based on lies could get nominated for Oscars.

'What was she like?' I asked.

'Who?'

'Jackson Wells's wife.'

'Mousey, like I said. Funny, I can't remember her clearly. She wasn't one of those trainer's wives who run the whole stable. Mouths like cesspits, some of them had in the old days. Jackson Wells's wife, you wouldn't have known she existed. I hear she's halfway to a whore in the book, poor little bitch.'

'Did she hang herself?'

'Search me,' Valentine said. 'I only shod the horses. The fuss died down pretty fast for lack of clues and evidence, but of course it did Jackson Wells in as a trainer. I mean, would *you* send your horses to a man who'd maybe killed his wife?'

'No.'

'Nor did anyone else.'

'The book says she had a lover,' I said.

'Did she?' Valentine pondered. 'First I've heard of it,' he said. 'But then, Dorothea could have a lover here under my nose and I wouldn't care. Good luck to her, if she did.'

'You're a wicked old man, Valentine.'

'Nobody's an angel,' he said.

I looked at his empty chair and remembered his desperate half-whisper . . . 'I killed the Cornish boy . . .'

Maybe the Cornish Boy was a horse.

Steps sounded on the path outside and the doorbell rang, ding-dong. I waited so as not to appear to be usurping Paul's desired status as head of the household, but it was in fact Dorothea who went to answer the summons.

'Come in, Robbie,' she said, the loud relief in her voice reaching me clearly. 'How dear of you to come.'

'That son of yours!' The doctor's voice held dislike.

'Sorry, sorry,' Dorothea said placatingly.

'Not your fault.'

Dorothea let him in and closed the front door, and I opened the door of Valentine's sitting-room to say hello.

Robbie Gill shook my hand perfunctorily. 'Glad you've got company,' he told Dorothea. 'Now, about Valentine?'

All three of us went quietly into the old man's dimly-lit room, followed importantly by Paul who immediately flooded the scene again with the overhead bulb. Perhaps it was only the director in me, I thought, that found this harsh insistence unpalatable. Certainly

Robbie Gill made no protest but set about establishing clinically what was evident to any eye, that Valentine – the he who had lived in that chemical shell – had left it.

'What time did he die?' he asked Dorothea, his pen poised over a clipboard.

'I don't know to the minute,' she said unhappily.

'Around one o'clock,' I said.

'Mother was asleep,' Paul accused unforgivingly. 'She confessed it. She doesn't know when he died.'

Robbie Gill gave him an expressionless stare and without comment wrote 0100 on his clipboard, showing it to me and Dorothea.

'I'll see to the paperwork for you,' he said to Dorothea. 'But you'll need to get an undertaker.'

'Leave it to me,' Paul interrupted. 'I'll take charge of all that.'

No one demurred. Taking important charge of relatively minor matters suited Paul's character perfectly: and perhaps, I thought, he would be so fulfillingly involved that he would forget about the books. There was no harm, however, in seeking to give Dorothea a close line of defence.

'How about,' I suggested to her, 'letting me go across to your friend Betty's house, and asking her to come over to keep you company?'

'Good idea,' Robbie Gill agreed emphatically.

'No need for that!' Paul objected.

'It's a bit *early*, dear,' Dorothea protested, looking at the clock, but seeming hopeful nevertheless.

I crossed the road to the friend's house and woke the friend's husband, whose initial irritation turned to a resigned shrug.

'Poor old sod,' he said, apparently referring to Valentine. 'We'll look after Dorothea.'

'Her son Paul is with her,' I told him.

'Betty,' he said intensely, 'will be over *straight away*.'

I smiled at the owner of the bristly chin and the crumpled pyjamas and dressing gown. Paul had a galvanic effect on everyone else's good nature, it seemed.

I waited until Betty had bustled across, plump and loving like Dorothea, and until Robbie Gill had left, during which period Paul half a dozen times told me I had no need to remain. While he was at one point busy patronising the doctor, Dorothea confided to me guiltily that she had *locked* Valentine's sitting-room door, dear, just in case, and had hidden the key in the pink vase in her bedroom.

I kissed her cheek, smiling, and drove off to work, half an hour late again but offering no apology.

Rehearsal and lighting took all morning. Each of the non-speaking characters, Jockey Club members, had to be positioned in his armchair and taken through the responses to Nash Rourke's long vehement defence.

'Act scandalised here,' I prompted, 'then disbelieving, then throw up hands, throw down pencil, look angry, you think the man's guilty and lying. Right everyone, we go through it again.'

And again and again, with Nash's stand-in repeating the speech and pausing step by forward step for Moncrieff's lighting plans to be finalised. Cibber, at the head of the table, kept making fruity jokes as usual and running down the government in the normal bored manner of an old character actor who'd long abandoned hopes of Hamlet. Cibber – I called most of the cast by their script names as I found it less confusing all round – Cibber was going to give a crack-up later of such truth and misery that he would garner good critical mentions while detesting me for a long time after, but as yet he coasted along on 'heard the one about the sperm and the lawyer, old boy?'

Cibber had been chosen by the casting director because of his upper-class appearance and voice; and I had no complaints about these, but only with his facile assumption that they were *enough*, when to me they were merely a start.

We broke briefly for lunch. Nash Rourke arrived in good time for make-up, and did one silent walk-through under the lights, for Moncrieff to check he had the same colour temperatures as with the stand-in.

Owing to Nash having rehearsed in private the evening before, the 'Jockey Club members' were not prepared for what they were going to see, and as I particularly wanted to record their spontaneous reactions in advance of their rehearsed version, I announced that the first take was in this case not to be considered to be a rehearsal, but would be the real thing: that action, failing only the set falling to pieces, would continue from start to finish, whatever was seeming to go wrong.

'Continuous,' I said. '*No stops*. Right?'

Everyone nodded, even if doubt could be spotted here and there. Except for unrepeatable effects involving five hundred extras, first takes were rarely those seen on the screen.

With the world-weariness of unlimited experience, Nash understood what I wanted, but that didn't guarantee that he would deliver. That day, however, from some motive of his own, he decided generously to go along with the all-out take one, and performed with such vibrating power that the mouths round the table fell open with real incredulity. Moncrieff said the hairs on his own neck stood up, let alone those of the cast. Cibber instinctively slid down in his chair as Nash came to a thunderous halt leaning over him, and after a second or two of dead silence, when I said a shade breathlessly, 'Cut, and print,' the crews and actors as if of one mind *applauded*.

Nash shrugged it off. 'Well, it's strongly written . . .'

He retraced his steps to leave the horseshoe and came over to where I stood.

'Well?' he said.

I was practically speechless.

'Go on,' Nash said. 'Say it. Say "Do it again".'

His eyes smiled.

'Do it again,' I said.

We repositioned and reloaded the cameras and repeated the scene twice more. All three takes went miraculously without glitches, and all three were printable, but it wasn't only I who thought the first electric beyond insulation.

'That man could murder,' Moncrieff said of Nash thoughtfully.

'He was acting.'

'No.' He shivered slightly. 'I mean, in fact.'

# CHAPTER FOUR

Howard had heard that the enquiry scene had given a galvanising, positively animating jolt to the whole production. He'd been told, by about ten different people, that Nash had said 'It's strongly written': and Howard knew that he hadn't written what Nash had yelled.

'*You*,' he said furiously, facing me after dinner across a small table in the Bedford Lodge Hotel bar, far too public a venue for his emotions, '*you* changed the script.'

'Well,' I said peaceably, 'not very much. Most of it was your words exactly.'

'But not the feeling,' he complained. 'You wilfully misinterpreted my intention. You told Nash to lose control and threaten Cibber. *You* told him to look like a killer, you must have done, otherwise he wouldn't have thought of it, not from what I wrote.'

'Look, Howard,' I said with resignation, 'we'd better come once and for all to an understanding. I don't want to quarrel with you. I want us to work together to produce a good film, but you did sign a contract – '

'What *you* think is a good film,' he interrupted, 'and what *I* think is a film truthful to my book, are totally opposite. All *you* care about is how much money it makes.'

I took a large bracing mouthful of post-prandial cognac (to hell with the non-alcohol ethos) and decided to explain a few basic facts of movie life to the unrealistic idealist opposite me, his prim round glasses gleaming over earnest brown eyes and his small mouth contracting further in pique.

'I'm a name,' he insisted. 'My readers expect subtlety, understatement and psychological depth. What you're giving them is sex and violence.'

'Have another vodka and cranberry juice?'

'No.'

'Howard,' I said, 'don't you understand what you agreed to? O'Hara put together a package that brought finance from one of the top seven studios. However much one may regret it, they don't fund moody films to play in art houses. They are strictly in the business for profit. The bottom line, Howard.'

'Obscene,' he said, disapprovingly.

I said, 'O'Hara's chief bargaining promise with the big-seven movie company was that we would, between us, produce a film that at least wouldn't *lose* them money. Your own soft-focus view of an ancient scandal obviously worked fine as a novel, and there's much of that that I've insisted on retaining. I've fought for you, whatever you may think.'

'What, precisely, have you retained?' he demanded, hurting.

'You wrote the whole first quarter as a semi-ghost story about the dream lovers of the wife who ended up hanged.'

'Yes.'

'Her dreams and illusions are in the screenplay,' I reminded him. 'Her lovers are jockeys, the way you wrote them. But who were the real jockeys? Did they ride the horses her husband trained?'

'They were in her mind.'

'But why did she hang, Howard? Was she topped by one of the dream lovers? Did she do it herself? Did her husband kill her?'

After a pause he said, 'No one knows.'

'I know they don't,' I said. 'At least, no one ever told. But an ending of no explanation at all isn't going to get people paying to see the film.'

He said sarcastically, 'That bottom line again.'

'I'll give you the dream lovers,' I said. 'And you'll allow me an earthly explanation.'

'That's not fair.'

I gazed at him. He was old enough to know that few things were fair. Most five-year-olds had already discovered it.

'What we are dealing with here,' I said, changing tack, 'is three versions of the same story.'

'What do you mean?'

'We have the story you wrote in your book. We have the story we're shooting in the film. And somewhere out of sight, way back in history, is what actually happened. Three views of the same facts.'

Howard didn't argue.

I said, 'By Sunday, Howard, I'd like you to come up with a rational explanation of the wife's death.'

'But it's already Thursday evening!' he exclaimed, horrified.

'You've had literally years to work it out.'

'But no one knows!'

'Then guess.'

'I can't,' he protested belligerently, 'I've tried.'

'Then I'll do it,' I said. 'I'll work with you on the necessary scenes. We'll use most of your script as written, but your inconclusive ending is impossible.'

'But it's what *happened*. There wasn't any ending to the story.'

'For the film, there has to be.'

'Don't you *care* about the facts?'

'Perhaps, if we look closely enough,' I said, only half meaning it, 'we might ourselves uncover those facts. What if we actually could find out what really happened?'

'You can't,' Howard said flatly. 'No one knows.'

'No one's saying. That's different.' I paused. 'What did Jackson Wells tell you, when you went to see him?'

O'Hara had asked Howard the same thing, he'd told me, and Howard, to O'Hara's utter disbelief, had said he hadn't consulted Jackson Wells at all. Howard hadn't thought it necessary. Howard didn't want to risk unwelcome anti-climactic disclosures from Jackson Wells that might upset his lyrical tale of the dream lovers and the semi-mystical death.

Moncrieff, strolling into the bar, seeing us, and crossing without hesitation to join us, saved Howard from having to answer.

Howard and Moncrieff disliked each other without making much overt display of it. Moncrieff, no reader of novels, thought Howard a prissy, impractical, pseudo-intellectual nuisance on the set. Howard's expression made no attempt to disguise his disparagement of Moncrieff's unkempt appearance with the small straggly beard that was halfway between an artistic statement and a lazy approach to shaving.

Neither of them had the least understanding of the other's function. Moncrieff, endlessly creative within the effects of lighting, needed to be given the actors, the scene and the intention of the storyline, but his enormous input was a moonshot outside the range of Howard's comprehension. Each of them, being acclaimed as individualists, wholly believed that it was he who was indispensable to any chance of esteem for the finished film.

As Nash Rourke tended to think the same, also O'Hara, also myself and also the film editor who would cut some of his own opinions into our work, it was unlikely that anyone would end up wholly satisfied, even if the public approved. Howard, though he didn't seem to appreciate it, at least had more control of his own work than most authors.

'What about those dream lovers, then?' Moncrieff asked abrasively.

Howard became predictably defensive. 'The wife imagines them. You don't need to worry about it.'

'Oh, yes, he does,' I corrected mildly. '*She* may be imagining the jockeys, but we, the onlookers, are going to see them standing in her bedroom.'

Howard looked aghast, to Moncrieff's amusement.

'One at a time,' I explained. 'She sees one in her bedroom. Another time, she sees another. And another. We have three tall ultra-handsome unknowns coming to dress up as the dream lovers. They won't look like real jockeys. They don't speak, and don't worry, Howard, they won't get into bed. The wife watches her husband from her bedroom window as he rides out with his string of horses to their morning exercise, then she turns into the room and conjures up her dream jockey lover. Moncrieff will light the jockey to make it clear that he's imaginary. Another day the wife will wave to her husband, and then turn and imagine a *different* lover.'

Moncrieff nodded. 'Easy.'

'She dances with the third lover. Slowly, orgasmically. She's transported,' I said.

Moncrieff happily nodded again.

'So there you are, Howard,' I said. 'The lovers are how you wrote them. No sex.'

'All highly unlikely,' Moncrieff laughed. 'Any jockey worth his salt would have her nightie off before her husband was out of the stable yard.'

'She hanged,' I said. 'No dream.'

Both of them stared, silenced.

*Why* did she hang, I wondered. The further we went with the filming, the more I wanted to know, yet until then it had been the results of that death, the accusations against her husband, and his handling of them, that had been the focus both of Howard's book and, more especially, of our film version.

I gave a mental shrug. I hadn't time for any inept detective work, trying to unearth a secret twenty-six years buried. I had only to bully Howard into inventing a good reason and giving Nash a huge satisfactory last scene in which he discovered the truth – Howard's version of the truth – to end the film in perhaps cynical heroism.

'What made you write the book?' I asked Howard.

'You know what did. A newspaper article.'

'Do you still have it?'

He looked surprised and, as usual, displeased. 'Yes, I suppose so,' he said grudgingly, 'but not here.'

'What paper was it in?'

'I don't see that it matters.'

Howard himself, in the ensuing pause, seemed to agree that he'd been unnecessarily ungracious.

'The *Daily Cable*,' he said. 'It was an obituary of the member of the Jockey Club that I called Cibber in the book.'

I nodded. That much I knew. 'What was Cibber's real name?'

'Visborough.' He spelled it.

'And who wrote the obituary?' I asked.

'I've no idea,' Howard replied, still obstructively but this time with a surprise that gave his statement credence.

'Didn't you follow it up?' I asked.

'Of course not.' Howard became condescending. 'You've no idea how a creative author writes. The *inconclusiveness* of the obituary was its own inspiration. I received the *idea* from the obituary and the book grew in my mind.'

'So,' Moncrieff said, 'you never even tried to find out what really happened?'

'Of course not. But I didn't *alter* the account given in the obituary, not like O'Hara and Thomas have made

69

me alter things for the film.' He was acridly bitter. 'My readers will *hate* the film.'

'No, they won't,' I said, 'and hundreds of thousands of new readers will buy your paperbacks.'

He liked that idea, however he might carp. He preened, smirking. Moncrieff's dislike of him visibly grew.

Howard had had enough of Moncrieff, and of me too, no doubt. He got to his feet and left us, making no pretence of social civility.

'He's an oaf,' Moncrieff said, 'and he's belly-aching all over the place, to anyone who will listen, about the bastardising of his masterpiece. A few dream lovers won't shut him up.'

'Who has he been belly-aching *to*?' I asked.

'Does it matter?'

'Yes, it does. His contract forbids him to make adverse criticism of the film in public until six months after it has had a general release. If he's talking to the actors and the crews, that's one thing. If he's complaining to strangers, say in the bar here, I'll have to shut him up.'

'But can you?' Moncrieff asked with doubt.

'There are prickly punitive clauses in his contract. I had a sight of it, so I'd know what I could ask of him, and what I couldn't.'

Moncrieff whistled softly through his teeth. 'Did O'Hara write the contract?'

'Among others. It's pretty standard in most respects. Howard's agent agreed to it, and Howard signed it.' I sighed. 'I'll remind him tactfully tomorrow.'

Moncrieff tired of the subject. 'About tomorrow,' he

said. 'Still the six-thirty dawn call out in the stable yard?'

'Definitely. The horses have to be exercised. I told all the stable lads this evening we'd be shooting them mounting and riding out through the gate to the exercise ground. They'll be wearing their normal clothes: jeans, anoraks, crash helmets. I reminded them not to look at the cameras. We'll take the overall scene of the lads mounting. Nash will come out of the house and be given a leg-up onto his mount. We'll rehearse it a couple of times, not more. I don't want to keep the horses circling too long. When Nash is mounted and comfortable the assistant trainer can lead the string out through the gate. Nash waits for them to go, and follows, last. As he leaves, he'll look backwards and up to the window from where his wife is supposedly watching. You've arranged for a camera crew up there to do the wife's point of view? Ed will be up there, supervising.'

Moncrieff nodded.

I said, 'We'll cut the main shot once Nash is through the gate. I hope we won't have to do many retakes, but when we're satisfied, the string can go on and get their regular exercise, and Nash can come back and dismount. We're going to be repeating the whole thing on Saturday. We'll need a new view from the wife's room and different jackets et cetera on Nash and the lads. We'll need close shots of hooves on the gravel, that sort of thing.'

Moncrieff nodded. 'And Sunday?'

'The Jockey Club people are letting us film out on the gallops, as there won't be many real horses-in-training working that day. You and I will go out by car on the roads on Saturday with a map for you to position the cameras. I know already where best to put them.'

'So you should, if you were brought up here.'

'Mm. Sunday afternoon, the horses go to Huntingdon racecourse. I hope to hell we have three fine mornings.'

'What if it rains?'

'If it's just drizzle, we go ahead with filming. Horses do go out in all weathers, you know.'

'You don't say.'

'Tomorrow afternoon,' I said, 'we'll be indoors up in the enquiry-room set again, like today. The schedule you've got is unchanged. There are more exchanges between Cibber, Nash and others. Apart from the wide establishing shots, it's mostly short close-ups of them speaking. The usual thing. We'll complete Nash's shots first. If the others don't fluff their lines too much, we might get through most of it tomorrow. Otherwise we'll have to carry on on Saturday afternoon as well.'

'OK.'

Moncrieff and I finished our drinks and went our separate ways, I upstairs to my room to make an arranged phone call to O'Hara in London.

'How did the Jockey Club scene go?' he asked immediately.

'Nash wowed them.'

'Good, then.'

'I think ... well, we'll have to see the rushes tomorrow ... but I think it was a sit-up-and-take-notice performance.'

'Good boy.'

'Yes, he was.'

'No, I meant . . . well, never mind. How's everything else?'

'All right, but,' I paused, 'we need a better ending.'

'I agree that the proposed ending's too weak. Hasn't Howard any ideas?'

'He *likes* the weak ending.'

'Lean on him,' O'Hara said.

'Yes. Um, you know he based his book on the obituary of the man he called Cibber? His real name was Visborough.' I spelled it, as Howard had done. 'Well, could you get me a copy of that obituary? It was published in the *Daily Cable*, Howard says. It must have been at least three years ago. Howard doesn't know who wrote it. He never followed anything up in any way. He says simply that the obituary, and especially its inconclusiveness, was what jolted his imagination into writing the book.'

'You don't ask much!'

'The *Daily Cable* must have a cuttings library. You'll certainly be able to get that obituary. Could you fax it to me here at Bedford Lodge? If I knew exactly what started Howard's imagination working in the first place, perhaps I could help him find an explosive denouement.'

'You'll have the obituary tomorrow,' O'Hara promised.

'Thanks.'

'How's your friend?' he asked.

'What friend?'

'The one who's dying.'

'Oh.' I paused. 'He died during last night.'

'Bad luck.'

'He was old. Eighty something. A blacksmith turned top racing journalist, grand old character, great unusual life. Pity we can't make a film of *him*.'

'Films of good people don't have much appeal.'

'Ain't that the truth.'

'What was his name?'

'Valentine Clark,' I said. 'The *Daily Cable* might do an obituary of him too, you never know. He wrote for the *Racing Gazette*. Everyone in racing knew him. And . . . um . . . he knew the real trainer, Jackson Wells, the basis of the character that Nash is playing.'

'Did he?' O'Hara's attention sharpened down the line. 'So you surely asked him what he knew of the hanging?'

'Yes, I did. He knew no more than anyone else. The police dropped the case for lack of leads. Valentine said Jackson Wells's wife was an unmemorable mouse. He couldn't tell me anything helpful. It was all so very long ago.'

O'Hara almost laughed. 'It was very long ago for *you*, Thomas, because you're young. I'll bet twenty-six years is yesterday to Jackson Wells himself.'

'I . . . er . . .' I said diffidently, 'I did think of going to see him.'

'Jackson Wells?'

'Yes. Well, Valentine, my dead friend, he was originally a blacksmith, as I told you. He used to shoe my grandfather's horses regularly, and he did say he'd also sometimes shod the horses Jackson Wells trained. So perhaps I could make some excuse . . . following Valentine's death ... to make a nostalgic visit to Jackson Wells. What do you think?'

'Go at once,' O'Hara said.

'He won't want to talk about the wife who hanged. He has a new life now and a second wife.'

'Try, anyway,' O'Hara said.

'Yes, I thought so. But he lives near Oxford ... it'll take me half a day.'

'Worth it,' O'Hara said. 'I'll OK the extra time.'

'Good.'

'Goodnight,' he said. 'I've a lady waiting.'

'Good luck.'

He cursed me – 'You son of a bitch' – and disconnected.

I'd always loved early mornings in racing stables. I'd been down in my grandfather's yard dawn by dawn for years, half my day lived before the first school bell. I tended, for the film, to make the horses more of a priority in my attention than perhaps I should have, moving about the yard, in close contact with the creatures I'd grown up among, and felt at home with.

I'd ridden as an amateur jockey in jump races from the age of sixteen, with most of my family expecting horses in some way to be my life for ever, but fate and finance – or lack of it – had found me at twenty engaged in organising horses in Arizona for the cavalry in a Western drama. By twenty-one I'd become the director of a bad minor film about rodeo riders, but that had led to the same post in a noble native-American saga that had modestly hit the jackpot. After that I'd spent a year working for film editors, learning their craft, followed by another year on soundtracks and music, and by twenty-six I'd been let loose as director on an unconsidered romance between a boy and a puma that had made astonishing profits. O'Hara had been the producer: I had never since been long out of work. 'The boy's lucky,' O'Hara would say, selling my name. 'You can't buy luck. Trust me.'

For this present film I'd suggested to O'Hara early in the pre-production stage that this time we should *buy*, not rent or borrow for fees, our stableful of horses.

'Too expensive,' he'd objected automatically.

'Not necessarily,' I'd contradicted. 'We can buy cheap horses. There are hundreds that have never done well in races, but they *look* like good thoroughbreds, and that's what's important. Also we won't have any problems with insurance or recompense for injuries, we can travel them where and when we like, and we can work them without anxious owners fluttering round to fuss about their feed or exercise. We can sell them again, at the end.'

One of O'Hara's chief virtues, in my eyes, was his ability to evaluate facts very fast and come up with quick decisions. So, 'Buy them,' he said, and he'd liberated sufficient funds for a bloodstock agency to acquire the fourteen good-looking no-hopers currently eating oats and hay in our yard.

The actors' unions having agreed we should use real-life stable personnel for the horses, I'd recruited a young assistant trainer from a prestigious Newmarket yard and installed him in charge of our whole horse

76

operation, giving him the title of horsemaster and also the riding but non-speaking role of assistant trainer in the film.

He was already busy getting lads and horses ready for the morning action when I arrived in the yard at dawn. Moncrieff's crew had laid felt carpeting over the gravel to silence the progress of the rolling camera dolly. He himself had strategically planted his lighting. Ed, he reported, was already in position upstairs.

The weather was cold and windy with dark scudding clouds. Moncrieff liked the moodiness, humming happily as he arranged for ominous shadows to fall across Nash's stand-in, who looked hopelessly un-trainerlike in riding gear. When Nash himself – in character – strode out of the house and yelled bad-tempered instructions to the lads it was as real as any such bona fide moment I'd ever seen.

There were annoyances with the camera truck – one of its wheels squeaked despite the felt path. Oil and oaths fixed it. Moncrieff and I fretted at the delay because of light values. Nash seemed less irritated than resigned.

Only two takes were necessary of the assistant trainer giving Nash a leg-up onto his hack; the horse amazingly stood still. Nash wheeled away and sat on his mount in and out of shot while the assistant trainer heaved himself into his own saddle and led the circling string of by now mounted lads out through wide open stable gates onto the Newmarket training grounds beyond. Nash followed last, remembering to look back and up to the bedroom window. When his horse had walked him well out of sight I yelled 'Cut', and the whole string ambled back into the yard, the hooves scrunching on the gravel, the lads joshing each other like kids out of school.

'How did it go?' I asked Moncrieff. 'Cameras OK?'

'OK.'

'Print, then.' I walked among the horses to speak to their riders. 'That was good,' I said. 'We'll do it again, now, though. Two snaps are better than one.'

They nodded. By then they all considered themselves expert film-makers. The second take didn't go as smoothly, but that didn't necessarily matter: we would use the version that looked more natural on film.

I followed them on foot out of the gate to where Nash and all the lads were circling, awaiting my verdict.

'Same again tomorrow morning,' I said, patting horses' necks. 'Different clothes. Off you all go, then. Remember not to get in the way of any real racehorses. Walk and trot only on the grounds we've been allotted.'

The string filed off to exercise and Nash returned to the yard, dismounting and handing his reins to the lad left behind for the purpose.

'Is it still on for tomorrow?' he asked, turning in my direction.

'Doncaster, do you mean?'

He nodded.

'Of course it is,' I said. 'The stewards have asked you to their lunch, so you can use their box all afternoon and have as much or as little privacy as you want. They've sent tickets for two, for you to take a companion.'

'Who?'

'Whoever you like.'

'You, then.'

'*What?* I meant a friend, or perhaps Silva?' Silva was the bewitching actress he'd tumbled around with in bed.

'Not her,' he said vehemently. 'You. Why not? And don't say you'll still be doing close shots in the enquiry room. Let's make damned sure they all get completed this afternoon. I want you because you know the drill on a British racecourse, and the racing people know *you*.'

Green lights got what they wanted. Moreover, I discovered it was what I wanted also.

'Fine, then,' I said. 'Helicopter at eleven-thirty.'

Watching his familiar back walk off to his ever-waiting Rolls, I called Bedford Lodge from my mobile phone and by persuasive perseverance got the staff to find Howard Tyler, who was in the bar.

'Just a word, Howard,' I said.

'Not *more* script changes?' He was acidly sarcastic.

'No. Um . . . simply a word of warning.'

'I don't need your words of warning.'

'Good, then. But . . . er . . . I just thought I might remind you, knowing how you feel, that you agreed not to bellyache about the film until after its release.'

'I'll say what I damned well please.'

'It's your privilege. I don't suppose you care about the penalties in your contract.'

'What penalties?'

'Most film contracts include them,' I said. 'I'm sure yours does. Film companies routinely seek ways to stop a disgruntled writer from sabotaging the whole film just

79

because he or she dislikes the changes made to the original work. They put in clauses allowing themselves to recover substantial damages.'

After a lengthy pause Howard said, 'I never signed such a contract.'

'Fine, then, but you might check with your agent.'

'You're trying to frighten me!' he complained.

'I'm just suggesting you might want to be careful.'

Silence. Howard simply put down his receiver. So much for tactful advice!

True to his intention, Nash did make damned sure that we completed the enquiry-room shots that day, even if not until past eight in the evening. In want of a shower and a reviving drink, I drove back to Bedford Lodge and found waiting for me a long fax from O'Hara, starting with the *Daily Cable* obituary.

Rupert Visborough's life was dedicated to serving his country, the neighbourhood and the Sport of Kings.

Commissioned into the Scots Guards, he retired with the rank of major to enter local politics in his home county of Cambridgeshire. Many committees benefited from his expert chairmanship, including . . .

The list was long, virtuous and unexciting.

A landowner, he was elected a member of the Jockey Club following the death of his father, Sir Ralph Visborough, knighted for his patronage of many animal charities.

Highly respected by all who knew him, Rupert Visborough felt obliged to remove his name from a shortlist of those being considered for selection as parliamentary candidate, a consequence of his having inadvertently been involved in an unexplained death closely touching his family.

His wife's sister, married to Newmarket trainer Jackson Wells, was found hanged in one of the loose boxes in her husband's stable yard. Exhaustive police enquiries failed to find either a reason for suicide, or any motive or suspect for murder. Jackson Wells maintained his innocence throughout. The Jockey Club, conducting its own private enquiry, concluded there was no justification for withdrawing Wells's licence to train. Rupert Visborough, present at the enquiry, was justifiably bitter at the negative impact of the death on his own expectations.

Reports that Jackson Wells's wife was entertaining lovers unknown to her husband could not be substantiated. Her sister – Visborough's wife – described the dead woman as 'fey' and 'a day-dreamer'. She said that as she and her sister had not been close she could offer no useful suggestions.

Who knows what Rupert Visborough might not have achieved in life had these events not happened? Conjecture that he himself knew more of the facts behind the tragedy than he felt willing to disclose clung to his name despite his strongest denials. The death of his sister-in-law is unresolved to this day.

Visborough died last Wednesday of a cerebral haemorrhage, aged 76, with his great potential sadly unfulfilled.

He is survived by his wife, and by their son and daughter.

O'Hara had handwritten across the bottom, 'Pious load of shit! No one on the paper knows who wrote it. Their obits often come in from outside.'

The pages of fax continued, however.

O'Hara's handwriting stated, 'This paragraph appeared in the *Cable*'s irreverent gossip column on the same day as the obituary.'

> Secrets going to grave in the Visborough family? It seems Rupert (76), Jockey Club member, dead on Wednesday of a stroke, never discovered how his sister-in-law hanged twenty-three years ago in who-dunnit circs. Bereaved husband, Jackson Wells, now remarried and raising rape near Oxford, had 'no comment' re the Visborough demise. Answers to the 23-year-old mystery *must* exist. Send us info.

O'Hara's handwriting: 'The Cable got about 6 replies, all no good. End of story as far as they are concerned. But at great expense they searched their microfilmed records and found these accounts, filed and printed at the time of the hanging.'

The first mention had earned a single minor paragraph: 'Newmarket trainer's wife hanged'.

For almost two weeks after that there had been daily revelations, many along the lines of 'did she jump or was she pushed?' and equally many about the unfairness – and personal bitterness – of the nipping in the bud effect of Visborough's ambitions for a political career.

A hanging in the family, it seemed, had discouraged not only racehorse owners; the blight had spread beyond Jackson Wells to canvassers and prospective voters.

The story had extinguished itself from lack of fuel. The last mention of Jackson Wells's wife announced untruthfully, 'The police expect to make an arrest within a few days.' And after that, silence.

The basic question remained unanswered – *why* did she hang?

I had dinner and went to bed and dreamed about them, Visborough as Cibber, his cuckolding wife as the pretty actress Silva, Nash as Jackson Wells and the fey, hanged woman as a wisp of muslin, a blowing curtain by the window.

No insight. No inspiration. No solution.

# CHAPTER FIVE

Delays plagued the going-out-to-exercise scene the next morning. One of the horses, feeling fractious, dumped his lad and kicked one of the camera-operating crew. Light bulbs failed in mid-shot. One of the stable lads loudly asked a silly question while the cameras were rolling, and a sound engineer, who should have known better, strolled, smoking, into the next take.

Nash, emerging from the house, forgot to bring with him the crash helmet he was supposed to put on before he mounted. He flicked his fingers in frustration and retraced his steps.

By the time we finally achieved a printable result it was no longer dawn or anywhere near it. Moncrieff, cursing, juggled relays of coloured filters to damp down the exuberant sun. I looked at my watch and thought about the helicopter.

'Once more,' I shouted generally. 'And for Christ's sake, get it right. Don't come back, go on out to exercise. Everyone ready?'

'Cameras rolling,' Moncrieff said.

I yelled, 'Action', and yet again the lads led their long-suffering charges out of the loose boxes, hauled themselves into the saddle, formed a straggly line and skittered out of the gate. Nash, following them, forgot to look up at the window.

I yelled, 'Cut' and said to Moncrieff, 'Print.'

Nash came back swearing.

'Never mind,' I said. 'We'll cut it in. Would you ride out again and turn and look up *after* you're through the gate, as if the other horses had gone out of shot ahead of you? We'll also do a close shot of that look.'

'Right now?'

'Yes,' I said. 'Now, because of having the same light. And how about a touch of exasperation with the wife?'

The close shot of the exasperation proved well worth the extra time taken in raising a camera high. Even Moncrieff smiled.

All Nash said was, 'I hope the Doncaster stewards wait lunch.'

He whisked off in the Rolls but when I followed a minute or two later I found him still standing in the hotel lobby reading a newspaper, rigidly concentrated.

'Nash?' I enquired tentatively.

He lowered the paper, thrust it into my hands and in explosive fury said, '*Shit!*' Then he turned on his heel and stalked off, leaving me to discover what had upset him.

I saw. I read, and felt equally murderous.


BUMMER OF A FILM ON THE TURF

First reports of 'Unstable Times', now in front of cameras in Newmarket, speak of rows, discord and screeching nerves.

Author Howard Tyler's vibrant tale, ten weeks on

bestseller lists, is mangled beyond recognition, my sources tell me. Nash Rourke, superstar, rues his involvement: says 'Director Thomas Lyon (30), ineffectual, arrogant, insists on disastrous last-minute script changes.'

Lyon vows to solve a 26-year-old real-life mystery, basis of Tyler's masterpiece. The police failed at the time. Who is Lyon kidding?

Naturally those closely touched by the tragic unexplained hanging death of a leading Newmarket trainer's wife are distressed to have cold embers fanned to hurtful inaccurate reheat.

Lyon's version so far has the hanged wife's trainer-husband – Rourke – tumbling her sister, prompting apoplectic revenge from consequently cuckolded top Jockey Club steward, later ga-ga. None of this happened.

Why do the giants of Hollywood entrust a prestigious film-of-the-book to the incompetent mercies of an over-hyped bully-boy? Why is this ludicrous buffoon still strutting his stuff on the Heath? Who's allowing him to waste millions of dollars on this pathetic travesty of a great work?

Isn't Master Thomas Lyon ripe for the overdue boot?

There was a large photograph of Nash, looking grim.

Blindly angry, I went up to my rooms and found the telephone ringing when I walked in.

Before I could speak into the receiver, Nash's voice said, 'I didn't say that, Thomas.'

'You wouldn't.'

86

'I'll kill that son of a bitch, Tyler.'

'Leave him to O'Hara.'

'Are we still going to Doncaster?'

'We certainly are,' I said. Anywhere but Newmarket, I thought. 'Ready in half an hour?'

'I'll be down in the lobby.'

I phoned O'Hara's mobile phone and reached only his message service.

I said, 'Read the *Daily Drumbeat*, page sixteen, feature column headed, "Hot from the Stars". Nash and I are going to the sports. I'll have my mobile. Take Prozak.'

Howard Tyler's phone rang and rang in his room, unanswered.

I showered in record time, put on steward-lunching clothes and went down to ask questions of the helpful soul behind the reception desk.

'Mr Tyler isn't here,' she confirmed. 'He left.'

'*When* did he leave?'

'Actually,' she said, 'he picked up a newspaper from the desk here and went into the dining-room to have breakfast, as he always does. It's so nice to have him here, and Mr Rourke too, we can hardly believe it ... So Mr Tyler hurried out of the dining-room five minutes later – he didn't eat his breakfast – he went upstairs and came down with his suitcase and said he didn't know when he'd come back.' She looked worried. 'I didn't ask him for payment. I hope I haven't done wrong, but I understood everything should be charged to the film company.'

'Don't worry about that,' I reassured her. 'Did Mr Tyler say where he was going?'

He hadn't, of course. He'd been in a great hurry. The receptionist had asked him if he'd felt ill, but he hadn't answered. He'd taken the newspaper with him, but the staff had had another copy. They had all read the column. She'd thought it best to show it to Mr Rourke. Her virtuousness nearly choked her.

'What will happen, do you think?' Nash asked, ready for the races, listening to a repeat from the receptionist.

'Short-term, we've got Howard off our backs.'

We went out to the Rolls and along to where the helicopter waited.

'I'll sue the bastard,' Nash said furiously, strapping himself in, 'saying I rue my involvement!'

'Did you?'

'Did I what?'

'Say it.'

'Shit, Thomas. I said I was sorry not to be staying home with my wife. And that was on day one. I don't in the least regret it now.'

'She could have come with you.'

He shrugged. We both knew why his wife had stayed at home: her insecurity in a four-months pregnancy with complications. She'd been annoyed with him for agreeing to Newmarket. He'd made too public an apology.

'As for all that trash I was supposed to say about you personally . . .'

'Howard put his own words into your mouth,' I said. 'Forget it.'

The helicopter lifted off from the Newmarket grass and swung round north-west.

However glibly I might say 'forget it', I had uncomfortable suspicions that the parent movie company, our source of finance, would come thundering down like a posse to lynch me from the nearest cross-beam. Any bad odour clinging to their investment called for dismissals to exorcise it. O'Hara might have to dump me: might even want to.

Bye-bye career, I thought. It had been great while it lasted. I couldn't believe what was happening.

Smart move on Howard's part to decamp out of reach of my fists. I could have killed him. I sat quietly in the helicopter looking out at Lincolnshire passing beneath and felt queasy from the turmoil in my gut.

I accepted that in general the most disliked person in the making of any film was the director. The director required people to do things they considered un-necessary/ridiculous/wrong. Directors (a) demanded too much from actors and (b) ignored their well-thought-out interpretations. Directors were never satisfied, wasted time on detail, worked everyone to death, ignored injured feelings, made no allowance for techni-cal difficulties, expected the impossible, screamed at people.

I accepted also on the other hand that a director needed an overall vision of the work in progress, even if details got changed en route. A director had to fight to bring that vision to revelatory life. Excessive sym-pathy and tolerance on the set were unproductive, vacillating decisions wasted money and inconsistency left an enterprise rudderless. A successful movie was a tight ship.

It was more in my nature to be a persuader than an ogre, but sometimes, as with Howard, when persuasion failed to work, the ogre surfaced. I knew, too, that it was what O'Hara expected and in fact required of me. Use your power, he'd said.

Now everyone working on the film would read the piece in the *Drumbeat*. Half of Newmarket also. Even if O'Hara left me in charge, my job would be difficult to impossible, all my authority gone. If I had to, I would fight to get that back.

The helicopter landed near the Doncaster winning post, where a senior official was waiting to give Nash a suitable greeting and to lead him to the mandarins. The minute I followed him onto the grass my mobile phone buzzed, and I told him to go ahead, I would join him after I'd talked to O'Hara; if it were in fact O'Hara.

He looked at me straightly and asked the official to pause for my call.

I answered the phone's summons. 'Thomas,' I said.

'Thomas!' O'Hara's voice was loud with annoyance. 'Where are you?' Nash could hear him shouting: he winced.

'Doncaster racecourse.'

'I've had Hollywood on the line. It's not yet five in the morning there but the company is already furious. Someone made a phone call and then sent a fax of the *Drumbeat*.'

I said stupidly, 'A *fax*?'

'A fax,' he confirmed.

'Who sent it?'

'The mogul I talked to didn't say.'

I swallowed. My heart raced. The hand holding the instrument visibly trembled beside my eye. Calm down, I thought.

'Who did Tyler talk to?' O'Hara demanded furiously.

'I don't know.'

'You don't *know*?'

'No. He was grumbling to everyone who would listen. He may not have known he was spouting to a journalist – or to someone who *knew* a journalist.'

'What does he say about it?'

'The hotel says he blasted off the minute he saw the paper. No one knows where he's gone.'

'I tried his home number,' O'Hara shouted. 'They say he's in Newmarket.'

'More likely the moon.'

'The mogul I talked to is one of the very top guys, and he wants your head.'

This was it, I thought numbly: and I couldn't think of anything to say. I needed an impassioned plea in mitigation. Drew a blank.

'Are you there, Thomas?'

'Yes.'

'He says you're fired.'

I was silent.

'Hell's teeth, Thomas, defend yourself.'

'I warned Howard yesterday not to shoot his mouth off, but I think now that he'd already done it.'

'Two weeks ago he tried to get the moguls to fire you, if you remember. I pacified them then. But *this*!' Words failed him.

I began finally to protest. 'We're on target for time. We're within budget. The company themselves insisted on story changes. I'm making a commercial motion picture, and it isn't true that there are rows and discord, except with Howard himself.'

'What's he saying?' Nash demanded impatiently.

'I'm sacked.'

Nash snatched the phone out of my hand.

'O'Hara? This is Nash. You tell those brain-deads who are our masters that I did not say what the *Drumbeat* says I did. Your boy is doing an OK job on this movie and if you take him off it at this stage you *will* get a bummer of a film, and what's more, they can whistle for me to sign with them ever again.'

Aghast, I snatched the phone back. 'Nash, you can't do that. O'Hara, don't listen to him.'

'Put him back on the line.'

I handed the phone over, shaking my head. Nash listened to O'Hara for a while and finally said, 'You told me to trust him. I do. This movie has a good feel. Now you trust *me*, trust my nose in these matters.'

He listened a bit longer, said 'Right' and pressed the power-off button.

'O'Hara says he'll call you back in five hours when they will have talked it through in Hollywood. They're going to hold a breakfast meeting there at nine o'clock, when the big-wigs are all up. O'Hara will sit in on a conference call.'

'Thank you,' I said.

He smiled briefly. 'My reputation is at stake here, same as yours. I don't want my green light turning amber.'

'It never will.'

'Bad reviews give me indigestion.'

We walked with the patient official across the track and up to the stewards' privacy. Heads turned sharply all the way as racegoer after racegoer did a double take at the sight of Nash. We had asked for no advance publicity – the parent film company was security hyper-conscious – so that only the top echelon knew whom to expect. I was glad, I found, to have an anonymous face.

They hadn't waited lunch. Even for mega-stars, racing time tables couldn't be changed. About twenty stewards and friends were at their roast beef and suitable Yorkshire pudding.

From behind the forks the welcome was as warm and impressed as the most inflated ego could desire, and Nash's ego, as I was progressively discovering, was far more normal and unassuming than seemed consistent with his eminence.

I'd been in awe of him before I'd met him. I'd metaphorically approached him on my knees, and I'd found, not the temperamental perfectionist I'd been ominously told to expect, but essentially the man I'd seen him play over and over again on the screen, a man, whatever the role or the make-up, of sane intelligence, mentally tough.

I forlornly hoped that the Doncaster stewards and their wives and other guests weren't avid readers of *Drumbeat*'s 'Hot from the Stars', and with relief I saw that the two papers most in evidence were the *Racing Gazette* and the *Daily Cable*, both of them lying open at the obituary page for Valentine.

Nash and I shook a fair number of hands and were seated in prestigious places, and while Nash asked a dumbstruck waitress for fizzy mineral water, nearly causing her to faint from her proximity to the sexiest eyes in screendom, I read both farewells to Valentine, and found they'd done the old man proud. Cremation, the *Gazette* also noted, was set for 11 a.m., Monday, and a memorial service would be arranged later. If I were truly out of work, I thought gloomily, I could go to both.

By the coffee stage, the *Drumbeat*'s pages were fluttering across the table and inevitably someone commiserated with Nash over the mess his director was making of his film. My own identity, remarked on round the table behind sheltering hands, produced universally disapproving stares.

Nash said with authority, his expert voice production easily capable of silencing other conversations, 'Never believe what you read in the papers. We're making an excellent film in Newmarket. We're being bad-mouthed by a spiteful little man. I did *not* say what I am reported to have said, and I have complete confidence in Thomas here. I shall complain to the paper and demand they print a retraction.'

'Sue them,' someone said.

'Perhaps I will.'

'And as for you, Thomas,' said one of the stewards whom I knew personally, '*you* must definitely sue.'

I said, 'I'm not sure that I can.'

'Of course you can!' He stabbed at the pages with a forefinger. 'This is defamatory in the extreme.'

I said, 'It's difficult to sue anyone for asking questions.'

'*What?*'

'Those defamations are written carefully in the form of questions. The question marks tend to take the certainty out of the slurs.'

'I don't believe it!'

A head further along the large table was gravely

94

nodding. 'A scurrilous suggestion, if it is expressed as a question, may or may not be considered libel. There are grey areas.'

My steward friend said blankly, 'That's not justice!'

'It's the law.'

'You knew that?' Nash said to me.

'Mm.'

'Did Howard know it?'

'Whoever wrote that piece certainly did.'

Nash said, '*Shit!*' and not a single face objected.

'What Nash really needs,' I said, 'is a reliable tip for the Lincoln.'

They laughed and with relief turned to the serious business of the day. I half-heard the knowledgeable form-talk and thought that five hours could be a long torture. Barely forty minutes of it had so far passed. My pulse still raced from anxiety. My whole professional life probably hung on whether the moguls who would be bidden to the breakfast table were putting in a good night's sleep. Saturday morning. Golf day. I would be doubly unpopular.

I went down with Nash and a couple of the stewards' other lunch guests to see the horses walking round the parade ring before the first race. Nash looked at the horses: the racecrowd progressively looked at Nash. He seemed to take the staring for granted, just as he would have done back home in Hollywood, and he signed a few autographs for wide-eyed teenagers with pleasant politeness.

'How do I put a bet on?' he asked me, signing away.

'I'll do it for you if you like. Which horse, how much?'

'Hell knows.' He raised his eyes briefly and pointed to a horse being at that point mounted by a jockey in scarlet and yellow stripes. 'That one. Twenty.'

'Will you be all right if I leave you?'

'I'm a grown boy, you know.'

Grinning, I turned away, walked to the Tote, and bet twenty pounds to win on the horse called Wasp. Nash, waiting for me to retrieve him, returned with me to the stewards' room, from where we watched Wasp finish an unobtrusive fifth.

'I owe you,' Nash said. 'Pick me one yourself for the next race.'

The races as always were being shown on closed-circuit television on sets throughout the bars and the grandstands. A set in the stewards' room was busy with a replay of the just-finished race, Wasp still finishing fifth, the jockey busy to the end.

I stared breathlessly at the screen.

'Thomas? *Thomas*,' Nash said forcefully in my ear, 'come back from wherever you've gone.'

'Television,' I said.

Nash said ironically, 'It's been around a while, you know.'

'Yes, but ...' I picked up a copy of the *Racing Gazette* that was lying on the table and turned from Valentine's obituary to the pages laying out the Doncaster programme. Television coverage of the day's sport, I saw, was, as I'd hoped, by courtesy of a commercial station that provided full day-by-day racing for grateful millions. For the big-race opening of the Flat season, they would be there in force.

'Thomas,' Nash repeated.

'Er . . .' I said, 'how badly do you want to save our film? Or, in fact . . . me?'

'Not badly enough to jump off a cliff.'

'How about an interview on TV?'

He stared.

I said, 'What if you could say on television that we're *not* making a bummer of a movie? Would you want to do it?'

'Sure,' he said easily, 'but it wouldn't reach every reader of the *Drumbeat*.'

'No. But what if O'Hara could get the interview transmitted to Hollywood? How about the moguls seeing it at breakfast? Your own face on the screen might tip things where O'Hara's assurances might not. Only . . . how do you feel about trying?'

'Hell, Thomas, get on with it.'

I went out onto the viewing balcony and pressed the buttons to get O'Hara: and let me not get his message service, I prayed.

He answered immediately himself, as if waiting for calls.

'It's Thomas,' I said.

'It's too early to hear from Hollywood.'

'No. It's something else.' I told him what I'd suggested to Nash, and he put his finger at once on the snags.

'First of all,' he said doubtfully, 'you'd have to get the TV company to interview Nash.'

'I could do that. It's getting the interview onto the screen in the Hollywood conference room that I'm not sure of. Live pictures get transmitted regularly from England to the States, but I don't know the pathways.

If we could get to an LA station we could have a tape rushed round for our moguls to play on a VCR . . .'

'Thomas, stop. I can fix the LA end. The transmission from England . . .' he paused, sucking his teeth. 'What station are we talking about?'

I told him. 'The people they'll have here are an outside broadcast unit. They'll have engineers and camera crews and a producer or two and three or four interviewers and commentators, but they won't have the authority or the equipment to transmit overseas. The OK would have to come from their headquarters, which are in London. They'll have Doncaster races on their screen there. They can transmit to anywhere. Their number will be in the phone book . . .'

'And you need me to use my clout.' He sounded resigned, seeing difficulties.

'Um,' I said, 'if you want *Unstable Times* to reach the cinema, it might be worth trying. I mean, it's your picture too, you know. Your head on the block for engaging me.'

'I see that.' He paused. 'All right, I'll start. It's a hell of a long shot.'

'They've been known to win.'

'Is Nash with you?'

'Five paces away.'

'Get him, would you?'

Nash came outside and took the phone. 'I'll do the interview. Thomas says he can fix it, no problem.' He listened. 'Yeah. Yeah. If he says he can, I guess he can. He doesn't promise what he can't deliver. O'Hara, you get off your ass and put Thomas and me into that meeting. It's damn stupid to let that son-of-a-bitch Tyler sink the ship.' He listened again, then said, 'Get it done, O'Hara. Hang the expense. I'll not be beaten by that *scribbler*.'

I listened in awe to the switched-on power of the ultimate green light and humbly thanked the fates that he saw me as an ally, not a villain.

He disconnected, handed the phone back to me and said, 'Where do we find our interviewer?'

'Follow me.' I tried to make it sound light-hearted, but I was no great actor. Nash silently came with me down to the unsaddling enclosure, from where the runners of the just-run race had already departed.

'Do you know who you are looking for?' he asked, as I turned my head one way and another. 'Can't you ask?'

'I don't need to,' I said, conscious, even if Nash ignored it, of everyone looking at *him*. 'This television company travels with a race-caller, a paddock commentator who talks about the runners for the next race, and someone who interviews the winning jockeys and trainers afterwards, and it's him I'm looking for ... and I know him.'

'That's something.'

'And there he is,' I said, spotting him. 'Coming?'

I slid then between the groups of people chatting in the railed area outside the weighing-room; slid where the groups parted like the Red Sea to clear a path for Nash. My acquaintance, the interviewer, began to say hello to me, saw who I was with and ended with his mouth open.

'Nash,' I introduced, 'this is Greg Compass: Greg ... Nash Rourke.'

Greg came to his senses like any seasoned television performer should and with genuine welcome shook the hand that had fired a hundred harmless bullets.

'He's here to see the Lincoln,' I explained. 'How about some inside information?'

'Gallico,' Greg suggested promptly. 'He's bursting out of his skin, so they say.' He looked thoughtfully at Nash and without pressing him asked, 'Do you mind if I say you're here? I expect Thomas told you I do the ghastly chat stuff for all the couch potatoes?'

'I did tell him, yes.'

'Thomas and I,' Greg explained, 'used to ride against each other, when I was a jockey and we were young.'

'You're all so tall,' Nash exclaimed.

'Jump jockeys are mostly taller. Ex-jump jockeys get to be racing commentators or journalists, things like that. Live it first. Talk about it after.' He was comically self-deprecating, though in fact he'd been a top career jockey, not an amateur like me. He was forty, slender, striking, stylish. He took a breath. 'Well . . .'

'You can certainly say I'm here,' Nash assured him.

'Great. Um . . .' He hesitated.

'Ask him,' I said, half-smiling.

Greg glanced at me and back to Nash. 'I suppose . . . I couldn't get you in front of my camera?'

Nash gave me a dry sideways look and in his best slay-them gravelly bass said that he saw no reason why not.

'I did hear you were in Newmarket, making a film,' Greg said. 'I suppose I can say so?'

'Sure. Thomas is directing it.'

'Yes. Word gets around.'

I pulled a folded *Drumbeat* page from my pocket and handed it to Greg.

'If you'll let him,' I said, 'Nash would very briefly like to contradict what's written in that "Hot from the Stars" column.'

Greg read it through quickly, his expression darkening from simple curiosity to indignation.

'Difficult to sue,' he exclaimed. 'It's all questions. Is it true?'

'It's true the film story is different from the book,' I said.

Nash assured him, 'I didn't say those things and I don't think them. The film is going well. All I'd like to say, if you'll let me, is that one shouldn't believe newspapers.'

'Thomas?' Greg raised his eyebrows at me. 'You're using me, aren't you?'

'Yes. But that column's assassinating me. If Nash can say on screen that it's not true, we can beam him to the money-men in Hollywood and hope to prevent them from taking the column seriously.'

He thought it over. He sighed. 'All right, then, but very casual, OK? I'll put you both together in shot.'

'Innocence by association,' I said gratefully.

'Always a bright boy.' He looked at his watch. 'How about after the Lincoln? An hour from now. After I've talked to the winning trainer and jockey and the owners, if they're here. We could slot it in at that point. I'll tell my producer. Thomas, you remember where the camera is? Come there after the Lincoln. And Thomas, you owe me.'

'Two seats for the première,' I said. 'Without you, there may not be one.'

'Four seats.'

'A whole row,' I said.

'Done.' Greg looked at Nash. 'What is this over-hyped buffoon of an ineffectual bullyboy really like as a director?'

'Worse,' Nash said.


We did the interview, Nash and I side by side. Greg introduced us to the viewers, asked if Nash had backed the winner of the Lincoln – Gallico – congratulated him and said he hoped Nash was enjoying his visit to Britain.

Nash said, 'I'm making a film here. Very enjoyable.' He nodded affably. He added a few details casually, as Greg had wanted, but left no listeners in doubt that the racing film we were making in Newmarket was going well.

'Didn't I read an uncomplimentary report . . .?' Greg prompted quizzically.

'Yes,' Nash agreed, nodding. 'Words were put into my mouth that I never said. So what else is new? Never believe newspapers.'

'You're playing a trainer, aren't you?' Greg asked the questions we had asked him to ask as if he'd just that minute thought of them. 'How's it going with the riding?'

'I can sit on a horse,' Nash smiled. 'I can't ride like Thomas.'

'Do you ride in the film?' Greg asked me helpfully.

'No, he doesn't,' Nash said, 'but he takes a horse out on the Heath to gallop it sometimes. Still, I can beat him at golf.'

The affection in his voice said more than a thousand words. Greg wound up the interview good-naturedly and expertly handed on the couch potatoes to the paddock commentator for profiles of the next race's runners.

'Thank you,' I said, 'very much.'

'A row of seats,' he nodded. 'Don't forget.' He paused, and added cynically, 'Do you play golf, Thomas?'

'No.'

'I can always beat him,' Nash confirmed.

'You're a double act!' Greg said.

O'Hara had watched the interview in the television company's headquarters in London, and he buzzed my telephone before I'd found a quiet spot for reaching him.

'Brilliant!' he said, almost laughing. 'Brotherly love all over the screen. Not a dry eye in the house.'

'Will it work?'

'Of course it will work.'

'Will it get to the meeting in time?'

'Cancel the anxiety, Thomas. The people here have been real helpful. Their fee would launch a Hubble telescope, but the moguls will see the show with their wheaties.'

'Thanks, O'Hara.'

'Give me Nash.'

I handed the phone over and watched Nash deliver a series of nods and yeses.

'Yes, of course he suggested my lines,' Nash said, 'and he got that pal of his to ask the right questions. How? Hell knows. The old jockey network, I guess.'

The last few races crawled by and, having thanked our hosts, we flew back to Newmarket with still no further word from O'Hara. After-breakfast time in Los Angeles. What were the moguls doing?

'Stop biting your nails,' Nash said.

His chauffeured Rolls took us back to Bedford Lodge, where Nash suggested I join him in his rooms so that we might both hear what O'Hara might report.

The film company had engaged four comfortable suites in the hotel; the best for Nash, one for Silva, one for me and one (often empty) for O'Hara or other visiting mogul. Rooms in the hotel were provided for Moncrieff and for Howard: the rest of the approximately sixty people working on the film, those in scenesetting, wardrobe, make-up, those in technical trades, those who were assistants or production staff or couriers, all those inescapably involved were staying in various other hotels, motels or private lodgings. Most of the stable lads were housed in a hostel. The horsemaster/assistant trainer went home to his wife. The overall logistics of keeping everyone fed and working within union guidelines were, thankfully, not my job.

Nash's rooms looked out over pleasant gardens and provided large armchairs fit for soothing limbs made weary by hours of pretending to be someone else; or rather by hours of waiting around in order to pretend to be someone else, for five minutes or so, now and then. Moncrieff and I might work frantically non-stop. Actors stood around getting bored, waiting for us to be ready. Actors, lengthily immobile, grew tired, while Moncrieff and I did not.

Nash sank into his favourite armchair and for about the four-hundredth time looked at his watch.

Five hours had gone. Almost six. I'd spent a great deal of the time sweating.

My mobile phone buzzed. My mouth went dry. Buzz, buzz.

'Answer it!' Nash commanded crossly, seeing my reluctance.

I said, 'Hello.' More of a croak.

'Thomas?' O'Hara said. 'You're not fired.'

Silence.

'Thomas? Did you hear? Get on with the film.'

'I . . . er . . .'

'For hell's sake! Is Nash there?'

I handed the phone to the green light whose reaction to the news was a robust, 'I should damn well think so. Yes, of course he's been worried, he's only human.'

He gave me the phone back. O'Hara said, 'There are strings attached. I have to spend more time in Newmarket supervising you. One of the big boys is coming to visit, in order to be satisfied that their money is being spent reasonably. They waffled on for far too long about who they could put in to direct in your place. But in the end your television clip did the trick. Nash convinced them. They still think he can do no wrong. If Nash is happy, they'll keep you on.'

'Thanks.'

'I'm coming back to Newmarket tomorrow. It's a goddam nuisance as I was planning to fly to LA, but there it is. Like you said, it's my head on the block alongside yours. What will you be doing tomorrow morning?'

'Horses galloping on the Heath.'

'And Nash?'

'Sitting on a horse, watching. In the afternoon, we ferry the horses to Huntingdon racecourse. Monday we set up and rehearse the crowd scenes at the races. Some of the crews are moving to motels around Huntingdon, but Nash and I, and a few others, are staying in our rooms here in Newmarket.'

'How far is it?'

'Only about thirty-eight miles. Where do you want to sleep?'

'Newmarket.' No hesitation. 'Get yourself a driver, Thomas. I don't want you falling asleep at the wheel with those long hours you work.'

'I like to drive myself, and it's not very far.'

'Get a driver.'

It was an order. I said OK. I was grateful to be still employed. He said, 'See you, fellow,' and I said, 'Thanks, O'Hara,' and he left one further report: 'Howard will have his claws well clipped. Stupid son of a bitch.'

'There you go,' Nash said, smiling, when I switched the phone off. 'Drink? Eat with me, why not?'

Nash had most of his meals alone upstairs, brought by room service. Unlike most actors he had a solitary streak to which, because of his wife's absence, he had given free rein. Surprised, therefore, but pleased not to be dining alone myself, I stayed for soup, lamb and claret and a step into a positive friendship that I wouldn't, a couple of weeks earlier, have thought likely.

Relaxed after the day's troubles, I decided to make a brief call on Dorothea, to see if she needed anything, before my scheduled meeting with Moncrieff to plan the morning's activities on the Heath.

I expected to find a quiet sorrowful house. Instead, when I arrived there, I found flashing lights, a police car, and an ambulance.

# CHAPTER SIX

A policeman barred my attempt to walk up the concrete path.

'What happened?' I asked.

'Clear the path, please, sir.' He was young, big, businesslike, and unsympathetic with unknown members of the public. He had kept – and was keeping – a small crowd of onlookers from stepping too close to the goings-on.

I tried again. 'The people who live here are my friends.'

'Stand back, if you please, sir.' He scarcely looked at me, unintentionally impressive, a large physical barrier that I had no inclination to fight.

I retreated through the curious crowd and from behind them used my constant companion, the portable telephone, to ring Dorothea's number. After what seemed a very long time a distressed woman's voice said, 'Hello.'

'Dorothea?' I said. 'It's Thomas.'

'Oh. Oh, no, I'm Betty. Where are you, Thomas? Can you come?' I explained I was outside but obstructed and in a few seconds she was hurrying down the path to collect me. The large policeman stepped aside, shrugging, not caring one way or the other, and I hastened with Betty towards the front door.

'What's happened?' I asked her.

'Someone broke in. It's *terrible* ... they've nearly killed Dorothea ... how *could* they? Dr Gill has just come and the police too and there's so much blood and they're taking photographs and it's all *unbelievable* ...'

We went into the house which looked inside as if it had been swept through by a tornado.

Valentine's bedroom by the front door had been wrecked: drawers were upturned on the floor, their contents scattered. The wardrobe stood open, empty. Pictures had been torn from the walls, their frames smashed. Mattress and pillows were ripped, guts spilling.

'It's all like this,' Betty wailed. 'Even the bathrooms and the kitchen. I must go back to Dorothea ... I'm afraid she'll die ...'

She left me and vanished into Dorothea's bedroom where I with hesitation followed, stepping round a wide drying sea of blood in the hall.

I needn't have felt I might be intruding: the room was full of people. Robbie Gill obstructed my view of most of Dorothea, who was lying unspeaking but in shoes and stockings on the sliced ruins of her bed. Two ambulancemen filled half the available space with a stretcher on wheels. A uniformed policewoman and a photographer were busy. Betty threaded a way into the throng, beckoning me to follow.

Robbie Gill glanced up, saw me, nodded recognition and took a pace back with the result that I saw all of

Dorothea, and became sickened and overwhelmingly angry.

She was bleeding, swollen and unconscious, with great gashes in the flesh of her cheek and forehead and a red mess where her mouth was.

'Her right arm's broken,' Robbie Gill dictated to the note-taking policewoman. 'She has internal injuries . . .' He stopped. Even for a doctor, it was too much. Dorothea's clothes were ripped open, her old breasts and stomach bare, two slashed wounds on her body bleeding copiously, one so deep that a bulge of intestines protruded through the abdomen wall, a glistening pale swelling island in a wet scarlet ocean. The smell of blood was overpowering.

Robbie Gill took sterile dressings from his bag and told everyone except the policewoman to leave. She herself looked over-pale, but stood her ground as the rest of us silently obeyed.

Betty was shaking, tears on her cheeks.

'I came over to make sure she'd given herself something to eat. She doesn't take care of herself, now Valentine's gone. I came in through the back door, into the kitchen, and it's *wrecked* . . . it's terrible . . . and I *found* her, she was bleeding on the floor in the hall, and I thought she was dead . . . so I phoned Dr Gill because his number is right beside the phone in the kitchen, and he brought the police here and the ambulancemen . . . and they carried her into the bedroom. Do you think she'll be all right?' Her anxiety shook her. 'She won't die, not like this. How *could* anyone do this?'

I had imagined and I had filmed scenes as bad or worse, but the blood we'd used had often been lipstick dissolved in oil – to give it viscosity – and intestines made of inflated sausage skin, and sweat sprayed through an atomiser onto grey-greasepainted faces.

More people came, apparently plain-clothes policemen. Betty and I retreated to Dorothea's sitting-room where, again, comprehensive chaos paralysed thought.

'How could anyone *do* this?' Betty repeated numbly. '*Why* would anyone do it?'

'Did she have anything valuable?' I asked.

'Of course she didn't. Just her little knick-knacks. Trinkets and souvenirs. They've even torn the photo of her and Bill's wedding. How *could* they?' She picked up the ruins of a photo frame, crying for her friend's pain. 'And her pretty pink vase ... it's in splinters. She loved that vase.'

I stared at the pink pieces, and then went down on one knee and fruitlessly searched the carpet around them.

'I've put the key in the pink vase in my sitting-room.'

Dorothea's voice spoke clearly in my memory. The key of Valentine's study, in safekeeping to prevent her son Paul from taking the books.

Bitterly but silently swearing I went along the passage and pushed open the study's half-closed door. The key was in the lock. Inside, Valentine's sanctum had been ravaged like the rest of the house; everything breakable had been demolished, everything soft slashed, all his photographs destroyed.

Every book had gone.

I opened the cupboard where I knew he kept the scrapbooks containing every column he'd ever written for newspapers.

Every shelf was bare.

Betty, trembling, put her hand on my arm and said, 'Dorothea told me Valentine wanted you to have his books. Where have they gone?'

With Paul, I automatically thought. But he *couldn't* have inflicted such wounds on his mother. A pompous, bombastic man, yes; but not to this extent vicious.

I asked Betty, 'Where is Paul? Her son.'

'Oh, dear! Oh, dear! He went home yesterday. He doesn't know ... And I don't know his number ...' She swayed. 'I can't bear it.'

'Don't worry,' I said. 'Sit down. I'll find his number. I'll get you some tea. Where's your husband?'

'It's his darts night ... at the pub.'

'Which pub?'

'Oh, dear ... The Dragon.'

First things first, I thought, heading for the kitchen. Hot sweet tea prevented a lot of breakdowns from shock. No figure of authority stopped me, though the little house seemed crowded with them. I took the cup and saucer to Betty who held them clattering in both hands as she sat in Valentine's room.

In the old man's fortunately unshredded phone book I looked up The Dragon's number and spoiled Betty's husband's treble twenty by asking him to come home quickly. Then I searched around for Paul's number and ran it to earth on the notepad attached to the extension phone in the kitchen.

Paul answered, and I listened to his obnoxious voice with relief. If he were at home in Surrey he couldn't have attacked his mother a hundred miles away in Newmarket, not with her wounds so recent and bleed-

112

ing. Even if she lived, she couldn't have mentally recovered from being attacked by her own son.

He sounded as appalled as he ought to be. He announced he would set off at once.

'I don't know which hospital they'll take her to,' I said.

'Is she going to die?' he interrupted.

'Like I told you, I don't know. Hold on for a bit and I'll get Dr Gill to talk to you.'

'Useless man!'

'Stay on the line,' I said. 'Wait.'

I left the kitchen, found the plain-clothes men starting to blow dust on things for fingerprints and hovered until Dorothea's door opened to let out the police-woman who was beckoning to the men to bring back the stretcher.

I said to her, 'Mrs Pannier's son is on the telephone. Please can Dr Gill talk to him?'

She looked at me vaguely and retreated into Doro-thea's room with the ambulance people, but it seemed that she did pass on the message because presently Robbie Gill opened the bedroom door again and asked me if Paul were actually on the line.

'Yes,' I confirmed. 'He's waiting to talk to you.'

'Tell him I won't be long.'

I relayed the message to Paul. He was impatiently displeased. I told him to wait and left him. Angry and anxious about Dorothea, and concerned about the missing books, I found reassuring Paul impossible. I couldn't even be decently sympathetic. I was sure he wouldn't give the books back unless I took him to court, and even then I had no list of what I'd lost.

113

Robbie Gill accompanied Dorothea on the rolling stretcher right out to the ambulance, solicitously making sure she was gently treated. Then, looking stern, he came back into the house, strode down the hall to where I waited by the kitchen door, walked over to the central table and picked up the receiver.

'Mr Pannier?' he asked, then grimaced crossly as Paul spoke on the other end.

'Mr Pannier,' Robbie said forcefully, 'your mother has been beaten about the head. She's unconscious from those blows. Her right arm is broken. In addition, she has knife wounds to her body. I am sending her to Cambridge . . .' he named the hospital . . . 'where she will receive the best attention. I cannot tell you whether or not she will survive.' He listened with disgust to Paul's reply. 'No, she was not sexually assaulted. I have done everything possible. I suggest you check with the hospital later. It is now out of my hands.' He thrust the receiver back into its cradle, compressed his mouth as if physically restraining himself from swearing, and squeezed his eyes with finger and thumb.

'How is she really?' I asked.

He shrugged wearily, his expression relaxing. 'I don't know. She put up a fight, I should think. Tried to defend herself with her arm. It's odd . . . it's almost as if she had *two* assailants . . . one that hit her arm and her head with something hard and jagged, and one that used a knife. Or perhaps there was only one assailant, but with two weapons.'

'It's a useless question,' I said, 'but *why* attack her?'

'A dear good old lady! The world's grown vicious.

Old ladies get attacked. I detest that son of hers. I shouldn't say that. Pay no attention. He wanted to know if she'd been raped.'

'He's the ultimate four-letter case.'

'The police want to know why the whole house is in this state.' He waved an arm at the devastation around. 'How do I know? They weren't poor, they weren't rich. Poor old bodies. They relied on you lately, you know. They loved you, in a way. Pity *you* weren't their son.'

'Valentine was part of my childhood.'

'Yes. He told me.'

'Well . . . what happens next?'

'The police are talking about attempted murder, because of the knife wounds. But . . . I don't know . . .'

'What?' I prompted, as he hesitated.

'It may be fanciful . . . I don't know if I'll say it to the police . . . but it would have taken so little to finish her off. Just one stab in the right place.' He paused. 'You saw her, didn't you?'

'Yes, when you moved back from her bed.'

He nodded. 'I thought so. You saw those slashes. Two of them, one relatively superficial, one very deep. The first one cut her clothes open. Why wasn't there a third? You know what I think? I think it was an *aborted* murder. I think he changed his mind.'

I stared.

'You can call me crazy,' he said.

'No, I think you're clever.'

'I've seen knife murders. They often look like frenzy. Dozens of stab wounds. Deranged mind at work. They can't stop. Do you see?'

115

'Yes,' I said.

'I don't know why I'm telling you. Pay no attention. With luck Dorothea will live to tell us herself.'

'How much luck does she need?'

'Frankly,' he said dispiritedly, 'quite a lot. Concussion's unpredictable. I don't think she has intracranial bleeding, but I can't be sure. But that abdominal wound ... it's bad ... it depends on infection ... and she's eighty next month ... but she's well in herself ... healthy for her age, I mean. I've grown fond of them both, though I used to fight with Valentine on the surface, obstinate old cuss.'

I thought Robbie Gill a good doctor, and I said so. He brushed off my words.

'Can I ask you something?' I said.

'Of course.'

'Well ... how long ago was Dorothea attacked?'

'How long ago?'

'Yes. I mean, was she attacked *before* the trashing of the house? All this damage must have taken quite a while to achieve. Or had she been out, and come back at the wrong moment? Or did someone try to beat some information out of her and go too far, and then pull the place apart looking for whatever he wanted?'

'Hey, slow down,' he protested. 'You think like a policeman.'

Like a film-maker, I thought. I said again, 'How long since she was attacked?'

He pursed his lips. 'The house was trashed first.'

We digested it in silence.

'You're sure?' I asked finally.

Gill said, 'Judging from the comparatively small

116

amount of swelling and the rate of bleeding, Dorothea hadn't been in that state very long before her friend Betty found her. I came at once when Betty phoned me. I wasn't much longer than five minutes on the way. Betty might be lucky that she didn't arrive here ten minutes sooner.' He sighed. 'It isn't our problem, I'm glad to say. We can leave it to the police.'

'Yes.'

He looked at his watch and said it had been a long day, and I agreed with that too. When he told the police he was leaving, they decided to take his fingerprints. They took mine also, and Betty's: for elimination, they said. They wrote brief statements from Betty and me, and we told them Paul's fingerprints would be everywhere, like our own.

Betty's husband came to collect her with wide consoling arms, and at length I drove back to Bedford Lodge and downed a medicinal large one with Moncrieff.

Summoned by Ed on my say-so, all available crews, technicians, wardrobe people and actors (except Nash) gathered in the stable yard at dawn on Sunday morning.

I mounted a wooden chair to address them and, in the fresh ever-moving East Anglian air, wondered how Shakespeare could have expected Henry V's words before Agincourt to be heard by any but the nearest knights, given the clinking noises of armour on horseback and the absence of microphones.

I at least had a megaphone, equipment perhaps overfamiliar to my audience.

'I expect,' I said loudly, when movement in the company had diminished to restless impatience, 'that most of you have by now read yesterday's "Hot from the Stars" column in the *Daily Drumbeat*.'

I reaped stares, nods, and a good many sardonic smiles. No overt sneers. Something, at least.

'As you can guess,' I went on, 'the column badly disturbed our parent company in Hollywood. Fortunately our producer assured them that you are all doing a very good job here. Some of you may like it, some may not, but Hollywood has confirmed that I continue to direct. Nash Rourke has told them he is in favour of this. In consequence, nothing has changed. Whether or not you agree with the *Drumbeat*'s assessment of my character, if you want to continue to be employed on this enterprise, you will please make a private commitment to give this film your best shot. For all our sakes, the creation of a well-made, visually exciting commercial motion picture should take priority over any personal feelings. I want you to be able in the future to say with *satisfaction* that you worked on this film. So it's back to business as usual, which means will the lads now saddle the horses and everyone else continue with the schedule that Ed has distributed. OK? Good.'

I lowered the megaphone, stepped off the chair and turned my back to the company to join Moncrieff, who had been standing behind me in support.

'Socked it to them,' he approved with irony. 'We could make a film of making this film.'

'Or a book,' I said.

Our female star, Silva Shawn, loped across the stable

yard to join us. As usual, when not dressed in character, she wore flapping dark voluminous layers of clothes reaching to her ankles, with black Doc Marten boots below and a charcoal hat above, a hat that looked like a soft collapsed topper sitting on her eyebrows. She walked with long strides and arrived at most meetings with her shapely chin thrust forward in the body language of belittle-me-if-you-dare.

O'Hara had strongly warned me not to pay her any compliment she could possibly construe as sexual harassment, which I found difficult to comply with, as the adjectives which sprang first and naturally to my mind, apart from delicious, were divine, bewitching and ultra-desirable: but 'Never call her darling,' O'Hara had instructed.

'Why did you pick her if she's so touchy?' I'd asked him, and he had said succinctly, 'She can act.'

To date, her acting in the film had chiefly consisted of the notably explicit bedroom scenes with Nash (punctuated by No, no, no, moans from Howard) that we had captured the previous week. We had in fact faithfully adhered to Howard's script in the matter of words: what infuriated him was that I had ignored his intention to have Nash and Silva deliver their lines fully clothed. He had set their restrained show of affection in the drawing-room. I had transferred it to the bedroom, letting the verbal restraint remain, but contrasting it with growing physical desire. Silva, without self-consciousness ('bodies are natural'), had allowed delicately lit shots of her nudity in the bathroom. The rushes had quickened many pulses, including my own.

Whether she chose to admit it or not, there was a sensual quality in Silva's acting diametrically opposite to her chosen off-screen stance.

She had been away from Newmarket for the past week fulfilling an unbreakable commitment somewhere else, but was due to ride a horse on the Heath that morning, making use of an equestrian skill she was proud of. As happened in almost all films, we were not shooting the scenes chronologically: the coming encounter between the trainer and Cibber's wife was their first, their meeting, all innocence at the start but with, in no time, a promise developing in their eyes.

Silva said disapprovingly, 'I hope you got me a good horse.'

'He's fast,' I said, nodding.

'And good looking?'

'Of course.'

'And well trained?'

'I've been riding him myself.'

Without comment she transferred her near-universal disapproval to Moncrieff, whom she considered a male chauvinist despite his spectacular ability to make even ugly women look beautiful on screen.

After so many years spent studying female curves one might have expected Moncrieff to have grown an impervious skin, but every time we'd worked together he had fallen in love with the leading lady, and Silva looked like being no exception.

'Platonic,' I'd advised him. 'Strictly hands off. OK?'

'She needs me,' he'd pleaded.

'Light her and leave her.'

'Such cheekbones!'

Silva had fortunately so far given him the reverse of encouragement. I'd noticed from the first day I met her that she looked with more favour on men with suits, ties, short haircuts and clean-shaven faces, an inclination that should ensure the comparative invisibility of straggle-bearded, shambling, sloppily-dressed Moncrieff.

'I think,' I said to Silva politely, 'they're expecting you in make-up.'

She demanded, 'Are you telling me I'm late?'

I shook my head. 'The meeting has set everyone back. But I hope to finish the Heath scenes by lunchtime.'

She loped off, skirts flapping, making her own sort of statement.

'Gorgeous,' Moncrieff breathed.

'Dangerous,' I said.

Nash arrived, yawning, in his Rolls, and went into the house to the wardrobe and make-up departments. He was followed into the stable yard almost immediately by a man of very similar build, riding a bicycle which braked hard with a spraying of gravel beside Moncrieff and me.

'Morning,' the newcomer said briefly, dismounting. No deference in sight.

'Good morning, Ivan,' I answered.

'Are we still in business?'

'You're late,' I said.

He rightly took the comment as disapproval and wordlessly retreated, with his bicycle, into the house.

'I don't like him,' Moncrieff said. 'Saucy bugger.'

'Never mind. Make him look like St George, a shining champion.'

Nash himself had great presence just sitting on a horse but any speed faster than a walk revealed deficiencies, so for distance shots of him trotting or cantering we were using a stuntman, Ivan, instead. Ivan made a living riding in front of cameras and had picked up a truculent manner that would prevent his ever getting further in his profession. He had a habit, I'd been told, of holding forth in pubs about how *close* he was to Nash Rourke, for whom he had doubled on an earlier picture. Nash this, Nash that, Nash and I . . . In actual fact, they met seldom and conversed less. Ivan had mushroomed a relationship from a few short businesslike exchanges.

Trainers in many other racing centres drove out in Land-Rovers to watch their strings work, but on Newmarket's mainly roadless Heath it was still the norm to oversee everything from horseback and there was no doubt Nash looked more imposing in the saddle than operating a four-wheel drive. The mega-star's sex appeal brought in the pennies. My job was to make it powerful while looking natural, which in Nash's case wasn't hard.

Moncrieff was driven off up one of the few roads in a camera truck, with a second crew following, to positions we'd agreed the previous evening. The string of horses would canter up a hill, be followed broadside by one camera and head-on by a second as they came over the brow into the low-in-the-sky sunlight; rather, I hoped, like an orchestral flourish of brass after a muted but lyrical introduction. I often heard sound-tracks in my head long before any composer approached them.

Ed, knowing to the minute when to start the action, remained down by the stable. Though I could easily have driven, I chose to ride up onto the Heath to join Moncrieff; and I rode the horse we'd allotted to Silva, to get its back down: that is to say, to warm him up so that he would go sweetly with her and not buck. Silva might be proud of her riding, but O'Hara wouldn't thank me for getting her dumped on her exquisite backside.

The terrible Ivan was to canter alone to the brow of the hill, riding Nash's usual mount. He was to stop there, turn his horse, and stand silhouetted against the brightening sky. I'd asked him particularly not to waste the precious light-slot by getting it wrong.

He'd been insulted that I should expect him to get it wrong.

'Don't then,' I said.

I joined Moncrieff by the truck positioned halfway up the hill, and breathed sighs of relief when Ivan obliged us with a beautifully ridden canter up the hill, stopping and turning at the right place, horse and rider stark and splendidly black against a halo of gold.

'Holy Moses,' Moncrieff said, intently looking through the lens. 'It's a beaut.' He ran a long fifteen seconds' worth before cutting.

'Again?' I suggested.

Moncrieff checked that the film had run properly through the camera gate and shook his head. 'It was about perfect.'

'Great. Print. Let's reload fresh stock for the next long shot of the rest of the horses.'

I called down to Ed on our walkie-talkie system, told him to stick to schedule, had the shot numbered as always by the clapper board operator and watched while the string was filmed streaming uphill at a fast canter. I called up the out-of-sight camera over the brow of the hill to start rolling, but perfection was an elusive quality and it was only after I'd ridden over the hill myself to organise things from up there, only after some huffing and puffing and two retakes, that I got my flourish of trumpets.

With the crowd shots at last in the can, everyone on horseback milled around waiting for clearance and instructions. Ivan was still importantly riding Nash's horse, but a little apart, and I myself was now down on foot conferring with Moncrieff, eyes concentrating on his records of exposed footage.

I didn't see what happened. I heard an indignant shout from Ivan and a clamour from other voices. I sensed and felt a lot of startled movement among the riders, but at first I assumed it to be the sort of everyday commotion when one in a company of horses lets fly with his heels at another.

Ivan, swearing, was picking himself up off the ground. One horse with its rider detached itself from the group and raced off over the hill in the direction of Newmarket town. I thought with irritation that I'd need to rap a knuckle or two and grudged the waste of time.

Ivan came storming up to me with his complaint.

'That *madman*,' he said furiously, 'came at me with a knife!'

'He can't have done.'

'Look, then.' He raised his left arm so that I could see his jacket, the tweed coat identical to that usually worn in the training scenes by Nash. At about waist level the cloth was cut open for seven or eight inches from front to back.

'I'm telling you!' Ivan was rigid with fear on top of indignation. 'He had a *knife*.'

Convinced and enormously alarmed, I glanced instinctively to find the horse I'd been riding, but he was being led around a good way off. Nearest in the matter of transport stood one of the camera trucks, though pointing in the wrong direction. I scrambled behind its steering wheel, made a stunt-worthy three-point turn and raced across the turf in the direction of Newmarket, coming into view of the fleeing horseman in the distance as soon as I was over the hilltop.

He was too far ahead for me to have a realistic chance of catching up with him. Over grass, a horse was as fast as the truck; and he had only to reach the town and to slow to a walk to become instantly invisible, as Newmarket was threaded through and through with special paths known as horse-walks which had been purpose-laid to allow strings of horses to transfer to the gallops on the Heath from their stables in the town without having to disrupt traffic on the roads. Any rider moving slowly on a horse-walk became an unremarkable part of the general scenery, even on a Sunday morning.

It crossed my mind that I should perhaps try to catch him on film, but the camera on the truck was bolted to face backwards, as normally it was driven along in front

125

of its subject, filming advancing cars, people or horses. If I stopped to turn the truck and change places to operate the camera my quarry would be too far off even for blow-ups, if not entirely out of sight.

I was just about to give up when the distant horse was suddenly and violently reined to a halt, the rider reversing his direction and starting back towards me. The truck's engine raced. His head came up. He seemed to see me speeding down the hill towards him. He whirled his horse round again and galloped towards Newmarket at an even faster pace than before.

Even though the distance between us had closed, he'd travelled too far towards safety. It was already hard to distinguish his outline against the buildings ahead. I had to admit to myself that I wasn't going to catch him, and if so I would settle for second best and try to discover what had made him stop and reverse.

I braked the truck to a standstill as near as I could judge to the place where he'd turned, then jumped out onto the grass, trying to see what he might have seen, that could have been important enough to interrupt his flight.

He'd been facing the town. I looked that way and could see nothing to alarm him. There seemed no reason for him to have doubled back, but no one escaping at that pace would have stopped unless he had to.

If I were filming it . . . why might he stop?

Because he'd *dropped* something.

The uphill stretch of well-grassed exercise ground was as wide as an airport runway and almost as long. I couldn't be sure I was in the right place. If the rider had

126

dropped something small I could search all day. If he had dropped something insignificant I wouldn't see any importance in anything I might come across. Yet he had *stopped*.

I took a few irresolute strides. There was simply too much space. Grass all round; miles of it. I looked up the hill, to the brow, and saw all the film horses and riders standing there, like Indians appearing on the skyline in an old pioneer movie. The sun was rising behind them.

I'd dropped my walkie-talkie up there in my hurry. I decided to drive the truck back up the hill, having left a mark where I was currently standing, and get all the lads to walk down in that strung-out sideways fashion, to see if they could find anything odd on the ground.

I marked the spot by taking off my light blue sweater and dropping it in a heap: anything smaller couldn't be seen. I walked back to climb into the truck.

The sun rose brilliantly over the hill, and in the grass twenty paces ahead of me, something *glinted*.

I went on foot to see what it was, as nothing should glint where racehorses worked; and I stood transfixed and breathless.

The escaping rider had dropped his *knife*.

No wonder he'd tried to retrieve it. I stared down at the thing which lay on the turf in front of my toes, and felt both awed and repelled. It was no ordinary knife. It had a wide double-edged blade about eight inches long, joined to a handle consisting of a bar with four finger holes like substantial rings attached to one side of it. The blade was steel and the grip yellowish, like dulled brass. Overall the knife, about a foot long, was thick, strong, frightening and infinitely deadly.

I looked up the hill. The lads still stood there, awaiting instructions.

One behaves as one is, I suppose. I returned to the truck, climbed into it and drove it round until it stood over the knife, so that no one could pick up that weapon or dislodge it; so that no horse could step on it and get cut.

Then I hopped into the back of the truck, set the camera rolling, and filmed the line of horsemen standing black against the risen sun.

Even though I was again staring unemployment in its implacable face, it seemed a shame to waste such a shot.

# CHAPTER SEVEN

I rearranged the day.

Everyone returned to the stable yard except Moncrieff, whom I left stationed behind the steering wheel of the camera truck with strict instructions not to move the wheels even if it were demanded of him by irate men whose job it was to keep vehicles off the Heath. I had transgressed appallingly, I told him, by driving on the hallowed gallops. He was not to budge the truck an inch.

'Why not?'

I explained why not.

'Knife?' he said disbelievingly.

'Someone really did mean harm to Nash.'

'Impossible!' Moncrieff exclaimed, though more in protest than disbelief.

'Tennis players, skaters, John Lennon,' I said. 'Who's safe?'

'Shit.'

Without choice, though reluctantly, I phoned the police, headlines bannering themselves in my head – 'Jinx strikes Newmarket film again'. *Shit*, indeed. I met them in the stable yard where all the lads were waiting in groups and Ivan had come to grandiose terms with his possible nearness to injury.

The policemen who presently arrived were different from those who had come to attend Dorothea. I wondered how odd it would strike the force eventually to have been called to two knife incidents within twenty-four hours, however unconnected the events might appear. I wondered if they would realise I'd been on the scene of both.

Nash, beseeched by Ed, came out of the house in costume and make-up and stood side by side with Ivan. The policemen looked from one to the other and came, as we all had, to the only possible conclusion. In carefully matched riding breeches, tweed jacket and large buckled crash helmet, they looked from ten paces identical. Only the slash along the side of Ivan's jacket distinguished them easily.

I said to Nash, '*This* may put paid to the film.'

'No one is hurt.'

'Someone was out to get you.'

'They didn't manage it,' he said.

'You're pretty calm.'

'Thomas, I've lived through years of danger of this sort. We all do. The world's full of crazy fanatics. If you let it worry you, you'd never go out.' He looked across to where the police were writing down what the lads were telling them. 'Are we going on with today's work?'

I hesitated. 'How will Silva react?'

'Tough.'

I smothered a smile. 'Do you want to come out on the Heath and see what someone intended to stick into

130

you? And do you realise that from now on you have to have a bodyguard?'

'No. I never have a bodyguard.'

'No bodyguard, no film. Very likely, no film anyway, once Hollywood gets to hear of this.'

He looked at his watch. 'It's the middle of the night over there.'

'You'll go on, then?'

'Yes, I will.'

'In that case, as soon as we can,' I said gratefully.

Ed came across and said the police wanted to speak to the person really in charge. I went over: they were both older than I and seemed to be looking around for a father figure to relate to. I was not, it appeared, their idea of authority. O'Hara would have fitted their bill.

The lads had told them that an extra horseman had joined their group while they were haphazardly circling after their third canter over the hill. They'd thought nothing much of it, as with film-making the normal routine of training-stable life was not adhered to. The newcomer, dressed in jeans, anorak and crash helmet, had blended in with themselves. It was only when Ivan's horse had reared away, and Ivan himself had shouted and fallen off, that they'd thought anything was wrong. No one seemed to have seen the slash of the blade.

They couldn't do much towards describing the extra man. Crash helmets with heavy chin straps effectively hid half the face. The newcomer also, they remembered, had been wearing jockey's goggles, as many of them frequently did themselves to shield their eyes from dust and kicked-up debris. They thought he might have been wearing gloves: nothing unusual in that, either.

131

Had I anything to add, the police wanted to know.

'He could ride well,' I said.

They seemed to find that unimportant, being used to the many skills of Newmarket, though I thought it significant.

'He wasn't a jockey,' I said. 'He was too heavy. Too thickset.'

Description of features? I shook my head. I hadn't seen his face, only his back view galloping away.

I waited until they had let the lads and the camera crew disperse out of earshot before I told them about the knife.

We drove up the road to get as near as possible to the camera truck which still stuck out like an illegal sore thumb. Thanks only to its being Sunday, I guessed, no groundsmen were hopping up and down in rage. Leading the police vehicle, I took Nash with me in my car, breaking all the film company's rigid insurance instructions. What with one thing and another, who cared?

Moncrieff backed the camera truck ten feet. The police peered in silence at the revealed peril. Moncrieff looked shocked. Nash grew still.

'He dropped it,' I explained. 'He turned to come back for it. Then he saw me chasing him and decided on flight.'

Nash said, 'He lunged at Ivan with *that*?'

I nodded. 'You'll have a bodyguard from now on.'

He looked at me and made no further protest. One of the policemen produced a large paper bag and with care not to smudge possible fingerprints lifted the knife from the grass.

'There weren't any touts,' I remarked.

'What?' asked Nash.

'Every day except Sunday there are watchers down there on the edge of the town, with binoculars.' I pointed. 'Information is their trade. They know every horse on the Heath. They pass tit-bits of training progress to newspapermen and to bookmakers. If they'd only been here today, our knifeman wouldn't have been able to vanish so easily.'

One of the policemen nodded. 'So who knew, sir, that Mr Rourke would be out here this Sunday morning?'

'About sixty people,' I said. 'Everyone working on the film knows the shooting schedule a couple of days in advance.' I paused. 'There *were* a few people out watching, as there always are with film-making, but we have staff moving them away as far as possible if we don't want them in shot. Then, too, we started work today before sunrise.' I looked round the Heath. Despite our activity, few people were about. Cars went past us on the road without slowing. The Heath looked wide and peaceful, the last place for death.

As Nash had pointed out, no one had been hurt. The police took their notes, the knife and their possible theories back into Newmarket and, with a feeling of imminent doom sitting like vultures on our shoulders, I summoned the camera crews back to work and made the magical initial meeting of Nash and Silva come to life.

It was nearly three in the afternoon by the time we'd finished on the Heath. Just as I returned to the stables four large motor horseboxes arrived to transport to

Huntingdon racecourse all the horses, their saddles, bridles, rugs and other gear and their feed and bedding, besides the lads and their own travel bags. Our horse-master seemed to be managing fine. Despite the early morning upset everyone involved seemed to hum in a holiday mood.

O'Hara banished the temporary euphoria, arriving in the yard by car and scrambling out angrily to demand of me loudly, 'What in hell's teeth's going on?'

'Going to Huntingdon,' I said.

'*Thomas*. I'm not talking about goddam Huntingdon. It's on the car radio that some maniac attacked Nash with a knife. What in buggery happened?'

I tried to tell him but he was too agitated to listen.

'Where's Nash?' he demanded.

'In the house getting his make-up off.'

He strode impatiently away and through the house's rear door, leaving me to re-start the transportation and set the wagon-train rolling, even though the pioneers no longer sang.

Moncrieff was supposed to be having a rare after-noon off. I told him he deserved it and to scarper, which he rapidly did, hoping O'Hara wouldn't reappear too soon.

Alone for a change, I leaned against the bottom half of a stable door, listening to the unaccustomed silence and thinking of knives. Valentine's old voice murmured in my head . . . 'I left the knife with Derry . . .'

The world was full of knives.

Who was Derry?

O'Hara and Nash came out of the house together looking more cheerful than I'd feared.

134

'I spent half the night talking to Hollywood,' O'Hara announced. 'I reminded them that yanking the director in mid-film almost inevitably led to critical disaster, as reviewers always latch onto that fact firstly and spend most of their column speculating on how much better it would have been to have left things alone.'

'However untrue,' Nash commented dryly.

'In this case,' O'Hara told him firmly, 'you said, if I remember, that if they sacked Thomas they sacked you too.'

'Yeah. Crazy.'

O'Hara nodded. 'Anyway, I'll be plugging the line that the attack on the stuntman is *positive* publicity, not bad. By the time this movie gets to distribution, the public will be fired up to see it.'

He sounded, I thought, as though he had had to convince himself first, but I was certainly not going to argue.

I asked instead, 'Do you need me around, then, for the next several hours?'

'I guess not.' He sounded doubtful, stifling curiosity.

'Late Sunday afternoon,' I explained, 'is a fairly mellow time for surprise calls on farmers.'

O'Hara worked it out. 'Jackson Wells!'

'Right.' I turned to Nash. 'Do you want to meet the man you're playing?'

'No, I do *not*,' he said positively. 'I do *not* want to pick up the crusty mannerisms of some bitter old grouch.'

As I didn't want him to, either, I felt relieved rather than regretful. I said, 'I'll be back by ten this evening. I've a meeting scheduled then with Moncrieff and Ziggy Keene.'

'Ziggy who?' Nash asked.

'Stuntman,' I said. 'No one better on a horse.'

'Better than Ivan?'

I smiled. 'He costs ten times as much and he's worth twenty.'

'This beach business?' O'Hara asked.

I nodded.

'What beach business?' Nash wanted to know.

'Don't ask,' O'Hara told him humorously. 'Our boy has visions. Sometimes they work.'

'What vision?' Nash asked me,

'He can't tell you,' O'Hara answered for me. 'But when he sees it, so will we.'

Nash sighed. O'Hara went on, 'Talking of seeing, when will today's dailies be ready?'

'Tomorrow morning, as usual,' I assured him. 'When the van comes back.'

'Good.'

We were sending our exposed film to London every day by courier, to have it processed there overnight in a laboratory specialising in Technicolor. The film travelled each way in a London-based van, with the driver and an accompanying guard spending their nights in London and their days in Newmarket: and so far the arrangement had thankfully proved hitchless.

Each day, after seeing the previous day's rushes, I entered on a complicated chart the scenes and takes that I thought we should use on screen, roughly editing the film as I went along. It both clarified my own mind and saved a great deal of time in the overall editing period later on. Some directors liked to work with the film's appointed editor always at hand making decisions throughout on the dailies, but I preferred to do it myself, even if sometimes it took half the night, as it gave me more control over the eventual product. The rough cut, the bones and shape of the finished film, would be in that way my own work.

Stand or fall, my own work. Life on the leaning tower.

I set off westwards from Newmarket with only a vague idea of where I was headed and an even vaguer idea of what I would say when I got there.

Perhaps postponing the moment, but anyway because the city lay on my route, I drove first into Cambridge and stopped at the hospital housing Dorothea. Enquiries on the telephone had produced merely 'She's comfortable' reports, which could mean anything from near death to doped to the eyeballs and, predictably, my arrival at the nurses' desk gained me no access to their patient.

'Sorry, no visitors.'

Nothing would budge them. Positively no visitors, except for her son. I could probably speak to *him*, if I liked.

'Is he here?' I asked, wondering why I should be surprised. Nothing, after all, would unstick Paul from a full-blown crisis.

One of the nurses obligingly went to tell him of my presence, coming back with him in tow.

'Mother is not well enough to see you,' he announced proprietorially. 'Also, she is sleeping.'

We eyed each other in mutual dislike.

'How is she?' I asked. 'What do the doctors say?'

'She is in intensive care.' His bulletin voice sounded over-pompous, even for him.

I waited. In the end he amplified, 'Unless there are complications, she will recover.'

*Great*, I thought. 'Has she said who attacked her?'

'She is not yet lucid.'

I waited again, but this time without results. After he began to show signs of simply walking off to end the exchange, I said, 'Have you seen the state of her house?'

He answered with a frown, 'I went there this morning. The police took my fingerprints!' He sounded outraged.

'They took mine also,' I said mildly. 'Please return my books.'

'Do *what*?'

'Return Valentine's books and papers.'

He stared with a mixture of indignation and hatred. 'I didn't take Valentine's books. *You* did.'

'I did *not*.'

He glared righteously. 'Mother locked the door and refused – *refused* – to give me the key. Her own son!'

'The key was in the open door last night,' I said. 'And the books had gone.'

'Because *you* had taken them. I certainly did *not*.'

I began to believe his protestations of innocence, unlikely as they were.

But if he hadn't taken the things, who on earth had? The damage inside the house and the attack on Dorothea spoke of violence and speed. Moving a wall of books and cupboardfuls of papers out of the house spoke of thoroughness and time. And Robbie Gill had been sure the rampage had happened before the attack on Dorothea.

None of it made any sense.

'Why,' I asked, 'were you so extremely anxious to get your hands on those books?'

Somewhere in his brain warning bells sounded. I'd directed too many actors not to recognise the twitch of eye muscles that I'd so often prompted. Paul, I thought, had a motive beyond greed, but apart from seeing that it existed, I was not going to get any further.

'It's best to keep family possessions in the family,' he pontificated, and fired a final shot before stalking off. 'In view of my mother's condition, the cremation planned for tomorrow morning has been indefinitely postponed. And do not plague her or me by coming here again. She is old and frail and *I* will look after her.'

I watched his large back-view bustle away, self-importance in every stride, the fronts of his suit jacket swinging out sideways in the motion.

I called loudly after him, 'Paul!'

He stopped reluctantly and turned, standing four-square in the hospital passage and not returning. 'What is it now?'

A forty-two-inch waist at least, I thought. A heavy leather belt held up his dark grey trousers. Cream shirt, diagonally striped tie. The podgy chin tilted upwards aggressively.

'What do you want?'

'Nothing,' I said. 'Never mind.'

He shrugged heavily with exasperation, and I went

thoughtfully out to my car with my mind on telephones. I wore my mobile clipped to my belt, ready at all times. Paul, I'd noticed, carried a similar mobile, similarly clipped to his heavy belt.

Yesterday evening, I remembered, I'd been glad for Dorothea's sake that Paul had answered from his Surrey home when I'd told him of the attack on his mother. Surrey was rock-solid alibi land.

If I'd liked or even trusted Paul it wouldn't have occurred to me to check. As it was, I strove to remember the number I'd called, but could get no further than the first four digits and the last two, which wasn't going to connect me anywhere.

I rang the operator and asked if the four first numbers were a regional exchange in Surrey.

'No, sir,' a crisp female voice said. 'Those numbers are used for mobile telephones.'

Frozen, I asked if she could find me Paul Pannier's mobile number: he lived near Godalming; the last two digits were seven seven. Obligingly, after a short pause for searching, she told me the numbers I'd forgotten, and I wrote them down and made my call.

Paul answered curtly, 'Yes?'

I said nothing.

Paul said, 'Who are you? What do you want?'

I didn't speak.

'I can't hear you,' he said crossly, and switched off his instrument.

So much for Surrey, I thought grimly. But even Paul – *even Paul* – couldn't have slashed open his mother.

Sons had been known to murder their mothers . . .

But not fat forty-five-year-old men with inflated self-esteem.

Disturbed, I drove westwards to Oxfordshire and set about looking for Jackson Wells.


With help again from directory enquiries I discovered his general location and, by asking at garages and from people out walking dogs, I arrived in the end at Batwillow Farm, south of Abingdon, south of Oxford, sleepy and peaceful in the late Sunday afternoon .

I bumped slowly down a rutted unmade lane which ended in an untidy space outside a creeper-grown house. Weeds flourished. A set of old tyres leaned against a rotting wooden shed. An unsteady-looking stack of fencing timber seemed to be weathering into disintegration. A crusty old grouch of a man leaned on a farm gate and stared at me with disfavour.

Climbing out of the car and feeling depressed already, I asked, 'Mr Wells?'

'Eh?'

He was deaf.

'Mr Wells,' I shouted.

'Aye.'

'Can I talk to you?' I shouted.

Hopeless, I thought.

The old man hadn't heard. I tried again. He merely stared at me impassively, and then pointed at the house.

Unsure of what he intended, I nevertheless walked across to the obvious point of access and pressed a conspicuous doorbell.

There was no gentle ding-dong as with Dorothea:

the clamour of the bell inside Batwillow Farm set one's teeth rattling. The door was soon opened by a fair young blonde girl with pony-tailed hair and to-die-for skin.

I said, 'I'd like to talk to Mr Jackson Wells.'

'OK,' she nodded. 'Hang on.' She retreated into a hallway and turned left out of my sight, prompting the appearance presently of a lean loose-limbed blond man looking less than fifty.

'You wanted me?' he enquired.

I looked back to where the old deaf grump still leaned on the gate.

'My father,' the blond man said, following my gaze.

'Mr Jackson Wells?'

'That's me,' he said.

'Oh!'

He grinned at my relief with an easy-going light-heartedness a hundred miles from my expectations. He waited, untroubled, for me to introduce myself, and then said slowly, 'Have I seen you somewhere before?'

'I don't think so.'

'On the television,' he said doubtfully.

'Oh. Well – were you watching the Lincoln at Don-caster yesterday?'

'Yes, I was, but ...' He wrinkled his forehead, not clearly remembering.

'My name,' I said, 'is Thomas Lyon, and I was a friend of Valentine Clark.'

A cloud crossed Jackson Wells's sunny landscape.

'Poor old bugger died this week,' he said. My name finally registered. 'Thomas Lyon. Not him that's making the film?'

'Him,' I agreed.

'I did see you on the telly yesterday, then, with Nash Rourke.'

He summed me up in a short silence, and rubbed the top of his nose indecisively on the back of his hand.

I said, 'I don't want to do you any harm in the making of this film. I came to ask you if there is anything you particularly don't want said. Because sometimes,' I explained, 'one can invent things – or think one invents them – that turn out to be damagingly true.'

He thought it over and finally said, 'You'd better come in, I reckon.'

'Thank you.'

He led me into a small room near the door; a room unlived in and furnished only with an upright piano, a piano stool, a hard wooden chair and a closed cupboard. He himself sat on the piano stool and waved me to the chair.

'Do you play?' I asked civilly, indicating the piano.

'My daughter does. Lucy, you met her.'

'Mm,' I nodded. I took a breath; said, 'Actually, I came to ask you about Yvonne.'

'Who?'

'Yvonne. Your wife.'

'Sonia,' he said heavily. 'Her name was Sonia.'

'It was Yvonne in Howard Tyler's book.'

'Aye,' he agreed. 'Yvonne. I read it. The book.'

He seemed to feel no anger or grief, so I asked, 'What did you think of it?'

Unexpectedly, he laughed. 'Load of rubbish. Dream

lovers! And that upper-class wimp in the book, that was supposed to be me! Cobblers.'

'You're going to be far from a wimp in the film.'

'Is it true, then? Nash Rourke is *me*?'

'He's the man whose wife is found hanged, yes.'

'You know what?' The sunniness shone in his manner and the smile in his eyes surely couldn't be faked. 'It's all so bloody long ago. I don't give a piss what you say in the film. I can hardly remember Sonia, and that's a fact. It was a different life. I left it behind. Did a bunk, if you like. I got fed up with the whole bloody shooting match. See, I was twenty-two when I married Sonia and not yet twenty-five when she died, and I was only a kid really. A kid playing at being a big Newmarket racehorse trainer. After that business, people started taking their horses away, so I packed it in and came here instead, and this life's OK, mate, no regrets.'

As he seemed to discuss it quite easily I asked, 'Why . . . er . . . why did your wife die?'

'Call her Sonia. I don't think of her as my wife. My wife's here in this house. Lucy's mother. We've been wed twenty-three years now and we'll stay that way.'

There was an obvious self-contentment in his whole personality. He had the weathered complexion and thread-veined cheeks of an outdoors man, his eyebrows dramatically blond against the tanned skin. Blue eyes held no guile. His teeth looked naturally good, even and white. No tension showed in his long limbs or sturdy neck. I thought him no great brain, but one of nature's lucky accidents, a person who could be happy with little.

'Do you mind me asking about her?' I said.

'Sonia? Not really. I can't tell you why she died, though, because I don't know.'

That was, I thought, the first lie he'd told me.

'The police had me in,' he smiled. 'Helping with their enquiries, they told the press. So of course everyone thought I'd done it. Questions! Days of them. I just said I didn't know why she died. I said it over and over. They did go on a bit. They thought they'd get me to confess, see?' He laughed. 'Seems they do sometimes get fools to confess to things they haven't done. I can't see how that happens, can you? If you haven't done something, you just keep on saying it. In England, leastwise. No actual thumbscrews, see? They ban actual thumbscrews here, see?' He laughed again at his joke. 'I told them to piss off and find out who really killed her, but they never managed *that*. They couldn't see farther than getting me to confess. I mean, it was daft. Would *you* confess to murdering someone if you hadn't?'

'I don't think so.'

''Course you wouldn't. Hour after hour of it! I stopped listening. I wouldn't let them work me up into a state. I just sat there like a lump and told them to piss off at regular intervals.'

'They must have loved it,' I said dryly.

'You're taking the mickey!'

'Indeed, I'm not,' I assured him. 'I think you were great.'

'I was young,' he said cheerfully. 'They kept waking me up in the night. Silly sods didn't realise I was often up half the night with sick horses. Colic. Stuff like that.

I just nodded off when they frothed on about Sonia. It narked them no end.'

'Mm,' I agreed, and asked tentatively, 'Did you *see* . . . Sonia . . . I mean . . . er . . .'

'Did I see her hanging? No, I didn't. I saw her in the morgue, hours after they took her down. They'd made her look peaceful by then.'

'So it wasn't you who found her?'

'No. Reckon I was lucky, there. One of my stable lads found her while I was driving north to York races. The police drove me back and they'd already decided I'd killed her. She'd been in a box we weren't using at that point. The lad that found her brought his food up for a week after, poor sod.'

'Did you think she'd hanged herself?'

'It wasn't like her.' He showed a very long-lived old doubt. 'There was a stack of hay bales there she could have jumped off of.' He shook his head. 'No one ever did know the truth of it and, tell you no lie, it's better that way. I read in that *Drumbeat* rag that you're trying to find out. Well, I'd just as soon you didn't, to be honest. I don't want my wife and Lucy stirred up. Not fair to them, it isn't. You just get on and make up what story you like for your film. As long as you don't make out I killed her, it'll be all right with me.'

'In the film you do *not* kill her,' I said.

'That's fine, then.'

'But I have to say why she died.'

He said without heat, 'I told you, I don't know why she died.'

'Yes, I know you did, but you must have *thought* about it.'

146

He gave me an unadulteratedly carefree smile and no information, and I had a clear picture of what the interrogating police had faced all those years ago: a happy unbroachable brick wall.

'In Howard Tyler's book,' I said, 'Yvonne daydreams about jockey lovers. Where ... I mean ... have you any idea where he got that idea?'

Internally this time, Jackson Wells laughed. 'Howard Tyler didn't ask me about that.'

'No,' I agreed. 'He told me he hadn't tried to see you at all.'

'No, he didn't. First I knew of it, people were saying that that book, *Unstable Times*, was about me and Sonia.'

'And did she ... well ... daydream?'

Again the secret, intense amusement. 'I don't know,' he said. 'She might have done. That whole marriage, it was a sort of make-believe. We were kids playing at grown-ups. That writer, he got us dead wrong. I'm not complaining, mind.'

'But the dream lovers are so striking,' I persisted. 'Where did he get the idea?'

Jackson Wells thought it over without any apparent anxiety.

'I reckon,' he told me at length, 'you should ask that stuck-up sister of hers.'

'Sister ... do you mean Rupert Visborough's widow?'

He nodded. 'Audrey. Sonia's sister. Audrey was married to a member of the Jockey Club and never let me forget it. Audrey told Sonia not to waste herself on me. I wasn't good enough for her, see?' He grinned, not

147

caring. 'When I read that book I heard Audrey's prissy voice all through it.'

Stunned by the simple depth of that perception I sat in silence wondering what to ask him next; wondering whether I should or could ask why the hanging death of an obscure young sister-in-law had so thoroughly and permanently blighted Rupert Visborough's chances of political life.

How unacceptable in Westminster, in fact, were mysteriously dead relations? Disreputable family misfortunes might prove an embarrassment, but if the sins of sons and daughters could be forgiven, surely the more distant unsolved death should have been but a hiccup.

Before I'd found the words, the door opened to reveal Lucy, sunny like her father.

'Mum wants to know if you want anything, like for instance drinks.'

I took it as the dismissal Mum had intended, and stood up.

Jackson Wells introduced me to his daughter with 'Lucy, this is Thomas Lyon, the personification-of-evil film-maker, according to yesterday's *Drumbeat*.'

Her eyes widened and, with her father's quiet mischief, she said, 'I saw you on the telly with no horns or tails in sight! How cool to be making a film with Nash Rourke.'

I said, 'Do you want to be in it?'

'What do you mean?'

I explained that we were recruiting the local inhabitants of Huntingdon to be 'crowd' at our version of a race meeting held on the course.

'We need people to ooh and aah . . .'

'And scream "shift your arse"?' she grinned.

'Exactly.'

'Dad?'

Her father's instinct was to say no. As he shook his head I said, 'No one needs to know who you are. Give your name as Batwillow . . . and, incidentally, what is a batwillow?'

'A tree you make cricket bats from,' Lucy said, as if my question revealed my stupidity.

'You're kidding me?'

'Certainly not,' her father said. 'Where do you think cricket bats come from? They grow on trees.'

They watched my face. 'We grow the willows in wetlands near the brook,' he said. 'This farm has grown batwillows for generations.'

Growing cricket bats, it seemed to me, entirely fitted his nature: wide shoulders hitting carefree sixes over the boundary with fast balls solidly blocked to prevent the breaking of the wicket.

Lucy's mother appeared with curiosity in the doorway, a friendly woman in fawn trousers and an enormous brown sweater over a cream polo-neck. Unconscious style, I thought, just like her daughter.

Jackson Wells explained my presence. His wife enjoyed the tale.

'Of course, we'll all come,' she said decisively, 'if you promise we'll see Nash Rourke!'

'How corny can you get?' Lucy demanded of her.

I said, 'Tomorrow at two o'clock we hold crowd rehearsals. Nash might be there, can't promise. On Tuesday and Wednesday we shoot the crowd scenes.

We offer breakfast, lunch and expenses to everyone who turns up, and Nash Rourke will definitely be there.'

'It's near a two-hour drive from here to Huntingdon racecourse,' Jackson Wells protested.

'You're outvoted, Dad,' Lucy told him. 'What time Tuesday? Would it be OK if we miss tomorrow's rehearsal?'

I gave them one of my cards, writing on the back 'Priority entry. Batwillow family.' 'Nine in the morning, on Tuesday,' I said. 'Follow the crowd, who'll know what to do. When we break for lunch, use this card, and find me.'

'Wow,' Lucy said.

She had freckles on her nose. Quizzical blue eyes. I wondered how mature she was on the piano.

I said to her father, 'Do you know why anyone would do violence to get this film abandoned?'

He answered blandly, 'Like I heard on the radio? Someone tried to take a knife to your star? Total madman. To my knowledge, no one's afraid of your film.'

I thought that that was probably the second lie he'd told me, or at least the second I'd noticed.

Lucy said, 'Can Dad's brother come as well?'

Her father made a dismissive gesture and said, 'He wouldn't want to.'

'Yes, he would.' To me she said, 'My Uncle Ridley lives in Newmarket. He goes to the cinema all the time, and he'd *rave* to be in a film with Nash Rourke.'

'Then bring him in with you,' I agreed. 'We need the largest crowd we can get.'

Her parents, I saw, didn't share her enthusiasm for her Uncle Ridley.

'Is he free,' I asked, fishing, 'to spend a day at Huntingdon on Tuesday or Wednesday?'

Lucy guilelessly answered, 'Uncle Ridley bums around, Dad says.'

Her father shook his head at her shortage of worldliness and amplified, 'My brother Ridley breaks in horses and acts as a general nagsman. He's not exactly high-powered, but he makes a living.'

I smiled, half interested. 'I'll be glad to meet him.' I paused, and returned to what more closely concerned me. 'Could you lend me a photo of ... er ... Sonia? Just so we don't make Yvonne too like her in the film.'

'Haven't got one,' Jackson Wells said promptly.

'Not even ... Excuse me,' I said to Mrs Wells apologetically, '... not even a wedding photo?'

'No,' Jackson Wells said. 'They got lost when I moved here.' His eyes were wide with innocence, and for the third time I didn't believe him.

# CHAPTER EIGHT

Driving towards Newmarket and working out times, I thought I might squeeze in an empty half-hour before my ten o'clock meeting, and accordingly telephoned Dr Robbie Gill, whose number I did remember clearly from Dorothea's heavy black help-summoning handwriting.

'Do you feel,' I asked, 'like a quick jar somewhere?'

'When?'

I'd worked it out. 'I'm in my car. I'll hit Newmarket around nine-thirty. Any good? I have to be at Bedford Lodge at ten.'

'Is it important?'

'Interesting,' I said. 'About Dorothea's attacker.'

'I'll square it with my wife.' His voice smiled, as if that were no problem. 'I'll come to Bedford Lodge at nine-thirty and wait in the lounge.'

'Great.'

'I heard someone attacked Nash Rourke with a knife.'

'As good as. It was his stand-in, though. And no harm done.'

'So I gathered. Nine-thirty, then.'

He clicked off, his Scottish voice as brusque as ever: and red-headed and terrier-like, he was patiently waiting in the entrance lounge when I got back to Bedford Lodge.

'Come upstairs,' I said, shaking his hand. 'What do you drink?'

'Diet coke.'

I got room service to bring up his fizzy tipple and for myself poured cognac from a resident bottle. This film, I thought fleetingly, was driving me towards forty per cent proof.

'Well,' I said, waving him to an armchair in the neat sitting-room, 'I went to see Dorothea in Cambridge this afternoon and found my way barred by our friend Paul.'

Robbie Gill grimaced. 'She's basically my patient, and he's barring my way too, as far as possible.'

'What can I do to preserve her from being shanghaied by him as soon as she's capable of being transported by ambulance? She told him, and me, that she didn't want to move into this retirement home he's arranging for her, but he pays no attention.'

'He's a pest.'

'Can't you slap a "don't move this patient" notice on Dorothea?'

He considered it doubtfully. 'No one would move her at present. But a few days from now . . .'

'Any which way,' I said.

'How much do you care?'

'A good deal.'

'I mean . . . moneywise.'

I looked at him over my brandy glass. 'Are you saying that an application of funds might do the trick?'

He replied forthrightly, as was his Scottish nature. 'I'm saying that as her doctor I could, with her permission, shift her into a private nursing home of my choice if I could guarantee the bills would be paid.'

'Would it break me?'

He mentioned an alarming sum and waited without censure for me to find it too much.

'You have no obligation,' he remarked.

'I'm not poor, either,' I said. 'Don't tell her who's paying.'

He nodded. 'I'll say it's free on the National Health. She'll accept that.'

'Go ahead, then.'

He downed his diet coke. 'Is that the lot?'

'No,' I said. 'If I draw something for you, tell me what you think.' I took a large sheet of writing paper, laid it on the coffee table, and drew a picture of the knife I'd found on the Heath. A wickedly knobbed hand grip on eight sharp inches of steel.

He looked at the drawing in motionless silence.

'Well?' I asked.

'A knuckle-duster,' he said, 'that grew into a knife.'

'And Dorothea's injuries?' I suggested. He stared at me. I said, 'Not two assailants. Not two weapons. This one, that's both a blunt instrument *and* a blade.'

'Dear God.'

'Who would own such a thing?' I asked him. He shook his head mutely.

'Do you know anyone called Derry?'

He looked completely perplexed.

I said, 'Valentine once mentioned leaving a knife with someone called Derry.'

Robbie Gill frowned, thinking. 'I don't know any Derry.'

I sighed. Too many people knew nothing.

He said abruptly, 'How old are you?'

'Thirty. And you?'

'Thirty-six.' He smiled wryly. 'Too old to conquer the world.'

'So am I.'

'Ridiculous!'

'Steven Spielberg,' I said, 'was twenty-seven when he made *Jaws*. I'm not him. Nor Visconti, nor Fellini, nor Lucas. Just a jobbing storyteller.'

'And Alexander the Great died at thirty-three.'

'Of diet coke?' I asked.

He laughed. 'Is it true that in America, if you die of old age, it's your fault?'

I nodded gravely. 'You should have jogged more. Or not smoked, or checked your cholesterol, or abstained from the juice.'

'And then what?'

'And then you exist miserably for years with tubes.'

He laughed and rose to go. 'I'm embarrassed,' he said, 'but my wife wants Nash Rourke's autograph.'

'Done,' I promised. 'How soon can you realistically move Dorothea?'

He thought it over. 'She was attacked yesterday evening. She's been sleepy from anaesthetic all day today. It was a bad wound ... they had to remove part of the intestine before repairing the abdomen wall. If all goes well she'll be fully awake tomorrow and briefly on her feet the day after, but I'd say it will be another week before she could travel.'

'I'd like to see her,' I said. 'The wretched Paul must sleep *sometimes*.'

'I'll fix it. Phone me tomorrow evening.'


Moncrieff, Ziggy Keene and I set off at four-thirty the next morning, heading north and east to the Norfolk coast.

Ed, instructed by O'Hara, had found me a driver, a silent young man who took my car along smoothly and followed the instructions I gave him as I map-read beside him in the front passenger seat.

Moncrieff and Ziggy slept in the back. Into the boot we'd packed the heavy camera Moncrieff could carry on his shoulders like a toy, also a cold-box full of raw film and a hot-box full of coffee and breakfast. The outside air was cold; the warm car soporific. I was glad, after a while, of the driver.

We cleared Norwich and headed across the flat lands towards the North Sea, skirting the Broads and sliding eventually through the still-sleeping village of Happisburgh and slowing down a narrow lane that ended in sand dunes.

Moncrieff and Ziggy climbed stiffly out of the car and shivered. It was still completely dark outside the range of the car's lights, and the coastal breeze was as unrelenting as ever.

'You said to bring warm clothes,' Moncrieff complained, zipping himself into a fur-lined parka. 'You said nothing about playing Inuits.' He pulled the fur-lined hood over his head and thrust his hands into Arctic-issue gauntlets.

Leaving the driver with his own separate breakfast in the car, the three of us walked onwards through the sand dunes towards the open shore, Moncrieff carrying the camera and the film box, I leading with the hot-box and Ziggy between us toting polystyrene rectangles for sitting insulation on cold salt-laden ground.

'How did you find this godforsaken place?' Moncrieff grumbled.

'I used to come here as a boy.'

'Suppose it had sprouted casinos?'

'I checked.'

Beyond the range of the car's lights we paused to establish night vision, then went on slowly until the sand dunes fell away, the breeze freshened, and the sound of the restless waves spoke of timeless desolation.

'OK,' I said, 'if there's any shelter, sit in it.'

Moncrieff groaned, took a pallet from Ziggy and folded himself with oaths into a shallow hollow on the sea side of the last dune. Ziggy, tougher and taciturn, found a similar place near him.

Ziggy, Ukrainian by birth, had from the nursery proved so spectacularly acrobatic on horses that he had been sent to the Moscow Circus school at the age of eight, and there, far from his rural roots, had received a first-class education along with endless practice in his special skill. Every pupil in the school, boys and girls alike, received daily ballet lessons to teach graceful movement in the circus ring. Ziggy could in consequence have joined any ballet company anywhere, but nothing interested him except horses.

Ziggy at twenty-two had left the circus behind:

circuses everywhere had left town. Never political, though a favoured son, he had somehow travelled with his trade to America, and it was there that I'd seen him first, turning somersaults on a cantering horse one afternoon in an ill-attended practice for the Ringling Brothers in Madison Square Garden.

I'd offered him a job in my rodeo film and, despite union protests, I'd secured him. I'd shortened his unpronounceable surname to Keene, and he'd quickly earned such a brilliant reputation in the horse stunt business that nowadays I had to beg him for his time.

Slender, light and wiry, he took the Norfolk chill in his stride. Child's play, I supposed, after the Russian steppes. Alternately morose and laughing, he was intensely Ukrainian in temperament, and often told me he would return soon to his roots, a threat receding as years passed. His roots, as perhaps he acknowledged, were no longer there.

At a fairly brief meeting the evening before, I'd outlined what we were looking for.

'Film the sunrise!' Moncrieff exclaimed lugubriously, 'We don't have to drive seventy miles for that! What's wrong with the Heath outside the door?'

'You'll see.'

'And the weather forecast?'

'Cold, windy and clear.'

His objections, I knew, were not from the heart. Every lighting cameraman knew that directors could be both unreasonable and unmovable when it came to specific locations. If I'd demanded the slopes of K2, he would have sworn and strapped on his crampons.

I said, 'As it's the time of the vernal equinox, the sun

will rise due east. And that' – I consulted the small compass I'd brought – 'is straight over there.' I pointed. 'At the moment, looking directly out to sea, we are facing a bit further north. The coast runs from north-west to south-east, so when the sun rises, horses galloping along the sand from our left will be back-lit, but will also have the sun very slightly in their faces.'

Moncrieff nodded.

'Can you catch gleams of sun in their eyes?'

'Close?'

'Heads, necks and manes in shot.'

'Thomas,' Ziggy said, the bass notes in his voice always a surprise from the slightness of his body, 'you ask for wild horses.'

I'd asked him the previous evening to picture them and to suggest where we might find some. The trouble with sudden visions was that I'd had no idea of the scene while we were at the pre-production stage, and so had not arranged a wild herd in advance. Wild horses didn't grow on batwillows.

Circus horses, Ziggy had said. Too fat and sleek, I'd objected. Moorland ponies no good, he'd said: too slow and stupid. Think, I'd urged him. Tell me in the morning.

'Thomas,' Ziggy said, as always emphasising the second syllable of my name, 'I think it must be *Viking* horses, from Norway.'

I gazed at him. 'Did you know that Viking ships once regularly raided this coast?'

'Yes, Thomas.'

Viking horses. Perfect. Where on earth could I get any? From Norway, of course. So easy.

I asked him, 'Have you ever worked with Norwegian horses?'

'No, Thomas. But I think they are not true wild. They are not ridden, but they are, I think, handled.'

'Could you ride one without a saddle?'

'Of course.' There wasn't a horse alive, his expression said, that wouldn't do what he asked.

'You could ride one in a nightgown and a long blonde wig?'

'Of course.'

'Bare feet?'

He nodded.

'The woman is *dreaming* she is riding the wild horse. It must be romantic, not real.'

'Thomas, she will *float* on the horse.'

I believed him. He was simply the best. Even Moncrieff stopped grumbling about our mission.

We ate our hot vacuum-packed bacon breakfast rolls and drank steaming coffee while the black sky slowly greyed and lightened and grew softly crimson far out at sea.

With adjusted eyes we watched the world take shape. Around us and at our backs the irregularly heaped sand dunes were revealed as being patches of scrubby marram grass, fringes of long dried stalks leaning in the wind. Slightly below us the sand remained powdery, unwashed by the tide, but blowing back to add to the dunes; and below that, hard-packed sand stretched away to distant white-fringed waves.

The tide, I reckoned, was as low as it ever went. Too low, really, for the best dramatic effect. One week ahead, the tide at dawn would be high, covering the

160

sand. We needed, I thought, to arrange to film the horses on a mid-tide day: better, I supposed, during an ebb tide, as a flooding tide could race over these flat sands and maroon the cameras. Say ten days to the next mid-tide ebb at dawn. Too soon. Add two weeks to the next opportunity; twenty-four days. Perhaps.

I told Ziggy the time frame. 'We need the horses here on the beach twenty-four days from now. Or else fourteen days later; thirty-eight days. OK?'

'I understand,' he agreed.

'I'll send an agent to Norway to arrange the horses and the transport. Will you go with him, to make sure we get the sort of horses we need?'

He nodded. 'Best to have ten,' he said. 'Or twelve.'

'See what you can find.'

Moncrieff stirred, abandoning breakfast in favour of art. Faint horizontal threads of clouds were growing a fiercer red against the still grey sky, and as he busied himself with camera speed and focus, the streaks intensified to scarlet and to orange and to gold, until the whole sky was a breath-gripping symphony of sizzling colour, the prelude to the earth's daily spin towards the empowerment of life.

I had always loved sunrise: was always renewed in spirit. For all my life I'd felt cheated if I'd slept through dawn. The primaeval winter solstice on bitter Salisbury Plain had raised my childhood's goose pimples long before I understood why; and it had ever seemed to me that dawn-worship was the most logical of primitive beliefs.

The glittering ball rimmed over the horizon and hurt one's eyes. The brilliant streaks of cloud flattened to

161

grey. The whole sun, somehow losing its magic, never-theless lit a shimmering pathway across the ruffled surface of the sea, and Moncrieff went on filming, breathing deeply with satisfaction. Slowly on the wind, he and I became aware of a deep rhythmic humming that grew into a melody seeming age-old and sad: and as if of one mind we understood and laughed.

Ziggy was *singing*.

This was a dangerous coast as, flat as it looked, a few miles out to sea unrelenting sandbars paralleled the shore; underwater invisible hazards, shipwrecking the unwary. Graveyards in the coastal villages were heaped with memorials to sailors drowned before accurate depth charts were invented.

Too much background music, I decided, would ruin the atmospheric quality of this historic shore. All we would need would be the wind, the waves, the clip of the horses' hooves, and perhaps Ziggy's own distant song, or maybe a haunting plaintive chant from Norway. This was to be a dream: did one ever hear whole orchestras in dreams?


Fulfilled in all sorts of ways, the three of us were driven back to Newmarket where everyday reality returned to the hotel lobby in the unwelcome shape of our author, Howard Tyler.

Howard was not repentant but incensed. The round glasses flashed as if with their own anger. The prissy little mouth puckered with injured feelings of injustice. Howard the great writer could produce temper tan-trums like a toddler.

Moncrieff, at the sight of him, evaporated into the woodwork. Ziggy, communing only with himself, loped off on foot towards the Heath and horses. Howard stood in my path, flushed with grievance.

'O'Hara says the company will sue me for breach of contract!' he complained. 'It's not *fair*.'

I said reasonably, 'But you *did* breach your contract.'

'No, I didn't!'

'Where did the *Drumbeat* get its opinions from?'

Howard opened his baby lips and closed them again.

'Your contract,' I reminded him, 'forbids you to talk about the film to outsiders. I did warn you.'

'But O'Hara can't sue me!'

I sighed. 'You signed with a major business corporation, not personally with O'Hara. The corporation has lawyers with flints for souls whose job it is to recover for the company any money they can squeeze from the most minor breaches of contract. They are not kind compassionate fellows who will pat you forgivingly on the back. They can imagine damages you never thought of. You opened your undisciplined mouth to some avidly listening ear, and whether you've done any real box-office damage or not, they're going to act as if you've cost the company millions, and they'll try to recover every penny they are contracted to pay you, and if you're really unlucky, more.'

It seemed finally to get through to him that his gripe would prove expensive.

'Then *do* something,' he insisted. 'Tell them no harm was done.'

'You as near as dammit cost me not just this job but any work in the future.'

'All I said was . . .' his voice died.

'All you said was that I was a tyrannical buffoon wasting the film company's money.'

'Well . . . I didn't mean it.'

'That's almost worse.'

'Yes . . . but . . . you've *mangled* my book. And as an author I have *moral* rights.' The air of triumph accompanying these last words made my next statement sound perhaps more brutal than I would have let it if he'd shown the slightest regret.

With vanishing patience I said, 'Moral rights give an author the right to object to derogatory alterations being made to his work. Moral rights can be waived, and invariably this waiver is included in agreements between screenplay writers and film production companies. Often the screenplay writer is given the right to remove his name from the credits if he hates the film enough, but in your case, Howard, it's your name they're specifically paying for, and you waived that right also.'

Stunned, he asked, 'How do you know?'

'I was given a sight of your contract. I had to know where we each stood.'

'*When?*' he demanded. 'When did you see it?'

'Before I signed a contract myself.'

'You mean . . . *weeks* ago?'

'Three months or more.'

He began to look bewildered. 'Then . . . what can I do?'

'Pray,' I said dryly. 'But for a start, you can say who you talked to. You can say how you got in touch with the writer of "Hot from the Stars". Who did you reach?'

'But I . . .' He seemed not far from tears. 'I *didn't*. I mean, I didn't tell the *Drumbeat*. I didn't.'

'Who, then?'

'Well, just a friend.'

'A *friend*? And the friend told the *Drumbeat*?'

He said miserably, 'I suppose so.'

We had been standing all this time in the lobby with Monday morning coming and going around us. I waved him now towards the lounge area and found a pair of convenient armchairs.

'I want some coffee,' he said, looking round for a waiter.

'Have some later, I haven't got time. Who did you talk to?'

'I don't think I should say.'

I felt like shaking him. 'Howard, I'll throw you to the corporation wolves. And besides that, I'll sue you personally for defamation.'

'She said questions weren't libellous.'

'She, whoever she is, got it at least half wrong. I don't want to waste time and energy suing you, Howard, but if you don't cough up some answers pronto you'll get a writ in tomorrow's mail.' I took a breath. 'So, who is *she*?'

After a long pause in which I hoped he faced a few realities, he said, 'Alison Visborough.'

'Who?'

'Alison Vis – '

'Yes, yes,' I interrupted. 'I thought her name was Audrey.'

'That's her mother.'

I shook my head to clear it, feeling I'd left my senses back on Happisburgh beach.

'Let's get this straight,' I said. 'You poured out your grudges to Alison Visborough, whose mother is Audrey Visborough, who is the widow of the deceased Rupert Visborough, known in your book as Cibber. Right so far?'

He nodded unhappily.

'And,' I said, 'when you read Rupert Visborough's obituary, and got the idea for your book, you did *not* go to see Jackson Wells, whose wife hanged, but you *did* go to see the dead woman's sister, Audrey Visborough.'

'Well . . . I suppose so.'

'Yes or no?'

'Yes.'

'And it was she who told you about her sister having dream lovers?'

'Er . . .'

'*Howard!*'

'Look,' he said, with a recurrence of petulance, 'I don't have to answer all these questions.'

'Why ever not?'

'They wouldn't like it.'

'Audrey and Alison wouldn't, do you mean?'

He nodded. 'And Roddy.'

'Who's Roddy?'

'Alison's brother.'

Give me strength, I thought. I said, 'Is this right? Rupert Visborough married Audrey; they had a daughter Alison and a son Roddy?'

'I don't see why you make it sound so difficult.'

'But you didn't put the children in your book.'

'They're not *children*,' Howard objected. 'They're as old as I am.'

166

Howard was forty-five.

'When you bitched to Alison,' I asked, 'why did she get your complaints printed in the *Drumbeat*? And how?'

He stood up abruptly. 'I didn't know she was going to do it. I didn't ask her to. If you want to know, I was shocked when I read the paper. I didn't mean what I said to her to be published like that.'

'Have you talked to her since?'

He said defensively, 'She thought she was helping me.'

'Shit,' I said.

He took offence and stalked off, heading for the way out to the world.

With a feeling of medium irritation I went upstairs and found my message light flashing. O'Hara, it seemed, would be pleased by my appearance in his suite.

I walked the carpeted passages. 'Did you know,' he asked, opening his door to my knock, 'that Howard is back?'

We discussed Howard. O'Hara's use of words was profligate.

'Howard told me,' I said, only half successfully damming O'Hara's flow, 'that he poured out his woes to a lady friend who promptly relayed them to the *Drumbeat* but without his knowledge.'

'What?'

I told O'Hara about the Visboroughs.

He repeated in disbelief, '*Audrey, Alison and Roddy?*'

'And God knows who else.'

'Howard,' he pronounced heavily, 'is off his trolley.'

'He's naive. Doesn't make him a bad writer.'

O'Hara agreed gloomily. 'Dream lovers are naive.' He thought things over. 'I'll have to discuss his breach of contract again with the moguls. I suppose you've never met this disastrous Alison?'

I shook my head.

'Someone will have to switch on her lights.'

'Mm,' I paused. 'You?'

O'Hara ducked it. 'What time do you have, yourself?'

'Oh, no,' I protested. 'We know her opinion of *me*.'

'All the same,' O'Hara smiled, 'if you want to, you can charm the birds off the trees.'

'I don't know where she lives.'

'I'll find out,' he promised, 'and you can do the damage control.'

He seemed all of a sudden happier. Suing Howard would have dragged on and on and could well have alienated the very lending-library customers his name was supposed to attract into the cinema. Never attack anyone, old Valentine had once written, unless you've counted the cost of winning.

O'Hara asked if I'd found Jackson Wells, but seemed disappointed in the sweetness and light of his household.

'Do you think he murdered his wife?' he asked curiously.

'No one could ever prove it.'

'But do *you* think he did?'

I paused. 'I don't know.'

O'Hara shrugged the thought away and, as he wanted to see the previous day's rushes, we drove along to the stable yard. There, in the vast house, one small room had been rigged for projection, with a screen and six chairs but no luxury. The windows were blacked out to foil peepers, and the reels of previously printed film were secured in racks in there by every fancy lock and fireproofing invented. The moguls had in this case spent lavishly: no one could afford to start shooting all over again.

That morning I worked the projector myself. O'Hara sat impassively while the horses galloped up the training hill and breasted it into sunlight. I'd been right, I saw, about the third attempt, and my flourish of trumpets looked great. Moncrieff had stopped the cameras after that. The only shot left on the reel was the one I'd made myself; the line of horses on the skyline, black against sunshine. The worst of luck, I thought, that with all that raw film in our possession, we had no footage at all that included the rider whose frightful knife had slashed at Ivan.

O'Hara cursed over it, but hindsight, as always, was an unfruitful regret.

I left that reel for the regular projectionist to rewind, and set going the stuff we'd done later, the 'first meeting' of Nash and Silva.

As always with dailies, the sound quality was imperfect; marrying the eventual soundtrack to the pictures came later, in the post-production stage. Dailies, in any case, with two or three or more takes printed of a single scene, could only be judged by experts, rather like wine buyers discerning an eventual vintage in the harsh juice straight from fermentation. O'Hara even made appropriate sucking noises with his teeth as he watched Silva

169

joltingly rein-in her horse, nearly knocking down Nash as he, the trainer, stood near his own horses; watched her dismount, jerk off her helmet and speak her lines with the character's initial aggravation awakening to quick sexual interest; watched the smile curve the blissful mouth in a way that would quadruple her sticker price next time out.

'Good girl,' O'Hara murmured, pleased.

Nash, bareheaded in riding clothes, did his own lines in platinum, close to priceless.

Howard, goaded into writing this scene, which had of course not appeared in the book, had nevertheless written exchanges of a quality entirely to justify his high placing in the film's credits. Moncrieff had lit the faces with creative skill and had, as agreed, shot the horses slightly out of focus to give sharp prominence to each human figure in close-up. Somehow the uncaring, oblivious nature of the horses lent contrast and comment to the vivid emotion developing near them. A brief, fleeting impression, but an addition to the mood. Not bad, overall.

The reel ended, I switched the projector off and the regular lights on and waited for O'Hara's verdict.

'Tell you something,' he said casually, 'if you're not careful we'll have a success on our hands.'

'A bit early to say.' I was pleased, all the same, at his compliment.

'How do you get on personally with Silva?' O'Hara asked, standing and stretching, preparing to leave.

'She does ride very well,' I said. 'I told her that I thought so.'

170

'And you did not, I hope, tell her she rides as well as any man.'

I laughed. 'I'm not suicidal.'

'She looks good on screen.'

I nodded. 'You were right, she can act. She knows where the camera is. She's professional, she listens to me, she did the nude scene on the closed set last week with cool naturalness, she's ambitious in a sensible way and I can tiptoe round the feminism.'

'And do you like her?'

'It's not necessary.'

'No, but do you?'

I smiled. 'If I told her I liked her she'd smack my face.'

'That's no answer.'

'Then yes, I do like her. Actually, very much. But she doesn't want to be liked. She wants to be thought a good actress. Which she is. A merry-go-round, don't you think?'

'She's sleeping with me,' O'Hara said.

I looked, in a moment of stillness, at the craggy strength of his face and physique, understood the magnetic sexual quality of power, and said without resentment, 'Are you telling me, hands off?'

He calmly nodded. 'Hands off.'

'OK.'

He made no more of it. It altered little. We went upstairs to see how far the art director and his department had gone with dismantling the Jockey Club enquiry-room set, ready to construct an approximation of the Athenaeum dining-room in the space.

Several of the upstairs walls had earlier been removed, with steel joists now holding up the roof. Many of the ceilings also had been cut out to allow for overhead lights and cameras. The house's owner was warming himself with his nicely stuffed bank account while trusting his beams and plaster would reassert themselves later.

The Athenaeum dining-room remained embryonic but would be ready with tables, waiters and roast beef on our return from Huntingdon.

O'Hara said, 'I met Moncrieff in the passage at the hotel this morning after you returned from the ocean. Incredibly, he was *humming*. He said he'd seen a revelation and that you were sending Ziggy to import a herd of wild horses from Norway. Say it's not true.'

I laughed. 'It's true. Viking horses. If we have ten or twelve, we can make them look like fifty. I'll send Ziggy with an agent to find some. They'll come over in horseboxes on the ferry from Bergen.'

'But,' O'Hara asked reasonably, 'wouldn't it be cheaper to use *local* wild horses?'

'First of all,' I said, 'there aren't any. Second, genuine Viking horses will be worth their weight in publicity.'

O'Hara picked his way across wobbling scraps of scenery and stood looking out of a high window at the grey-green expanse of the Heath. He turned eventually: I couldn't see his expression against the light.

'I'll arrange it,' he said. 'I'll send Ziggy. You just get on with the movie.'

I said with satisfaction, 'Right,' and we made our way as colleagues down to the stable yard, signing out as usual with the guard on the outer door and crossing to the car.

'Did you know,' I said conversationally, 'that they used to hang witches?'

O'Hara stopped in mid-stride and after a pause said, 'Howard didn't suggest such a thing in the book, did he?'

'No. I'm surprised, really, that he didn't. It would have gelled with the dream lovers, don't you think?'

O'Hara blinked.

'The last witch was hanged in Merrie England in 1685,' I said. 'By then they had strung up over a thousand people accused of witchcraft, mostly women. I looked it up. Witchcraft itself went on for a long time after that. Goya was painting witches flying, around the year eighteen hundred. People still follow the old practices to this day. I'd think it improbable that a witch-hanging took place in Newmarket only twenty-six years ago, but there's no harm in Howard inserting a scene or two to sow doubt.'

# CHAPTER NINE

Unexpectedly glad after all to have a driver, I travelled to Huntingdon making notes for the rehearsals ahead and thinking over my second conversation with Howard. He had been in his room when I returned with O'Hara and had agreed to come along to my sitting-room, but with bad grace.

'Howard,' I pointed out, 'your name is immovable on this film. You can write brilliantly. Whether or not you disapprove of its plot, the *words* in this film are mostly yours, and you'll be judged by them.'

'Some are *yours*,' he objected.

'I prefer yours. I only write what you won't.'

He could glare, but not dispute it.

'So,' I said without fuss, 'please will you write a scene suggesting that the dead wife was hanged for being a witch.'

He was outraged. 'But she *wasn't* a witch.'

'How do you know?'

'She was Audrey Visborough's sister!' His tone said that that settled matters beyond doubt.

'Think it over, Howard. Put the thought into someone's mouth. Into someone's head. Just a shot of a magazine article might do the trick. Headline – "Is witchcraft dead?" Something like that. But don't place your scene in the Jockey Club enquiry room, they've already struck that set.'

Howard looked as if he might comply: he even looked interested.

'Her real name was Sonia,' I said.

'Yes, I know.'

'Did the Visboroughs tell you?'

'Why shouldn't they?' His prickles rose protectively. 'They were all very helpful.'

I forbore to say that the *Drumbeat* was as unhelpful as one could get, and went on my way.

My assistant director, Ed, who normally had one assistant of his own, now had, as usual for crowd scenes, several extra deputised helpers. The townspeople of Huntingdon, having streamed to the racecourse in highly satisfactory numbers, were being divided, positioned and generally jollied along by Ed who had been given, and had passed on, my emphatic instruction that the people who had come should be *happy*, and should want to return the next day, and the next. Lollipops were to be dangled. Fun was to be had. Nash – ah, Nash *himself* – would sign autographs now and then.

The people in charge of Huntingdon racecourse had been welcoming and obliging. Contracts, payment, insurance, safety precautions, police: all had been arranged. Provided we finished and vacated the place by Friday, they would give us, if they could, everything we asked for. Repairs, if any were needed, could then be done before they opened the gates to bona fide racing the following Monday.

Our horses, our jockeys, our crowds, our drama, had realistically to play their parts by Thursday evening. Tight, but possible.

I prayed for it not to rain.

Ed chose people to stand in the parade ring in groups, looking like owners and trainers. Others were directed to crowd round and stare. Genuine professional steeplechase jockeys appeared in the parade ring in racing colours and scattered to each group. They weren't the absolute top jockeys, but tough, reliably expert and being well paid. Our lads led round the horses, saddled, rugged and carrying number cloths. It all began to look like a race meeting.

The real thing, of course, would be filmed separately on the following Monday, with Ed in charge of wide, establishing shots of full stands, large crowd movement and bookmakers shouting the odds. Cut in with our own scenes, the joins of real to acted would be invisible – given no rain.

Cibber stood in the parade ring with his wife (Silva), and I positioned Nash's stand-in within easy scowling distance. Moncrieff rolled his camera around on a dolly to get interesting architectural background. It all, as ever, took time, but as soon as possible I sent the townspeople home. Boredom was my enemy; bore them, and they wouldn't return. Every child received a helium balloon on leaving (UNSTABLE TIMES in blue on silver), given with jokes and thanks.

The jockeys had been asked to stay in the parade

ring for a briefing. I found them standing stiffly in a group there, their attitude distrustful and surly.

Not understanding this, I began, 'Just pretend it's a normal race tomorrow. Do everything you normally do on the way down to the start.'

One of them almost belligerently interrupted, 'Is it true you raced once as an amateur?'

'Well, yes, for three seasons.'

'Why did you stop?'

I frowned. It wasn't their business to ask such questions, and certainly not like an inquisition, but I needed their cooperation, so I said mildly, 'I went to Hollywood to make films of horses instead.'

Silence.

'What's the matter?' I asked.

After a long pause, one of them told me, 'It says about you in the *Drumbeat* . . .'

'Ah.' Light arrived. I looked at the cool faces, all highly cynical. I needed these jockeys to ride their hearts out the next day; and I could see with absolute clarity that they weren't going to.

How odd, I thought, that I'd feared losing my authority over the film crews, but in fact had had little difficulty in re-establishing it, only to find now that I'd lost it among men I thought I understood. I asked if they'd watched the Lincoln and seen me talking to Greg Compass. None had. They'd been too busy working, they said. They'd been riding in races.

I said, 'If any of you has doubts about doing a good job for me tomorrow, I'll race him here and now.'

I didn't know I was going to say it until I did. Once said, there was no going back.

They stared.

I said, 'I'm not incompetent or a buffoon or a tyrant. Newspapers tell lies. Surely you know?'

They loosened up a little and a few began staring at their boots instead of my face, but one of them slowly and silently unbuttoned his shiny green and white striped shirt. He took it off and held it out. Underneath he wore the usual thin blue sweater, with a white stock round his neck.

I unclipped the walkie-talkie from my belt and whistled up Ed.

'Where are you?' I asked.

'In the stables.'

'Good. Send three of the horses back, will you, with racing saddles and bridles, each led by a lad.'

'Sure. Which three?'

'The three fastest,' I said. 'And find the doctor we brought with us. Ask him to come to the parade ring.'

'You don't have to be an effing hero,' one of the jockeys said. 'We get your point.'

The one who'd removed his colours, however, still held them out as a challenge.

I unzipped my navy windproof jacket, took it off, and dropped it on the grass. I pulled off my sweater, ditto, and unbuttoned my shirt, which followed. I wore no jersey underneath, but I didn't feel my bare skin chill in the wind: too much else to think about. I put on the offered green and white stripes and pointed to the stock. Silently, it was handed over, and I tied it neatly, thanking my stars that I remembered how.

As it had been only a rehearsal that afternoon, and

all on foot, no one carried a whip and none of the jockeys was wearing the normal shock-absorbing body protector that shielded fallen riders from horses' hooves. No one mentioned this absence. I buttoned the shirt and pushed the tails down inside my trousers; and I was passed a crash helmet with a scarlet cap.

Ed, in the distance, was walking back with three horses.

Moncrieff suddenly arrived at my elbow and demanded, 'What in hell are you doing?'

'Going for a ride.' I put on the helmet and left the strap hanging.

'You can't!'

'Be a pal and don't film it in case I fall off.'

Moncrieff threw his arms out and appealed to the jockeys. 'You can't let him. Tell him to stop.'

'They've read the *Drumbeat*,' I said succinctly, 'and do we want one hell of a race tomorrow, or do we not?'

Moncrieff understood all right, but made ineffectual noises about insurance, and moguls, and O'Hara, and what would happen to the movie if I broke my neck.

'Do shut up,' I said.

'Thomas!'

I grinned at him. I said to the jockeys, 'Two of you might care to race with me. Sorry I can't take you all on, but we have to race the whole string tomorrow and they'll need to be fresh. So just two. Whoever you like. We'll go one circuit over the fences, not the hurdles, just as long as there's no one roaming about on the course where they shouldn't be.'

Silence.

Privately amused, I waited until Ed had drawn near with the horses and had got over his shock at my explicit clothes.

'Ed, get a car out onto that road beside the far rails,' I showed him where, 'and drive round behind us. Take our doctor with you in case one of us falls.' I pointed. 'There he is. He's coming now.'

Ed looked stricken. I unclipped both the walkie-talkie and my mobile phone from my belt, and gave them to him to look after.

'I don't believe this,' Moncrieff said.

A jockey said, 'We could lose our licences, racing you.'

'No, you can't,' I contradicted. 'You're employed by the film company, and you're out here for a rehearsal. We have permission from everyone for you to jump round the course. You're just doing it a day earlier than planned. There's a doctor in attendance, as we promised in your agreements. Who'll come with me?'

They had lost the worst of their antagonism but I'd thrown the challenge back in their faces, and they weren't having *that*. Two of them started for the horses and left me the third.

'O'Hara will *kill* you,' Moncrieff told me.

It so happened that they'd left me the horse that Silva had ridden the previous morning: the undisputed fastest of our bunch. I'd ridden him often at a canter and, according to his history, he was supposed to know how to jump.

'You haven't any breeches or boots,' Ed said, looking with bewilderment at my ordinary trousers and brown shoes.

180

'The horse won't mind,' I said. A little light-headedness, I thought, wasn't a bad idea in the circumstances.

The horse's lad gave me a leg up, as he'd done many times. I tightened the girth and lengthened the stirrup leathers, and buckled the strap of my helmet.

The two jockeys holding me to my word were mounted and ready. I laughed down at the ring of other faces that had suddenly reverted to a better humour.

'You're a right lot of bastards,' I said, and I got several grins back.

As none of the gates was locked we walked the horses without hindrance out to the track. The one-and-a-half-mile circuit ran right-handed, with nine assorted jumps on the way. I hadn't raced for eleven years. I was crazy. It felt great.

Nasty long words like irresponsibility swam like worms into the saner regions of my mind. I did carry this multi-million motion picture on my shoulders. I did know, arrogance aside, that the soufflé I was building would collapse if the cooker were switched off.

All the same, it seemed to me somehow that I'd grown old a long time ago after too brief a youth. For perhaps three minutes I would go back to my teens.

Ed, car and doctor followed us onto the course.

One of my opponents asked me, 'How much do you weigh?'

'Enough to give me an excuse for losing.'

'Bugger that,' he said, and pointed his horse towards the task and dug him in the flanks with his heels.

I followed him immediately. I'd have no second chance, and I felt the old controlled recklessness swamp through brain and body as if I'd never been away.

I thought of the man in front as Blue, because of his colours, and the one behind me as Red. We'd had all the shiny shirts especially made for the film for eye-appeal and distinguishability, and the wardrobe people had given us the goods.

Both Blue and Red were younger than I and had not yet started their careers by the time I'd left. They were intent, I saw at once, on making no allowances, and indeed, if they had done so, the whole enterprise would have been without purpose. I simply dredged my memory for a skill that had once come naturally, and judged my horse's stride before the first of the fences with an easy practice I'd thought long forgotten.

There was speed and there was silence. No banter, no swearing from the others. Only the thud of hooves and the brush through the dark birch of the fences. Only the gritting determination and the old exaltation.

My God, I thought in mid-air, why ever did I give this up? But I knew the answer. At nineteen I'd been too tall and growing too heavy, and starving down to a professional riding weight had made me feel ill.

Half a mile and two jumps later I felt the first quiver of unfitness in my muscles and remembered that both Blue and Red had been at racing peak for several months. The speed they took in their stride used all my strength. We'd rounded the bottom turn and had straightened three abreast into the long far side before I seriously considered that I'd been a fool – or at least definitely foolhardy – to set off on this roller-coaster, and I jumped the next four close-together fences con-centrating mainly on desperately keeping my weight as far forward as possible.

Riding with one's centre of gravity over the horse's shoulder was best for speed aerodynamically, but placed the jockey in a prime position for being catapulted off forwards if his mount hit a fence. The alternative was to slow the pace before jumping, sit back, let the reins slide long through one's fingers, and maybe raise an arm up and back to maintain balance before landing. An habitually raised arm, termed 'calling a cab', was the trade-mark of amateurism. To do it once couldn't be helped, but five or six raised arms would bring me pity, not in the least what I was out there trying to earn. I was going to go over Huntingdon's jumps with my weight forward if it killed me.

Which of course it might.

With this last mordant thought, and with straining muscles and labouring lungs, I reached the long last bend towards home: two more fences to jump, and the run-in and winning post after.

Experienced jockeys that they were, Blue and Red had waited for that last bend before piling on the ultimate pressure. I quickened with them, determined only not to be ignominiously tailed-off, and my mount responded, as most thoroughbreds do, with an inbred compulsion to put his head in front.

I don't know about the others, but I rode over the last two fences as if it mattered like the Grand National; but even so, it wasn't enough. We finished in order, Red, Green, Blue, flat out past the winning post, with half a length and half a length between first and second and second and third.

We pulled up and trotted back to the gate. I felt weak enough for falling off. I breathed deeply through my nose, having told many actors in my time that the most reliable evidence of exhaustion was to gasp with the mouth open.

With Blue and Red leading the way, we rejoined the other jockeys. No one said much. We dismounted and gave the reins to the lads. I could feel my fingers trembling as I unbuckled the helmet and hoped the jockeys couldn't see. I took off the helmet, returning it to the man who'd lent it, and brushed sweat off my forehead with my thumb. Still no sound above half-heard murmurs. I unbuttoned the striped colours, forcing my hands to the task, and fumbled too much over untying the stock. Still with breaths heaving in my belly, I handed shirt and stock back, and took my own clothes from someone who'd lifted them from the grass. I hadn't the strength to put them on, but simply held them over my arm.

It struck me that what everyone was feeling, including myself, was chiefly embarrassment, so I made my best stab at lightness.

'OK!' I said. 'Tomorrow, then? You'll race?'

Blue said, 'Yes', and the others nodded.

'Fine. See you.'

I raised a smile that was genuine, even if only half wattage, and turned away to walk over to where Moncrieff, curse him, was trying to pretend he hadn't had a video camera on his shoulder the whole time.

A voice behind me called, 'Mr Lyon.'

I paused and turned. Mr Lyon, indeed! A surprise.

The one with the green and white stripes said, 'You did make your point.'

I managed a better smile and a flap of a hand and plodded across the grass to Moncrieff.

'Shit,' he said.

'Anything but. We might now get a brilliant race tomorrow. They're not going to let themselves do worse than a panting amateur.'

'Put your shirt on, you'll die of cold.'

But not of a broken neck, I thought, and felt warm and spent and thunderously happy.

Ed gave me back the mobile phone saying that O'Hara had called while he, Ed, was driving round the course, and had wanted to know where I was.

'What did you tell him?' I asked.

'I said you were riding. He wants you to call him back.'

'Right.'

I set off towards my car and its driver and called O'Hara as I went. He had spent time with Howard, it seemed, who was now enthusiastic over the witchcraft angle and wanted it emphasised. Scenes were positively dripping off his pen.

'Yeah,' I said, 'but restrain him. Witches do not hang *themselves*, and we still need our designated murderer.'

'You have,' O'Hara said dryly, 'a habit of putting your finger on the button.' He paused briefly. 'Howard told me where Alison Visborough lives.'

'Did you bargain with him? A deal?'

'It's possible,' O'Hara said stiffly, 'that we may not wring the last cent out of him.'

I smiled.

'Anyhow, go see her, will you? Some place in Leicestershire.'

'When? We're shooting all day tomorrow.'

'Uh, now. Howard phoned her. She's expecting you.'

'*Now?* Can't someone else do it?'

I'd been up since four that morning and it was by now five-forty in the afternoon and I needed a shower and I felt knackered, to put it politely. Leicestershire began a lot of miles in the wrong direction.

O'Hara said, 'I thought you'd be interested to meet her, and she has her mother living with her.'

'The Audrey?'

O'Hara confirmed it. 'Silva's character in the movie.'

'Well . . . yes, I'm interested. OK, I'll go. What's the address?'

He told it to me in detail, phone number included. 'Howard's busting a gut trying to be helpful.'

'I'll bet.'

O'Hara said, changing the subject, 'Ed said you were riding?'

Amused by his oblique question, I answered, 'I rode round the course with a couple of the jockeys for them to see what we'll be needing tomorrow.'

'You take care.'

'Sure,' I said. 'Always.'

We said goodbye and I walked onwards to the car, making another phone call, this time to Robbie Gill.

'Thomas Lyon,' I said, when I reached him. 'How's my girl?'

'Still in intensive care. I've liaised with her surgeon. He's slapped a "Do not move" notice on her, which should hold while she needs drip feeds. Two or three days, anyway. I can't stand that son of hers. What a bully!'

'What's he been doing?'

'The nurses threaten a mutiny. He's so bloody *lordly*.'

'Is Dorothea awake yet?'

'Yes, she's talked briefly to the police. Apparently the last thing she remembers is setting off to walk home from supper with a widowed friend who lives only a quarter of a mile away. They watch TV together sometimes and she felt like company with Valentine gone. Lucky she wasn't at home earlier.'

'I guess so. Perhaps.'

'Perhaps,' he agreed.

'Anything else?' I asked.

'Nothing. I asked the police. They gave me the sort of guff which means they haven't a clue.'

'I'd like to see her.'

'I told her that you'd been asking. She was obviously pleased. Perhaps tomorrow evening, or the next day.'

'I'll phone you,' I said.

I reached the car, delivered the change of plans to the driver and consulted the road map. A matter of turn right onto the A14, go north-west, skirt Kettering, press onwards. Forty miles perhaps to Market Harborough. Wake me when we reach that point, I said, and went to sleep on the back seat.

Alison Visborough's hideaway proclaimed her personality from the gateposts onwards. A crumbling tarmac drive led to an old two-storey house, brick-built, possibly eighteenth century, but without distinction. Fields near the house were divided into many paddocks, all fenced with weathered wooden rails, some occupied by well-muscled but plain horses. A larger paddock to one side held a variety of flakily-painted gates, poles and fake walls, the paraphernalia of show jumping. At the far end, a man in a tweed jacket and high-domed black riding hat cantered a horse slowly round in a circle, looking down and concentrating on the leading foreleg, practising dressage. A child, watching him, held a workaday pony by the reins. Lesson, it appeared, being given and received.

Everything about the place looked tidy and efficient and spoke of a possible shortage of funds.

My driver drew up outside the undemonstrative front door. He had said he would check that we had arrived at the right place, but he had no need to. The door opened before he could reach it, to reveal a full-bosomed middle-aged woman dressed in jodhpurs, shirt and dull green sweater, accompanied by two half-grown Labrador dogs.

'Mr Lyon?' Her voice reached me, loud, imperious, displeased.

My driver gestured to the car, out of which I unen-thusiastically climbed.

'I'm Thomas Lyon,' I said, approaching her.

She shook my hand as an unwelcome social obligation and similarly invited me into her house, leaving my driver to look after himself.

'I am Alison Visborough. Howard warned me to expect you,' she announced, leading me into a cold tidy room furnished with hard-stuffed, blue-green armchairs and sofas which looked inviting but repelled boarders, so to speak. I perched on the inhospitable edge of one of them, and she on another. The dogs had been unceremoniously left in the hall.

'You are younger than I expected,' she pronounced, her vowels unselfconsciously plummy. 'Are you sure you are who you say?'

'Quite often.'

She stared.

I said, 'I'm not the ogre you described to the *Drumbeat*.'

'You were driving Howard to despair,' she said crisply. 'Something had to be done. I did not expect all this fuss. Still less did I intend to bring trouble to Howard. He has explained that your wretched film company are angry with me, but when I perceive an injustice, I must speak out.'

'Always?' I asked with interest.

'Of course.'

'And does it often get you into trouble?'

'I am not to be deterred by opposition.'

'For Howard's sake,' I said, 'could you write a short apology to the film company?'

She shook her head indignantly, then thought it over, and finally looked indecisive, an unusual state for her, I guessed.

She had short dark hair with grey advancing, also unafraid brown eyes, weathered skin, no lipstick and ringless work-roughened hands. A woman hard on herself and on everyone else, but admired by Howard.

I asked, 'Who did you talk to, who works for the *Drumbeat*?'

She hesitated again and looked not over-pleased. 'I didn't say,' she grudgingly answered, 'exactly what she wrote in the paper.'

'She?'

'She's an old acquaintance. We went to the same school. She works on the "Hot from the Stars" team, and I thought it would *help* Howard in his fight against you. *She* didn't write what was printed. She just passed on the information to one of the columnists, as she always does. She gathers the material, you see, and then it gets *sensationalised*, she explained to me, by someone whose job it is to do that.'

Sensationalised. What a process! Yet without it, I supposed, Howard's gripe wouldn't have been worth the space.

'How long,' I enquired, 'have you known Howard?'

'Why do you want to know?'

'I only wondered about the length of your commitment to him.'

With a touch of the belligerence I was coming to expect, she said, 'I can be committed to a good cause within five minutes.'

'I'm sure.'

'Actually, we've known Howard since he came to visit us after Daddy died.'

The word Daddy came naturally: it was only I who found it odd and incongruous in someone of her age.

'He came to see your mother?'

'Principally, I suppose so.'

'Because of the obituary?'

She nodded. 'Howard found it interesting.'

'Mm.' I paused. 'Have you any idea who wrote that obituary?'

'Why do you want to know?'

I shrugged. 'Interest. It seemed to me it was written from personal feelings.'

'I see.' She let seconds pass, then said, 'I wrote that myself. It was edited by the paper, but the gist of it was mine.'

'Was it?' I was non-committal. 'You wrote about your father's potential career being blighted by Sonia's death?'

'Yes, I did.'

'You wrote as if you cared.'

'Of *course* I cared,' she said vehemently. 'Daddy would never discuss it with me, but I knew he was bitter.'

'Uh,' I said, 'but why did Sonia's death make him give up politics?'

Impatiently, as if it were self-evident, she said, 'Scandal, of course. But he would never talk about it. He would never have let this film be made. Rodbury and I were also against it, but we were powerless. The book was Howard's, not ours. Our name, Daddy's name, doesn't appear in it. Howard says you *forced* him to make the ridiculously untrue changes to his work, so of *course* I felt someone had to stop you. For Howard's sake and, yes, for Daddy's memory, I had to do it.'

And nearly succeeded, I thought.

I said, without trying to defend either myself or film company policy, 'Excuse me, but who is Rodbury?'

'My brother, Roddy.'

Roddy, of course.

'Could I possibly,' I asked, 'meet your mother?'

'What for?'

'To pay my respects.'

It hung in the balance, but it wasn't left to her to decide. The half-closed door was pushed open by a walking stick in the hands of a thin seventyish lady with a limp. She advanced slowly and forbiddingly and, while I rose to my feet, informed me that I was a monster.

'You are the person, aren't you,' she accused with tight lips, 'who says I was unfaithful to my husband with Jackson Wells? *Jackson Wells!*' There was a world of outraged class-distinction in her thin voice. 'Dreadful man! I *warned* my sister not to marry him, but she was headstrong and wouldn't listen. He wasn't good enough for her. And as for you thinking that I . . . I . . .' Words almost failed her. 'I could hardly even be *civil* to the man – and he was almost twenty years *younger* than I.'

She shook with vibrant disapproval. Her daughter rose, took her mother's arm and helped her towards one of the chairs whose overstuffed firmness suddenly made sense.

She had short white curling hair and high cheek-bones, and must once have been pretty, but either pain or a general disapproval of life had given her mouth a pinched bad-tempered downturn. I thought of Silva and her glowing beauty, and reckoned the two women would probably not want to meet.

I said without emphasis, 'The film company discussed with Howard Tyler the changes they wished made to certain elements of the published book. I did not myself

arrange them. I was engaged after the main changes
had been agreed. Still, I think they were necessary and
that they'll make a strong and entertaining motion
picture, even though I understand your reservations.'

'*Reservations!*'

'Disapproval, then. But as your own name is
nowhere used, and as the film is fiction, not many will
connect you to it.'

'Don't be ridiculous. We are the laughing stock of
Newmarket.'

'I don't think so,' I said. 'It was all so long ago. But I
would like to ask you a question, and I do hope you
will help with the answer, as it might soften for you
your understandable outrage. Did your sister Sonia lead
the strong fantasy life that Howard gave her in the
book? Was she a dreamy young woman in real life?'

While the older woman hesitated, Alison said, 'I've
never met her husband and I don't remember her much
at all. I was only fourteen.'

'Sixteen,' her mother corrected sharply.

Alison darted a barb of irritation at her mother, who
looked faintly complacent. An uneasy mother–daughter
friction existed, I saw, that was only half-stifled by good
manners. Alison, odd though it seemed for one of her
disposition, was woman enough to want me to believe
her younger.

'Dreams?' I prompted.

'My sister,' Audrey Visborough pronounced repressively, 'tended to fall for any man in breeches. She
would drool over men she could never have. Very silly.
I daresay I mentioned it to Howard when he first came

193

here. Jackson Wells looked good in breeches and of course he was flattered when Sonia made eyes at him. It was no basis for a marriage.'

I said, 'Er . . .' without opinion.

'I at least prevented my daughter from making the same mistake.'

Alison, the unmarried daughter, flashed her a glance full of old and bitter resentment.

I cleared my throat diplomatically and asked, 'Do you by any chance have a photograph of your sister?'

'I don't think so.'

'Not even from when you were both young?'

Audrey said severely, 'Sonia was a late and unexpected child, born when I was already grown. She was pleasant enough to begin with, I suppose. I didn't see much of her. Then I married Rupert, and really . . . ! Sonia's behaviour became *insupportable*. She wouldn't *listen* to me.'

'But . . . when she died in that way . . . ?' I left the question open, ready for any response.

Audrey shuddered a little. 'Horrible,' she said, but the word and the shudder were automatic, the emotion dead from age.

'Do you have any idea why she died?' I asked.

'We have said over and over again that we do not.'

'And,' Alison added in the same manner, 'it is disgraceful that you and your film should be intruding on our lives.'

Audrey nodded vigorously: mother and daughter were agreed on that, at least.

I asked Alison, 'For Howard's sake, then, will you

194

write the short note of explanation to the film company?'

With asperity she countered, 'You don't care about Howard. You just care about yourself.'

With patience I spoke the truth. 'Howard writes a good screenplay. His name is on the film. If he is worried about being sued by the film company he will not do himself justice in scenes which still need expanding. He admires you, Miss Visborough. Give him a chance to do his best work.'

She blinked, rose to her sturdy feet, and left the room, closing the door behind her.

Her mother gave a cough of implacable distrust and said, 'May I ask why you want a photograph of my sister?'

'It would help because then I could be sure the actress who plays her in the film will not look like her. If your sister had red hair, for instance, we could get the actress a black wig.'

Every response seemed to be squeezed out of her against her will. She said, however, 'My sister had naturally mousey-brown hair. She disliked it and dyed it any colour she could think of. My husband had a fierce disagreement with her once when she came here with a green crewcut.'

I managed not to smile. 'Upsetting,' I said.

'I do not care what you say about Sonia,' she went on, 'but I mind very much that you are denigrating my husband's achievements. Ga-ga! He was *never* ga-ga. He was a man of sense and wisdom, with a spotless reputation.'

And I had no need to wonder what he'd looked like, as there were photographs of Rupert Visborough at various ages in silver frames on almost every surface in the room. He'd been handsome, upright and humourless: no twinkle in any of the eyes. I thought with a small twinge of guilt that I was going to make of Cibber something Visborough had never been; a charging bull travelling out of control to self-destruction.

The sitting-room door opened to reveal, not Alison returning, but an unprepossessing man in hacking jacket and jodhpurs who entered as if thoroughly at home, crossing to a tray holding glasses and a single bottle of whisky. He poured from bottle to glass and took a swig before looking me over and waiting for an introduction.

'Roddy,' Audrey Visborough said from conditioned social reflex, 'this man is Thomas Lyon, who is making that wretched film.'

Roddy Visborough had his glass to his face so that I couldn't see his expression, but his body stiffened in annoyance. He was, I thought, the dressage rider from the show-jumping paddock: a man of medium height, neither fat nor thin, uncharismatic, with scanty grey-brown hair, going bald.

He lowered the glass to chest level and offensively said, 'Bugger off.' He said it phonetically, as bugger *orf*.

Audrey Visborough made not the slightest protest. She remarked, merely, 'Mr Lyon is leaving shortly.'

Her son sank the rest of his undiluted drink and poured a second. 'What are you doing here?' he said. 'You're upsetting my mother.'

I answered, 'I came to help straighten things out for Howard Tyler.'

'Oh, him.' Roddy Visborough smiled superciliously. 'Seems keen on Alison. I can't think what he sees in her.'

His mother made no comment.

I thought that what Howard saw in Alison was a staunch woman who took a realistic but none too happy view of the world. There had been unlikelier alliances.

Alison herself returned with a white envelope which she held out for me to take. I thanked her: she nodded unenthusiastically and turned to her brother, asking, 'How did the lesson go?'

'The child's stupid.'

'We need her custom.'

'I do not need your criticism.'

Alison looked as if this level of brotherly love was customary. To me, rather to my surprise, she explained, 'We prepare horses and riders for eventing and show jumping. We keep horses and ponies here at livery.'

'I see.'

'*I* don't live here,' Roddy said with a sort of throttled grudge. 'I have a cottage down the road. I only work here.'

'He's the show jumper,' Alison said, as if I should have heard of him. 'I employ him to teach.'

'Ah,' I said vaguely.

'This house is mine,' Alison said. 'Daddy left our family home to me in his will. Mummy, of course, is now my guest.'

I looked carefully at Alison's face. Under the no-nonsense exterior she let me see a buried but definite glimmer of mischief, of extreme satisfaction, of perhaps the sweetest revenge for a lifetime of snubs.

# CHAPTER TEN

Next morning I awoke with a groan, every muscle stiffly lecturing me on the folly of proving points. I winced down towards my car but was stopped in the lobby by Nash, O'Hara and Moncrieff, who seemed to have been holding a conference.

O'Hara didn't say good morning, he said, 'You're goddam crazy, you know that.'

I turned disillusioned eyes on Moncrieff, who said, 'Yeah, well, nothing's off the record, you're always saying so yourself.'

Nash said, 'Midnight last night, when you'd gone to bed, Moncrieff played us the video.'

I pinched sleepy eyes between finger and thumb and asked O'Hara if he'd faxed Alison's letter to Hollywood, as he'd intended.

He nodded. 'If Howard stays in line, he's off the hook.'

'Good.' I paused. 'OK. Today, then. It's not raining. We can shoot the race as planned. We can only do it once, so anyone loading fogged film or getting his f-stops wrong will be blindfolded for the firing squad. Moncrieff, I'll sincerely kill you if your crews bugger it up.'

O'Hara said, 'Did you phone that TV guy, Greg Compass, yesterday?'

I thought back and nodded. 'From Huntingdon. I couldn't reach him.'

'He sent a message. The reception desk says you didn't call down for it.'

He handed me a piece of paper on which a phone number was written, and a time, 9 a.m.

By nine o'clock, each of us travelling in his own car with driver, we had long reached Huntingdon race-course. Greg, as good as his message, answered immediately I phoned.

I said, 'I wanted to thank you for Saturday.'

'No sweat. I gather you're still running things.'

'Sort of.' I explained about the Huntingdon scenes and invited him to come and drape his familiar figure in shot, if he cared to.

'When?'

'Today, tomorrow or Thursday. Any or all.'

'Too busy,' he said.

'Never mind, then.'

'Fee?'

'Of course.'

'I'll be with you tomorrow.' He laughed and clicked off, and I wondered if it would cost me another row of seats.

I drove round the track with Moncrieff to check the positions of the cameras and, in places, lights. Apart from our own two usual crews, we had rented three more cameras on dollies and planted two others, unmanned, in the fences for close action. Moncrieff himself would be on the camera truck, driving round ahead of the horses, filming them from head on. The last of the rented equipment was high on the stands from where it would follow the action from start to winning post. As always with scenes that could only be shot once, there would be glitches, but enough, I fervently hoped, would be usable.

Ed having briefed the jockeys to wait for me, I found them gathered in the jockeys' changing room, kitted as for an ordinary race. Fourteen of them. Every single one.

'Morning,' I said, matter of factly.

'Morning.'

No one referred to the day before. I said, 'I know Ed's given you the gen but we'll just go over it once more. From your point of view, it will be a race like most others. Two miles over fences. You'll circle around at the starting gate, and the starter will call you into line. The starter is an actor. He's been well rehearsed, but if he makes a balls of it, don't stop and go back. Just keep on racing.' I paused. 'Same as usual, there's a groundsman and an ambulanceman at every fence. The groundsmen and the ambulancemen are the real thing. The ambulance is real. So is the doctor. So is the vet. All the spectators out on the course and at the fences will be professional extras. All the crowds on the stands will be townspeople. OK so far?'

They nodded.

'Our fourteen horses are all fairly fit but, as you know, they were chosen for a safe jumping record and bought cheaply. They won't break any sound barriers, and the three of them that raced yesterday may not stay the course today. If you want to you can draw lots in a minute to see who gets which horse; one to fourteen on the number cloths.'

The faces were businesslike. They agreed to draw lots.

'This race won't work,' I said, 'unless you yourselves make it good. You want to be able to show the video of it all to your families, let alone see it in the cinema. You'll all get a CD or video tape later.'

'Who's got to win?' one of them asked.

'Didn't Ed tell you?'

They shook their heads.

'It's got to be a bona fide race. Whoever wins, those are the colours we'll put on the actor who's playing the jockey in close-up. This actor looks OK sitting on a horse and he can trot at a pinch. Sorry, but it's he who'll be led into the unsaddling enclosure in the winner's colours. But ... er ... to make up for it, the one of you who wins this race will get a percentage same as usual. When you pull up, come off the course through the usual gate. All the also-rans can unsaddle in the usual place. There'll be some extras there acting as owners and trainers. The lads will take the horses. Just behave as normal. The first four will be led off towards the winner's enclosure. Any questions?'

'What if we fall?' It was Blue who asked.

'Why did you all turn up?'

Some laughed and some swore. No tension any more.

'Have fun,' I said.

One asked, 'And where will you be?'

I said with audible regret, 'I'll be watching from the

ground.' I paused. 'If you can possibly avoid it, don't give us any flagrant grounds for an enquiry. There's no enquiry in the script. Try not to cross. OK?'

I went outdoors through the deserted weighing-room that on a real race day would have been crowded with officials and trainers, and I watched for a moment the helpful people of Huntingdon arrive in droves, all dressed in racegoing clothes and carrying, in impressive numbers, binoculars. Ed, I saw, had done a fine job.

One of the film personnel came up to me and handed me an envelope, saying it was urgent. I thanked him perfunctorily, and he'd gone before I'd opened the message.

I unfolded the inside sheet of contents, and read the words:

Stop making this film or you will die by the knife today.

Oh, delightful.

It looked like a computer printout on anonymous white office paper.

O'Hara appeared, wanting to discuss a detail or two, and asked what was the matter. 'Why are you frozen?'

I gave him the missive. 'I've had death threats before,' I pointed out.

'Those were after the movie had been distributed. But we have to take this seriously.' He flicked the page with a fingernail. 'What are we going to do about it?'

'What do you suggest?'

'If you leave the set,' O'Hara said plainly, 'the movie

automatically goes into recess. It would give us all time to find this bozo and slap him behind bars.'

'We can't stop the filming,' I said. 'After the *Drumbeat* article and the knife on the Heath ... one more panic and the moguls will take complete fright and yank the whole movie for ever.'

O'Hara suspected it was true, but worriedly said, 'This letter doesn't just say you'll die, it says you'll die *today*.'

'Mm.'

'Thomas, you're no good to us dead.'

'What strikes me,' I said, half-smiling at his pragmatism, 'is that whoever sent this note doesn't actually want to kill me, he wants to stop the film without being driven to drastic action. If he – or, I suppose, she – meant to stop the film by killing me, why not just do it? Why the preliminary melodrama? We'll ignore it and press on.'

'I'll at least get you a bodyguard, like Nash.'

Nash, that day, had not one but two bodyguards in attendance but, as I reminded O'Hara, both of these bodyguards were well known to us.

'If you bring in a stranger, you're risking what you're trying to avoid,' I said. 'In classic cases, it's the bodyguards themselves that kill the victim.' I tried a lie that I hoped would be true, and said, 'I don't think I'm in much danger, so just forget it.'

'Difficult.' He was mildly relieved, all the same, by my decision.

'Keep the paper,' I told him, 'and keep the envelope.' I gave it to him. 'And let's get on with the film.'

'I still don't like it.'

Nor did I, much; but delivering a death *threat* took little organisation or courage, and delivering a death by knife took both.

The knife intended for Nash had been incompetently dropped. Cling to that. Forget – for Christ's sake forget – the intestines spilling out of Dorothea.

'Who gave you the letter?' O'Hara asked.

'One of the grips. I've seen him around but I don't know his name.'

There was never time to know the names of the between sixty and a hundred people working on a film on location. I hadn't learned even the names of the horses, neither their registered names, nor the names the lads called them, nor their invented names for the film. I didn't know the jockeys' names, nor those of the bit-part actors. It was faces I remembered, horses' faces, jockeys' faces, actors' faces from way back: my memory had always been chiefly visual.

I did forget for a while about the death threat: too much else to do.

As always with scenes involving two or three hundred people, the race took forever to set up. I spent ages on the walkie-talkie checking the status of each far-flung section but, at last, towards noon, everything seemed to be ready. The lads brought the horses from the stables and the jockeys mounted their balloted numbers and cantered down to the start.

I decided to ride on the camera truck with Moncrieff, to be nearer the action: and to guard my back, I cravenly and privately acknowledged.

Ed, equipped with loudspeaker, alerted the Huntingdon multitude to put on raceday faces and cheer the finish. The commentary, we had explained, would be missing; we had to record it separately and afterwards. Nevertheless, Ed urged, cheer whoever won.

Eventually it was he who shouted, 'Action', the command reverberating through the stands, and I, with raised pulse, who found myself begging unknown deities for perfection.

There were flaws, of course. One of the rented cameras jammed, and one of the two planted in fences got kicked to oblivion by a horse, but the race started tidily, and it was joyously clear from the first that my quasi-colleagues were playing fair.

They had seen me on the truck, when it was positioned for the start, seen me sitting on the edge of the roof of the cab, to get the best of views. They'd waved, in a way, I thought, to reassure me, and I'd waved back; and they did indeed ride their hearts out all the way round.

We had the truck driven for a lot of the way so that the camera was barely six feet from the leading horses' heads, then speeded it up to give a longer view, then slowed again, varying the angles.

Two horses fell on the backstretch second time round. I looked back with anxiety, but both jockeys got to their feet, the loose horses adding the unpremeditated facets that in the end proved the contest real.

The other riders again piled on the pressure rounding the last bend, and again they rode flat out over the last two fences and stretched every sinew to win. The finish was even faster and closer than the day before, but distinguishably Blue, Green with White Stripes, and Yellow crossed the line in the first three places; and as the truck slowed I could hear the crowd shouting them home as if they'd gambled their shirts. Those jockeys had ridden with an outpouring of courage that left me dry-mouthed and breathless, grateful beyond expression, bursting with admiration.

As agreed, when they jogged the tired horses back to unsaddle, another of Moncrieff's cameras continued to film them. I couldn't walk into shot to thank them, and thanks, in any form, would have been inadequate.

'Hell's teeth,' Moncrieff exclaimed, moved by the proximity to the speed and sweating commitment. 'And they do that for a *living*?'

'Day in, day out, several times an afternoon.'

'Crazy.'

'There's nothing like it,' I said.

We changed the actor-jockey into Blue's colours and had him led into the winner's enclosure, to applause from a throng of mixed extras and townspeople. We had to do the unsaddling at that point, while the horses still steamed and sweated and stamped from the excitement of racing. We filmed Nash patting the winner's neck. We filmed the actor-jockey unbuckling the saddle while showing, to my mind, a lot too much clumsiness. We filmed the four horses being rugged and led away by the lads; and we broke for lunch.

Nash, bodyguard close, signed a host of good-natured autographs, mostly on the racecards we'd lavishly distributed.

O'Hara, again at my elbow, breathed in my ear, 'Satisfied?'

'Are you?'

'Nash and I watched the race from up in the stewards' box. Nash says those first three jockeys rode beyond the call of duty.'

'Yes, they did.'

'He says it will give fantastic bite to the victory of *his* horse over Cibber's.'

'It'll drive Cibber mad.'

'The final straw?'

'Almost. Cibber can't stand to have his best horse beaten into second place like that by the man he hates.'

'When I read the revised script, I thought Howard had overdone the hate. I couldn't see any race inducing that level of paranoia.'

'Hate can corrode the soul to disintegration.'

'Maybe. But to show that, you needed an *exceptional* race ...' His voice tailed off momentarily. '... and I guess you got it,' he finished, 'in your own way.'

I half-smiled. 'Let's find some lunch.'

'You're having it in the stewards' box with Nash and me. Do you realise I could have come up behind you just now and put a knife through your ribs? Do you realise we have roughly three hundred strangers here wandering around?'

I did realise. I went with him and lunched high up in safety.

By the time we returned to ground level and to work, one of Ed's assistants had found the grip who'd passed on the letter. Some kid had given it to him. What kid? He looked around, bewildered. Kids were all over the place. The grip had no recollection of age, sex or

207

clothes. He'd been busy with the unloading of scenery for the following day.

'Shit,' O'Hara said.

Another of the film personnel approached as if apologetically and held out a card towards me. 'Some people called Batwillow say you're expecting them.' He looked across to where the little group stood. Jackson Wells, his wife and Lucy, and a man I didn't know.

I took the card and waved them over and had time only to say to O'Hara, 'This is our hanged lady's real husband,' before shaking their hands. They had come dressed for the races and Jackson Wells himself, in tweeds and trilby, looked indefinably more a trainer than a farmer. He introduced the stranger as 'Ridley Wells, my brother.' I shook a leathery hand.

Ridley Wells was altogether less striking than Jackson, both in colouring and personality, and he was also, I thought, less intelligent. He blinked a lot. He was dressed in riding clothes as if he had come straight from his work, which Jackson described to O'Hara as 'teaching difficult horses better manners'.

Ridley nodded, and in an accent stronger than his brother's, said self-pityingly, 'I'm out in all weathers on Newmarket Heath, but it's a thankless sort of job. I can ride better than most, but no one pays me enough. How about employing me in this film?'

Jackson resignedly shook his head at Ridley's underlying chip-on-the-shoulder attitude. O'Hara said sorry, no job. Ridley looked as if he'd been badly treated; a habitual expression, I guessed. I could see why Jackson hadn't welcomed Ridley's inclusion in the day's proceedings.

Jackson still had, it seemed, the old professional trainer's eye, because after a few 'nice days' and so on, he said, 'That was some race those jocks rode. More electrifying than most of the real thing.'

'Could you see that?' O'Hara asked interestedly.

'Didn't you hear the cheering? That was no act, either. "Cheer the winner," we were told, but the cheers came easy as pie.'

'Be darned,' O'Hara said, no horseman himself. He looked at my guests thoughtfully and said impulsively to me, 'Keep the Batwillow family around you, why not?'

He meant, use them as bodyguards. He hadn't heard Jackson Wells tell me he'd have preferred not to have the film made. I felt safe, though, with his wife and daughter, so I wrapped them as a living shield around me, Mrs Wells on one arm, Lucy on the other, and walked them all off to meet Nash.

Although Nash hadn't wanted to meet the man he was playing, I introduced them straightforwardly, 'Jackson Wells – Nash Rourke,' and watched them shake hands with mutual reservations.

They were in several ways superficially alike: same build, same age bracket, same firm facial muscles. Jackson was blond where Nash was darker, and sunnily open, where Nash, from long mega-star status, had grown self-protectively wary. Easier with the women, Nash autographed racecards for wife and daughter and effortlessly melted their hearts. He signed for Ridley also, and didn't take to him.

We were due to film Nash walking up the steps to the stands to watch (supposedly) his horse run in the race. Slightly to O'Hara's dismay, he invited Mrs Wells and Lucy to stand near him, in front of the bodyguards, for the scene. Ridley, unasked, followed them up the steps, which left Jackson Wells marooned on his feet by my side, looking as if he wished he hadn't come.

'It hasn't occurred to your wife,' I said.

'What hasn't?' he said, but he knew what I meant.

'That she's standing next to you, twenty-six years ago.'

'They're the wrong age,' he said brusquely. 'We were all kids at the time. And you're right, I don't like it.'

He bore it, however, standing rigid but quiet, while Nash, taking over from his stand-in, walked up the steps and turned on exactly the right spot to bring his face into Moncrieff's careful lighting. We shot the scene three times and I marked the first and third takes to be printed: and O'Hara stood all the while at my left elbow, riding shotgun, so to speak.

I grinned at him. 'I could get me some armour,' I said.

'It's no laughing matter.'

'No.'

One can't somehow believe in one's own imminent death. I hadn't stopped the film and I went on shooting bits of it all afternoon; and for ages at a time, like ten minutes, I stopped thinking about steel.

At one point, waiting as ever for lights and camera to be ready, I found myself a little apart from the centre of activity, standing beside Lucy, gazing into her amazing blue eyes and wondering how old she was.

She said suddenly, 'You asked Dad for a photo of Sonia so that you didn't copy her exactly in the film.'

'That's right. He hadn't kept any.'

'No,' she agreed. 'But ... well ... I've got one. I found it one day jammed at the back of a drawer. I meant to give it to Dad, but he won't talk about Sonia. He won't let us mention her, ever. So I just kept it.' She opened the small handbag swinging from her shoulder and handed me a creased but clearly distinguishable snapshot of a pretty girl and a good-looking young man, not Jackson. 'You won't make Yvonne look like her, will you?'

Shaking my head, I turned the photo over and read the pencilled information on the back, 'Sonia and Pig.'

'Who is Pig?' I asked.

'No idea,' Lucy said. 'I've never heard Dad mention him. But that's Dad's handwriting, so he must have known him, long ago.'

'Long ago before you were born.'

'I'm eighteen,' she said.

I felt old. I said, 'Could I borrow the photo for a while?'

She looked doubtful. 'I don't want to lose it.'

'Until tomorrow?' I suggested. 'If you came here again tomorrow . . .'

'I don't think there's a chance. Dad didn't really want to come at all. He only gave in to Mum so that she could meet Nash Rourke.'

'Could you and your mother come tomorrow?'

'She won't do anything if Dad doesn't like it.'

'And you?'

'I don't have a car of my own.'

'Lend me the photo for an hour, then.'

She brightened and agreed, and I gave the photo to

Moncrieff with an on-my-knees expression, begging him to do me a clear negative from which we could get a positive print. It would take the usual day for travelling to London to the laboratory for development, but with reasonable luck I'd have it back in the morning.

In the morning. Die today. Shut up, I thought.

'Do you,' I asked Lucy later, 'have a computer and a printer at home?'

'Of course we do,' she answered, puzzled. 'No one can farm without one, nowadays. The paperwork drives Dad *loco*. Why do you ask?'

'Just wondered. We use one here all the time.' I enlarged on it, defusing my enquiry. 'Every inch of film, every lens used, every focal stop . . . we have a script supervisor entering the lot. We can lay our hands on any frame of film that way, and also make sure we have continuity if we shoot the next scene days later.'

She nodded in partial understanding and said, 'And who are all those odd people you see on the credits? Grips, gaffers . . . who are they?'

'Grips move scenery. The gaffer is in charge of the lighting equipment. The most important chap at the moment is the production manager. He's the person who arranges for vehicles and scenery and props and all sorts of things to be in the right place when we need them.'

'And you,' she said with unflattering doubt, 'are in overall charge of the whole thing?'

'I and the producer.' I pointed to O'Hara. 'No us, no film.'

She said baldly, 'Dad said so, but Mum thought you were too young.'

'Are you always so frank?'

'Sixteen was hell,' she said. 'Tongue-tied. Not long ago I broke out of the egg.'

'Congratulations.'

'Dad says I talk nonsense.'

'No better time for it. Stay and have dinner. I'll take you home later.'

'Sorry.' The response was automatic, the blue eyes full of the warnings she'd been given about date-rape and such. 'Not on our own.'

I smiled wryly. I'd thought only of not being knifed, not of bed. I'm losing it, I thought, wanting my life saved by an eighteen-year-old still half in the cradle. I fetched her snap from Moncrieff – thumbs up, he said – and returned it to her.

'I didn't mean,' she said awkwardly, sixteen surfacing again after all. 'I mean, I don't want to offend you . . .'

'But no casting couches. It's all right.'

She blushed and retreated, sane and confused, to her parents, and I thought bed wouldn't have been such a bad idea after all.

The trouble with making films, I acknowledged, was the way the occupation gobbled time. For the three months of any pre-production, I worked flat out to put the film together, choosing locations, getting the feel – the vision – in place, altering the screenplay, living with the characters. During production, like now, I worked seven days a week with little sleep. Post-production – the recording of music and sound effects, the cutting together of scenes and parts of scenes to make an impact and tell a story, the debates and the meetings and the previews – all of those often had to be scrambled into just a further three months. And with one film done, another crowded on my heels. I'd made three films lately in under two years. This new one had by far the biggest budget. I loved the work, I was lucky to be wanted, I felt no flicker of regret: I just didn't seem to have time to look for a wife.

One day, I guessed, it might happen like a thunderbolt. The skies, however, had to date vouchsafed only scattered showers, and Lucy looked like a continuing drought.

Someone unexpectedly knocked my elbow. I whirled round with surging heartbeat and found myself face to face with Moncrieff.

'Jumpy!' he said, watching me reach for composure. 'What were you expecting? A tiger?'

'With claws,' I agreed. I got things under control and we discussed the next scene.

'Are you all right?' Moncrieff asked, puzzled. 'Not ill?'

Not ill, I thought, but plain scared. I said, 'Everything's fine. But ... er ... some nutter wants to get the film stopped, and if you see anyone in my area raising a blunt instrument, give me a holler.'

His eyebrows rose. 'Is that why O'Hara has been standing behind you whenever he can?'

'I guess so.'

He thought it over. 'Nasty knife, that, on the gallops.' A pause. 'It got effing close to Ivan.'

'Do me a favour and don't remind me.'

'Just keep my eyes open?'

'Got it.'

We lit and shot some non-speaking takes of Nash's emotions during the race. The block of crowd behind

214

him, mostly bona fide extras but some townspeople, also Mrs Wells, Lucy, Ridley and Nash's bodyguards, responded faithfully to Ed's exhortations, looking for each shot to where he pointed, oohing and aahing, showing anxiety, showing excitement and finally cheering wildly as they watched in memory the horses racing to the finish.

All of the faces except Nash's would be very slightly out of focus, thanks to Moncrieff's wizardry with lenses. One of his favourite lenses had to be focused principally on the light in the actor's eyes. Everything else on the actor's head would be a tiny shade fuzzy, his neck, hair, the lot.

'The daylight's going,' Moncrieff told me eventually, though to any eye but his the change was too slight to notice. 'We should wrap for today.'

Ed through his megaphone thanked the citizens of Huntingdon for their work and invited them back for the morrow. They clapped. Happy faces all round. Nash signed autographs with the bodyguards at his shoulders.

Lucy, glowing with the day's pleasures, walked to where I was checking through the following day's schedule with O'Hara, and handed me a flat white box about a foot long by three inches wide, fastened shut with a rubber band.

'What is it?' I asked.

'I don't know,' she said. 'A boy asked me to give it to you.'

'What boy?'

'Just a boy. A present, he said. Aren't you going to open it?'

O'Hara took it out of my hands, stripped off the

rubber band and cautiously opened the box himself. Inside, on a bed of crunched-up white office paper, lay a knife.

I swallowed. The knife had a handle of dark polished wood, ridged round and round to give a good grip. There was a businesslike black hilt and a narrow black blade nearly six inches long: all in all, good looking and efficient.

'Wow,' Lucy said. 'It's beautiful.'

O'Hara closed the box without touching the knife and, restoring the rubber band, stuck it in his outside jacket pocket. I thought it was better to get a knife in a box than in the body.

'We should stop all boys from leaving,' O'Hara said, but he could see, as I could, that it was already too late. Half of the crowd had already walked homewards through the gates.

'Is something the matter?' Lucy asked, frowning, sensing our alarm.

'No,' I smiled at the blue eyes. 'I hope you've had a good day.'

'Spectacular!'

I kissed her cheek. In public, she allowed it. She said, 'I'd better go, Dad's waiting,' and made a carefree departure, waving.

O'Hara took the white box from his pocket and carefully opened it again, picking out of the raised lid a folded strip of the same white paper. He handed it to me and I looked at its message.

Again a computer print out, it said, 'Tomorrow'.

*

O'Hara and I walked out together towards the cars and I told him about Dorothea and her injuries. I described again for him, as I had two days earlier, the knife that had been dropped on the Heath.

He stopped dead in mid-stride. 'Are you saying,' he demanded, 'that your friend was attacked with *that* knife? The one on the Heath?'

'I don't know.'

'But,' he protested, bemused, 'what possible connection could there be between her and our film?'

'I don't know.'

'It can't have been the same knife.' He walked on, troubled but certain.

'The only connection,' I said, going with him, 'is the fact that long ago Dorothea's brother Valentine put shoes on Jackson Wells's racehorses.'

'Much too distant to have any significance.'

'And Valentine said he once gave a knife to someone called Derry.'

'Hell's teeth, Thomas, you're rambling.'

'Yes. Valentine was at the time.'

'Valentine was what?'

'Rambling,' I said. 'Delirious.'

*I killed the Cornish boy . . .*

Too many knives.

'You are *not*,' O'Hara said strongly, 'going to get knifed tomorrow.'

'Good.'

He laughed. 'You're a jackass, Thomas.'

He wanted me to travel in his car, but I called Robbie Gill's mobile and found I could briefly see Dorothea, if I arrived by seven.

At the hospital the egregious Paul had positioned himself in a chair outside the single room into which Dorothea had been moved. He rose heavily to his feet at the sight of me, but to my surprise made none of the objections I was expecting.

'My mother wants to see you,' he said disapprovingly. 'I've told her I don't want you here, but all she does is cry.'

There had been, I thought, a subtle change in Paul. His pompous inner certainty seemed to have rocked: the external bombast sounded much the same, but half its fire had gone.

'You're not to tire her,' he lectured. 'Five minutes, that's all.'

Paul himself opened Dorothea's door, and came in with me purposefully.

Dorothea lay on a high bed, her head supported by a bank of pillows, her old face almost as colourless as the cotton except for dark disturbing bruises and threadlike minutely stitched cuts. There were tubes, a bag delivering drops of blood, another bag of clear liquid, and a system that allowed her to run painkillers into her veins when she needed it. Her hold on life looked negligible. Her eyes were closed and her white body was motionless, even the slow rise and fall of her chest seeming too slight to register on the covering sheet.

'Dorothea,' I said quietly. 'It's Thomas. I've come.'

Very faintly, she smiled.

Paul's loud voice broke her peace. 'I've told him, Mother, that he has five minutes. And, of course, I will remain here at hand.'

218

Dorothea, murmuring, said she wanted to talk to me alone.

'Don't be silly, Mother.'

Two tears appeared below her eyelids and trembled in the lashes.

'Oh, for heaven's sake,' Paul said brusquely. 'She does that all the time.' He turned on his heel and gave her her wish, seeming hurt at her rejection. 'Five minutes,' he threatened as a parting shot.

'Paul's gone,' I said, as the door closed behind him. 'How are you feeling?'

'So tired, dear.' Her voice, though still a murmur, was perfectly clear. 'I don't remember how I got here.'

'No, I've been told. Robbie Gill told me.'

'Robbie Gill is very kind.'

'Yes.'

'Hold my hand, dear.'

I pulled the visitor's chair to her side and did as she asked, vividly remembering Valentine's grasp of my wrist, exactly a week ago. Dorothea, however, had no sins to confess.

'Paul told me,' she said, 'that someone tore my house apart, looking for something.'

'I'm afraid so. Yes, I saw it.'

'What were they looking for?'

'Don't you know?'

'No, dear. The police asked me. It must have been something Valentine had. Sometimes I think I know. Sometimes I think I hear him shouting at me, to tell him. Then it all goes away again.'

'Who was shouting?'

She said doubtfully, 'Paul was shouting.'

'Oh, no.'

'He does shout, you know. He means well. He's my son, my sweet baby.' Tears of weakness and regret ran down her cheeks. 'Why do precious little babies grow . . .?' Her question ended in a quiet sob, unanswerable. 'He wants to look after me.'

I said, 'Did Robbie Gill talk to you about a nursing home?'

'So kind. I'd like to go there. But Paul says . . .' She stopped, fluttering a white hand exhaustedly. 'I haven't the strength to argue.'

'Let Robbie Gill move you,' I urged. 'In a day or two, when you're stronger.'

'Paul says . . .' She stopped, the effort of opposing him too much.

'Just rest,' I said. 'Don't worry. Just lie and drift and get stronger.'

'So kind, dear.' She lay quiet for a long minute, then said, 'I'm sure I know what he was looking for, but I can't remember it.'

'What Paul was looking for?'

'No, dear. Not Paul.' She frowned. 'It's all jumbled up.' After another pause she said, 'How many knives did I have?'

'How many . . .?'

'The police asked me. How many knives in the kitchen. I can't remember.'

'No one knows how many knives they have in the kitchen.'

'No. They said there weren't any knives in the house with blood on them.'

'Yes, I see.'

220

'Perhaps when I go home I'll see which knife is missing.'

'Yes, perhaps. Would you like me to tidy your house up a bit?'

'I can't ask you.'

'I'd like to do it.'

'Paul wants to. He keeps asking. He gets so angry with me, but I don't know who has the key. So silly, isn't it? I can't go home because I haven't got the key.'

'I'll find the key,' I said. 'Is there anything you want from there?'

'No, dear. I just want to be at home with Valentine.' The slow tears came. 'Valentine's dead.'

I stroked her soft hand.

'It was a photo album,' she said suddenly, opening her eyes.

'What was?'

'What they were looking for.' She looked at me worriedly, pale blue shadows round her eyes.

'What photo album?'

'I don't know. I haven't got one, just some old snaps I keep in a box. Some pictures of Paul when he was little. I never had a camera, but friends gave me snaps...'

'Where's the box?'

'In my bedroom. But it's not an *album* ... I didn't think of it before. Everything's so confusing.'

'Mm. Don't let it worry you. And Robbie Gill will be cross if I tire you, let alone Paul.'

A smile shone briefly in the old eyes. 'I might as well be tired. I've nothing else to do.'

I laughed. 'It's just a shame,' I said, 'that Paul took

Valentine's books after all. He swears he didn't, but he must have done because they aren't in the house.'

Dorothea frowned. 'No, dear, Paul didn't take them.'

'Didn't he?' I was sceptical. 'Did he send someone else?'

'No, dear.' Her forehead wrinkled further. 'Valentine wanted you to have his books and I know he would have been furious if Paul had taken them because he wasn't very fond of Paul, only put up with him for my sake, such a pity.'

'So . . . who took them?'

'Bill.'

'Who?'

'Bill Robinson, dear. He has them safe.'

'But Dorothea, who is Bill Robinson, and where and why does he have the books?'

She smiled guiltily. 'I was afraid, you see, dear, that Paul would come back and persuade me to let him take them. He tires me out sometimes until I do what he wants, but he's my son, dear, after all . . . So I asked Bill Robinson to come and pick them all up and put them in his garage, and he's a chum of mine, dear, so he came and took them, and they'll be quite safe, dear, he's a nice young man, he mends motorbikes.'

# CHAPTER ELEVEN

I went to bed after midnight, thinking that although I had not died today, it was now already tomorrow.

Nash and I had eaten dinner together in harmony over his scenes-to-come in the parade ring, where his jockey would be wearing blue, while Cibber's would be in the green and white stripes.

After the evening preparation for the Jockey Club enquiry scene, Nash had, without baldly saying so, let me realise that he much preferred to rehearse everything with me in private, so that on set little needed to be asked or answered, his performances being already clear in his mind. I didn't know if he worked in this way with every director, but between the two of us it was notably fruitful in regard to his readiness for every shot. That we were saving time and running ahead of schedule was in this way chiefly his doing.

As usual I'd spent the last two hours of the evening with Moncrieff, putting together with him the plan of positions and lights for the parade-ring cameras, also for those catching the pre-race routines of horses being saddled and led from the saddling boxes, being led round the parade ring, being de-rugged and mounted.

Multiple cameras, though not cheap in themselves, also saved time: I would later cut together, from several lengthy shots, the snippets and pieces that in shorthand would give an overall impression of the whole pre-race tension. The slap of leather straps into buckles, the brushing of oil to gloss the hoof, the close shots of muscle moving below shining coat. It needed only two seconds of graphic visual image to flash an impression of urgency and intent, but it took maybe ten long minutes of filming to capture each.

Pace had a lot to do with good film-making. There would be no flash-flash-flash over the dream/fantasy sequences, only a slowly developing realisation of their significances.

Well . . . so I hoped.

While my silent young driver took me towards Huntingdon in the morning I thought of Dorothea's preservation of Valentine's books, and of the new uncertainty beneath Paul's bluster. He hadn't tried to cut short my visit to the patient: the five allowed minutes had stretched to ten, until I myself thought that she'd talked enough.

Paul had walked with me from her room to the hospital exit, his breath agitated and deep as if he wanted to say something but couldn't bring himself entirely to the point. I gave him time and opportunity, but he was not, as his uncle had been, desperate enough for confession.

Paul was shouting, Dorothea had said. For her sake, I hoped to God she'd got things mixed up.

At Huntingdon racecourse, before eight o'clock, the gates were already wide open to admit the local inhabitants. Breakfast, provided free for all-comers via the film's caterers, ran to endless hot dogs out of a raised-sided van. The weather, though cold, still smiled. Cheerful faces abounded. I needn't have worried that the townspeople would be too bored to return: word of mouth had acted positively and we ended with an even larger crowd than on the day before.

The publicity department of the film company had provided five hundred T-shirts, one to be given that day to thank every local helper on departure – (much to my amusement the front of each T-shirt carried the slogan, UNSTABLE TIMES in large letters, but if one looked closely at some extra tiny letters it read UNSTABLE AT ALL TIMES) – and I began to think they hadn't ordered enough.

The Huntingdon racecourse officials having been generous and helpful throughout, we had had unlimited access to everything we'd wanted. I was so keen not to abuse their welcome that I'd screwed O'Hara's arm to provide an army of scavengers to clean up all trash left by us.

'They'll have their own cleaning staff,' he'd protested. 'We're paying them, after all.'

'Goodwill is beyond price.'

He'd instructed the production manager to have the place left spotless.

The weighing-room and the jockeys' changing-rooms were already unlocked when I arrived on the course, and the wardrobe people were there too, laying out the jockeys' bright colours alongside their breeches and boots.

We had had all their gear made especially for the

film, not just the colours. Everything except the racing saddles, which had been hired, belonged to the company.

There were twenty sets across the board, as we'd allowed for tears and spares and hadn't, at time of ordering, known how many horses we would end with. In the changing-rooms I found that none of the jockeys had already arrived – they'd been called for nine o'clock – and I had no difficulty at all in scooping up what I wanted and locking myself privately into the bathroom.

I had taken with me two of the body protectors designed to save fallen jockeys from the worst effects of kicks. Stripped down to shirt and underpants, I put on the first and zipped it up the front.

In essence, the body protector was a blue cotton lightweight waistcoat padded throughout with flat poly-styrene oblongs, about six inches by four, by half an inch thick. The polystyrene pieces, stitched into place, covered the trunk from the neck to below the waist, with a further extension at the back to cover the coccyx at the base of the spine. From there a soft wide belt led forward between the legs to fasten to the vest in front, a scheme which prevented the protector from being displaced. Extra pieces led like epaulettes over the shoulders and down the upper arms, to be fastened round the arm with Velcro.

Although I'd taken the largest available, the protec-tor fitted tight and snugly. When I put the second on top, the front zip wouldn't meet to fasten across my chest; a problem I half solved by straining my trousers over both protectors and cinching my waist with my belt to hold everything together. I ended feeling like a hunch-shouldered quarterback, but with my ordinary sweater on top and my windproof blue jacket fastened over all, I didn't in the mirror look much bigger.

I had no idea how a jockey's kick protector would stand up to a knife, but psychologically an inch of polystyrene and four layers of sturdy cotton cloth was better than nothing, and I couldn't afford to spend the whole busy day worrying about something that would probably not happen.

I'd happily ridden flat out over jumps round the racecourse without a body protector, risking my neck. I would as happily have done it again. Odd how fear had different faces.

Outside, Moncrieff had already positioned his camera on its dolly for the first scene of the day, which was the exodus of the jockeys from the weighing-room on their way out to the parade ring before the race. Halfway along their path a child extra was to dash forward to offer an autograph book to the actor-jockey. Ed, directing a second camera, would film the jockey's friendly reaction in close-up, registering his face, his blue colours, and his nice-guy status, while the other jockeys went on their way through the shot behind him.

In the event we shot the sequence twice, though thanks to rehearsal it went smoothly the first time. Insurance, though, to my mind, was never wasted.

Between the two takes, I talked to the jockeys, joining them where they waited in the weighing-room. I thanked them for their brilliant race the day before and they made nothing of it, joking. All prickliness had vanished absolutely. They called me Thomas. They said several of them would be racing over the course for real at the Huntingdon meeting the following Monday, but it would be the old nitty-gritty, not the joys of make-believe land. Any time I made another racing film, they said with typically mocking humour, they would stampede in the opposite direction.

When they were recalled for the retake walk to the parade ring, I went out before them and watched from beside Moncrieff: then with the two printable shots in the can Moncrieff took the camera and crew into the parade ring itself, where the camera could swivel on a turntable to take an almost 360-degrees view of the horses being led round. I stood in the centre of the ring beside him, overseeing things.

As always it was the setting up that took the time: the positioning of extras playing the small groups of owners and trainers, the extras playing racing officials and stewards, the townspeople filling the viewing steps round the ring, the rehearsing of the jockeys so that each went to an allotted owner, the ensuring that the jockeys of the two deadly rivals would arrive in the ring together – the actor-jockey in blue, the other in green and white stripes – and part at a designated spot to join the two groups containing Nash and Cibber.

Nash's main two bodyguards, dressed as owners, carried binoculars as if they would rather have had guns. The apparently elderly lady completing that group was a twenty-eight-year-old martial arts champion with lioness instincts.

Cibber's group included Silva dressed as befitted a Jockey Club member's wife in well-cut wool coat, knee-high boots and fur hat; warm and pretty in the chill wind. Cibber's 'trainer', off-course, taught judo. O'Hara had taken these precautions. My own shadow, the one he'd insisted on, the evening before, stood beside me in the ring, looking dim. He was supposed to be a black-belt but I had more faith in polystyrene.

Later in the day we would do close-ups of Cibber's acrid fury at having to suffer Nash, his wife's lover, in unbearable proximity: close-ups of Silva looking lovingly at Nash, goading poor Cibber further; close-ups of Nash behaving with good manners, neutral towards Cibber, circumspect with Silva; short essential close shots that would take an age to light.

Meanwhile, with the horses being led round the ring and with everyone in their allotted places, we filmed the entry of the jockeys. Miraculously they all went to the right groups, touched their caps to the owners, made pretence conversations, watched the horses; behaved as jockeys do. The actor-jockey in blue joined Nash. Green and white stripes went to Cibber. No one tripped over cables, no one wandered inappropriately into shot, no one swore.

'Hallelujah,' Moncrieff breathed, sweating beside me when Ed yelled 'Cut.'

'And print,' I added. 'And do it again.'

We broke for lunch. Nash, in the centre of the parade ring, signed autographs one by one for a well-behaved but apparently endless single line of people, shepherded closely by one of Ed's assistants. O'Hara, the bodyguard and the lioness formed a human wall round the mega-star's back.

We ate again, Nash, O'Hara and I, up high in the stewards' box.

Threats to the film apart, it had been a satisfactory morning; we all knew that the scenes had gone well.

O'Hara said, 'Howard's here, did you know?'

'Howard!' Nash exclaimed with disgust.

'A very quiet Howard,' O'Hara amplified, grimly amused. 'Howard is putty in our hands.'

'I don't think his views have changed,' I said. 'He's been frightened. He'll keep his mouth shut. I'd describe it as a plug in a volcano. There's no doubt he passionately meant what he said to Alison Visborough. He stirred her up enough to relay his gripes to her friend on the *Drumbeat* and what he said to her, that's how he still feels.'

'But,' O'Hara protested, 'he wouldn't want the film actually stopped, would he?'

'His full screenplay fee became payable on the first day of principal photography – the first day of filming in Newmarket. It's normal, of course, and it's in his contract. Finished or abandoned, the film can't earn him more money, unless it makes unlikely zillions. And I think he still wants me sacked. He's still convinced I'm butchering his bestseller.'

'Which you are,' Nash smiled.

'Yes. You don't get good meat without a good butcher.'

O'Hara liked it. 'I'll tell Howard that.'

'Better not,' I said resignedly, knowing that he would.

O'Hara's mobile phone buzzed, and he answered it. 'What? What did you say? I can't hear you. Slow down.'

He listened a brief moment more and passed the instrument to me. 'It's Ziggy,' he said. 'You talk to him. He goes too fast for me.'

'Where is he?' I asked.

O'Hara shrugged. 'He went to Norway yesterday morning. I outlined what you wanted to an agent, who whisked him off at once.'

Ziggy's voice on the telephone was as staccato as automatic rifle fire, and just as fast.

'Hey,' I said after a while, 'have I got this straight? You've found ten wild Viking horses but they must come at once.'

'They cannot come at twenty-four days, or at thirty-eight days. They are not free. They are free only next week, for the right tides. They are coming on the ferry on Monday from Bergen to Immingham.'

'Newcastle,' I corrected.

'No. The Bergen ferry goes usually to Newcastle, but for horses it must be Immingham. It is better for us, they say. It is on the River Humber. They will leave Bergen on Sunday. They have a trainer and five grooms. They are all coming in big horse vans. They will bring the horses' food. They can work on Wednesday and Thursday and on Friday they must return to Immingham. It is all arranged, Thomas. Is it good?'

'Brilliant,' I said.

He laughed happily. 'Good horses. They will run wild without bridles, but they are trained. I have ridden one without a saddle, as you want. They are perfect.'

'Fantastic, Ziggy.'

'The trainer must know where we are to go from Immingham.'

'Er . . . are you meaning to travel with them?'

'Yes, Thomas. This week I work with the trainer. I learn his ways with the horses. They get to know me. I will practise with a blonde wig and a nightgown. It is arranged. The horses will not then panic. Is it good?'

I was practically speechless. Good hardly described it. 'You're a *genius*,' I said.

He said modestly, 'Yes, Thomas, I am.'

'I'll arrange where the horses are to go. Telephone again on Saturday.'

He said goodbye excitedly without giving me a number where I could call him back, but I supposed the agent might help in an emergency. I relayed Ziggy's news to O'Hara and Nash and said we would have to rearrange the following week's schedule, but that it shouldn't be much problem.

'We have the hanged-wife actress working next week,' O'Hara reminded me. 'We have to complete all her scenes in fourteen days.'

I would take her to the beach, I thought. I'd have the nightgown diaphanously blowing against the sunrise. I'd have her standing on the shore, and have Ziggy galloping for her on the horse. Insubstantial. Unreal. All in her mind.

Pray for a sunrise.

'Sonia,' I said.

'Yvonne,' O'Hara corrected. 'We have to call her Yvonne. That's her name in the book and in the script.'

I nodded. 'Howard wrote the usual hanging cliché of legs and shoes swaying unsupported, with onlookers displaying shock. But I've ideas for that.'

O'Hara was silent. Nash shuddered.

232

'Don't get us an NC-17 certificate,' Nash finally said. 'We'll have to cut that scene, if you do.'

'I'm to make it tastefully horrifying?'

They laughed.

'She did hang,' I said.

Downstairs again, one of the first people I saw was Lucy Wells, who was arguing with a man obstructing her way. I walked over and asked what was the matter.

'This man,' Lucy said heatedly, 'says he has instructions not to let anyone near you.'

O'Hara's order, the man explained. I reassured him about Lucy and bore her off, holding her arm.

'I thought you weren't coming today,' I said.

'Dad changed his mind. He and Mum are both here again. So is Uncle Ridley. Wild horses wouldn't keep him away, he said.'

'I'm glad to see you.'

'Sorry I was so uncouth.'

I smiled at her blue eyes. 'A wise child,' I said.

'I am *not* a child.'

'Stay beside me,' I said. 'I'll tell Moncrieff it's OK.'

'Who's Moncrieff?'

'The Director of Photography. Very important man.'

She looked at me dubiously when I introduced her to the untidy beard and the earthquake-victim clothes, but after allowing us one old-fashioned sideways look he took a fancy to her and let her get in his way without cursing.

She looked colourfully bright in a scarlet short coat over clean new blue jeans, and mentally bright with noticing eyes and a firm calm mouth. She watched the proceedings without senseless chatter.

233

'I told Dad about that knife,' she told me after a while.

'What did he say?'

'Funny, that's exactly what he said. He said, "What did he say?"'

'Did he?' I considered her guileless expression. 'And what did you say I said?'

Her forehead wrinkled. 'I told him the knife looked beautiful, but you hadn't said much at all. I told Dad it hadn't pleased the producer, O'Hara, and I didn't know why.'

'O'Hara doesn't like knives,' I said, dismissing it.

'Oh, I see. Dad said it might be because someone had tried to cut Nash Rourke, like he'd heard on the radio, but it was his stand-in, not Nash himself.'

'That, too,' I agreed.

'Dad said directors don't have a stand-in,' she was teasing, unaware, 'and you don't know which they are until someone points them out.'

'Or when they come to your home.'

'Goodness, yes. Did the photo of Sonia come out all right?'

'I'm sure it did, but I won't see it until I go back to Newmarket this evening.'

She said, hesitantly, 'I didn't tell Dad. He really wouldn't like it.'

'I won't mention it. The actress playing Yvonne – that's Nash's wife, in the film – starts work on set next week. I promise she won't look like the photo. She won't upset your father.'

She smiled her appreciation and thanks, exonerated

from her deception. I hoped no deadly harm would come to her, but in so many lives, it did.

First on the afternoon's schedule was the last of the wide crowd shots round the parade ring; the mounting of the jockeys onto their horses and their walk out towards the course. Even though the action would in the end be peripheral to the human story, we had to get the race-day sequences right to earn credibility. We positioned the owner-trainer groups again as before, each of them attended by their allotted jockey. Moncrieff checked the swivelling camera and gently moved Lucy out of shot.

Nash arrived in the ring trailing clouds of security and detoured to tell me a friend of mine was looking for me.

'Who?' I asked.

'Your TV pal from Doncaster.'

'Greg Compass?'

He nodded. 'Outside the weighing-room. He's been yacking with the jockeys. He'll meet you there, he said.'

'Great.'

We rehearsed the mounting scene twice and shot it three times from two camera angles until the horses grew restive, and then asked all the townspeople to go round to the course side of the stands, to watch the string cantering down to the start.

During the inevitable delay for camera-positioning I left Lucy with Moncrieff and walked over to the weighing-room to meet Greg, whom I found in a milk-of-human-kindness mood, dressed in an expensive grey suit and wide open to suggestions from me that he might like to earn an unexpected fee by briefly taking on his usual persona and interviewing the winning trainer; in other words, Nash.

'It won't be more than a few seconds on screen,' I said. 'Just enough to establish your pretty face.'

'Don't see why not.' He was amused and civilised; friendly.

'In half an hour?'

'Done.'

'Incidentally, do you yourself remember anything about the trainer whose wife was hanged, who we're making this saga about?'

'Jackson Wells?'

'Yes. He's here, himself, today. So is his present wife. So's his daughter. And his brother.'

'Before my time, old lad.'

'Not much,' I assured him. 'You must have been about sixteen when Jackson stopped training. You rode in your first race not long after that. So, did you hear anything from the older jockeys about ... well ... anything?'

He looked at me quizzically. 'I can't say I haven't thought about this since last Saturday, because of course I have. As far as I know, the book, *Unstable Times*, is sentimental balls. The jockeys who knew the real Yvonne were not dream lovers, they were a randy lot of activists.'

I smiled.

'You knew?' he asked.

'It sort of stands to reason. But they're still going to be dream lovers in the film.' I paused. 'Do you remember any names? Do you by any chance know *who*?'

'By the time I'd dried behind the ears in the changing-room, no one was saying *anything*. All scared at being sucked into a murder. Clams weren't in it.' He paused. 'If Jackson Wells himself is truly here today, I'd like to meet him.'

'His daughter says he's here.'

I refrained from asking him why he wanted to meet Jackson Wells but he told me anyway. 'Good television. Rivet the couch potatoes. Good publicity for your film.'

'Jackson Wells isn't keen on the film.'

Greg grinned. 'All the better, old lad.'

I returned to Moncrieff with Greg in tow and promptly lost Lucy's attention to the smooth commentator's allure. Lucy promised breathlessly to take him to find her father and, when they'd gone, Moncrieff and I went back to work.

We shot the scenes of the horses walking out onto the course and cantering off to the start. One of the horses bolted. One of the saddles slipped, dumping its rider. One of the rented cameras jammed. The crowd grew restive, the jockeys lost their cool and Moncrieff cursed.

We got it done in the end.

I walked with drained energy back towards the weighing-room and found O'Hara there, talking to Howard.

Howard, to my complete astonishment, had brought with him his three friends: Mrs Audrey Visborough, her daughter Alison and her son Roddy.

O'Hara gave me a wild look and said, 'Mrs Visborough wants us to stop making the film.'

I said to Howard, 'Are you mad?' which might not

have been tactful but summed up my exasperation. I'd been afraid of a stiletto through the heart, and Howard had brought clowns.

All three of them, however, wore unremarkable race going clothes, not white cone hats, bobbles and red noses. Audrey Visborough leaned on her cane and continued with her complaint.

'Your director, Thomas Lyon,' she flicked me a venomous glance, 'has obviously no intention whatever of either returning to the facts or of stopping making this travesty of a film. I demand that you order him to cease at once.'

Howard shuffled from foot to foot and ineffectually said, 'Er . . . Audrey.'

O'Hara, restraining himself amazingly, told her that he hadn't the power to stop the film himself (which I guessed he actually had) and that she should write her objections directly to the moguls of the film company: in other words, to the top.

She announced that she would do that, and demanded names and addresses. O'Hara obligingly handed her two or three business cards with helpful and soothing advice that slid over her consciousness without sticking. Audrey Visborough felt personally and implacably insulted by the film's plot, and nothing would satisfy her short of preventing its completion.

Alison stood to one side of her, nodding. Roddy looked weakly supportive but from the glances he gave his mother I would have guessed he cared a good deal less than she did about the scurrilous suggestion that she would *ever* have contemplated going to bed with the unspeakable lower-class Jackson Wells.

I said to Howard, 'Why on *earth* did you bring them here?'

'I couldn't stop them,' he said huffily. 'And I do agree with Audrey, of course, that you have made her almost *ill* with disgust.'

'You agreed to the plot changes,' I pointed out. 'And you yourself wrote the love scenes between Nash and Silva.'

'But they were supposed to be quiet, in the drawing-room, not rutting about in bed.' His voice whined with self pity. 'I wanted to *please* the Visborough family with this film.'

With a second twinge of guilt I reflected that his troubles with Audrey Visborough hadn't yet reached a peak.

I said to her daughter, Alison, 'Would you care to watch a scene being shot?'

'Me?' She was surprised and glanced at her mother before answering. 'It won't change our minds. This film is a disgrace.'

When I moved a pace away in irritation, however, she took a pace after me.

'Where are you going?' her mother demanded sharply. 'I need you here.'

Alison gave me a dark look and said, 'I'll work on Mr Lyon.'

She walked resolutely beside me, sensible in tweed suit and flat shoes, earnestly committed to just causes.

'Daddy,' she said, 'was a *good* man.'

'I'm sure.'

'Not easy going,' she went on with approbation. 'A man of principle. Some people found him boring, I know, but he was a good father to me. He believed that women are very badly treated by the English system of leaving family inheritances chiefly to sons, which is why he left his house to me.' She paused. 'Rodbury was furious. He's three years older than I am and he'd taken it for granted he would inherit everything. He had been generously treated all his life. Daddy bought all his showjumpers for him, and only insisted that Rodbury should earn his own keep by giving lessons. Perfectly reasonable, I thought, as Daddy wasn't unduly rich. He divided his money between the three of us. None of us is rich.' She paused again. 'I expect you wonder why I'm telling you this. It's because I want you to be fair to Daddy's memory.'

I couldn't be, not in the way she wanted.

I said, 'Think of this film as being about fictional people, not about your father and mother. The people in the film are not in the least like your parents. They are not *them*. They are inventions.'

'Mummy will never be persuaded.'

I took her with me into the parade ring where Moncrieff as ever was busy with lights.

'I'm going to show you two people,' I said to Alison. 'Tell me what you think.'

She looked puzzled, but her gaze followed where I pointed to a nearby couple, and she looked without emotion at Cibber, a sober fifty, and at lovely young Silva in her well-cut coat and polished narrow boots and bewitching fur hat.

'Well?' Alison demanded. 'They look nice enough. Who are they?'

'Mr and Mrs Cibber,' I said.

'*What?*' She whirled towards me, halfway to fury. Then, thinking better of a direct physical attack, turned back thoughtfully and simply stared.

'Beyond them,' I said, 'is Nash Rourke. He plays the character loosely based on Jackson Wells.'

Alison speechlessly stared at the broad-shouldered heart-throb whose benign intelligence was unmistakable from twenty feet.

'Come with me,' I said.

Dazed, she followed, and I took her to where Greg Compass and Lucy seemed finally to have found Lucy's father.

'These people,' I told Alison, 'are Greg Compass, who interviews racing people on TV.'

Alison briefly nodded in recognition.

'This family,' I said neutrally, 'are Mr and Mrs Jackson Wells and their daughter, Lucy.'

Alison's mouth opened but no words came out. Jackson Wells, good-looking and smiling, stood between his two wholesome, well-groomed women, waiting for me to complete the introduction.

'Alison Visborough,' I said.

Jackson Wells's sunny face darkened. He said, almost spitting, '*Her* daughter!'

'You see,' I said to Alison, 'Jackson Wells dislikes your mother as intensely as she dislikes *him*. No way in real life would they ever have had a love affair. The people in this film are *not them*.'

Alison remained dumb. I took her arm, wheeling her away.

'Your mother,' I said, 'is making herself ill. Persuade her to turn her back on what we are doing. Make her

241

interested in something else, and don't let her see the completed film. Believe that I mean no disrespect to her or to your father's memory. I am making a movie about fictional people. I have some sympathy with your mother's feelings, but she will not get the film abandoned.'

Alison found her voice. 'You are ruthless,' she said.

'Quite likely. However, I admire you, Miss Visborough, as Howard does. I admire your good sense and your loyalty to your father. I regret your anger but I can't remove its cause. Cibber in the film is not a nice man at all, I have to warn you. All I can say again is, don't identify him with your father.'

'Howard did!'

'Howard wrote Cibber as a good man without powerful emotions. There's no conflict or drama in that. Conflict is the essence of drama ... first lesson of film-making. Anyway, I apologise to you and your mother and brother, but until last week I hardly knew you existed.'

'Oh, Roddy!' she said without affection. 'Don't worry about *him*. He doesn't care very much. He and Daddy were pretty cold to each other. Too different, I suppose. Rodbury – and I call him by his full name because Roddy sounds like a nice little boy, but he would never let me join in his games when we were children, and other girls were so wrong when they said I was *lucky* having an older brother – ' She broke off abruptly. 'I don't know why I said that. I don't talk to people easily. Particularly not to people I disapprove of. Anyway, Rodbury wouldn't care what you said about Daddy as long as *he* didn't lose money over it.

He only pretends to Mummy that he cares, because he's always conning her into buying things for him.'

'He's not married?'

She shook her head. 'He boasts about girls. More talk than action, I sometimes think.'

I smiled at her forthright opinion and thought of her unfulfilled life: the disappointing brother, the adored but distant father, the mother who'd prevented a perhaps unsuitable match. An admirable woman overall.

'I like you, Miss Visborough,' I said.

She gave me a straight look. 'Stop the film, then.'

I thought of her feelings, and I thought of knives.

'I can't,' I said.


We completed the day's shooting schedule in time to hold the semi-planned good-public-relations final auto-graphing session outside the weighing-room. Nash, Silva and Cibber scribbled there with maximum charm.

Many Huntingdon residents were already wearing their UNSTABLE AT ALL TIMES T-shirts. Good humour abounded all around. The envisaged orderly line of autograph hunters dissolved into a friendly scrum. O'Hara signed books and racecards presented to him by people who knew a producer when they saw one, and I, too, signed my share. Howard modestly wrote in proffered copies of his book.

The happy crowd roamed around. Nash's body-guards were smiling. The lioness tried to stop him being kissed. My black-belt stood at my left hand so that I could sign with my right.

I felt a thud as if someone had cannoned into me, a

243

knock hard enough to send me stumbling forward onto one knee and from there overbalancing to the ground. I fell onto my right side and felt the first pain, sharp and alarming, and I understood with searing clarity that I had a knife blade in my body and that I had fallen onto its hilt, and driven it in further.

# CHAPTER TWELVE

O'Hara, laughing, stretched his hand down to help me up.

I took his hand in my right, and reflexly accepted his assistance, and he saw the strong wince round my eyes and stopped laughing.

'Did you hurt yourself?'

'No.' His pull had lifted me back to my knees. I said, 'Lend me your jacket.' He wore an old flying type of jacket, army-coloured, zip fronts hanging open. 'Jacket,' I repeated.

'What?' He leaned down towards me from his craggy height.

'Lend me your jacket.' I swallowed, making myself calm. 'Lend me your jacket and get my driver to bring my car right up here to the weighing-room.'

'Thomas!' He was progressively concerned, bringing his head lower to hear me better. 'What's the matter?'

Clear-headed beyond normal, I said distinctly, 'There is a knife in my side. Drape your jacket over my right shoulder, to hide it. Don't make a fuss. Don't frighten the moguls. Not a word to the press. Don't tell the police. I am not dead, and the film will go on.'

245

He listened and understood but could hardly believe it. 'Where's the knife?' he asked as if bewildered. 'You look all right.'

'It's somewhere under my arm, above my elbow. Do lend me your jacket.'

'I'll get our doctor.'

'No, O'Hara. *No*. Just the jacket.'

I put, I suppose, every scrap of the authority he'd given me into the words that were half plea, half order. In any case, without further objection, he took off his windproof jacket and draped it over my shoulder, revealing the heavy-knit army-coloured sweater he wore underneath.

Other eyes looked curiously our way. I put my left hand on O'Hara's arm, as he was facing me, and managed the endless inches to my feet. I concentrated on his eyes, at the same height as my own.

'The bastard,' I said carefully with obvious anger, 'is not going to succeed.'

'Right,' O'Hara said.

I relaxed infinitesimally, but in fact bloody-mindedness was the best anaesthetic invented, and too much sympathy would defeat me quicker than any pain from invaded ribs.

O'Hara sent one of Ed's assistants to bring my car and reassuringly told a few enquirers that I'd fallen and wrenched my shoulder but that it was nothing to worry about.

I saw a jumbled panorama of familiar faces and couldn't remember any of them having been near enough for attack. But crowd movement had been non-stop. Anyone I knew in England, or anyone they had employed – and professionals were for hire and invisible everywhere – could have stood among the autograph hunters and seized the moment. I concentrated mostly on remaining upright while rather wildly wondering what vital organs lay inwards from just above one's right elbow, and realising that though my skin might feel clammy from the shock waves of an outraged organism, I was not visibly leaking blood in any large quantities.

'Your forehead's sweating,' O'Hara observed.

'Never mind.'

'Let me get the doctor.'

'You'll get Greg Compass and television coverage, if you do.'

He was silent.

'I know a different doctor,' I promised. 'Where's the car?'

Ed returned with it pretty soon, though it seemed an age to me. I asked him to thank everyone and see to general security, and said we would complete the close-ups the next day.

He nodded merely and took over, and I edged gingerly into the rear seat of the car.

O'Hara climbed in on the other side. 'You don't need to,' I said.

'Yes, I do.'

I was glad enough of his company, and I gave him a number to call on his telephone, taking the mobile from him after he'd pressed buttons.

'Robbie?' I said, grateful not to get his message service. 'Thomas Lyon. Where are you?'

'Newmarket.'

'Um ... could you come to the hotel in an hour? Fairly urgent.'

'What sort of urgent?'

'Can't say, right now.'

O'Hara looked surprised, but I nodded towards our driver, who might be economical with words, but was far from deaf.

O'Hara looked understanding, but also worried. 'One of the moguls from LA has arrived at the hotel and will be waiting for us.'

'Oh.' I hesitated, then said, 'Robbie, can you make it Dorothea's house instead? It's for a Dorothea sort of job, though not so radical.'

'You've got someone with you, listening, that you don't want to know what you're talking about? And it's a knife wound?'

'Right,' I said, grateful for his quickness.

'Who's the patient?'

'I am.'

'Dear God ... have you got a key to Dorothea's house?'

'I'm sure her friend Betty must have one. She lives nearly opposite.'

'I know her,' he said briefly. 'One hour. Dorothea's house. How bad is it?'

'I don't know the internal geography well enough, but not too bad, I don't think.'

'Abdomen?' he asked worriedly.

'No. Higher, and to one side.'

'See you,' he said. 'Don't cough.'

I gave the phone back to O'Hara, who stifled all his questions with worry and difficulty. I sat sideways, propping myself as firmly as possible against the motion of the car, but all the same it was a long thirty-eight miles that time from Huntingdon to Newmarket.

I gave the driver directions to Dorothea's house. Robbie Gill's car was there already, Robbie himself opening the front door from inside when we pulled up, and coming down the path to meet us. O'Hara arranged with the driver to return for us in half an hour while I uncurled out of the car and steadied myself unobtrusively by holding Robbie's arm.

I said, 'We're not keen for publicity over this.'

'So I gathered. I haven't told anyone.'

He watched O'Hara get out of the car and give the driver a signal to depart, and I said briefly, 'O'Hara . . . Robbie Gill,' which seemed enough for them both.

We walked up the path slowly and into the empty but still ravaged house. Dorothea, Robbie said, had told him of my offer to start tidying up. We went into the kitchen where I sat on one of the chairs.

'Did you see the knife?' Robbie asked. 'How long was the blade?'

'It's still in me.'

He looked shocked. O'Hara said, 'This is some crazy boy.'

'O'Hara's producing the film,' I said. 'He would like me stitched up and back on set tomorrow morning.'

Robbie took O'Hara's jacket off my shoulder and knelt on the floor to take a closer look at the problem.

'This is like no knife I ever saw,' he pronounced.

'Like the one on the Heath?' I asked.

'Different.'

'Pull it out,' I said. 'It hurts.'

Instead he stood up and said something to O'Hara about anaesthetics.

'For Christ's sake,' I said impatiently, 'just ... pull ... it ... out.'

Robbie said, 'Let's take an inside look at the damage, then.'

He unzipped my dark blue windcheater and cut open my sweater with Dorothea's kitchen scissors, and came to the body protectors underneath.

'What on earth – ?'

'We had death threats,' I explained, 'so I thought ...' I closed my eyes briefly and opened them again. 'I borrowed two of the jockeys' body protectors. In case of kicks.'

'*Death threats?*'

O'Hara explained, and asked me, 'What made you think of these padded jackets?'

'Fear,' I said truthfully.

They almost laughed.

'Look,' I said reasonably, 'this knife had to go through my windproof jacket, a thick sweater, two body protectors designed to minimise impact and also one shirt in order to reach my skin. It has cut into me a bit but I'm not coughing blood and I don't feel any worse than I did an hour ago, so ... Robbie ... a bit of your well-known toughness ... please ...'

'Yes, all right,' he said.

He spread open the front of the body protectors and found my white shirt wet and scarlet. He pulled the shirt apart until he could see the blade itself, and he raised his eyes to me in what could only be called horror.

'What is it?' I said.

250

'This blade ... it's *inches* wide. It's pinning all the layers into your side.

'Go on then,' I said. 'Get it out.'

He opened the bag he'd brought with him and picked out a pre-prepared disposable syringe which he described briefly, sticking the needle into me, as a painkiller. After that he sorted out a surgical dressing in a sterile wrapping. The same as for Dorothea, I thought. He checked his watch to give the injection time to work, then tore off the wrapping and positioned the dressing ready inside my shirt and with his left hand tugged on the protruding handle of the knife.

I didn't budge and in spite of the injection it felt terrible.

'I can't get enough leverage from this angle,' Robbie said. He looked at O'Hara. 'You're strong,' he said. 'You pull it out.'

O'Hara stared at him, and then at me.

'Think of moguls,' I said.

He smiled twistedly and said to Robbie, 'Tell me when.'

'Now,' Robbie said, and O'Hara grasped the knife's handle and pulled until the blade came free.

Robbie quickly put the dressing in place and O'Hara stood as if stunned, holding in disbelief the object that had caused me such trouble.

'Sorry,' Robbie said to me.

I shook my head, dry mouthed.

O'Hara laid the knife on the kitchen table, on the discarded wrapping from the dressing, and we all spent a fairly long silence simply looking at it.

Overall it was about eight inches long, and half of

251

that was handle. The flat blade was almost three inches wide at the handle end, tapering to a sharp point. One long side of the triangular blade was a plain sharp cutting edge: the other was wickedly serrated. At its wide end the blade extended smoothly into a handle which had a space through it big enough to accommodate a whole hand. The actual grip, with undulations for fingers to give a better purchase, was given substance by bolted-on, palm-width pieces of dark, richly-polished wood: the rest was shiny metal.

'It's heavy,' O'Hara said blankly. 'It could rip you in half.'

A stud embellishing the wider end of the blade bore the one word, 'Fury'.

I picked up the awful weapon for a closer look and found it was indeed heavy (more than half a pound, we soon found, when Robbie weighed it on Dorothea's kitchen scales) and, according to letters stamped into it, had been made of stainless steel in Japan.

'What we need,' I said, putting it down, 'is a knife expert.'

'And what you need first,' Robbie said apologetically, 'is a row of staples to stop the bleeding.'

We took off all my protective layers for him to see what he was doing and he presently told me consolingly that the point of the blade had hit one of my ribs and had slid along it, not slicing down into soft tissue and through into the lung. 'The rib has been fractured by the blow but you are right, and lucky, because this injury should heal quite quickly.'

'Cheers,' I said flippantly, relieved all the same. 'Maybe tomorrow I'll get me a bullet-proof vest.'

252

Robbie mopped a good deal of dried blood from my skin, damping one of Dorothea's tea towels for the purpose, then helped me into my one relatively unharmed garment, the windproof jacket.

'You look as good as new,' he assured me, fitting together the bottom ends of the zip and closing it upwards.

'The mogul won't notice a thing,' O'Hara agreed, nodding. 'Are you fit enough to talk to him?'

I nodded. It was necessary to talk to him. Necessary to convince him that the company's money was safe in my hands. Necessary to confound all suggestion of 'jinx'.

I said, 'We do, all the same, have to find out just who is so fanatical about stopping the film that he – or she – will murder to achieve it. It's possible, I suppose, that the knife was meant only to frighten us, like yesterday's dagger, but if I hadn't been wearing the protectors...'

'No protection and an inch either way,' Robbie nodded, 'and you would likely have been history.'

'So,' I said, 'if we take it that my death was in fact intended, I absolutely *must* find out who and why. Find it out among ourselves, I mean, if we're not bringing in the police. Otherwise ...' I hesitated, then went on, '... if the reason for the attack on me still exists, which we have to assume is the case, they – he or she or they – may try again.'

I had the feeling that the thought had already occurred to both of them, but that to save my peace of mind they hadn't liked to say it aloud.

'No film is worth dying for,' O'Hara said.

'The film has stirred up mud that's been lying quiet for twenty-six years,' I said. 'That's what's happened. No point in regretting it. So now we have the choice of either pulling the plug on the film and retiring in disarray – and where is my future if I do that? – or ... er ... sifting through the mud for the facts.'

'But,' Robbie said doubtfully, 'could you really find any? I mean, when it all happened, when it was fresh, the police got nowhere.'

'The police are ordinary people,' I said. 'Not infallible supermen. If we try, and get nowhere also, then so be it.'

'But how do you start?'

'Like I said, we look for someone who knows about knives.'

It had been growing dark while we spoke. As Robbie crossed to flip the light switch, we heard the front door open and close, and footsteps coming heavily along the passage towards us.

It was Paul who appeared in the kitchen doorway: Paul annoyed, Paul suspicious, Paul's attention latching with furious astonishment onto my face. The indecisiveness of our last meeting had vanished. The bluster was back.

'And what do you think *you're* doing here?' he demanded. 'I've told you to stay away, you're not wanted.'

'I told Dorothea I would tidy up a bit.'

'I will tidy the house. I don't want you here. And as for you, Dr Gill, your services aren't needed. Clear out, all of you.'

It was O'Hara's first encounter with Paul Pannier; always a learning experience.

'And where did you get a key from?' he demanded aggrievedly. 'Or did you break in?' He looked at O'Hara directly for the first time and said, 'Who the hell are you? I want you all out of here at once.'

I said neutrally, 'It's your mother's house and I'm here with her permission.'

Paul wasn't listening. Paul's gaze had fallen on the table, and he was staring at the knife.

There was barely a smear of blood on it as it had been more or less wiped clean by its outward passage through many layers of polystyrene and cloth, so it seemed to be the knife itself, not its use, that was rendering Paul temporarily speechless.

He raised his eyes to meet my gaze, and there was no disguising his shock. His eyes looked as dark as his pudgy features were pale. His mouth had opened. He found nothing at all to say but turned on one foot and stamped away out of the kitchen down the hall and out through the front door, leaving it open behind him.

'Who was *he*?' O'Hara asked. 'And what was that all about?'

'His mother,' Robbie explained, 'was savagely cut with a knife in this house last Saturday. He may think that somehow we've found the weapon.'

'And have you?' O'Hara turned to me. 'What was it you were trying to tell me yesterday? But this isn't the knife you found on the Heath, is it?'

'No.'

He frowned. 'I don't understand any of it.'

That made two of us; but somewhere there had to be an explanation. Nothing happened without cause.

I asked Robbie Gill, who was tidying and closing his medical case, 'Do you know anyone called Bill Robinson who mends motorbikes?'

'Are you feeling all right?'

'Not a hundred per cent. Do you?'

'Bill Robinson who mends motorbikes? No.'

'You know the town. Who would know?'

'Are you serious?'

'He may have,' I explained briefly, 'what this house was torn apart for.'

'And that's all you're telling me?'

I nodded.

Robbie pulled the telephone towards him, consulted a notebook from his pocket, and pressed some numbers. He was passed on, relay by relay, to four more numbers but eventually pushed the phone away in satisfaction and told me, 'Bill Robinson works for Wrigley's garage, and lives somewhere in Exning Road. He tinkers with Harley Davidsons for a hobby.'

'Great,' I said.

'But,' O'Hara objected, 'what has any of this to do with our film?'

'Knives,' I said, 'and Valentine Clark knew Jackson Wells.'

'Good luck with the mud,' Robbie said.

The mogul proved to be a hard-nosed thin businessman in his forties with no desire even to look at the growing reels of printed film. He didn't like movies, he said. He despised film actors. He thought directors should be held in financial handcuffs. Venture capital was his field, he said, with every risk underwritten. Wrong field, I thought.

He had demanded in advance to have an accounting for every cent disbursed or committed since the first day of principal photography, with the result that O'Hara's production department had spent the whole day itemising such things as food, transport, pay for stable-lads, lipsticks and light bulbs.

We sat round the dining table in O'Hara's suite, I having made a detour to my own rooms to exchange my windproof jacket for a shirt and sweater. Robbie had stuck only a light dressing over the mended damage. I still felt a shade trembly, but apparently nothing showed. I concentrated on justifying Ziggy's fare and expenses in Norway, while sipping mineral water and longing for brandy.

'Wild horses!' the mogul exclaimed in near-outrage to O'Hara. 'You surely didn't sanction bringing horses all the way from Norway! They're not in the script.'

'They're in the hanged woman's fantasy,' O'Hara explained flatly. 'Her dream life is what the company thought best about the plot, and what you expect on the screen. Viking horses hold glamour for publicity, and will earn more than they cost.'

O'Hara's clout silenced the mogul, who scowled but seemed to realise that if he antagonised his high-grade producer beyond bearing, he would lose him and scupper the whole investment. In any event, he moderated his aggressive approach and nodded through the bonus for the winning jockey with barely a grimace.

The accounts audited, he wanted to discuss Howard.

I didn't.

O'Hara didn't.

Howard proving to be usefully out of the hotel, the subject died. I excused myself on the grounds of the regular evening meeting with Moncrieff, and the mogul said in parting that he trusted we would have no further 'incidents', and announced that he would be watching the action the next morning.

'Sure,' O'Hara agreed easily, hardly blinking. 'The schedule calls for dialogue and close-ups, and several establishing shots of people walking in and out of the weighing-room at Huntingdon racecourse. No crowd scenes, though, they're in the can. No jockeys, they've finished also. The horses will be shipped back here tomorrow afternoon. Thanks to fine weather and Thomas's good management, we'll be through with the racetrack scenes a day early.'

The mogul looked as if he'd bitten a wasp. I wondered, as I left, just what would make him happy.

The Moncrieff session swelled with the arrival of both Nash and Silva, each wanting to continue with the private rehearsals. Nash had brought his script. Silva wore no lipstick and a feminist expression. I wondered what she and O'Hara were like together in bed, a speculation that didn't advance my work any, but couldn't be helped.

We went through the scenes. Moncrieff and Nash discussed lighting. Silva thrust forward her divine jaw and to her pleasure Moncrieff assessed her facial bones in terms of planes and shadows.

258

I drank brandy and painkillers with dedication: possibly medicinally a bad combination, but a great distancer from tribulation. When everyone left I went to bed half-sitting up, and stayed awake through a lot of o'clocks, throbbing and thinking and deciding that in the near future I would stand with my back to a wall at all times.

O'Hara woke me from a troubled sleep by phoning at seven-thirty. Late.

'How are you doing?' he asked.

'Lousy.'

'It's raining.'

'Is it?' I yawned. 'That's good.'

'Moncrieff phoned the weather people. It should be dry this afternoon. So we could watch all the Huntingdon rushes this morning, when the van comes from London.'

'Yes . . . I thought the mogul couldn't be bothered.'

'He's going to London himself. He's not keen on waiting for Huntingdon this afternoon. He told me everything seems to be going all right with the movie now, and he'll report back to that effect.'

'Jeez.'

O'Hara chuckled. 'He thought you were business-like. That's his highest word of praise. He says I can go back to LA.'

'Oh.' I was surprised by the strength of my dismay. 'And are you going?'

'It's your movie,' he said.

I said, 'Stay.'

After a pause he said, 'If I go, it shows you're totally

in command.' Another pause. 'Think it over. We'll decide after the dailies. See you at eleven o'clock in the screening room. Will you be fit enough?'

'Yes.'

'I sure as hell wouldn't be,' he said, and disconnected.

By nine I'd decided against the great British breakfast and had located Wrigley's garage on a town road map: by nine-fifteen my driver had found it in reality. There was a canopy over the petrol pumps: shelter from rain.

Bill Robinson had long hair, a couple of pimples, a strong East Anglian accent, a short black leather jacket covered in gold studs and a belt of heavy tools strung round his small hips. He took in the fact that I had a chauffeur and offered opportunist respect.

'Wha' can I do for yer?' he enquired, chewing gum.

I grinned. 'Mrs Dorothea Pannier thinks you're a great guy.'

'Yeah?' He moved his head in pleasure, nodding. 'Not such a bad old duck herself.'

'Did you know she's in hospital?'

His good humour vanished. 'I heard some bastard carved her up.'

'I'm Thomas Lyon,' I said. 'She gave me your name.'

'Yeah?' He was wary. 'You're not from that son of hers? Right turd, that son of hers.'

I shook my head. 'Her brother Valentine left me his books in his will. She told me she'd trusted them to you for safekeeping.'

'Don't give them to no one, that's what she said.' His manner was determined and straightforward. I judged it would be a bad mistake to offer him money, which conferred on him saintly status in the modern scheme of things.

'How about,' I said, 'if we could get her on the phone?'

He could see nothing wrong in that, so I used the mobile to reach the hospital and then, with many clicks and delays, Dorothea herself.

She talked to Bill Robinson in his heavy leather gear and studs, and Bill Robinson's face shone with goodness and pleasure. Hope for the old world yet.

'She says,' he announced, giving me my phone back, 'that the sun shines out of your arse and the books are yours.'

'Great.'

'But they aren't here,' he said. 'They're in the garage at home.'

'When could I pick them up?'

'I could go home midday in my lunch hour.' He gazed briefly to one side at a gleaming monster of a motorbike, heavily wheel-chained to confound would-be thieves. 'I don't usually, but I could.'

I suggested buying an hour of his time at once from his boss and not waiting for lunch.

'Cor,' he said, awestruck; but his boss, a realist, accepted the suggestion, and the money, with alacrity, and Bill Robinson rode to his house in my car with undoubted enjoyment.

'How do you know Dorothea?' I asked on the way.

'My girlfriend lives next door to her,' he explained simply. 'We do errands sometimes for the old luv. Carry her shopping, and such. She gives us sweets like we were kids.'

'Er,' I said, 'how old are you, then?'

'Eighteen. What did you think of my bike?'

'I envy you.'

His smile was complacent, and none the worse for that. When we reached his home ('Ma will be out at work, the key's in this thing what looks like a stone'), he unlocked a padlock on the solid doors of a brick-built garage and revealed his true vocation, the care and construction of bikes.

'I buy wrecks and rebuild them,' he explained, as I stood inside the garage gazing at wheels, handlebars, twisted tubing, shining fragments. 'I rebuild them as good as new and then I sell them.'

'Brilliant,' I said absently. 'Do you want to be in a film?'

'Do I what?'

I explained that I was always looking for interesting backgrounds. Would he mind moving some of the parts of motorbikes out of the garage into his short driveway and getting on with some work while we filmed Nash Rourke walking down the street, thinking? 'No dialogue,' I said, 'just Nash strolling by and pausing for a second or two to watch the work in progress. The character he's playing will be walking through Newmarket, trying to make up his mind about something.' I was looking for real Newmarket backgrounds, I said.

'Nash *Rourke*! You're kidding me.'

'No. You'll meet him.'

'Mrs Pannier did say you were the one making the film they're talking about. It was in the *Drumbeat*.'

'The tyrannical bully-boy? Yes, that's me.'

262

He smiled broadly. 'Your books are in all those boxes.' He pointed to a large random row of cartons that announced their original contents as TV sets, electrical office equipment, microwave ovens and bread-making machines. 'A ton of paper, I shouldn't wonder. It took me the whole of Saturday morning to pack it all and shift it here, but Mrs Pannier, dear old duck, she made it worth my while.'

It was approbation rather than a hint, but I said I would do the same, particularly if he could tell me which box held what.

Not a snowball's chance, he said cheerfully. Why didn't I look?

The task was too much, both for the available time and my own depleted stamina. I said I'd wrenched my shoulder and couldn't lift the boxes, and asked him to stow as many as possible in the boot of the car. He looked resignedly at the rain but splashed backwards and forwards efficiently, joined after hesitation by my driver who buttoned his jacket closely and turned up his collar.

The car, including the front passenger seat, absorbed half of the boxes. I asked what he'd used to transport them on Saturday.

'My dad's little old pick-up,' he said. 'It needed three journeys. He takes it to work weekdays, so I can't borrow it till this evening.'

He agreed to load and deliver the rest of the boxes in the pick-up, and in cheerful spirits came along to the hotel and helped the porter there stack the cartons in the lobby.

'Do you mean it about me being in your film?' he asked on the way back to Wrigley's garage. 'And ... *when*?'

'Tomorrow, maybe,' I said. 'I'll send a message. I'll fix it with your boss, and the film company will pay you a fee for your help.'

'Cor,' he said.


Nash, Silva and Moncrieff all joined O'Hara and me to watch the Huntingdon rushes.

Even without much sound the crowd scenes looked like an everyday race meeting and the race itself was still remarkable for the Victoria Cross riding of the jockeys. The race had been filmed successfully by five cameras and semi-successfully by another. There was easily enough to cut together a contest to stir the pulses of people who'd never seen jump-racing at close quarters: even Silva gasped at one sequence, and Nash looked thoughtful. Moncrieff fussed about shadows in the wrong places, which no one else had noticed.

The close shots with dialogue showed Silva at her most enticing. I praised her interpretation, not her looks, and got a brief nod of acknowledgment. The two days' work, all in all, had been worth the effort.

After the end of the rushes the film developers had joined on the thirty seconds' worth Moncrieff had shot of Lucy's photo. Large and in sharp focus, the two faces appeared on the screen.

'Who are they?' O'Hara asked, perplexed.

'The girl on the left,' I said, 'is Yvonne. Or rather, she was Sonia Wells, the girl who hanged. The real one.'

'Christ,' O'Hara said.

'And who's the man?' Nash asked.

'His name is Pig, I think.' I explained about Lucy's photo. 'I promised her that Yvonne wouldn't look like Sonia.'

The girl on the screen had curly light-brown hair, not a green crewcut or other weirdness. We would give Yvonne a long straight blonde wig and hope for the best.

The screen ran clear. We switched on the lights, talked about what we'd seen and, as always, went back to work.

Later at Huntingdon a photographer, who'd been engaged by the company to chart progress for the publicity department, brought a set of eight- by ten-inch prints for O'Hara to see. He and I took them into the weighing-room and sat at a table there, minutely searching the snapshots with a magnifying glass.

We saw nothing of any help. There were photos of Nash signing in the end-of-the-day autograph session. A shot of Howard looking smug, inscribing his own book. Silva being film-star charming. Greg signing race-cards. A shot of O'Hara and myself standing together. The lens had been focused every time on the main subject's face: people around were present, but not warts and all.

'We need blow-ups of the crowd,' O'Hara said.

265

'We're not going to get nice clear views of the Fury.'

Morosely, he agreed, but ordered blow-ups anyway.

No more knives appeared, in or out of bodies. We filmed the remaining scenes and shipped out the horses. We made sure the whole place was shipshape, thanked Huntingdon racecourse management for their kindnesses, and were back in Newmarket soon after six o'clock.

The message light inexorably flashed in my sitting-room: whenever did it not?

Robbie Gill wanted me to phone him, urgently.

I got his answer service: he would be available at seven.

To fill in the time I opened the tops of a few of the cartons of Valentine's books, which now took up a good deal of the floorspace, as I'd particularly asked for them not to be put one on top of another. I'd forgotten, of course, that bending down used chest muscles also. On my knees, therefore, I began to inspect my inheritance.

There was too much of it. After the first three boxes had proved to hold part of the collection of biographies and racing histories, after I'd painstakingly taken out every volume, shaken it for insertions and replaced it, I saw the need for secretarial help; for a record keeper with a lap-top computer.

Lucy, I thought. If I had a fantasy, I would materialise her in my sitting-room, like Yvonne's dream lovers. Lucy knew how to work a computer.

Impulsively I phoned her father's house and put a proposition to his daughter.

'You told me you'd left school and are waiting to do a business course. Would you care for a two-week temporary job in Newmarket?' I explained what I needed. 'I am not trying to seduce you,' I said. 'You can bring a chaperon, you can stay anywhere you like, you can drive home every day to Oxfordshire if you prefer. I'll pay you fairly. If you don't want to do it, I'll get someone local.'

She said a shade breathlessly, 'Would I see Nash Rourke again?'

Wryly, I promised that she would. 'Every day.'

'He's ... he's ...'

'Yes,' I agreed, 'and he's married.'

'It's not *that*,' she said disgustedly. 'He's just ... nice.'

'True. What about the job?'

'I could start tomorrow.'

The boxes could wait that long, I thought.

At seven I phoned Robbie Gill's number again and reached him promptly.

'Which do you want first,' he asked, 'the good news or the appalling?'

'The good. I'm tired.'

'You don't surprise me. The good news is a list of names of knife experts. Three in London, two in Glasgow, four in Sheffield and one in Cambridge.' He read them all out and took away what little breath I could manage with a broken rib.

I said weakly, 'Say that Cambridge one again.'

He repeated it distinctly. 'Professor Meredith Derry, lecturer in mediaeval history, late of Trinity College, retired.'

*Derry*.
*Knives* . . .

'Do you want the appalling?' Robbie asked.

'I suppose I have to hear it?'

'Afraid so. Paul Pannier has been murdered.'

# CHAPTER THIRTEEN

'*Murdered?*'

''Fraid so.'

'Where? And . . . er . . . how?'

As if it were inevitable, the Scots voice informed me, 'He was killed in Dorothea's house . . . with a knife.'

I sighed; a groan. 'Does Dorothea know?'

'The police sent a policewoman to the hospital.'

'Poor, poor Dorothea.'

He said bluntly, 'She won't be bullied any more.'

'But she loved him,' I protested. 'She loved the baby he'd been. She loved her little son. She will be devastated.'

'Go and see her,' Robbie said. 'You seem to understand her. I never could see why she put up with him.'

She needed a hug, I thought. She needed someone to hold her while she wept. I said, 'What about Paul's wife, Janet?'

'The police have told her. She's on her way here now, I think.'

I looked at my watch. Five past seven. I was sore and hungry and had tomorrow's shots to discuss with Nash and Moncrieff. Still . . .

'Robbie,' I said, 'does Professor Derry have an address?'

'There's a phone number.' He read it out. 'What about Dorothea?'

'I'll go to see her now. I could be at the hospital in about forty minutes. Can you fix it that they'll let me see her?'

He could and would. Who had discovered Paul's murder, I asked.

'I did, damn it. At about three o'clock this afternoon I went to pick up a notebook that I left in Dorothea's kitchen last night. I called to get the key again from her friend Betty, but she said she didn't have the key any more, she'd given it to Paul this morning early. I went across to Dorothea's house and rang the bell – that ruddy quiet ding-dong – and no one came, so I went round the back and tried the kitchen door, and it was open.' He paused. 'Paul was lying in the hall on almost the exact spot where Betty found Dorothea. There wasn't any blood, though. He'd died at once and he'd been dead for hours. He was killed with what looked like one of Dorothea's big kitchen knives. It was still in him, driven deep into his chest from behind at a point not far above his right elbow . . .'

'*Robbie*,' I said, stunned.

'Yes. Almost the same place as you. The handle was sticking out. An ordinary chef's knife handle, nothing fancy. No Fury. So I phoned the police and they kept me hanging about in that house all afternoon, but I couldn't tell them why Paul had gone there. How could I know? I couldn't tell them anything except that it looked to me as if the knife had reached his heart and stopped it.'

I cleared my throat. 'You didn't tell them about . . . me?'

'No. You didn't want me to, did you?'

'I did not.'

'But things are different now,' he said dubiously.

'Not if the police find Paul's killer quickly.'

'I've got the impression that they don't know where to look. They'll be setting up an incident room, though. There will be all sorts of questions. You'd better be ready for them, because you were there in that house after Dorothea was attacked, and they have your fingerprints.'

'So they have.' I thought a bit and asked, 'Is it against the law not to report having a knife stuck into you?'

'I don't really know,' Robbie said, 'but I know it's mostly against the law to carry a knife like the Fury in a public place, which is what O'Hara did when the two of you took it away with you last night. He could be liable for a fine and six months in jail.'

'You're kidding?'

'No. There are fierce laws now about carrying offensive weapons, and you can't get anything much more offensive than a Fury.'

'Forget you ever saw it.'

'So easy.'

We had cleaned the kitchen the evening before by bundling the body protectors, my shirt, my sweater and Robbie's medical debris into a trash bag, knotting the top; and we'd taken it with us, casually adding it to the

271

heap of similar bags to one side of Bedford Lodge, from where mountains of rubbish and empty bottles were cleared daily.

Robbie in farewell said again he would tell the nurses it was OK to let me in to see Dorothea, and asked me to phone him back later.

Promising I would, I said goodbye to him and dialled the number of Professor Meredith Derry who, to my relief, could be brought to the phone and who would acquiesce to a half-hour's worth of knife-expertise, especially if I were paying a consultancy fee.

'Of course,' I said heartily. 'Double, if it can be this evening.'

'Come when you like,' the professor said, and gave me an address and directions.


Dorothea's grief was as deep and pulverising as I'd feared. The tears flowed the minute she saw me, weak endless silent tears, not howls and sobs of pain, but an intense mourning as much for times past as for present loss.

I put my arm round her for a while and then simply held her hand, and sat there in that fashion until she fumbled for a tissue lying on the bed and weakly blew her nose.

'Thomas.'

'Yes, I know. I'm so sorry.'

'He wanted what was best for me. He was a good son.'

'Yes,' I said.

'I didn't appreciate him enough . . .'

272

'Don't feel guilty,' I said.

'But I do. I can't help it. I should have let him take me with him as soon as Valentine died.'

'No,' I said. 'Stop it, dearest Dorothea. You are not to blame for anything. You mustn't blame yourself.'

'But *why*? Why would anyone want to kill my Paul?'

'The police will find out.'

'I can't *bear* it.' The tears came again, preventing speech.

I went out of her room to ask the nurses to give Dorothea a sedative. She had already been given one. No more without a doctor's say-so, they said.

'Then get a doctor,' I told them irritably. 'Her son's been murdered. She's feeling guilty.'

'Guilty? Why?'

It was too difficult to explain. 'She will be seriously ill by morning if you don't do something.'

I went back to Dorothea thinking I'd wasted my breath, but ten minutes later one of the nurses came in brightly and gave her an injection, which almost immediately sent her to sleep.

'That satisfy you?' the nurse asked me with a hint of sarcasm.

'Couldn't be better.'

I left the hospital and helped my driver find the way to Professor Derry. The driver was on time-and-a-half for evening work and said he was in no hurry at all to take me home.

Professor Derry's retirement was no gold-plated affair. He lived on the ground floor of a tall house divided horizontally into flats, himself occupying, it transpired, a study, a bedroom, a bathroom and a screened-off kitchen alcove, all small and heavy looking in brown wood, all the fading domain of an ancient academic living frugally.

He was white haired, physically stooped and frail, but with eyes and mind in sharp array. He waved me into his study, sat me down on a wooden chair with arms and asked how he could help.

'I came for information about knives.'

'Yes, yes,' he interrupted. 'You said that on the phone.'

I looked around but could see no phone in his room. There had, however, been one – a pay phone – out in the hallway, shared with the upstairs tenants.

I said, 'If I show you a drawing of a knife, could you tell me about it?'

'I can try.'

I took the drawing of the Heath knife out of my jacket pocket and handed it to him folded. He opened it, flattened it out and laid it aside on his desk.

'I have to tell you,' he said with many small, rapid lip movements, 'that I have recently already been consulted about a knife like this.'

'You are an acknowledged expert, sir.'

'Yes.' He studied my face. 'Why do you not ask who consulted me? Have you no curiosity? I don't like students who have no curiosity.'

'I imagine it was the police.'

The old voice cackled in a wheezy sort of laugh. 'I see I have to reassess.'

'No, sir. It was I who found the knife on Newmarket Heath. The police took it into custody. I didn't know

274

they had consulted you. It was curiosity, strong and undiluted, that brought me here.'

'What did you read?'

'I never went to university.'

'Pity.'

'Thank you, sir.'

'I was going to have some coffee. Do you want some coffee?'

'Yes. Thank you, I'd like some.'

He nodded busily, pulled aside the screen, and in his kitchen alcove heated water, spooned instant powder into cups and asked about milk and sugar. I stood and helped him, the small domesticity a signal of his willingness to impart.

'I didn't care for the two young policemen who came here,' he said unexpectedly. 'They called me Granddad. Patronising.'

'Stupid of them.'

'Yes. The shell grows old, but not the inhabiting intellect. People see the shell and call me Granddad. And *Dearie*. What do you think of *Dearie*?'

'I'd kill 'em.'

'Quite right.' He cackled again. We carried the cups across to the chairs. 'The knife the police brought here,' he said, 'is a modern replica of a trench knife issued to American soldiers in France in the First World War.'

'Wow,' I said.

'Don't use that ridiculous word.'

'No, sir.'

'The policemen asked why I thought it was a replica and not the real thing. I told them to open their eyes. They didn't like it.'

'Well . . . er . . . how did you know?'

He cackled. 'It had "Made in Taiwan" stamped into the metal. Go on, say it.'

I said, 'Taiwan wasn't called Taiwan in World War One.'

'Correct. It was Formosa. And at that point in its history, it was not an industrial island.' He sat and tasted his coffee, which, like mine, was weak. 'The police wanted to know who owned the knife. How could I possibly know? I said it wasn't legal in England to carry such a knife in a public place, and I asked where they had found it.'

'What did they say?'

'They didn't. They said it didn't concern me. Granddad.'

I told him in detail how the police had acquired their trophy and he said, mocking me, 'Wow.'

I was becoming accustomed to him and to his crowded room, aware now of the walls of bookshelves, so like Valentine's, and of his cluttered old antique walnut desk, of the single brass lamp with green metal shade throwing inadequate light, of rusty-green velvet curtains hanging from great brown rings on a pole, of an incongruously modern television set beside a worn old typewriter, of dried faded hydrangeas in a cloisonné vase and a brass Roman-numeralled clock ticking away the remains of a life.

The room, neat and orderly, smelled of old books, of old leather, of old coffee, of old pipe smoke, of old man. There was no heating, despite the chilly evening. An old three-barred electric fire stood black and cold. The professor wore a sweater, a scarf, a shabby tweed jacket with elbow patches, and indoor slippers of brown checked wool. Bifocals gave him sight, and he had meticulously shaved: he might be old and short of cash, but standards had nowhere slipped.

On the desk, in a silver frame, there was an indistinct old photograph of a younger himself standing beside a woman, both of them smiling.

'My wife,' he explained, seeing where I was looking. 'She died.'

'I'm sorry.'

'It happens,' he said. 'It was long ago.'

I drank my unexciting coffee, and he delicately brought up the subject of his fee.

'I haven't forgotten,' I said, 'but there's another knife I'd like to ask you about.'

'What knife?'

'Two knives, actually.' I paused. 'One has a handle of polished striped wood that I think may be rosewood. It has a black hilt and a black double-edged blade an inch wide and almost six inches long.'

'A *black* blade?'

I confirmed it. 'It's a strong, purposeful and good-looking weapon. Would you know it from that description?'

He put his empty cup carefully on his desk and took mine also.

He said, 'The best-known black-bladed knife is the British commando knife. Useful for killing sentries on dark nights.'

I nearly said 'Wow' again, not so much at the content of what he said, but at his acceptance that the purpose of such knives was death.

277

'They usually come in olive-khaki webbing sheaths,' he said, 'with a slot for a belt and cords for tying the bottom of the sheath round the leg.'

'The one I saw had no sheath,' I said.

'Pity. Was it authentic, or a replica?'

'I don't know.'

'Where did you see it?'

'It was given to me, in a box. I don't know who gave it, but I know where it is. I'll look for "Made in Taiwan".'

'There were thousands made in World War Two, but they are collectors' items now. And, of course, in Britain one can no longer sell, advertise or even give such knives since the Criminal Justice Act of 1988. A collection can be confiscated. No one who owns a collection will have it on display these days.'

'Really?'

He smiled dimly at my surprise. 'Where have you been, young man?'

'I live in California.'

'Ah. That explains it. Knives of all sorts are legal in the United States. Over there, they have clubs for aficionados, and monthly magazines, and shops and shows, and also one can buy almost any knife by mail order.' He paused. 'I would guess that the trench knife the police showed me came here illegally from America.'

I waited a few seconds, thinking things over, and then said, 'I'd like to draw another knife for you, if you have a piece of paper.'

He provided a notepad and I drew the Fury, giving it its name.

Derry looked at the drawing in ominous stillness, finally saying, 'Where did you see this?'

'In England.'

'Who owns it?'

'I don't know,' I said. 'I hoped you might.'

'No, I don't. As I said, anyone who owns such a thing in Britain keeps it invisible and secret.'

I sighed. I'd hoped much from Professor Derry.

'The knife you've drawn,' he said, 'is called the Armadillo. Fury is the manufacturer's mark. It's made of stainless steel in Japan. It is expensive, heavy and infinitely sharp and dangerous.'

'Mm.'

After a silence, I said, 'Professor, what sort of person likes to own such knives, even in secret? Or, perhaps, particularly in secret?'

'Almost anyone,' he said. 'It's easy to buy this knife in the United States. There are hundreds of thousands of knife buffs in the world. People collect guns, they collect knives, they like the feeling of power . . .' His voice faded on the edge of personal revelation and he looked down at the drawing as if unwilling for me to see his eyes.

'Do you,' I asked carefully, without inflection, 'own a collection? A collection left over, perhaps, from when it was legal?'

'You can't ask that,' he said.

A silence.

'The Armadillo,' he said, 'comes in a heavy black leather protective sheath with a button closure. The sheath is intended to be worn on a belt.'

'The one I saw had no sheath.'

'It isn't safe, let alone legal, to carry it without a sheath.'

'I don't think safety was of prime importance.'

'You talk in riddles, young man.'

'So do you, Professor. The subject is one of innuendo and mistrust.'

'I don't know that you wouldn't go to the police.'

'And I,' I said, 'don't know that you wouldn't.'

Another silence.

'I'll tell you something, young man,' Derry said. 'If you are in any danger from the person who owns these knives, be very careful.' He considered his words. 'Normally knives such as these would be locked away. I find it disturbing that one was *used* on Newmarket Heath.'

'Could the police trace its owner?'

'Extremely unlikely,' he said. 'They didn't know where to begin, and I couldn't help them.'

'And the Armadillo's owner?'

He shook his head. 'Thousands will have been made. The Fury Armadillo does, I believe, have a serial number. It would identify when a particular knife was made and one might even trace it to its first owner. But from there it could be sold, stolen or given several times. I cannot envisage these knives you've seen being allowed into the light of day if they were traceable.'

Depressing, I thought.

I said, 'Professor, please show me your collection.'

'Certainly not.'

A pause.

I said, 'I'll tell you where I saw the Armadillo.'

'Go on, then.'

His old face was firm, his eyes unblinking. He promised nothing, but I needed more.

'A man I knew was murdered today,' I said. 'He was killed in a house in Newmarket with an ordinary kitchen knife. It is his mother's house. Last Saturday, in the same house, his mother was badly slashed by a knife, but no weapons were found. She lived, and she's recovering in hospital. On the Heath, as I told you, we believe the star of our picture was an intended victim. The police are investigating all three of these things.'

He stared.

I went on. 'At first sight there seems to be no connection between today's murder and the attack on the Heath. I'm not sure, but I think that there may be.'

He frowned. 'Why do you think so?'

'A feeling. Too many knives all at once. And . . . well . . . do you remember Valentine Clark? He died of cancer a week ago today.'

Derry's stare grew ever more intense. When he didn't answer I said, 'It was Valentine's sister, Dorothea Pannier, who was slashed last Saturday, in the house she shared with Valentine. The house was ransacked. Today her son Paul, Valentine's nephew, went to the house and was killed there. There is indeed someone very dangerous roaming around and if the police find him – or her – quickly . . . great.'

Unguessable thoughts occupied the professor's mind for whole long minutes. Finally he said, 'I became interested in knives when I was a boy. Someone gave me a Swiss Army knife with many blades. I treasured it.' He smiled briefly with small mouth movements. 'I was a lonely child. The knife made me feel more able

281

to deal with the world. But there you are, that's how I think many people are drawn towards collecting, especially collecting weapons that one could use if one were . . . bolder, perhaps, or criminal. They are a crutch, a secret power.'

'I see,' I said, as he paused.

'Knives fascinated me,' Derry went on. 'They were my companions. I carried them everywhere. I had them strapped to my leg, or to my arm under my sleeve. I wore them on my belt. I felt warm with them, and more confident. Of course, it was adolescence . . . but as I grew older, I collected more, not less. I rationalised my feelings. I was a student, making a serious study, or so I thought. It went on for very many years, this sort of self-confidence. I became an acknowledged expert. I am, as you know, *consulted*.'

'Yes.'

'Slowly, some years ago, my need for knives vanished. You may say that at about sixty-five I finally grew up. Even so, I've kept my knowledge of knives current, because consultancy fees, though infrequent, are welcome.'

'Mm.'

'I do still own a collection, as you realise, but I seldom look at it. I have left it to a museum in my will. If those young policemen had known of its existence, they had the power to take it away.'

'I can't believe it!'

With the long-suffering smile of a tutor for a dim student, he pulled open a drawer in his desk, fumbled around a little and produced a photo-copied sheet of paper, finely printed, which he handed to me.

I read the heading. PREVENTION OF CRIME ACT 1953. OFFENSIVE WEAPONS.

'Take it and read it later,' he said. 'I give this to everyone who asks about knives. And now, young man, tell me where you saw the Armadillo.'

I paid my dues. I said, 'Someone stuck it into me. I saw it after it was pulled out.'

His mouth opened. I had really surprised him. He recovered a little and said, 'Was this a *game*?'

'I think I was supposed to die. The knife hit a rib, and here I am.'

'Great God.' He thought. 'Then the police have the Armadillo also?'

'No,' I said. 'I've good reasons for not going to the police. So I'm trusting you, Professor.'

'Tell me the reasons.'

I explained about the moguls and their horror of jinxes. I said I wanted to complete the film, which I couldn't do with police intervention.

'You are as obsessed as anybody,' Derry judged.

'Very likely.'

He wanted to know where and how I had – er, *acquired* – my first-hand knowledge of the knife in question, and I told him. I told him about the body protectors, and all about Robbie Gill's ministrations; all except the doctor's name.

When I stopped, I waited another long minute for his reaction. The old eyes watched me steadily.

He stood up. 'Come with me,' he said, and led the way through a brown door to an inner room, which proved to be his bedroom, a monastic-looking cell with a polished wood floor and a high old-fashioned iron bed with a white counterpane. There was a brown wooden wardrobe, a heavy chest of drawers and a single upright chair against plain white walls. The right ambience, I thought, for a mediaevalist.

He creaked down onto his knees by the bed as if about to say his prayers, but instead reached under the bedspread at floor level, and tugged.

A large wooden box on casters slowly rolled out, its dusty lid padlocked to the base. Roughly four feet long by three wide, it was at least a foot deep, and it looked formidably heavy.

The professor fumbled for a key ring which bore four keys only, and removed the padlock, opening the lid until it leaned back against the bed. Inside there was an expanse of green baize, and below that, when he removed it, row upon row of thin brown cardboard boxes, each bearing a neat white label with typewritten words identifying the contents. He looked them over, muttering that he hadn't inspected them for months, and picked out one of them, very much not at random.

'This,' he said, opening the narrow brown box, 'is a genuine commando knife, not a replica.'

The professor's commando knife was kept safe in bubble packing but, unwrapped, looked identical to the one sent to me as a warning, except that this one did have its sheath.

'I no longer,' he said unnecessarily, 'keep my knives on display. I packed them all away when my wife died, before I came here. She shared my interest, you see. She *grew* to be interested. I miss her.'

'I'm sure you do.'

He closed the commando knife away and opened other treasures.

'These two knives from Persia, they have a curved blade, and handles and sheaths of engraved silver with lapis lazuli inserts. These are from Japan ... these from America, with carved bone handles in the shape of animal heads. All hand-made, of course. All magnificent specimens.'

All lethal, I thought.

'This beautiful knife is Russian, nineteenth century,' he said at one point. 'Closed, like this, it resembles, as you see, a Fabergé egg, but in fact five separate blades open from it.' He pulled out the blades until they resembled a rosette of sharp leaves spreading out from the base of the egg-shaped grip, itself enamelled in blue and banded in fine gold.

'Er ...' I said, 'your collection must be valuable. Why don't you sell it?'

'Young man, read the paper I gave you. It can be *illegal* to sell these things. One may now only give them to museums, not even to other individuals, and then only to museums that don't make a profit from exhibiting them.'

'It's amazing!'

'It stops law-abiding people in their tracks, but criminals take no notice. The world is as mediaeval as ever. Didn't you know?'

'I suspected it.'

His laugh cackled. 'Help me lift the top tray onto the bed. I'll show you some curiosities.'

The top tray had a rope handle at each end. He

grasped one end, I the other and, at his say-so, we lifted together. The tray was heavy. Not good, from my point of view.

'What's the matter?' he demanded. 'Did that hurt you?'

'Just the Armadillo,' I apologised.

'Do you want to sit down?'

'No, I want to see your knives.'

He knelt on the floor again and opened more boxes, removing the bubble wrapping and putting each trophy into my hand for me to 'feel the balance'.

His 'curiosities' tended to be ever more fearsome. There were several knives along the lines of the American trench knife (the genuine thing, 1918) and a whole terrifying group of second cousins to the Armadillo, knives with whole-hand grips, semi-circular blades and rows of spikes, all dedicated to tearing an opponent to shreds.

As I gave each piece back to him he re-wrapped it and restored it to its box, tidying methodically as he went along.

He showed me a large crucifix fashioned in dark red cloisonné, handsome on a gold chain for use as a chest ornament, but hiding a dagger in its heart. He showed me an ordinary-looking belt that one could use to hold up one's trousers: ordinary except that the buckle, which slid easily out into my hand, proved to be the handle of a sharp triangular blade that could be pushed home to kill.

Professor Derry delivered a grave warning. 'Thomas . . .' (we had progressed from 'young man') 'Thomas, if a man – or woman – is truly obsessed with knives, you must expect that *anything* he or she carries on their person may be the sheath of a knife. One can get key rings, money clips, hair combs, all with hidden blades. Knives can be hidden even under the lapels of a coat, in special transparent sheaths designed to be stitched onto cloth. A dangerous fanatic will *feed* on this hidden power. Do you at all understand?'

'I'm beginning to.'

He nodded several times and asked if I would be able to help him replace the top tray.

'Before we do that, Professor, would you show me one more knife?'

'Well, yes, of course.' He looked vaguely at the seas of boxes. 'What sort of thing do you want?'

'Can I see the knife that Valentine Clark once gave you?'

After another of his tell-tale pauses, he said, 'I don't know what you're talking about.'

'You did know Valentine, didn't you?' I asked.

He levered himself to his feet and headed back into his study, switching off the bedroom light as he went: to save electricity, I supposed.

I followed him, and we resumed our former positions in his wooden armchairs. He asked for my connection with Valentine, and I told him about my childhood, and about Valentine recently leaving me his books. 'I read to him while he couldn't see. I was with him not long before he died.'

Reassured by my account, Derry felt able to talk. 'I knew Valentine quite well at one time. We met at one of those ridiculous fund-raising events, all for a good cause, where people stood around with tea or small glasses of bad wine, being civil and wishing they could go home. I hated those affairs. My dear wife had a soft heart and was always coaxing me to take her, and I couldn't deny her . . . So long ago. So long ago.'

I waited through his wave of regret and loneliness, unable to comfort the nostalgia.

'Thirty years ago, it must be,' he said, 'since we met Valentine. They were raising funds to stop the shipment of live horses to the Continent to be killed for meat. Valentine was one of the speakers. He and I just liked each other . . . and we came from such different backgrounds. I began reading his column in the newspapers, though I wasn't much interested in racing. But Valentine was so *wise* . . . and still an active blacksmith . . . a gust of fresh air, you see, when I was more used to the claustrophobia of university life. My dear wife liked him, and we met him and his wife several times, but it was Valentine and I who *talked*. He came from one sort of world and I from another, and it was perhaps because of that that we could discuss things with each other that we couldn't have mentioned to our colleagues.'

I asked without pressure, 'What sort of things?'

'Oh . . . medical, sometimes. Growing old. I would never have told you this once, but since I passed eighty I've lost almost all my inhibitions, I don't *care* so much about things. I told Valentine I was having impotency problems, and I was not yet sixty. Are you laughing?'

'No, sir,' I said truthfully.

'It was easy to ask Valentine for advice. One *trusted* him.'

'Yes.'

'We were the same age. I asked him if he had the

same problem but he told me his problem was the opposite, he was aroused by young women and had difficulty in controlling his urges.'

'*Valentine?*' I exclaimed, astonished.

'People hide things,' Derry said simply. 'My dear wife didn't really mind that I could no longer easily make love to her, but she used to joke to other people about how *sexy* I was. Such a dreadful word! She wanted people to admire me, she said.' He shook his head in love and sorrow. 'Valentine told me a doctor to go to. He himself knew of all sorts of ways to deal with impotence. He told me he'd learned a lot of them from stud farms! He said I must be more light-hearted and not think of impotence as an embarrassment or a tragedy. He told me it wasn't the end of the world.' He paused. 'Because of Valentine, I learned to be content.'

'He was great to so many people,' I said.

The professor nodded, still reminiscing. 'He told me something I've never been able to verify. He swore it was true. I've always *wondered* ... If I ask you something, Thomas, will you answer me truthfully?'

'Of course.'

'You may be too young.'

'Try me.'

'In confidence.'

'Yes.'

Nothing, I'd told Moncrieff, was ever off the record. But confessions were, surely?

The professor said, 'Valentine told me that restricting the flow of oxygen to the brain could result in an erection.'

289

He waited for my comment, which took a while to materialise. I hesitantly said, 'Er . . . I've heard of it.'

'Tell me, then.'

'I believe it's a perversion that comes under the general heading of auto-erotic mania. In this case, self-inflicted partial asphyxia.'

He said impatiently, 'Valentine told me that thirty years ago. What I'm asking you is, does it work?'

'First hand, I don't know.'

He said with a touch of bitterness, 'Because you've never needed to find out?'

'Well, not yet, no.'

'Then . . . has anyone told you?'

'Not first hand.'

He sighed. 'I could never face doing it. It's one of those things I'm never going to know.'

'There are others?'

'Don't be stupid, Thomas. I am a mediaevalist. I know the facts that were written down. I try to feel my way into that lost world. I cannot smell it, hear it, live it. I can't know its secret fears and its assumptions. I've spent a lifetime learning and teaching at second hand. If I went to sleep now and awoke in the year fourteen hundred, I wouldn't understand the language or know how to cook a meal. You've heard the old saying that if Jesus returned to do a replay of the Sermon on the Mount, no one now living would understand him, as he would be speaking ancient Hebrew with a Nazareth carpenter's accent? Well, I've wasted a lifetime on an unintelligible past.'

'No, Professor,' I protested.

'Yes,' he said resignedly. 'I don't think I any longer

care. And I no longer have anyone to talk to. I can't talk to boring social workers who think I need looking after, and who call me "dearie". But I find I'm talking to *you*, Thomas, and I'm an old fool who should know better.'

'Please go on talking,' I said. 'Go on about Valentine.'

'These last years, I haven't seen him much. His wife died. So did mine. You might think it would have drawn us together, but it didn't. I suppose it was our wives who had arranged our meetings. Valentine and I just drifted apart.'

'But,' I said, 'years ago ... he knew you were interested in knives?'

'Oh yes, of course. He was enthusiastic about my collection. He and his wife used to come over to our house and the women would chat together and I would show Valentine the knives.'

'He told me he gave you one.'

'He *told you* ...?'

'Yes.'

The professor frowned. 'I remember him saying I wasn't ever to say who had given me that knife. He said just to keep it in case he asked for it back ... but he never asked. I haven't thought about it. I'd forgotten it.' He paused. '*Why* do you want to see it?'

'Just curiosity ... and fondness for my old friend.'

The professor thought it over, and said, 'I suppose if he told you, he wouldn't mind.'

He got to his feet and returned to the bedroom, with me on his heels. The light went on dimly; an economical bulb.

'I'm afraid,' my host said doubtfully, 'that there are three levels of knives in this chest, and we have to lift out the second tray to reach the knife you want to see. Are you able to lift it out onto the floor? It doesn't have to go up onto the bed.'

I assured him I could, and did it left-handed, a shade better. The third layer, revealed, proved not to be of brown cardboard boxes but of longer parcels, each wrapped only in bubble plastic, and labelled.

'These are mostly swords,' Derry said. 'And sword-sticks, and a couple of umbrellas with swords in the handles. They were a defence against footpads a hundred or two hundred years ago. Now, of course, they are illegal. One has nowadays to allow oneself to be mugged.' He cackled gently. 'You mustn't hurt the poor robber, you know.'

He surveyed the labels, running his fingers along the rows.

'Here we are. "Present from V.C."' He lifted out a bubble-wrapped package, snapped open a sellotaped fastening and unrolled the parcel to reveal the contents.

'There you are,' Professor Derry said, 'that's Valentine's knife.'

I looked at it. It was like no knife I'd ever seen. It was at least fifteen inches long, possibly eighteen. Its blade, double-edged and clearly sharp, took up barely a third of the overall length and was of an elongated flat oval like a spear, with a sharp spear's point. The long handle was narrow and was twisted throughout its length in a close spiral. The end of the spiral had been flattened into a circular embellishment, perforated with several holes.

'It's not a knife,' I said. 'It's a spear.'

Derry smiled. 'It's not meant for throwing.'

'What was it for?'

'I don't know. Valentine simply asked me if I'd like to put it in my collection. It's hammered steel. Unique.'

'But where would he buy such a thing?'

'Buy it?' The full cackle rang out. 'Have you forgotten Valentine's trade? He was a smith. He didn't buy it. He *made* it.'

# CHAPTER FOURTEEN

Early Friday morning I worked in peace from four o'clock to six-thirty in the projection room, cutting scenes into rough order, a process that apart from anything else always told me what necessary establishing shots hadn't been provided for in the screenplay. A five-second shot here and there could replace, also, patches of dialogue that hadn't gone well. I made notes, fiddled about, hummed with contentment, clarified the vision.

By six-thirty Moncrieff was setting up the cameras in the stable yard, by seven the horses (back from Huntingdon) were out at exercise on the Heath, by seven-thirty the wardrobe and make-up departments were at work in the house, and at eight-thirty O'Hara's car swept into the yard with the horn blowing.

The lads, back from the Heath to groom and feed their charges, came out of the open-doored boxes at the summons. Wardrobe and make-up appeared. The camera crews paused to listen. Actors and extras stood around.

Satisfied, O'Hara borrowed Ed's megaphone and announced that the Hollywood company was pleased with the way things were going, and that as he himself was now leaving for Los Angeles, Thomas Lyon would be in sole charge of the production.

He handed the megaphone back to Ed, waved everyone away to resume work, and gave me a challenging stare.

'Well?' he said.

'I'd rather you stayed.'

'It's your film,' he insisted. 'But you will please not go anywhere without your driver and your bodyguard.' He looked around. 'Where are they, anyway?'

'I'm safe here,' I said.

'You are not to think you're safe *anywhere*, Thomas.' He handed me a key, explaining it was his hotel key. 'Use my rooms if you need them. The two knives are in the safe in there. The combination is four five, four five. Got it?'

'Yes . . . but how will I reach you?'

'Phone my secretary in LA. She'll know.'

'Don't go.'

He smiled. 'My airplane leaves at noon. See you, guy.'

He climbed into his car with finality and was driven away, and I felt like a junior general left in charge of a major battlefield, apprehensive, half confident, emotionally naked.

The schedule that morning was for some of the earliest scenes of the film, the arrival of the police to investigate the hanging. Moncrieff set about lighting the actors – some in and some out of police uniform – explaining exactly where he wanted them to stop and turn towards the camera. He and they would be working from the plans and diagrams we'd drawn the evening before on my return from Cambridge.

Leaving Ed to supervise, I drove back to Bedford Lodge for a quiet breakfast in my rooms and found my driver and black-belt distractedly pacing the lobby and fearing the sack.

'Calm down,' I said. 'Your day starts in an hour.'

'Mr O'Hara said . . .'

'One hour,' I reiterated, and went upstairs thinking that as they hadn't saved me from the Armadillo I might do equally well on my own.

Room service brought my breakfast and a visitor, Robbie Gill.

'I should be listening to chests and prescribing cough mixture,' he said. 'My receptionist is dealing with a seething line of disgruntled patients. Take your clothes off.'

'Do what?'

'Sweater and shirt off,' he repeated. 'Undo your trousers. I've come to save your unworthy life.'

Busily he unpacked things from his case, moving my croissant and coffee aside and eating my ham with his fingers.

'Hope you're not hungry,' he said, munching.

'Starving.'

'Too bad. Get undressed.'

'Er . . . what for?'

'Number one, fresh dressing. Number two, knifeproof vest. I tried to get a proper bullet-and-knife-proof vest but neither the police nor the army would let me have one without bureaucracy, so we'll have to trust to home made.'

296

I took off my sweater and shirt and he removed the dressing, raising his eyebrows at the revealed scenery but appearing not displeased.

'You're healing. Is it sore?'

'The broken rib is.'

'Only to be expected,' he added, and stuck on a new dressing. 'Now,' he said, 'what do you know about Delta-cast?'

'Nothing.'

'It's used instead of the old plaster of Paris for fractured arms and legs. It's rigid. It's a polymer, actually, and porous, so you won't itch. A knife won't go through it.'

'A bullet?'

'That's another matter.'

He worked for half an hour, during which time we discussed Dorothea and Paul, and came to no useful conclusions, though I explained how, via Bill Robinson, I was now surrounded by the army of boxes containing Valentine's books.

At the end of Robbie's work I was encased from chin to waist in a hard sleeveless jacket that I could take off and put on in two halves and fasten with strips of Velcro.

When I protested at its height round my neck he said merely, 'Do you want your throat cut? Wear a polonecked sweater. I brought you this thin white one, in case you hadn't got one.' He handed it over as if it were nothing.

'Thanks, Robbie,' I said, and he could hear I meant it.

He nodded briefly. 'I'd better get back to my mob of

297

coughers, or they'll lynch me.' He packed things away. 'Do you think your hanged lady was lynched?'

'No, I don't think so.'

'Did you trawl any useful mud with Professor Derry?'

'The knife that bust my rib is called an Armadillo. The one with the finger holes, from the Heath, is a replica from World War One. The police had already asked the professor about it.'

'Wow.'

'The professor's about eighty-five. He told me not to say wow.'

'He sounds a riot.'

'We got on fine, but he doesn't know who owns the Armadillo.'

'Take care,' he said, leaving. 'I'm around if you need me.'

I ate what was left of my breakfast, dressed slowly, shaved and gradually got used to living like a turtle inside a carapace.

At about the time I was ready to leave again the people at the reception desk phoned up to tell me that a young woman was asking for me. She thought I was expecting her. A Miss Lucy Wells.

'Oh, yes.' I'd temporarily forgotten her. 'Please send her up.'

Lucy had come in jeans, sweater, trainers and ponytail, chiefly with the cool eighteen-year-old young lady in charge but with occasional tongue-tied lapses. She looked blankly at the multitude of boxes and wanted to know where to begin.

I gave her a lap-top computer, a notebook, a biro and a big black marker pen.

'Give each box a big number,' I said, writing '1' with the marker pen on a microwave oven carton. 'Empty it out. Write a list of the contents on the pad, enter the list on the little computer and then put everything back, topping each box with the list of contents. On another page, write me a general list, saying, for example, "Box I, books, biographies of owners and trainers." OK?'

'Yes.'

'Shake out each book in case it has loose papers inside its pages, and don't throw anything away, not even pointless scraps.'

'All right.' She seemed puzzled, but I didn't amplify.

'Order lunch from room service,' I said. 'Don't leave any papers or books lying around when the waiter comes. OK?'

'Yes, but why?'

'Just do the job, Lucy. Here's the room key for here.' I gave it to her. 'If you leave this room, use the key to return. When I come back I'll bring Nash Rourke in for a drink.'

Her blue eyes widened. She wasn't a fool. She looked at the boxes and settled for the package I'd offered.

I went back to work, driver and bodyguard giving me a lot less confidence than Delta-cast. We spent all morning in the stable yard, with Nash patiently (both in and out of character) dealing with the actors playing at police.

The initial police doubts, called for in the script, took an age to get right. 'I don't want these policemen to

299

appear *thick*,' I pleaded, but it was the actors, I concluded, who were slow. I'd had no hand in casting minor
characters; the trick was to make the dumbest poodle
jump through the hoops.

Moncrieff swore non-stop. Nash could turn and get
the light across his forehead right every time, but Nash,
I reminded my fuming director of photography, wasn't
called a mega-star for nothing.

The level of muddle was not helped by the arrival of
the real police asking why my fresh fingerprints were all
over Dorothea's house. We could have played it for
laughs, but no one was funny. I proved to have an alibi
for whenever it was that Paul had died (they wouldn't
or couldn't say exactly when) but the stoppage ate up
my lunch hour.

Back at work we progressed at length to the first
arrival (by car) of Cibber, and to his planting of
suspicions against Nash in the (fictional) police mind.
Cibber was a good pro, but inclined still to tell inappropriate fruity jokes and waste time. 'Sorry, sorry,' he
would breezily say, fluffing his words without remorse.

I hung on grimly to forbearance and walked twice
out onto the Heath breathing deeply with sore rib
twinges while Moncrieff's men loaded the cameras for
the eighth take of a fairly simple sequence. I phoned
Wrigley's garage and asked if Bill Robinson could have
the afternoon off, and I spoke to Bill himself, thanking
him for the second safe delivery of the boxes and asking
him to open his home garage and bring bits of motorbike out onto his drive.

'We've decided to film your stuff after dark,' I said.

'Can you spare us the evening? And will you have your big bike at home?'

Natch, fine, yes indeedy, and cor, he said.

Tired and a shade dispirited I called it a day at five-thirty in the afternoon and invited Nash to my Bedford Lodge rooms for a reviver.

'Sure,' he agreed easily, and greeted Lucy with enough warmth to tongue-tie her into knock knees.

'How did you get on?' I asked her, explaining the task briefly to Nash; and she apologised for being slow and having completed only five boxes. She had just discovered that one of the boxes held some clippings about Sonia's death. Wasn't that extraordinary? Box six, she said. She hadn't had time to go through them.

'That's fine,' I said. 'Come again tomorrow, will you? Are you going right home at nights? Or perhaps staying with your Uncle Ridley?'

She made a face. 'Not with him. Actually,' she blushed perceptibly, 'I'm staying here in this hotel. They had a room free and Dad agreed. I hope that's all right?'

'It's splendid,' I said moderately, knowing enthusiasm would frighten her. 'What about Sunday, day after tomorrow?'

'I can stay until the job's finished,' she said. 'Dad said it was better.'

'Good for Dad,' Nash smiled.

'He's awfully interested,' Lucy said, and after a pause added, 'It's really odd, Mr Rourke, imagining you as my dad.'

Nash smiled, the eyelids crinkling. Despite his preg-

301

nant wife, he didn't look at all like anyone's dad, certainly not Lucy's.

We drank briefly together and split up, Nash yawning as he went and saying the slavedriver (T. Lyon) wanted him out working again in a couple of hours. Lucy, without making an issue of it, excused herself at the same time. Staying in the hotel, she was telling me, meant no more than convenience.

When she'd gone I looked at her master list of the boxes' contents. Since they had been well jumbled up on the journeys, and since she had started methodically at one end, the six boxes she'd worked on held mixed and random contents.

Box I. Form books. Flat racing.

Box II. Biographies, trainers, owners and jockeys.

Box III. Form books. National Hunt racing.

Box IV. Weekly columns, *Racing Gazette*.

Box V. Books, annuals, racing history.

With unstoppable curiosity I knelt on the floor and opened Box III, National Hunt form books, and found that by happy chance it contained the records of two of the years when I'd been racing.

A British racing form book, built up week by week throughout the season with loose-leaf inserts tied between soft leather covers, contained details of every single race run, identifying each runner by name, trainer, jockey, weight carried, age and sex, and giving a start-to-finish commentary of performance.

There was no gainsaying the form book. If the form

302

books said Mr T. Lyon (the Mr denoting amateur status) had finished fifth a long way back, it was no good Mr T. Lyon in memory thinking he'd ridden a close contest to be beaten by half a length. Mr T. Lyon, I read with nostalgia, had won a three-mile steeplechase by two lengths at Newbury, the horse carrying ten stone six. The underfoot conditions that day had been classified as 'soft', and the starting price had been 100–6, Mr T. Lyon's mount having unaccountably beaten the hot favourite (weighted out of it, carrying 20 lbs more). Mr T. Lyon, I remembered, had been ecstatic. The crowd, who'd mostly lost their bets, had been unenthusiastically silent.

I smiled. Here I was, twelve years later, clad in Delta-cast and trying not to be killed: and I didn't think I'd ever been happier than on that cold long-ago afternoon.

Valentine had put a red exclamation mark against my winner, which meant that he personally had fitted the horse with shoes especially for racing, probably on the morning of the race.

Horses wore thin aluminium shoes for racing, much lighter and thinner than the steel shoes they needed in the stable and out at exercise. Farriers would routinely change the shoes before and after a race.

Owing to chance, the form books in Box III went back only as far as my seventeenth birthday. For the Mr T. Lyon debut at sixteen to turn up, I would have to wait for Lucy.

I opened Box I, Flat racing form books, and found that in this instance the books were older. These, indeed, covered the few years when Jackson Wells had been training in Newmarket: one of them covered the year of Sonia's death.

Fascinated, I looked for Valentine's red dots (runners) and red exclamation marks (winners) and found my grandfather's name as trainer all over the place. Twenty-six years ago, when I'd been four. A whole generation ago. So many of them gone. So many horses, so many races, lost and forgotten.

Jackson Wells hadn't had large numbers of runners and precious few winners, as far as I could see. Jackson Wells hadn't had a regular jockey either: only successful wealthy stables could afford to retain a top-flighter. Several of the Wells horses had been ridden by a P. Falmouth, several others by D. Carsington, neither of whom I'd heard of, which wasn't surprising.

On the day of his wife's death, Jackson Wells had set off to York races where a horse from his stable had been entered. I looked up the actual day and found his horse hadn't started and was listed as a non-runner. Trainer Wells had been on his way back to Newmarket when they'd run the race without him.

I flicked forward through the pages. Valentine's dots for Jackson Wells were scattered and diminishing in number. There was only one exclamation mark, a minor race on a minor track, ridden by the minor jockey, D. Carsington.

'A winner is a winner,' my grandfather always said. 'Never despise the lowliest.'

I put the form books back in the box, dutifully collected my guardian shadows from the lobby, and went by car to Betty's house to ask if she by any chance had Dorothea's key. She shook her head. *Poor* Dorothea; that poor man, Paul.

Betty's husband wasn't grieving for Paul. If I wanted to start tidying Dorothea's house, he said, he could open her door in no time. Betty's husband was an all-round handyman. A little how's-your-father and a shove, he said, would circumvent most locks, and consequently he and I soon went from room to ravaged room righting the mess as best we could. The police, he said, had taken their photos and their fingerprints and left. The house, such as it was, and crammed with bad memories, was Dorothea's to come home to.

I spent most time in her bedroom, looking for the photographs she said she kept in a box. I couldn't find them. I told Betty's husband what I was looking for – Dorothea's only mementos of Paul when young – but neither of us succeeded.

'Poor love,' Betty's husband said. 'That son of hers was a brute, but she would never hear a strong word against him. Between you and me, he's no loss.'

'No . . . but who killed him?'

'Yeah, I see what you mean. Gives you a nasty feeling, doesn't it, some geezer running around with a knife?'

'Yes,' I said. 'It does.'


I stood in the dark street outside Bill Robinson's garage, with the black-belt at my back facing the crowd that had inevitably collected.

There were bright lights inside the garage where Bill Robinson himself stood, dressed in his accustomed black leather and studs and looking selfconscious. The monster Harley Davidson stood to one side. Pieces of a second, that Bill was rebuilding, lay in clumps on the drive. Moncrieff was busy pointing arc lamps and spots to give dramatic shadows and gleams, and Nash's stand-in walked to the designated point and looked towards the garage. Moncrieff lit his profile first, and then a three-quarter-face angle, one side bright, the other in darkness, only the liquid sheen of an eye showing.

Nash arrived, walked up beside me and watched.

'You pause,' I said. 'You're wondering how the hell you're going to get out of the fix you're in. You're psyching yourself up. OK?'

He nodded. He waved a hand towards the scene. 'It's striking,' he said, 'but why a bike?'

'It's what our movie is about.'

'How do you mean? There aren't any bikes in it, are there?'

'Fantasy,' I said. 'Our movie is about the need for fantasy.'

'The dream lovers?' he suggested doubtfully.

'Fantasy supplies what life doesn't,' I said casually. 'That boy there with his bike is eighteen, good natured, has a regular job, carries his elderly neighbour's shopping home for her, and in his fantasy life he's a hell raiser with roaring power between his legs and the gear and the studs. He's playing at what he wouldn't really like to be, but the imagining of it fills and satisfies him.'

Nash stood without moving. 'You sound as though you approve,' he said.

'Yes, I do. A good strong fantasy life, I'd guess, saves

countless people from boredom and depression. It gives them a feeling of being individual. They invent themselves. You know it perfectly well. You *are* a fantasy to most people.'

'What about serial killers? Aren't they fantasists?'

'There's a hell to every heaven.'

Moncrieff called, 'Ready, Thomas,' and Nash, without comment, went to the place from where he would walk into shot, and pause, and turn his head, and watch Bill Robinson live in his courage-inducing dreamland.

Ed went round explaining the necessity of silence to the neighbours. He shouted, 'Turn over.' The cameras reached speed. Ed yelled, 'Action.' Nash walked, stopped, turned his head. Perfect. Bill Robinson dropped a piece of exhaust pipe out of nervousness and said, 'Sorry.'

'Cut,' Ed said, disgusted.

'Don't say "sorry",' I told Bill Robinson, walking towards the garage to join him. 'It doesn't matter if you drop something. It doesn't matter if you swear. It's normal. Just don't say "sorry".'

He grinned. We shot the scene again and he fitted two shining pieces of metal together as if he hadn't got fifty people watching.

'Cut,' Ed yelled with approval, and the neighbours cheered. Nash shook Bill Robinson's hand and signed autographs. We sold a lot of future cinema tickets, and no one stuck a knife in my back. Not a bad evening, overall.

Returning to Bedford Lodge, Nash and I ate room-service dinner together.

'Go on,' he said, 'about the need for fantasy.'

'Oh ... I ...' I hesitated, and stopped, unwilling to sound a fool.

'Go on,' he urged. 'People say ... in fact *I* say ... that play-acting isn't a suitable occupation for a serious man. So tell me why it is.'

'You don't need me to tell you.'

'Tell me why you make fantasies, then.'

'Have some wine.'

'Don't duck the issue, dammit.'

'Well,' I said, pouring lavishly, 'I wanted to be a jockey but I grew too big. Anyway, one day I went to see a doctor about some damage I'd done to my shoulder in a racing fall, and she asked me what I wanted to do with my life. I said "be a jockey" and she lectured me crossly on wasting my time on earth frivolously. I asked her what occupation she would recommend and she sternly told me that the only profession truly helpful and worthwhile was medicine.'

'Rubbish!'

'She scorned me for wanting to be merely an entertainer.'

Nash shook his head.

'So,' I said, 'I rationalised it, I suppose. I'm still an entertainer and always will be, I guess, and I've persuaded myself that I do at least as much good as tranquillisers. Everyone can go where their mind takes them. You can live in imaginary places without feeling the real terror or the real pain. I make the images. I open the door. I can inflame ... and I can heal ... and comfort ... and get people to understand ... and, for

God's sake, don't remember a word of this. I've just made it up to entertain you.'

He drank his wine thoughtfully.

'And in this movie that we're engaged in,' I said, 'the dream lovers make the spurned wife's existence happier. They're the best way she can face her husband's affair with her own sister. They're her refuge . . . and her revenge.'

He smiled twistedly. 'My character's a shit, isn't he?'

'Human,' I said.

'And are you going to sell Howard on her suicide?'

I shook my head. 'I'm sure she didn't kill herself. But don't worry, your character will avenge her death and come up smelling of roses.'

'Has Howard written those extra scenes?'

'Not yet.'

'You're a rogue, Thomas, you know that?'

We finished dinner peaceably, and together with Moncrieff mapped out the next day's scenes, which were due to take place in the Athenaeum's look-alike dining-room, happily by now built and ready.


After that meeting I un-Velcroed my restricting knife-repeller with relief and washed without soaking the dressing, and in sleeping shorts thought I'd just take a quick look at the newspaper cuttings about Sonia's death before inching into bed: and two hours later, warmed by a dressing gown, I was still sitting in an armchair alternately amused and aghast and beginning to understand why Paul had desperately wanted to take away Valentine's books and why Valentine, perhaps, hadn't wanted him to have them. In leaving them to me, a comparative stranger, the old man had thought to safeguard the knowledge contained in them, since I couldn't have understood the significance of the clippings and might simply have thrown them away, a task he should have done himself but had left too late, until his progressing illness made action impossible.

Paul had wanted Valentine's books and papers, and Paul was dead. I looked at the Delta-cast jacket standing empty and mute on a table and felt a strong urge to fasten it on again, even at two in the morning.

In describing Sonia to me, Valentine had called her a mouse, but that couldn't have been how he'd thought of her when she was alive. The folder of clippings about her held two large photographs, both the likenesses of a vividly pretty young woman with a carefree spirit and, I would have said, considerable carnal knowledge.

One of the photographs was an expert, glossy, eight by ten black and white version of the coloured photo Lucy had lent me of 'Sonia and Pig'. In Valentine's photo the young man's presence had been deleted. Sonia smiled alone.

The second photo was of Sonia in her wedding dress, again alone, and again with nothing virginal about her eyes. My mother, of all people, had once instructed me about the difference: once a woman had slept with a man, she said, the woman would develop little pouches in her lower eyelids which would show when she smiled. Sonia was smiling in both pictures, and the small pouches were there unmistakably.

Valentine had said the book made her out to be a poor little bitch and, in saying that, he'd intended to mislead. The folder held clippings about her death from a myriad of newspapers and, in the most derogatory of the various accounts, in those most overtly speculatory about Mrs Wells's fidelity to Jackson, someone – and it had to have been Valentine himself – had stricken the accounts through and through with red biro and had written No! No! as if in pain.

I took everything out of the Sonia folder and found that beside the photos and the whole sheaf of newspaper cuttings, there were two frail dried roses, a brief note about shoeing which started 'Darling Valentine', and a wisp of creamy lace-edged panties.

Valentine had confessed he'd been too easily aroused by young women, Professor Derry had said. According to Valentine's own collection of memories, one of those young women had been Sonia Wells.

Poor old sod, I thought. He had been sixty, nearly, when she died. I was young enough to have considered sixty the far side of acute sexual obsession: Valentine enlightened even from beyond the grave.

The emotional vigour of the thick Sonia file blinded me for a long while to the slim folder underneath which lay at the bottom of the box: but this folder proved, when I read the contents carefully, to be raw explosive material in search of a detonator.

In search of myself.

I slept for five hours, put on the carapace, went back to work. Saturday morning. I struck it off in my mind's calendar as Day Nineteen of production, or almost a third of my time allowed.

It rained all day, which didn't matter as we were engaged indoors in the Athenaeum dining-room, shooting the scene where Cibber's suspicions of his wife's canoodling gelled into inescapable certainty. Cibber and Silva endlessly said yes please and no thank you to actor-waiters; chewed endless mouthfuls of food, and in Silva's case spitting them out immediately I said 'Cut'; drank endless sips of wine-coloured water; waved (in Cibber's case) to unidentified acquaintances across the room; conducted a conversation of concentrated spite with rigidly smiling lips and a vivid awareness of social status. Jockey Club membership, to Cibber, meant not publicly slapping your wife's face in the most conservative dining-room in London.

Howard, I thought, as I listened and watched, had surpassed himself in understanding and reproducing the constraints of class on the potentially dangerous ego of a rejected male.

Silva sneered at Cibber with her eyes, her mouth saccharine. Silva told him she couldn't bear his hands on her breasts. Cibber, destroyed within, looked around to make sure the waiters hadn't heard. Both players gave the film enormously good value for money.

Breaking for lunch, with the close-ups to do in the afternoon, I returned for a respite to Bedford Lodge and found Nash in my rooms sprawling in an armchair and having an easy time with Lucy. She, in consequence, had, as her morning's work, itemised the contents of barely one and a half cartons.

312

'Oh, hallo,' she greeted me from her knees, 'what would you like me to do with three boxfuls of huge old encyclopaedias?'

'How old?'

She pulled out one large volume and investigated. 'Forty years!' Her voice made forty years unimaginable. Nash reflexly winced.

'Just label them and leave them,' I said.

'Right. Oh . . . and I haven't come across any photo albums, that you wanted me to look for, but I did find a lot of snaps in an old chocolate box. What do you want me to do with those?'

'In a chocolate box . . .?'

'Well, yes. It's got flowers on the lid. Pretty old.'

'Er . . . where's the box?'

She opened a carton that had once held a fax machine, and from it produced several box files full of ancient racecards and newspaper clippings of winners that Valentine had regularly shod. 'Here's the chocolate box,' Lucy said, lifting out and handing me a faded and battered gold-coloured cardboard box with flowers like dahlias on the lid. 'I didn't make a list of the photos. Do you want me to?'

'No,' I said absently, taking off the lid and finding small ancient pictures inside, many in long-ago faded colours with curling edges. Pictures of Valentine and his wife, pictures of Dorothea and her husband, a photo or two of Meredith Derry and his wife, and several of Dorothea with her child: with her nice-looking little boy, Paul. Pictures when life was fine, before time loused it up.

313

'How about ordering us all some lunch?' I said.

Nash did the ordering. 'What do you want to drink, Thomas?'

'Lethe,' I said.

'Not until you've finished the movie.'

'What's Lethe?' Lucy asked.

Nash said, 'The river in the underworld that, if you drink it, makes you sleep and forget about living.'

'Oh.'

'For ever,' Nash added. 'But Thomas doesn't mean that.'

Lucy covered non-comprehension in activity with the marker pen.

At the bottom of the chocolate box, I came across a larger print, the colours still not razor sharp, but in a better state of preservation. It was of a group of young people, all looking about twenty. On the back of the photo were two simple words – 'The Gang'.

The Gang.

The Gang consisted of five young men and a girl.

I sat staring at it for long enough for the other two to notice.

'What is it?' Nash asked. 'What have you found?'

I handed the photo to Lucy, who glanced at it, did a double take and then exclaimed, 'Why, that's Dad, isn't it? How *young* he looks.' She turned the photo over. 'The Gang,' she read aloud. 'That's his handwriting, isn't it?'

'You'd know better than I would.'

'I'm sure of it.'

'Who are the people with him? Who are the Gang?' I asked.

314

She studied the picture. 'That's Sonia, isn't it? It must be.'

Nash took the photo out of Lucy's hand and peered at it himself, nodding. 'That's definitely your father, and the girl looks like the photo you lent us ... and that boy next to her, that's the other one in that photo ... that's surely "Pig".'

'I suppose so,' Lucy said doubtfully. 'And that one on the end, he looks like ...' She stopped, both unsure and disturbed.

'Like who?' I asked.

'He's not like that any more. He's, well ... *bloated* ... now. That's my Uncle Ridley. He looks lovely there. How *awful*, what time does to people.'

'Yes.' Nash and I said it in unison. An endless host of barely recognisable old actors and actresses lived on in Hollywood in inelastic skins, everything sagging but the memory of glamour, their youthful selves mocking them relentlessly from rented videos and movie channels.

'Who are the others?' I asked.

'I don't know them,' Lucy said, handing the photo back to me.

I said, 'They look people of your age.'

'Yes, they do.' She found it unremarkable. 'Do you want me to repack this box?'

'Yes, please. But leave out the chocolate box.'

'OK.'

Lunch came and we ate. Ziggy phoned the hotel from Norway.

'I cannot reach O'Hara's number,' he complained.

'He's gone back to LA,' I said. 'How are the horses?'

'Working well.'

'Good. The production department has found a disused stable yard for them to stay in, only ten miles from our beach.' I fished a piece of paper out of an inner pocket and spelled the address for him patiently, letter by letter. 'Phone me after you've landed at Immingham on Monday if you have any problems.'

'Yes, Thomas.'

'Well done, Ziggy.'

He laughed, pleased, and departed.

I left Nash and Lucy drinking coffee and, taking with me both 'The Gang' photo and the lower file from the previous night's reading, went along to O'Hara's suite, let myself in with his key and stowed Valentine's mementos in the safe, with the knives. All the rooms in the hotel were equipped with individual small safes, which each guest could set to open to his own choice of combination. I hardly liked to acknowledge the instinct for extra security that led me to use O'Hara's safe instead of my own, but anyway, I did it.

Still in O'Hara's rooms I looked up the number of Ridley Wells in the local phone directory, and tried it, but there was no answer.

On returning to my own rooms I found Nash, on the point of leaving, announcing that he was going to spend the afternoon watching racing on TV while betting by phone with a bookmaker I'd arranged for him.

'Is it still on, for tonight?' he asked, pausing in the doorway.

'Certainly is, if the rain stops, which it is supposed to.'

'How do you expect me to ride a horse in the goddam dark?'

'There will be moonlight. Moncrieff's arranging it.'

'What about goddam rabbit holes?'

'There aren't any on Newmarket's gallops,' I assured him.

'But what if I fall *off*?'

'We'll pick you up and put you back in the saddle.'

'I hate you sometimes, Thomas.' He grinned and went on his way. I left Lucy up to her elbows in decades of form books, collected my minders in the lobby and was bowled the short mile back to the stables.

On my way back to 'The Athenaeum' I detoured into the downstairs office, used chiefly by Ed, where we had the business paraphernalia of telephones, faxes, and large-capacity copier, and asked the young woman operating everything there to keep on trying Ridley Wells's number for me, and if he returned home and answered the summons, to put the call through to me upstairs immediately.

'But you said never to do that, in case the phone rang during a shot.'

'We can re-shoot,' I said. 'I want to catch this man. OK?'

She nodded, reassured, and I went upstairs to re-coax Cibber and Silva into their most venomous faces.

Ridley Wells answered his telephone at three-thirty, and sounded drunk.

I said, 'Do you remember you asked our producer, O'Hara, if we had any riding work for you in our film?'

'He said you hadn't.'

'Right. But now we have. Are you still interested?' I

mentioned a fee for a morning's work large enough to hook a bigger fish than Ridley, and he didn't even ask what the job entailed.

I said, 'We'll send a car for you tomorrow morning at seven. It will bring you to the stables where we're keeping our horses. You don't need to bring anything with you. We'll supply you with clothes from our wardrobe department. We'll supply the horse for you to ride. We don't want you to do anything out of the ordinary or dangerous on the horse. We're just short of a rider for a scene we're shooting tomorrow.'

'Got you,' he said grandly.

'Don't forget,' I insisted.

'Mum's the word, old boy.'

'No,' I said. 'Mum's *not* the word. If you're not sober in the morning, then no job and no fee.'

After a pause he said, 'Got you,' again, and I hoped he meant it.

When we'd finished the close-ups and the day's work was safely on its way to London for processing I ran the previous day's rushes in the screening room, happy for Bill Robinson's sake that he and his monster bike positively quivered with shining power, filling Nash's character with the determination he needed if he were to take action.

From fantasy, courage, I thought. I wanted the film to assert that old idea, but without ramming it down anyone's throat. I wanted people to see that they had always known it. To open doors. A door-opener; that was my function.

It stopped raining more or less at the time forecast – miraculous – and Moncrieff busied himself in the stable yard supervising the loading of cameras, films, lights and crews onto trucks for the 'moonlit' shots of Nash on the Heath.

Nash arrived to the minute, no surprise, and came out of the house half an hour later in riding clothes and night-time make-up, carrying his helmet and demanding a thoroughly tranquillised mount.

'If your fans could only hear you!' I remarked dryly.

'You, Thomas,' he said, smiling, 'can go try 6G in a brake turn at low level.'

I shook my head. Nash could fly fast jet aircraft – when not under a restrictive contract in mid-film – and I couldn't. Nash's pre-mega-star hair-raising CV included air force service in fighters, all part of his mystique.

'The scene comes a night or two before the motorbikes,' I said. 'You have been accused. You are worried. OK?'

He nodded. The screenplay had included the night-on-the-horse scene from the beginning, and he was prepared.

We drove the camera truck slowly up the road by the hill, Nash in the saddle beside us (the horse in dim 'moonlight') looking worried and thoughtful. We then filmed him sitting on the ground with his back to a wind-bent tree, the horse cropping grass nearby. We'd more or less finished when the thick clouds unexpectedly parted and blew in dramatic shapes across the real full moon, and Moncrieff turned his camera heavenwards for more than sixty seconds, and beamed at me triumphantly through his straggly beard.

The long day ended. Back at Bedford Lodge I found

319

three more boxes itemised, plus a note from Lucy saying she hoped I didn't mind but her parents wanted her home for Sunday after all. Back Monday, she wrote.

Box VIII. Form books. Flat racing.
Box IX. Horseshoes.
Box X. Encyclopaedias, A–F.

The horseshoes were actual horseshoes, each saved in a plastic bag and labelled with the name of the horse that had worn it, complete with winning date, racecourse and event. Valentine had been a true collector, squirrelling his successes away.

I pulled out the first of the encyclopaedias without anything particular in mind and, finding a slip of paper in it acting as a bookmark, opened it there. *Autocrat*: an absolute ruler. Multiple examples followed.

I closed the book, rested my head against the back of my armchair, decided it was time to take off the Delta-cast and drifted towards sleep.

The thought that galvanised me to full wakefulness seemed to come from nowhere but was a word seen peripherally, unconsidered.

Autocrat . . .

Further down the page came *Auto-erotism*.

I picked the volume out of the box and read the long entry. I learned much more than I wanted to about various forms of masturbation, though I could find nothing of much significance. Vaguely disappointed, I started to replace the bookmarker, but glanced at it and kept it in my hand. Valentine's bookmarker bore the one word 'Paraphilia'.

I didn't know what paraphilia was, but I searched through several unopened boxes and finally found the P volume of the encyclopaedia, following where Valentine had directed.

The P volume also had a bookmark, this time in the page for *Paraphilia*.

Paraphilia, I read, consisted of many manifestations of perverted love. One of them was listed as 'erotic strangulation – the starvation of blood to the brain to stimulate sexual arousal'.

Valentine's knowledge of self-asphyxia, the process he had described to Professor Derry, had come from this book.

'In 1791 in London,' I read, 'at the time of Haydn, a well-known musician died as a result of his leaning towards paraphilia. One Friday afternoon he engaged a prostitute to tie a leash round his neck which he could then tighten to the point of his satisfaction. Unfortunately he went too far and throttled himself. The prostitute reported his death and was tried for murder, but acquitted, as the musician's perversion was well known. The judge ordered the records of the case not to be published, in the interests of decency.'

One lived and learned, I thought tolerantly, putting the encyclopaedia back in its box. Poor old Professor Derry. Just as well, perhaps, that he hadn't acted on Valentine's information.

Before throwing them both away I glanced at Valentine's second bookmark. On the strip of white paper he'd written, 'Tell Derry this' and, lower down, 'Showed this to Pig'.

I went along to O'Hara's room, retrieved the folder

and 'The Gang' photograph from the safe, and sat in his armchair looking at them and thinking long and hard.

Eventually, I slept in his bed, as it was safer.

# CHAPTER FIFTEEN

The film company's car brought Ridley Wells to the stables on time and sober the next morning. We sent him into the house to the wardrobe department, and I took the opportunity to telephone Robbie Gill on my mobile.

I expected to get his message service at that early hour, but in fact he was awake and answered my summons himself.

'Still alive?' he asked chattily.

'Yes, thank you.'

'So what do you need?'

As always with Robbie, straight to the point.

'First,' I said, 'who gave you the list of knife specialists?'

'My professional colleague in the police force,' he said promptly. 'The doctor they call out locally. He's a randy joker, ex-rugger player, good for a laugh and a jar in the pub. I asked him for known knife specialists. He said the force had drawn up the list themselves recently and asked him if he could add to it. He couldn't. The people he knows who carry knives tend to be behind bars.'

'Did he attend Dorothea?'

'No, he was away. Anything else?'

'How is she?'

'Dorothea? Still sedated. Now Paul's gone, do you still want to pay for the nursing home?'

'Yes, I do, and I want to see her soon, like this afternoon.'

'No problem. Just go. She's still in a side ward because of Paul, but physically she's healing well. We could move her by Tuesday, I should think.'

'Good,' I said.

'Take care.'

I said wryly, 'I do.'

In the stable yard the lads were readying for morning exercise, saddling and bridling the horses. As it was Sunday, I told them, we would again have the Heath gallops more or less to ourselves, but we wouldn't be filming exactly the same scenes as the week before.

'You were all asked to wear what you did last Sunday,' I said. 'Did you all check with our continuity girl if you couldn't remember?'

I got nods.

'Fine. Then all of you will canter up the hill and stop where you stopped and circled last week. OK?'

More nods.

'You remember the rider who came from nowhere and made a slash at Ivan?'

They laughed. They wouldn't forget it.

'Right,' I said, 'today we don't have Ivan, but we're going to stage that attack ourselves, and put it into the film. Today it will be a fictional affair. OK? The knife

324

used will not be a real knife but one that's been made out of wood by our production department. What I want you to do is exactly the sort of thing you were doing last Sunday – circling, talking, paying not much attention to the stranger. Right?'

They understood without trouble. Our young horse-master said, 'Who is going to stand in for Ivan?'

'I am,' I said. 'I'm not as broad-shouldered as him or as Nash, but I'll be wearing a jacket like the one Nash usually wears as the trainer. I'll be riding the horse Ivan rode. When we're ready with the cameras, the man playing the knife-attacker will mount and ride that slow old bay that finished last in our race at Huntingdon. The lad who usually rides him will be standing behind the cameras, out of shot. Any questions?'

One asked, 'Are you going to chase him down the hill on the camera truck, like last week?'

'No,' I said. 'He will gallop off down the hill. The camera will film him.'

I handed over command, so to speak, to the horse-master, who organised the mounting and departure of the string. Ed and Moncrieff were already on the Heath. I went into the wardrobe section to put on Nash's jacket and, Ridley being ready, took him with me in my car up the road to the brow of the hill. Ridley and I, out of the car, walked over to the circling horses, stopping by the camera truck.

'What we need,' I told Ridley, 'is for you to ride into the group from somewhere over there ...' I pointed. 'Trot into the group, draw a make-believe knife from a sheath on your belt, slash at one of the group as if you intended to wound him badly, and then, in the ensuing mêlée, canter off over the brow of the hill and down the wide training ground towards the town. OK?'

Ridley stared, his eyes darkly intense.

'You will slash at *me*, OK? I'm standing in for Nash.'

Ridley said nothing.

'Of course,' I told him pleasantly, 'when this scene appears in the finished film it will not look like one smooth sequence. There will be flashes of the knife, of horses rearing, of jumbled movement and confusion. There will be a wound. There will be blood. We will fake those later.' Ed brought various props across to where I stood with Ridley, and handed them to him one by one.

'Make-believe knife in sheath on belt,' Ed said, as if reading from a list. 'Please put on the belt.'

As if mesmerised, Ridley obeyed.

'Please practise drawing the knife,' I said.

Ridley drew the knife and looked at it in horror. The production department had faithfully reproduced the American trench knife from my drawing, and although the object Ridley held was light-weight and of painted wood, from three paces it looked like a heavy knuckle-duster with a long blade attached to its index finger side.

'Fine,' I said non-committally. 'Put it back in its sheath.'

Ridley fumbled the knife back into place.

'Helmet,' Ed said, holding it out.

Ridley buckled on the helmet.

'Goggles,' Ed offered.

Ridley put them on slowly.

'Gloves.'

Ridley hesitated.

'Anything the matter?' I asked.

Ridley said 'No' hoarsely, and accepted a leg-up onto our slowest nag.

'Great,' I said, 'off you go, then. When Ed yells "Action", just trot straight towards me, draw the knife, take a slash, and canter away fast towards Newmarket. Do you want a rehearsal, or do you think you can get it right first time?'

The helmeted, be-goggled, gloved figure didn't respond.

'We'll take a bet you can get it right,' I said.

Ridley seemed incapable of action. I asked the lad whose horse he was riding to lead him over to the starting point, and then let go and clear the shot. While the lad intelligently followed the instruction, the lad on Nash's horse dismounted and gave me a leg-up. The cracked rib tugged sharply. I lengthened the stirrup leathers. Moncrieff opened his floodlights to bathe the scene and augment the daylight.

Ed yelled, 'Action.'

Ridley Wells kicked his horse into a canter, not a trot. He tugged the knife free with his right hand while holding the reins with his left. He steered his mount with his legs, expert that he was, and he aimed himself straight at me, as murderously intent as one could have hoped.

The 'knife' hit my coat and the carapace beneath and because the imitation blade had no slicing power, the impact knocked the weapon flying out of Ridley's grasp.

'I've dropped it,' he shouted, and I pointed to the brow of the hill and yelled at him, 'Never mind. Gallop.'

He galloped. He sat down low in the saddle and galloped as if it were a genuine escape.

The lads on their horses crowded to the top of the hill to watch, just as before, and this time I went after the fugitive on a horse, not in a truck.

The truck was being driven down the road, camera whirring. The sequence I finally cut together for the film showed 'Nash' closely chasing his assailant; Nash with a deep bleeding wound; Nash losing his quarry, blood dripping everywhere; Nash in pain.

'*Lovely stuff*,' O'Hara breathed when he saw it. '*God*, Thomas . . .'

On this Sunday morning, however, there was no blood. I had much the faster horse and I caught up with Ridley before he could vanish into Newmarket's streets.

He reined furiously to a halt. He tore off the gloves, the goggles and the helmet and threw them on the ground. He struggled out of the anorak we'd dressed him in and flung it away from him.

'I'll *kill* you,' he said.

I said, 'I'll send your fee.'

His bloated face wavered with irresolution as if he couldn't decide whether or not to attack me there and then, but sense or cowardice prevailed, and he dismounted in a practised slide, facing me, right foot lifting over the horse's neck. He let go of the reins. He turned his back on me and walked off unsteadily in the direction of Newmarket, as if he couldn't feel his feet on the ground.

I leaned forward, picked up the dangling reins and walked both horses back to the stables.

The lads came back from the hill chattering like starlings, wide eyed.

'That man looked just the same!' 'He was the same!' 'He looked like that man last week!' 'Didn't he look just like the same man?'

'Yes,' I said.

From the wardrobe department, where I shed Nash's coat and helmet, I paid a brief visit upstairs to where the production people were stacking the Athenaeum scenery to one side and filling the space instead with a reproduction of any horse's box in the stable yard.

As a real natural box was far too small for camera, crew, lights and technicians, let alone a couple of actors, we were fabricating our own version. It was as if a box had been divided into thirds, then spread apart, leaving a large centre area for camera manoeuvring. One third had the split door to the outer world (back projection of the stable yard), one portion contained a manger and water bucket. One, the largest, encompassed the place where a horse would normally stand.

The walls of the box were being constructed of actual white washed breeze blocks with an open ceiling of heavy rafters. Bales of hay, at present neatly stacked, would be placed on a platform on the rafters above the action. A floor of concrete sections covered with straw was being slotted into each setting. Artistic hoof marks and other signs of wear and habitation showed that this was a box often in use.

'How's it going?' I asked, looking round with approval.

'Ready in the morning,' they assured me. 'It'll be as solid as a rock, like you asked.'

'Great.'


Dorothea's cheeks were faintly pink; a great advance.

We had a few tears on my arrival, but not the racking distress of two days earlier. As her physical state had grown stronger, so had her strength of mind resurfaced. She thanked me for the flowers I'd brought her and said she was sick of a diet of tomato soup.

'They say it's good for me but I'm growing to hate it. It's true I can't eat meat and salad – have you ever endured a hospital salad? – but why not *mushroom*, or *chicken* soup? And none of it's home made, of course.'

She was longing, she said, to go to the nursing home dear Robbie Gill had suggested, and she hoped her daughter-in-law, Janet, would soon return home to Surrey.

'We don't like each other,' Dorothea confessed, sighing. 'Such a pity.'

'Mm,' I agreed. 'When you're well, will you go back to your house?'

Tears quivered in her eyes. 'Paul died there.'

Valentine also, I thought.

'Thomas ... I've been remembering things.' She sounded almost anxious. 'That night when I was attacked...'

'Yes?' I prompted, as she stopped. 'What do you remember?'

330

'Paul was shouting.'

'Yes, you told me.'

'There was another man there.'

I drew the visitor's chair to beside her bed and sat peacefully holding her hand, not wanting to alarm her and smothering my own urgent thoughts.

I said gently, 'Do you remember what he looked like?'

'I didn't know him. He was there with Paul when I got home from Mona's house ... I'd been watching television with her, you see, but we didn't like the programme and I went home early ... and I went in by the kitchen door as usual and I was so surprised and, well – *pleased*, of course – to see Paul, but he was so *strange*, dear, and almost *frightened*, but he couldn't have been frightened. Why should he have been frightened?'

'Perhaps because you'd come home while he and the other man were ransacking your house.'

'Well, dear, Paul shouted ... where was Valentine's photo album, and I'm sure I said he didn't have one, he just kept a few old snaps in a chocolate box, the same as I did, but Paul wouldn't believe me, he kept going on about an album.'

'So,' I said, 'did Valentine ever have an album?'

'No, dear, I'm sure he didn't. We were never a great family for photos, not like some people who don't believe a thing's happened unless they take snaps of it. Valentine had dozens of pictures of horses, but it was horses, you see, that were his life. Always horses. He never had any children, his Cathy *couldn't*, you see. He might have been keener on photos if he'd had children.

I keep quite a lot of photos in a box in my bedroom. Photos of us all, long ago. Pictures of Paul . . .'

Tears came again, and I didn't tell her I hadn't been able to find those pathetically few mementos in her bedroom. I would give her Valentine's chocolate box instead.

'Did Paul say why he wanted the photo album?' I asked.

'I don't think so, dear. Everything was happening so fast and the other man was so *angry*, and shouting too, and Paul said to me – so *frightening*, dear, but he said, "Tell him where the album is, he's got a knife."'

I asked quietly, 'Are you sure about that?'

'I believed it was a dream.'

'And now?'

'Well, now . . . I think he must have said it. I can hear my Paul's voice . . . oh, dear . . . oh, my darling little boy.'

I hugged her while she sobbed.

'That other man *hit* me,' she said, gulping. 'Hit my head . . . and Paul was shouting, "Tell him, tell him". . . and I saw . . . he really did have a knife, that man . . . or at least he was holding something shiny, but it wasn't a real knife, he had his fingers through it . . . dirty fingernails . . . it was horrid . . . and Paul was shouting, "Stop it . . . *don't* . . ." and I woke up in the hospital and I didn't know what had happened, but last night . . . well, dear, when I was waking up this morning and thinking about Paul, well, I sort of *remembered*.'

'Yes,' I said. I paused, consolidating earlier impressions. 'Dearest Dorothea,' I said. 'I think Paul saved your life.'

'Oh! Oh!' She was still crying, but after a while it was from radiant joy, not grinding regret.

'I think,' I said, 'that Paul was so horrified by seeing you attacked with that knife, that he prevented a fatal blow. Robbie Gill thought that the attack on you looked like an *interrupted* murder. He said that people who inflicted such awful knife wounds were usually in a frenzy, and simply couldn't stop. I think Paul stopped him.'

'Oh, *Thomas*!'

'But I'm afraid,' I said regretfully, 'that it means that Paul knew the man who attacked you, and he didn't identify him to the police. In fact, Paul pretended he was in Surrey when you were attacked.'

'Oh, dear.'

'And,' I said, 'Paul tried hard to prevent you from talking to me or to Robbie, or anyone else, until he was sure you remembered nothing about the attack.'

Dorothea's joy faded somewhat but, underneath, remained.

'He changed a bit,' I said. 'I think at one point he almost told me something, but I don't know what. I do believe, though, that he was feeling remorse over what had happened to you.'

'Oh, Thomas, I do hope so.'

'I'm sure of it,' I said, more positively than I felt.

She thought things over quietly for a while and then said, 'Paul would burst out sometimes with opinions as if he couldn't hold them in any more.'

'Did he?'

'He said . . . I didn't like to tell you, Thomas, but the other day – when he was here with me – he burst out

333

with, "*Why* did you ever have to make your film?" He was *bitter*. He said, "I would never have been attacked if you hadn't stirred everything up." Of course I asked *what* you had stirred up and he said, "It was all in the *Drumbeat*, but I was to forget what he'd said, only if anything happened to you it would be your own fault." He said . . . I'm really sorry . . . but he said he would be pleased if you were cut to ribbons like me . . . It wasn't like him, really it wasn't.'

'I did bolt him out of your house,' I reminded her. 'He didn't like me much for embarrassing him.'

'No, but . . . well, something was *worrying* him, I'm sure of it.'

I stood up and wandered over to the window, looking out aimlessly at the institutionally regular pattern of the windows in the building opposite and the scrubby patch of garden between. Two people in white coats walked slowly along a path, conversing. Extras playing doctors, I thought automatically – and realised I often saw even real life in terms of film.

I turned and asked Dorothea, 'While you've been here in the hospital, did Paul ask you about a photo album?'

'I don't think so, dear. Everything gets so muddled, though.' She paused. 'He said something about you having taken Valentine's books away, and I didn't tell him you hadn't. I didn't want to argue, you see, dear. I felt too tired.'

I told her I'd found a photo among Valentine's possessions which I had retrieved from her nice young friend, Bill Robinson – but I couldn't see that it was worth the damage to her house or to herself.

'If I show it to you,' I said, 'will you tell me who the people are?'

'Of course, dear, if I can.'

I took 'The Gang' photo out of my pocket and put it into her hand.

'I need my reading glasses,' she said, peering at it. 'That red case on the bedside table.'

I gave her her glasses and she looked without much reaction at the picture.

'Did one of those people attack you?' I asked.

'Oh no, none of those. He was much older. All these people are so young. Why!' she exclaimed, 'that's Paul! That one at the end, isn't that Paul? How young he was! So handsome, then.' She let the hand holding the photo rest on the sheet. 'I don't know any of the others. I wish Paul was here.'

Sighing, I took back the photo, replaced it in my pocket and produced the small memo pad I habitually carried.

I said, 'I don't want to upset you, but if I draw a knife will you tell me if it's the one that might have been used on you?'

'I don't want to see it.'

'Please, Dorothea.'

'Paul was killed with a knife,' she wailed, and cried for her son.

'Dearest Dorothea,' I said after a while, 'if it will help to find Paul's killer, will you look at my drawing?'

She shook her head. I put the drawing close to her hand and, after a long minute, she picked it up.

'How *horrid*,' she said, looking at it, 'I didn't see a

knife like that.' She sounded extremely relieved. 'It wasn't anything like that.'

I'd drawn for her the American trench knife from the Heath. I turned the paper over and drew the wicked Armadillo, serrated edge and all.

Dorothea looked at it, went white and didn't speak.

'I'm so sorry,' I said helplessly. 'But you didn't die. Paul loved you . . . He saved your life.'

I thought of the cataclysmic shock in Paul's face when he'd come to Dorothea's house and seen the Armadillo lying on the kitchen table. When he'd seen me sitting there, *alive*.

He'd blundered out of the house and gone away, and it was pointless now to speculate that if we'd stopped him, if we'd sat him down and made him talk, he might have lived. Paul had been near, once, to breaking open. Paul, I thought, had become a fragile danger, likely to crumble, likely to confess. Paul, overbearing, pompous, unlikeable, had lost his nerve and died of repentance.

My driver, with the black-belt beside him, aimed my car towards Oxfordshire while consulting from time to time my written directions, and I sat in the back seat looking again at 'The Gang' photo and remembering what both Dorothea and Lucy had said about it.

'They're so *young*.'

Young.

Jackson Wells, Ridley Wells, Paul Pannier, were all at least twenty-six years younger in the photo than the living men I'd met. Sonia had died twenty-six years earlier, and Sonia was alive in the picture.

336

Say the photo had been taken twenty-*seven* years ago – that made Jackson Wells about twenty-three, with all the others younger than that. Eighteen, nineteen, twenty: that sort of age. Sonia had died at twenty-one.

I had been four when she died and I hadn't heard of her, and I'd come back at thirty and wanted to know *why* she had died, and I had said I might try and find out, and in saying that I'd set off a chain reaction that had put Dorothea into hospital and Paul into his grave and had earned me a knife in the ribs . . . and whatever else might come.

I hadn't known there was a genie in the bottle, but genies once let out couldn't be put back.

My driver found Batwillow Farm and delivered me to Jackson Wells's door.

Lucy again answered the summons of the over-loud bell, her blue eyes widening with astonishment.

'I say,' she said, 'you didn't mind my coming home for the day, did you? You haven't come to drag me back by my ponytail?'

'No,' I smiled. 'I really wanted to talk to your father.'

'Oh, sure. Come in.'

I shook my head. 'I wonder if he would come out.'

'Oh? Well, I'll ask him.' Faintly puzzled, she disappeared into the house, to return soon with her blond, lean, farm-tanned enquiring parent looking exactly as he had looked there one week earlier.

'Come in,' he said, gesturing a welcome, happy-go-lucky.

'Come for a walk.'

He shrugged. 'If you like.' He stepped out of his

house and Lucy, unsure of herself, remained in the doorway.

Jackson eyed the two agile men sitting in my car and asked, 'Friends?'

'A driver and a bodyguard,' I answered. 'Film company issue.'

'Oh.'

We crossed from the house and came to rest by the five-barred gate on which deaf old Wells senior had been leaning the week before.

'Lucy's doing a good job,' I said. 'Did she tell you?'

'She likes talking to Nash Rourke.'

'They get on fine,' I agreed.

'I told her to be careful.'

I smiled. 'You've taught her well.' Too well, I thought. I said, 'Did she mention a photograph?'

He looked as if he didn't know whether to say yes or no, but in the end said, 'What photograph?'

'This one.' I brought it out of my pocket and gave it to him.

He looked at the front briefly and at the back, and met my eyes expressionlessly.

'Lucy says that's your handwriting,' I commented, taking the picture back.

'What if it is?'

'I'm not the police,' I said, 'and I haven't brought thumbscrews.'

He laughed, but the totally carefree manner of a week earlier had been undermined by wariness.

I said, 'Last week you told me no one knew why Sonia had died.'

'That's right.' The blue eyes shone, as ever, with innocence.

I shook my head. 'Everyone in that photo,' I said, 'knew why Sonia died.'

His utter stillness lasted until he'd manufactured a smile and a suitably scornful expression.

'Sonia is in that photo. What you said is codswallop.'

'Sonia knew,' I said.

'Are you saying she killed herself?' He looked almost hopeful, as well he might.

'Not really. She didn't intend to die. No one intended to kill her. She died by accident.'

'You know bloody nothing about it.'

I knew too much about it. I didn't want to do any more harm, and I didn't want to get myself killed, but Paul Pannier's death couldn't simply be ignored; and apart from considerations of justice, until his murderer had been caught I would be wearing Delta-cast.

'You all look so young in that photo,' I said. 'Golden girl, golden boys, all smiling, all with bright lives ahead. You were all kids then, like you told me. All playing at living, everything a game.' I named the light-hearted gang in the photo. 'There's you and Sonia, and your younger brother Ridley. There's Paul Pannier, your blacksmith's nephew. There's Roddy Visborough, the son of Sonia's sister, which made Sonia actually his aunt. And there's your jockey, P. Falmouth, known as Pig.' I paused. 'You were the eldest, twenty-two or twenty-three. Ridley, Paul, Roddy and Pig were all eighteen, nineteen or twenty when Sonia died, and she was only twenty-one.'

Jackson Wells said blankly, 'How do you know?'

'Newspaper reports. Doing sums. It hardly matters. What does matter is the immaturity of you all ... and the feeling some people have at that age that youth is eternal, caution is for oldies, and responsibility a dirty word. You went off to York and the others played a game ... and I think this whole gang, except you, were there when she died.'

'No,' he said sharply. 'It wasn't a gang thing. You're meaning gang rape. That didn't happen.'

'I know it didn't. The autopsy made it quite clear that there'd been no intercourse. The newspapers all pointed it out.'

'Well, then.'

I said carefully, 'I think one of those boys in some way throttled her, not meaning to do her harm, and they were all so frightened that they tried to make it look like suicide, by hanging her. And then they just – ran away.'

'No,' Jackson said numbly.

'I think,' I said, 'that to begin with you truly didn't know what had happened. When you talked to the police, when they tried to get you to confess, you could deal blithely with their questions because you knew you weren't guilty. You truly didn't know at that point whether or not she'd hanged herself, though you knew – and said – that it wasn't like her. I think that for quite a while it was a true mystery to you, but what is also evident is that you weren't psychologically pulverised by it. None of the newspaper reports – and I've now read a lot of them – not one says anything about a *distraught* young husband.'

340

'Well . . . I . . .'

'By then,' I suggested, 'you knew she had lovers. Not dream lovers. Real ones. The Gang. All casual. A joke. A game. I'd guess she never thought the sex act more than a passing delight, like ice cream, and there are plenty of people like that, though it's not them but the intense and the jealous that sell the tabloids. When Sonia died, your playing-at-marriage was already over. You told me so. You might have felt shock and regret at her death, but you were young and healthy and blessed with a resilient nature, and your grief was short.'

'You can't possibly know.'

'Am I right so far?'

'Well . . .'

'Tell me what happened afterwards,' I said. 'If you tell me, I promise not to put anything you say in the film. I'll keep the fictional story well away. But it would be better if I knew the truth because, like I told you before, I might reveal your innermost secrets simply by guessing. So tell me . . . and you won't find what you're afraid of on the screen.'

Jackson Wells surveyed his creeper-covered house and his untidy drive and yard, and no doubt thought of his pleasant existence with his second wife and of his pride in Lucy.

'You're right.' He sighed heavily. 'They were all there, and I didn't find out for weeks.'

I let time pass. He had taken the first great step: the rest would follow.

'Weeks afterwards, they began to unravel,' he said at length. 'They'd sworn to each other they would never

341

say a word. Never. But it got too much for them. Pig pissed off to Australia and left me with only Derek Carsington to ride my nags; not that it mattered much, the owners were leaving as if I had the pox, and then Ridley . . .' He paused. 'Ridley got drunk, which wasn't a rarity even in those days, and spilled his guts from every possible orifice. Ridley *disgusts* me but Lucy still thinks he's a laugh, which won't last much longer as he'd have his hand up her skirt by now except that I've told her always to wear jeans. No fun being a girl these days, not like Sonia, she loved skirts down to her ankles and no bra most of the time and a green crewcut – and why the *hell* am I telling you this?'

I thought he might be mourning Sonia twenty-six years too late; but maybe nothing was ever too late in that way.

'She was *fun*,' he said. 'Always good for a laugh.'

'Yes.'

'Ridley told me what they'd done.' The pain of the revelation showed sharply in the sunny face. 'I as good as killed him. I thrashed him. Hit him. Beat him with a riding whip. Anything I could lay my hands on. I kicked him unconscious.'

'That was grief,' I said.

'Anger.'

'Same thing.'

Jackson stared unseeingly at time past.

'I went to see Valentine to ask him what to do,' he said. 'Valentine was like a father to all of us. A better father than any of us had. Valentine loved Sonia like a daughter.'

342

I said nothing. The way Valentine had loved Sonia had had nothing to do with fatherhood.

'What did Valentine say?' I asked.

'He already knew! He said Paul had told him. Paul was in pieces, like Ridley. Paul had told his uncle everything. Valentine said they could all either live with what they'd done or go to the police . . . and he wouldn't choose for them.'

'Did Valentine know that Roddy Visborough had been there?'

'I told him,' Jackson said frankly. 'Sonia was Roddy's *aunt*. And whatever sort of sex orgy they'd all been planning – I mean, of course, it was nothing like that, forget I said it – Roddy couldn't be dragged in, they said it was impossible. She was his aunt!'

'You all knew Valentine well,' I said.

'Yes, of course. His old smithy was only just down the road from my yard. He was always in and out with the horses and we'd drop in there at his house, all of us. Like I said, he was a sort of father. Better than a father. But everything broke up. Training died on me, and Paul left Newmarket and moved away with his mother and father, and Roddy went off to go on the show jumping circuit . . . he'd been wanting to be an assistant race-horse trainer only he hadn't yet got a job, and Pig, like I said, he'd already gone off. And then Valentine was moving too. The old smithy needed impossible roof repairs, so he had it torn down and sold the land for building. I was there one day when he was watching the builders throw the junk of a lifetime down to fill up an old well that he had in the back there, that was a danger

343

to children, and I said things were never going to be the same again. And of course they weren't.'

'But they turned out all right for you.'

'Well, yes, they did.' He couldn't repress his grin for long. 'And Valentine became the Grand Old Man of racing, and Roddy Visborough's won enough silver cups for an avalanche. Ridley's still bumming about and I help him out from time to time, and Paul got married . . .' He stopped uncertainly.

'And Paul got killed,' I said baldly.

He was silent.

'Do you know who killed him?' I asked.

'No.' He stared. 'Do you?'

I didn't answer directly. I said, 'Did any of them tell Valentine – or you – which of the four of them throttled Sonia?'

'It was an accident.'

'Whose accident?'

'She was going to let them put their hands round her neck. She was laughing, they all agreed about that. They were sort of high, but not on drugs.'

'On excitement,' I said.

His blue eyes widened. 'They were all going to . . . that's what broke them up . . . they were all going to have a turn with her, and she wanted it . . . she bet they couldn't all manage it, not like that when the lads had all ridden out for second morning exercise, not before they came back again in an hour, and not with all of the gang watching and cheering each other on, and not in a box on hay as a bed . . . and they were all crazy, and so was she . . . and Pig put his hands round her neck and kissed her . . . and squeezed . . . and she choked . . . he

344

went on too long ... and she went dark ... her skin went dark, and by the time they realised ... they couldn't bring her back ...' His voice died, and after a while he said, 'You're not surprised, are you?'

'I won't put it in the film.'

'I was so angry,' he said. 'How *could* they? How could she let them? It wasn't drugs ...'

'Do you realise,' I asked, 'that it's almost always men who die in that sort of asphyxia?'

'Oh, God ... They wanted to see if it worked the same for women.'

The total foolishness of it blankly silenced us both.

I took a breath. I said, 'The *Drumbeat* said I couldn't solve Sonia's death, and I have. So now I'll find out who killed Paul Pannier.'

He pushed himself away from the gate explosively, shouting back at me, '*How?* Leave it alone. Leave all of us alone. Don't make this pissing film.'

His raised voice brought my judo keeper out of the car like an uncoiling eel. Jackson looked both surprised and alarmed, even as I made soothing hand gestures to calm my minder's reflexes.

I said to Jackson, 'My bodyguard's like a growling dog. Pay no attention. The film company insists on him because others beside you want this movie stopped.'

'That bitch Audrey, Sonia's sneering sister, I bet *she* does, for one.'

'She above all,' I agreed.

Lucy reappeared at the front door and called to her father, 'Dad, Uncle Ridley's on the phone.'

'Tell him I'll come in a minute.'

I said, as she dematerialised, 'Your brother rode on the Heath this morning, for the film. He won't be pleased with me.'

'Why not?'

'He'll tell you.'

'I wish you'd never come,' he said bitterly, and strode off towards his house, his safe haven, his two normal nice women.

I spent the journey back to Newmarket knowing I'd been rash, but not really regretting it. I might think I knew who'd killed Paul, but proving it was different. The police would have to prove it, but I could at least direct their gaze.

I thought of one particular newspaper clipping that I'd found in the file now resting in O'Hara's safe.

Valentine had written it for his occasional gossip column. The paper was dated six weeks after Sonia's death, and didn't mention her.

It said:

Newmarket sources tell me that the jockey P.G. Falmouth (19), familiarly known as 'Pig', has gone to Australia, and is seeking a work-permit to ride there, hoping to settle. Born and raised near the town of his name in Cornwall, Pig Falmouth moved to Newmarket two years ago, where his attractive personality and dedication to winning soon earned him many friends. Undoubtedly he would have prospered in England as his experience increased, but we wish him great success in his new venture overseas.

This item was accompanied by a smiling picture of a fresh-faced, good-looking young man in jockey's helmet and colours; but it was the headline of the section that had been for me the drench of ice-cold understanding.

'Exit,' it said, 'of the Cornish boy.'

# CHAPTER SIXTEEN

We filmed the hanging scene the following morning, Monday, in the cut-and-separated loose box upstairs in the house.

Moncrieff flung a rope over the rafters and swung on it himself to test the set's robustness, but owing to the solid breeze blocks and huge metal angle-iron braces anchoring the new walls to the old floor, there wasn't the slightest quiver in the scenery, to the audible relief of the production department. The straw-covered concrete in the set sections deadened all hollow give-away underfoot echoing noises, those reality-destroying clatterings across the floors of many a supposedly well-built Hollywood 'mansion'.

'Where did you get to after our very brief meeting last night?' Moncrieff enquired. 'Howard was looking all over the hotel for you.'

'Was he?'

'Your car brought you back, you ate a room-service sandwich while we discussed today's work, and then you vanished.'

'Did I? Well, I'm here now.'

'I told Howard you would be sure to be here this morning.'

'Thanks so much.'

Moncrieff grinned. 'Howard was *anxious*.'

'Mm. Did the Yvonne girl get here?'

'Down in make-up,' Moncrieff nodded lasciviously. 'And is she a dish.'

'Long blonde hair?'

He nodded. 'The wig you ordered. Where did you get to, in fact?'

'Around,' I said vaguely. I'd slipped my minder and walked a roundabout way, via the Heath, to the stables, booking in with the guard on the house door and telling him I wanted to work undisturbed and, if anyone asked, to say I wasn't there.

'Sure thing, Mr Lyon,' he promised, used to my vagaries, so I'd gone privately into the downstairs office and phoned Robbie Gill.

'Sorry to bother you on Sunday evening,' I apologised.

'I was only watching the telly. How can I help?'

I said, 'Is Dorothea well enough to be moved tomorrow instead of Tuesday?'

'Did you see her today? What did you think?'

'She's longing to go to the nursing home, she said, and a lot of her toughness of spirit is back. But medically . . . could she go?'

'Hm . . .'

'She's remembered a good deal more about being stabbed,' I said. 'She saw the attacker's face, but she doesn't know him. She also saw the knife that cut her.'

'*God*,' Robbie exclaimed, 'that knuckle-duster thing?'

'No. It was the one that ended in me.'

'*Christ.*'

'So, move her tomorrow if you can. Give her a false name in the nursing home. She's at risk.'

'Bloody hell.'

'She remembers that Paul interrupted the attack on her and effectively saved her life. It's comforting her. She's amazing. She's had three terrible things happen, but she'll be all right, I think.'

'Spunky old woman. Don't worry, I'll shift her.'

'Great.' I paused. 'You remember the police took our fingerprints to match them with the prints in Dorothea's house?'

'Of course I do. They took Dorothea's and her friend Betty's and her husband's and worked out Valentine's from his razor.'

'And,' I said, 'there were others they couldn't match.'

'Sure. Several, I believe. I asked my police friend how their enquiries were progressing. Dead stop, I would guess.'

'Mm,' I said. 'Some of the prints they couldn't match would have been O'Hara's, and some would have been Bill Robinson's.' I explained Bill Robinson. 'And there has to be another – Dorothea's attacker didn't wear gloves.'

Robbie said breathlessly, 'Are you sure?'

'Yes. She said she saw his hand through the knife and he had dirty fingernails.'

'*Jeeze.*'

'When he went to her house he didn't expect her to be there. He didn't plan in advance to attack her. He went to search with Paul for something Valentine might

350

have had and I guess they ripped the place to bits from fury and frustration that they couldn't find anything. Anyway, his prints must be all over the place.'

Robbie, perplexed, asked, 'Whose?'

'I'll tell you when I'm sure.'

'Don't get yourself killed.'

'Of course not,' I said.

Yvonne came upstairs at the required time, and proved to be the regulation issue semi-anorexic Californian waif beloved of moguls, a culture concept a cosmos away from the real laughing reckless Sonia.

Sonia, at her death, had worn, according to the more conservative newspapers, 'a rose-red satin slip', and, according to the titillators, in blackest type, 'A shiny scarlet mini with shoe-string shoulder straps, and black finely-strapped sandals with high rhinestone heels.'

No wonder, I'd thought, that suicide had been in doubt.

Yvonne of the dream lovers was wearing a loose white day-dress described in American fashion circles as a 'float': that is to say, it softly outlined only what it touched. She also wore, at my request, chandelier pearl and gold earrings and a long pearl necklace nearly to her waist.

She looked beautifully ethereal and spoke like Texas.

'This morning,' I said, 'we're shooting the scenes in the right sequence. That's to say, first you enter through that split door.' I pointed. 'There will be back-lighting. When Moncrieff is ready, I'd like you to stand in the doorway and turn your head slowly until we say stop, then if you'll remember that position and stop your head right there for the take, we will get a dramatic effect. You will be entering but looking back. OK? I expect you know your lines.'

She gave me a limpid unintelligent wide-eyed look: great for the film, not so good for technical speed while we made it.

'They say,' she said, 'you get mad if you have to shoot a scene more than three times. That so?'

'Absolutely so.'

'Guess I'd better concentrate then.'

'Honey child,' I said in her accent, 'you do just that and I'll earn you talk-show spots.'

'The Today Show?'

'Nothing's impossible.'

Calculation clouded the peerless violet eyes and she went quietly off to one side and studied her script.

Battle lines drawn, we proceeded. When Moncrieff was satisfied with his light placement we stood Yvonne in the doorway and moved her inch by inch until the light outside the door shone through her flimsy float to reveal her body to the camera inside: too flat-chested for my interest, but of the dreamy otherworld unreality I'd hoped for.

'Jeeze,' Moncrieff murmured, looking through his lens.

I said, 'Can you put a glint on those earrings?'

'You don't ask much!'

He positioned an inkie – an inkie-dinkie, meaning a very small spotlight – to give a glitter below her ears.

'Great,' I said. 'Everyone ready? We'll do a rehearsal. Yvonne, don't forget you're being followed by an earthy man who is parsecs away from a dream lover. You are already laughing at him in your mind, though not openly, as he has power to make Nash's life – that's to say, your film husband's life – very difficult. Just imagine you're being followed by a man you sexually despise but can't be rude to . . .'

Yvonne giggled. 'Who needs to act? I meet them every day.'

'I'll bet you do,' Moncrieff said under his breath.

'Right then,' I said, trying not to laugh, 'we'll do a walk-through. Ready? And . . .' a pause, 'go.'

Yvonne got it dead right at the second rehearsal and then we shot the scene for real twice, both times fit to print.

'You're a doll,' I told her. She liked it, where Silva might have said 'sexism' or 'harassment'. I liked women, all sorts; I'd simply discovered, as I had with male actors, that it saved time to accept, not fight, their views of themselves in the world.

In the scene Yvonne, talking to a man out of shot, had been saying she'd promised to prepare the loose box for a soon-to-arrive horse, a job she'd forgotten earlier but was now doing before joining her husband at a drinks party, to be held somewhere on his way home from the races.

So silly about her white sandals, she said, on the rough flooring. Would he please help her move the stack of hay bales, since – eyelashes fluttering – he was so much *bigger* and *stronger* than little Yvonne?

'I'd lie down and die for her,' Moncrieff observed.

'He more or less did.'

'Such a cynic,' Moncrieff told me, moving lights to a point high among the rafters.

I rehearsed Yvonne through the scene where she

353

realised the man meant business against her wishes. We trekked through surprise, discomfort, revulsion and, dangerously, mockery. I made sure she understood – and could personally relate to – every step.

'Most directors just yell at me,' she said at one point, when she'd fluffed her lines in rehearsal for the fifth or sixth time.

'You look stunning,' I said. 'All you need to do is *act stunned*. Then *laugh* at him. Some men can't bear women laughing at them. He's full of lust for you, and you think he's *funny*. What you're doing is mocking him to madness. He's going to kill you.'

Total comprehension lit her sweet features. 'Get out the strait-jacket,' she said.

'Yvonne, I love you.'

We took a long series of shots of her face, one emotion at a time, and many of negative messages of body language and of the growth of fright, of panic, of desperate disbelief: enough to cut together the ultimate terror of approaching unexpected death.

We gave Yvonne a rest for lunch, while Moncrieff and I filmed the crews slapping heavy ropes sharply over the rafters, and tying frightful knots, to show the violence, the speed, the lack of mercy that I wanted. Naturally each segment took many minutes to stage and get right, but later, in cinemas, with every successful impression strung together – slap, slap, slap – the horror of the hanging would strike the popcorn crunchers silent.

I sat beside Yvonne on a hay bale. I said, 'This afternoon we are going to tie your wrists together with that thick rope now hanging free from that rafter.'

She took it easily.

'The man has by now frightened you so much that you are almost relieved that it is your wrists he has tied.'

She nodded.

'But suddenly he pulls some slack into the rope leading from the rafter, and he loops the slack round your neck, and does it a second time, and pulls the rope tight until your pearls break and slide down inside your dress, and he leans all his weight on the free end of rope swinging from the rafter, and . . . er . . . he lifts you off your feet . . . and hangs you.'

Big-eyed, she said, 'What do I say? Do I beg? It doesn't say this.'

'You don't say anything,' I said. 'You scream.'

'*Scream?*'

'Yes. Can you?'

She opened her mouth and screamed up a hair-raising scale, alarming everyone on set and bringing them galloping to her rescue.

She giggled.

'No one rescued Yvonne,' I said regretfully, 'but no one will forget that scream.'

We filmed a brutal hanging, but short of the dreaded 'NC-17' or '18' certificates. We showed no black asphyxiated face, no terrible bloating. I got Yvonne to wriggle frantically while we suspended her from the wrists, but I filmed her only from the roped neck to her feet that frantically stretched down to the out-of-reach floor. We arranged for one of her white shoes to fall off. We turned the camera onto the shoe while the shadow of her last paroxysms fell across the white-washed walls, and we filmed her broken pearls and one twisted earring in the straw with her bare jerking toes just above.

That done, I let her down and hugged her gratefully; and told her she was marvellous, ravishing, brilliant, moving, could play Ophelia in her sleep and would *undoubtedly* appear on the Today Show (which fortunately, later, she did).

I'd planned from the beginning to shoot the hanging separate from the murderer just in case we needed to make a radical plot re-think at a later stage. By filming murder and murderer apart, one could slot in anyone's face behind the rope. That afternoon, however, I'd invited Cibber to learn the murderer's few lines, and he arrived on set with them only vaguely in his mind, while he expansively smoked a large cigar and exercised his fruity larynx on inappropriate jokes.

He patted Yvonne's bottom. Silly old buffoon, I thought, and set about turning him into a lecherous bull.

I positioned him in the manger section, and gave him an ashtray to prevent his setting fire to the straw. We placed Yvonne so that her white dress, on the edge of the frame and out of focus from being too near the camera, nonetheless established her presence.

Moncrieff, concentrating on the lighting, added a sheet of blue gelatine across one of the spots. He looked through the lens and smiled, and I looked also, and there it was, the actor blinking, bored, waiting for us while we fiddled, but with the probability of his guilt revealed by a trick of light.

Cibber, as first written by Howard, had been a pillar

of the Jockey Club, an upright, unfortunate victim of events. Reluctantly Howard, bowing to the film company, had agreed to write a (mild!) liaison between Cibber's wife (Silva) and Nash Rourke. Equally reluctantly he had agreed that Cibber should persecute Nash for supposedly having hanged his (Nash's) wife Yvonne. Howard still didn't know that it would be Cibber himself that did the hanging. I would have trouble with Howard. Nothing new.

To me, the character of Cibber lay at the centre of the film's dynamic. The Cibber I saw was a man constrained by his position in society; a man forced by upbringing, by wealth, by the expectations of his peers to mould himself into a righteous puritan, difficult to love, incapable of loving. Cibber couldn't in consequence stand ridicule; couldn't bear to know his wife had rejected him for a lover, couldn't have waiters hearing his wife mock him. Cibber expected people to do his bidding. He was, above all, accustomed to deference.

Yet Cibber, underneath, was a raw and passionate man. Cibber hanged Yvonne in a burst of uncontrollable rage when she laughed at his attempt at rape. Appalled, unable to face his own guilt, Cibber persecuted Nash to the point of paranoia and beyond. Cibber, eventually, would be totally destroyed and mentally wrecked when Nash, after many tries, found that the one way to defeat his persecutor was to trap him into earning pitying sneers. Cibber would, at the end, disintegrate into catatonic schizophrenia.

I looked at Cibber the actor and wondered how I could ever dig out of him Cibber the man.

I started that afternoon by blowing away his complacency and telling him he didn't understand lust.

He was indignant. 'Of course I do.'

'The lust I want is uncontrollable. It's out of control, frenetic, frantic, raging, berserk. It's *murderous*.'

'And you expect *me* to show all that?'

'No, I don't. I don't think you can. I don't think you have the technique. I don't think you're a good enough actor.'

Cibber froze. He stubbed out the cigar: and he produced for the camera that day a conception of lust that made one understand and pity his ungovernable compulsion even while he killed for having it mocked.

He would never be a grandee type-cast actor again.

'I hate you,' he said.


Lucy was busy with the boxes when, on returning to the hotel, I opened the door of my sitting-room and went in, leaving it ajar.

She was on her knees among the boxes and looked up as if guiltily, faintly blushing.

'Sorry for the mess,' she said, flustered. 'I didn't think you'd be back before six o'clock, as usual. I'll just tidy this lot away. And shall I close the door?'

'No, leave it open.'

Books and papers were scattered over much of the floor, and many of them, I was interested to see, had come out of boxes she had already investigated and itemised. The folder of clippings about Sonia's death lay open on the table: the harmless clippings only, as Valentine's totally revealing souvenirs were out of sight in O'Hara's safe.

'You had some messages,' Lucy said jerkily, picking up and reading from a notebook. 'Howard Tyler wants to see you. Someone called Ziggy – I think – wanted you to know the horses had come without trouble through Immingham and had reached their stable. Does that sound right? Robbie – he wouldn't give any other name – said to tell you the move had been accomplished. And the film crew you sent to Huntingdon races got some good crowd and bookmaker shots, they said.'

'Thanks.'

I viewed the general clutter on the floor and mildly asked, 'What are you looking for?'

'Oh.' The blush deepened. 'Dad said ... I mean, I hope you won't mind, but my Uncle Ridley came in to see me.'

'In here?'

'Yes. I didn't know he was coming. He just knocked on the door and walked straight in when I opened it. I said you might not be pleased, and he said he didn't care a f—. I mean, he didn't care what you thought.'

'Did your father send him?'

'I don't know if he *sent* him. He told him where I was and what I was doing.'

I hid from her my inner satisfaction. I had rather hoped to stir Ridley to action; hoped Jackson would perform the service.

'What did Ridley want?' I asked.

'He said I wasn't to tell you.' She stood up, her blue eyes troubled. 'I don't like it ... and I don't know what I should do.'

'Perch on something and relax.' I lowered myself stiffly into an armchair and eased my constricted neck. 'Bad back,' I said, explaining it away. 'Nothing to fuss over. What did Ridley want?'

She sat doubtfully sideways on the edge of the table, swinging a free leg. The ubiquitous jeans were accompanied that day by a big blue sweater across which white lambs gambolled: nothing could possibly have been less threatening.

She made up her mind. 'He wanted that photo of the Gang that you showed Dad yesterday. And he wanted anything Valentine had written about Sonia. He emptied out all this stuff. And,' her forehead wrinkled, 'he wanted the *knives*.'

'What knives?'

'He wouldn't tell me. I asked him if he wanted that one a boy asked me to give you at Huntingdon, and he said that one and others.'

'What did you say?'

'I said I hadn't seen any others and anyhow, if you had anything like that you would keep it locked away safely ... and ... well ... he told me to wheedle out of you the combination you're using for the safe here. He tried to open it, you see ...' She stopped miserably. 'I *know* I should never have let him in. What is it all *about*?'

'Cheer up,' I said, 'while I think.'

'Shall I tidy the boxes?'

'Yes, do.'

First catch your sprat . . .

'Lucy,' I said, 'why did you tell me what Ridley wanted?'

She looked uncomfortable. 'Do you mean, why am I not loyal to my uncle?'

'Yes, I do mean that.'

'I didn't like him saying *wheedle*. And . . . well . . . he's not as nice as he used to be.'

I smiled. 'Good. Well, if I tell you the combination number, will you please tell Ridley? And also tell him how clever you were, the way you wheedled it out of me! And tell him you do think I have knives in the safe.'

She hesitated.

I said, 'Give your allegiance one way or the other, but stick to one.'

She said solemnly, 'I give it to you.'

'Then the combination is seven three five two.'

'Now?' she asked, stretching towards the telephone.

'Now.'

She spoke to her uncle. She blushed deeply while she lied, but she would have convinced me, let alone Ridley.

When she put down the telephone I said, 'When I've finished all the work on this film, which will be in another four and a half months, I should think, would you like to spend a holiday in California? Not,' I went on hastily, 'with any conditions or expectations attached. Just a holiday. You could bring your mother, if you like. I thought you might find it interesting, that's all.'

Her uncertainty over this suggestion was endearing.

361

I was everything she'd been taught to fear, a young healthy male in a position of power, out for any conquest he could make.

'I won't try to seduce you,' I promised lightly. But I might end by marrying her, I thought unexpectedly, when she was older. I'd been forever bombarded by actresses. An Oxfordshire farmer's freckled-nosed blue-eyed daughter who played the piano and lapsed occasionally into sixteen-year-old awkwardness seemed in contrast an unrealistic and unlikely future.

There was no thunderbolt: just an insidious hungry delight that never went away.

Her first response was abrupt and typical. 'I can't afford it.'

'Never mind, then.'

'But ... er ... yes.'

'Lucy!'

The blush persisted. 'You'll turn out to be a frog.'

'Kermit's not bad,' I said, assessingly.

She giggled. 'What do you want me to do with the boxes?'

Her work on the boxes had been originally my pathway to her father. I might not need her to work on them any longer, but I'd grown to like finding her here in my rooms.

'I hope you'll go on with the cataloguing tomorrow,' I said.

'All right.'

'But this evening I have to work on the film ... er, alone.'

She seemed slightly disappointed but mostly relieved. A daring step forward ... half a cautious step back. But we would get there one day, I thought, and was content and even reassured by the wait.

We left through the still slightly open doorway and I walked down the passage a little way before waving her down the stairs; and, returning, I stopped to talk to my bodyguard whom O'Hara, for the company, had by now installed in the room opposite my own.

My bodyguard, half Asian, had straight black hair, black shiny eyes and no visible feelings. He might be young, agile, well-trained and fast on his feet, but he was also unimaginative and hadn't saved me from the Armadillo.

When I pushed open his unlocked door to reveal him sitting wide awake in an upright chair facing me, he said at once, 'Your door has all the time been open, Mr Lyon.'

I nodded. I'd arranged with him that if he saw my door closed he was to use my key and enter my rooms immediately. I couldn't think of a clearer or more simple demand for help.

'Have you eaten?' I asked.

'Yes, Mr Lyon.'

I tried a smile. No response.

'Don't go to sleep,' I said tamely.

'No, Mr Lyon.'

O'Hara must have dug him up from central casting, I thought. Bad choice.

I retreated into my sitting-room, left the door six inches open, drank a small amount of brandy and answered a telephone call from Howard.

He was predictably raging.

'Cibber told me you've made him the murderer! It's

impossible! You can't do it. I won't allow it! What will the Visboroughs say?'

I pointed out that we could slot in a different murderer, if we wanted to.

'Cibber says you tore him to *shreds*.'

'Cibber gave the performance of his life,' I contradicted: and indeed, of the film's eventual four Oscar nominations, Cibber won the award for Best Supporting Actor – graciously forgiving me about a year later.

I promised Howard, 'We'll hold a full script conference tomorrow morning. You, me, Nash and Moncrieff.'

'I want you to stop the film!'

'I don't have that authority.'

'What if you're *dead*?' he demanded.

I said after a moment, 'The company will finish the movie with another director. Killing me, believe me, Howard, would give this film massive publicity, but it would not stop it.'

'It's not *fair*,' he said, as if he'd learned nothing, and I said, 'See you in the morning,' and disconnected in despair.

The safe in my sitting-room, as in O'Hara's, was out of casual sight in a fitment that housed a large TV set above and a mini-bar as well as the safe below. The mini-bar held small quantities of drinks for needy travellers, spirits, wine, champagne and beer, also chocolate and nuts. The safe – my safe – held nothing. I programmed it to open at seven three five two, entrusted 'The Gang' photo into its safekeeping, and closed its door.

364

I sat then in the armchair in my bedroom and waited for a long time, and thought about the obligations of the confessional, and about how totally, or how little, I myself was bound by Valentine's dying and frantic admissions.

I felt the weight of the obligation of priesthood that so many priests themselves took lightly, knowing that their role absolved them from any dire responsibility, even while they dispensed regular indulgences. I had had no right to hear Valentine's confession nor to pardon his sins, and I had done both. I'd absolved him. '*In nomine Patris . . . ego te absolvo.*'

I could not evade feeling an absolute obligation to the spirit of those words. I should not – and could not – save myself with the knowledge he'd entrusted to me as a priest when he was dying. On the other hand, I could in good conscience use what he'd left me in his will.

I hadn't come across, in his books and papers, any one single revelation that could have been found by ransacking his house. The pieces had been there, but obscured and devious. I'd sorted those out a good deal by luck. I wished there were a more conclusive artifact than 'The Gang' photo with which to bait the safe, but I'd come to the conclusion that there wasn't one. Valentine hadn't written down his ultimate sin; he'd confessed it in his last lucid breaths but he had never meant it to live after him. He hadn't left any exact concrete record of his twenty-six-year-old secret.

Two and a half hours after I'd talked to Howard, my visitor arrived. He came to my sitting-room door calling my name, and when I didn't at first reply he walked in boldly and closed the door behind him. I heard it latch. I heard him open the fitment and press the buttons to open the safe.

I ambled to my bedroom door and greeted him.

'Hello, Roddy.'

He was dressed in blazer, shirt and tie. He looked a pillar of show-jumping rectitude; and he held 'The Gang' photo.

'Looking for something?' I asked.

'Er . . .' Roddy Visborough said civilly, 'yes, actually. Bit of an imposition, I'm afraid, but one of the children I teach has begged me to get Nash Rourke's autograph. Howard swears you'll ask him for it.'

He laid the photo on the table and came towards me holding out an autograph album and a pen.

It was so very unexpected that I forgot Professor Derry's warning – *anything* he possesses may hide a knife – and I let him get too close.

He dropped the autograph book at my feet, and when I automatically looked down at it, he pulled his gold-coloured pen apart with a movement too fast for me to follow, and lunged at me with it.

The revealed stiletto point went straight through my jersey and shirt and hit solid polymer over my heart.

Himself flummoxed, disbelieving, Roddy dropped the pen and reached for his tie, and with a tug produced from under it a much larger knife, fearsomely lethal, which I later saw to be a triangular blade like a flat trowel fixed to a bar which led between his fingers to a grip within his hand.

At the time I saw only the triangular blade that seemed to grow like an integral part of his fist, the wide end across his knuckles, the point protruding five or more inches ahead.

He slashed at my throat instantly and found Robbie's handiwork foiling him there also, and with one quick movement flicked the blade higher so that it cut my chin and ran sharply up across my cheek to above my ear.

I hadn't meant to have to fight him. I wasn't good at it. And how could anyone fight an opponent so appallingly armed, when one had no defence except fists?

He meant to kill me. I saw it in his face. He was going to get blood on his elegant clothes. One thinks such stupid *non sequiturs* at moments of maximum peril. He worked out that I wore a body protector from neck to waist and aimed at more vulnerable areas and punched his awful triangular blade into my left arm several times as I tried to shield my eyes from damage while unsuccessfully trying to get behind him to put my right arm round his throat.

I tried to evade him. We circled the bedroom. He sought to keep himself between me and the door while he killed me.

There were scarlet splatters all over the place; a scarlet river down my left hand. I yelled with what breath I could muster for my damned bodyguard to come to my rescue and nothing happened except that I began to believe that whatever happened to Roddy afterwards I wouldn't be there to care.

I tugged the bedspread off the bed and threw it at him, and by good fortune it landed over his right hand. I sprang at him. I rolled against him, wrapping his right arm closely. I overbalanced him: I put one leg behind his and levered him backwards off his feet, and scrambled with him on the floor, enveloping him ever more deeply in the bedspread until he was cocooned in it, until I lay over him bleeding while he tried to heave me off.

I don't know what would eventually have happened, but at that moment my bodyguard finally showed up.

He arrived in the bedroom doorway, saying enquiringly, 'Mr Lyon?'

I was past answering him sensibly. I said, 'Fetch someone.' Hardly a Nash Rourke-hero sort of speech.

He took me literally, anyway. I vaguely heard him talking on the sitting-room telephone and soon my rooms seemed full of people. Moncrieff, Nash himself, large men from the Bedford Lodge kitchen staff who sat on the wriggling bedspread, and eventually people saying they were policemen and paramedics and so on.

I apologised to the hotel manager for the blood. Oh, well.

'Where the hell were you?' I asked my bodyguard. 'Didn't you see that my door was shut?'

'Yes, Mr Lyon.'

'Well then?'

'But, Mr Lyon,' he said in righteous self-justification, 'sometimes I have to go to the bathroom.'

# CHAPTER SEVENTEEN

Early on Thursday morning I sat on a windy sand dune waiting for the sun to rise over Happisburgh beach.

O'Hara, back in a panic from LA, sat shivering beside me. About forty people, the various location crews, came and went from the vehicles parked close behind the dunes, and out on the wet expanse of firm sand left clean and unmarked by the ebbing tide, Moncrieff worked the cameras, lights and gantry that had been taken out there bolted onto a caterpillar-tracked orange beach-cleaning monster that could bull-doze wrecks if need be.

Far off to the left, Ziggy waited with the Viking horses. Between him and us, Ed commanded a second camera crew, one that would give us side-on shots.

We had held a rehearsal on the ebb tide the evening before and knew from the churned-up state of the sand afterwards that we needed to get the first shoot right. Ziggy was confident, Moncrieff was confident, O'Hara was confident: I fidgeted.

We needed a decent sunrise. We could fudge together an impression by using the blazing shots of the sky from the previous week; we could shine lights to get gleams in the horses' eyes, but we needed luck and the real thing to get the effect I truly wanted.

I thought over the events of the past few days. There had been a micro-surgeon in the Cambridge hospital who'd sewn up my face with a hundred tiny black stitches that at present looked as if a millipede was climbing from my chin to my hairline, but which he swore would leave hardly a scar. The gouges in my left arm had given him and me more trouble, but at least they were out of sight. He expected everything to be healed in a week.

Robbie Gill visited the hospital briefly early on Tuesday morning, taking away with him the Delta-cast jacket that had puzzled the night-nursing staff the evening before. He didn't explain why I'd been wearing it beyond. 'An experiment in porosity – interesting.' He also told me he'd mentioned to his police colleague that Dorothea could now identify her attacker, and that as two knife nuts suddenly active in Newmarket were unlikely, why didn't they try her with a photo?

I'd spent Tuesday afternoon talking to policemen, and by then (during Monday night) I'd decided what to say and what not.

I heard later that they had already searched Roddy Visborough's cottage in Leicestershire and had found it packed with hidden unusual knives. They asked why I thought Roddy had attacked me.

'He wanted the film stopped. He believes it harms his family's reputation.'

They thought it not a good enough reason for attempted murder and, sighing at the vagaries of the world, I agreed with them. Did I know of any other reason? Sorry, no.

Roddy Visborough, I was certain, would give them no other reason. Roddy Visborough would not say, 'I was afraid Thomas Lyon would find out that I connived at a fake hanging of my aunt to cover up a sex orgy.'

Roddy, 'the' show jumper, had had too much to lose. Roddy, Paul and Ridley must all have been aghast when their buried crime started coming back to haunt them. They'd tried to frighten me off first with threats, and when those hadn't worked, with terminal action.

With knives.

The police asked if I knew that Mr Visborough's fingerprints had been found all over Mrs Pannier's house, along with my own? How *extraordinary*! I said; I'd never seen Mr Visborough in her house.

They said that, acting on information, they had that morning interviewed Mrs Pannier who had identified a police photograph of Mr Visborough as being the man who had attacked her.

'*Amazing*,' I said.

They asked if I knew why Mrs Pannier had been attacked by Mr Visborough. No, I didn't.

What connection was there between her and me?

'I used to read to her blind brother,' I said. 'He died of cancer . . .'

They knew.

They wondered if the knife I'd found on the Heath, that was now in their possession, had anything to do with what had happened to me.

'We all believed it was an attempt to get the film abandoned,' I said. 'That's all.'

371

I believed also, though I didn't say so, that it was Roddy who had given Ridley the trench knife and told him to frighten off Nash and, through him, the film.

I believed Roddy had coerced Paul to ransack Dorothea's house with him, both of them looking for any give-away account Valentine might have left of Sonia's death.

Roddy had been the strongest of the three of them, and the most afraid.

Prompted by Lucy, Ridley had obligingly passed on to Roddy the combination of my safe, and had told him that I knew far too much.

Roddy, as I'd hoped, had revealed himself and his involvement, the mackerel coming to the sprat. I had lured him to come, had hoped he might bring with him another esoteric knife: I hadn't meant to get myself so cut.

The police went away as if dissatisfied, but they were sure at the very least of two convictions for grievous bodily harm, and if, with all the modern available detection techniques, they couldn't prove Roddy Visborough had killed Paul Pannier, too bad. As for motive, they might conclude Paul had threatened in remorse to give Roddy away to the police for attacking Dorothea: near enough for belief. Near enough, anyway, for Dorothea to believe it, and be comforted.

On Wednesday morning I discharged myself from the hospital and returned to Newmarket to be confronted by a furious Howard and an extremely upset Alison Visborough.

'I *told* you you shouldn't have made changes to my book,' Howard raged. 'Now see what you've done! Roddy is going to *prison*.'

Alison looked in disbelief at the long millipede track up my face. 'Rodbury wouldn't have done that!'

'Rodbury did,' I said dryly. 'Did he always have knives?'

She hesitated. She was fair minded under the outrage. 'I suppose ... perhaps ... he was secretive ...'

'And he wouldn't let you join in his games.'

She said 'Oh,' blankly, and began re-evaluating her brother's psyche.

Sitting on the Norfolk dunes I thought of her father, Rupert, and of his aborted political career. I thought it almost certain that the scandal that had caused his retreat was not that his sister-in-law had been mysteriously hanged, but that he'd learned – perhaps from Valentine or even from Jackson Wells – that his own son had been present at the mid-morning cover-up hanging, having intended to have sexual relations with his aunt. Rupert, upright man, had given his son show jumpers with which to redeem himself, but had stopped short of loving forgiveness and had left his own house to his daughter. Poor Rupert Visborough ... he hadn't deserved to become Cibber, but at least he would never know.

O'Hara, huddling into his padded ex-army jacket, said that while I'd been out on the beach rehearsing the previous evening, he'd got the projectionist to show him the rushes of the hanging.

'What sort of certificate did we earn?' I asked. 'PG-13? That's what we ideally want.'

'Depends on the cutting. What gave you that view of her death?'

'Howard holds forth on the catharsis of the primal scream.'

'Shit, Thomas. That death wasn't any sort of therapy. That hanging had gut-churning vigour.'

'Good.'

O'Hara blew on his fingers. 'I hope these damn horses are worth this frigging cold.'

The eastern sky turned from black to grey. I picked up the walkie-talkie and spoke again to Ed and also to Ziggy. Everything was ready. I wasn't to worry. All would be well.

I thought of Valentine's powerful muscles, years ago.

I had kept faith with his confession. No one through me would ever learn his truth.

*I left the knife with Derry. . . .*

Valentine's strength had fashioned for his great friend Professor Derry a unique knife to add to his collection: a steel knife with a spear head and a candy-twisted handle, unlike any ordinary weapon.

*I killed the Cornish boy. . . .*

One of the Gang, perhaps even Pig Falmouth himself, had told Valentine how Sonia had died, and in an overwhelming, towering tidal wave of anger and grief and guilt he had snatched up the spear and plunged it deep into the jockey's body.

It had to have happened in some way like that. Valentine had loved Sonia in secret. He'd learned about paraphilia to solve Derry's impotence problem, and he'd shown the encyclopaedia article to Pig, no doubt light-heartedly – 'I say, Pig, just look at this!' – and Pig had told his friends.

*I destroyed all their lives . . .* I guessed he might have meant he ruined their lives by giving them the idea of

374

their fatal game. They had destroyed their own lives, but guilt could lack logic.

Valentine had killed Pig Falmouth in the wild, uncontainable sort of anger and grief that had caused Jackson Wells to beat his brother Ridley near to death: and Valentine himself had then written the gossip column that reported Pig's departure to work in Australia, that everyone had believed.

Pig Falmouth, I guessed, had lain for twenty-six years at the bottom of the well that Valentine had had a firm of builders fill in to make it safe for children. Valentine had stood with Jackson Wells and watched them throw the junk of years down the hole to obliterate the carefree boy who had kissed and killed his golden girl.

Valentine had at the end unloaded his soul's burden of murder.

I laid them both to rest.


The sky's amorphous grey was slowly suffused with a dull soft crimson in the east.

Moncrieff was holding a light meter to measure the changing intensity in minutes with the dedication that won him *Unstable Times'* second Oscar, for Cinematography. Howard, nominated for Best Adapted Screenplay, lost the award by inches, as did our fourth nominee, the Art Director. O'Hara and the moguls were happy, however, and I got allotted a big-budget epic with mega-star Nash.

Over Happisburgh beach the crimson in the sky blossomed to scarlet and coloured the waves pink.

There were fewer cloud streaks than the week before, fewer brilliant gold halos against the vermilion. We would merge the two sunrises, I thought.

Away to our right, far behind Moncrieff and his cameras, the trainer of the Viking horses had spread out on the sands great bowls of horse-nuts: the wild horses would race, on our signal, to reach their breakfast, as they had been trained.

Moncrieff, raising meters high, greeted the dawn like an ancient prophet. When he lowered his arms, I was to cue the action.

The blinding sun swam upwards. Moncrieff's arms swept down.

I said, 'Action, Ed,' and 'Now, Ziggy,' into my walkie-talkie, and away down the beach the horses began their run.

We had dressed Ziggy in an all-over body suit of grey Lycra, to which, ballet trained, he'd adapted instantly. Over the body suit he wore a floating shapeless gown of translucent white silk voile, and on his head the light blonde wig. His own dark features had been transformed to blondeness by the make-up department, and he was riding, as he'd promised, without shoes, saddle or reins.

The horses accelerated, bursting into the wide silence of the deserted seascape with the thud and suction of their galloping hooves.

Ziggy knelt on his horse's withers, his head forward above the horse's straining neck. Gown and hair streamed out, gathering to themselves all the light, the grey-clad man inside seeming almost invisible, a misty shadow.

Moncrieff ran two head-on cameras, one set for a speed of thirty-six frames, a second, slow motion.

The rising sun shone in the horses' eyes. Light gleamed on the flying manes. The heads of the wild herd plunged forward in the urgency of racing, in the untamed compulsion to be *first*, to lead the pack. The herd parted and swept round Moncrieff, the plunging bodies close, the Viking heads wild and free.

Ziggy rode between Moncrieff and the maximum brilliance of light. On the finished film it looked as if the flying figure had evaporated there, had been absorbed and assimilated in luminescence; had become a part of the sun.

'Jesus *Christ*,' O'Hara said, when he saw it.

I cut some of the shots of the hanging scene into the wild horse sequences for the ending of the film.

Yvonne's scream dissolved into the high thin forlorn cry of a wheeling seagull.

The young woman of the fantasy lovers dreamed she was riding the wild horses as she swung to her death.

# 10lb PENALTY

With thanks to my grandson
MATTHEW FRANCIS
aged eighteen

and to

Weatherbys
and
No. 10 Downing Street

# CHAPTER ONE

Glue-sniffing jockeys don't win the Derby.

I'd never sniffed glue in my life.

All the same, I stood before the man whose horses I rode and listened to him telling me he had no further use for my services. He sat behind his large antique paper-covered desk fidgeting with his clean fingernails. His hands were a yellowish white, very smooth.

'I have it on good authority,' he said.

'But I don't!' I protested in bewilderment. 'I've never sniffed glue or anything else. Certainly not cocaine. I've never even smoked pot. It's not true.'

He looked at me coldly with the knowing eyes of a rich, powerful, assured and physically bulky man who had inherited a good brain and a chunk of merchant bank, and trained racehorses prestigiously out of obsession.

I was not yet eighteen at that point and, I now know, immature for my age, though of course I wasn't aware of it at the time. I felt helpless, though, in the face of his inaccurate certainty, and had no idea how to deal with it.

'Sir Vivian...' I began with desperation, but he effortlessly cut me off with his heavier authoritative voice.

'You can clear off at once, Benedict,' he said. 'I'll not have my stable contaminated by rumours of a drug-taking jockey, even if he is an amateur and not much good.' He saw me flinch but went on relentlessly. 'You'll never be a top race rider. You're too big, for one thing, or at least you will be in a year or two and, frankly, you look clumsy on a horse. All arms and legs. In your hands, the most collected jumper turns in a sprawling performance. With that and an unsatisfactory reputation... well, I no longer want you associated with my stable.'

I stared at him numbly, hurt more deeply by his fairly brutal assessment of my lack of riding ability, which could perhaps be substantiated, rather than by the accusations of drug-taking, which couldn't.

Around me the familiar walls of his stable office seemed to recede, leaving me isolated with a thumping heart and no feeling below the ankles. All the framed photographs of past winners, all the bookshelves and the olive-green wallpaper faded away. I saw only the stony faces spelling out the effective end of my long-held dream of winning all races from the Grand National down.

I expect seventeen is a better age than most to be

chopped off at the ambitious knees. It just didn't feel like it at that moment of the slice of the axe.

'Outside that window,' said Sir Vivian Durridge, pointing, 'a car is waiting for you. The driver says he has a message for you. He's been waiting a good hour or more, while you've been out at riding exercise.'

I followed the direction of his finger, and saw, some way across the raked gravel of the imposing entrance driveway to his porticoed domain, a large black car inhabited solely by a chauffeur in a peaked cap.

'Who is it?' I asked blankly.

Vivian Durridge either didn't know or wasn't telling. He said merely, 'On your way out, you can ask him.'

'But, sir . . .' I began again, and dried to fresh silence in the continuing negation of his distrust.

'I advise you to clean up your act,' he said, making a gesture that directed me to leave. 'And now, I have work to do.'

He looked steadfastly down at his desk and ignored me, and after a few seconds I walked unsteadily over to the high polished door with its gilded knob and let myself out.

It was unfair. I had not cried much in my life but I felt weak then and near to weeping. No one before had pitilessly accused me of something I hadn't done. No one had so ruthlessly despised my riding. I still had a thin skin.

No other good trainer would let me into his stable if Vivian Durridge had kicked me out of his.

In a mist of bewildered misery I crossed the wide Durridge entrance hall, made my way through the heavy front door and crunched across the gravel to where the car and chauffeur waited.

I knew neither of them. The August morning sun gleamed on black spotless bodywork, and the chauffeur with the shiny black peak to his cap let down the window beside him and stretched out a black uniformed arm, silently offering me a white unaddressed envelope.

I took it. The flap was only lightly glued. I peeled it open, drew out a single white card from inside, and read the brief message.

'*Get in the car.*'

Underneath an afterthought had been added.

'*Please.*'

I looked back towards the big house from which I'd been so roughly banned and saw Vivian Durridge standing by his window, watching me. He made no movement: no reconsidering action, no farewell.

I understood none of it.

The handwriting on the card was my father's.


I sat on the back seat of the car for almost an hour while the chauffeur drove at a slow pace through

Sussex, south of London, approaching finally the seaside spread of Brighton.

He would answer none of my questions except to say that he was following instructions, and after a while I stopped asking. Short of jumping out and running free at any of the few traffic-light stops, it seemed I was going to go wherever my father had ordained, and as I had no fear of him I would, from long conditioned habit, do what he asked.

I thought chiefly – and in a mixture of rage and unhappiness – of the scene in Durridge's study, his words circling endlessly in memory and not getting more bearable as time went by.

The black car drifted past Regency town houses and open-fronted souvenir shops, past old grandeur and new-world commercialism, and sighed to a stop on the sea front outside the main door of a large hotel of ancient French architectural pedigree with bright beach towels drying on its decorative wrought-iron balconies.

Porters appeared solicitously. The chauffeur climbed out of his seat and ceremoniously opened the door beside me and, thus prompted, I stood up into the sea air, hearing gulls crying and voices in the distance calling on the wet ebb-tide strand, smelling the salt on the wind and unexpectedly feeling the lift of spirits of the sandcastle holidays of childhood.

The chauffeur made me a small sketch of a bow and pointed at the hotel's main door, and then, still without explaining, he returned to his driving seat and at a convenient moment inserted himself into the flow of traffic and smoothly slid away.

'Luggage, sir?' one of the porters suggested. He was barely older than myself.

I shook my head. For luggage I wore the clothes suitable for first-lot August morning exercise with the Durridge string: jodhpurs, jodhpur boots, short-sleeved sports shirt and harlequin-printed lightweight zipped jacket (unzipped). I carried by its chin-strap my shiny blue helmet. With a conscious effort I walked these inappropriate garments into the grand hotel, but I needn't have worried: the once-formal lobby buzzed like a beehive with people looking normal in cut-off shorts, flip-flop sandals and message-laden T-shirts. The composed woman at the reception desk gave my riding clothes an incurious but definite assessment like a click on an identification parade and answered my slightly hoarse enquiry.

'Mr George Juliard?' she repeated. 'Who shall I say is asking for him?'

'His son.'

She picked up a telephone receiver, pressed buttons, spoke, listened, gave me the news.

'Please go up. Room four-twelve. The lift is to your left.'

My father was standing in an open doorway as I walked down a passage to locate four-twelve. I stopped as I approached him and watched him inspect me, as he customarily did, from my dark curly hair (impervious to straightening by water), to my brown eyes, thin face, lean frame, five foot eleven (or thereabouts) of long legs to unpolished boots: not in any way an impressive experience for an ambitious parent.

'Ben,' he said. He breathed down his nose as if accepting a burden. 'Come in.'

He tried hard always to be a good father, but gave no weight to my infrequent assurances that he succeeded. I was a child he hadn't wanted, the accidental consequence of his teenage infatuation with a woman biologically just old enough to be his own mother. On the day I went to Brighton I was almost as old as he had been when he fathered me.

Over the years I'd gleaned the details. There had been a hullabaloo in both extended families when they were told of the pregnancy, an even worse fuss (product of the times) when my mother refused an abortion, and a frosty turning of backs at the hasty (and happy) wedding.

The marriage-day photograph was the only record I had of my mother, who ironically died of pre-eclampsia at my birth, leaving her very young husband literally holding the baby with his envisaged bright future in ruins, so it was said.

George Juliard, however, who wasn't considered bright for nothing, promptly rearranged his whole life, jettisoning the intended Oxford degree and career in law, persuading his dead wife's sister to add me to her already large family of four sons, and setting forth into the City to learn how to make money. He had paid from the beginning for my keep and later for my education and had further fulfilled his duties by turning up at parent–teacher meetings and punctiliously sending me cards and gifts at Christmas and birthdays. A year ago for my birthday he'd given me an air ticket to America so that I could spend the summer holidays on a horse farm in Virginia owned by the family of a school friend. Many fathers had done less.

I followed him into four-twelve and found without surprise that I was in the sitting-room of a suite directly facing the sea, the English Channel stretching blue-grey to the horizon. When George Juliard had set out with the goal of making money, he had spectacularly hit his target.

'Have you had breakfast?' he asked.

'I'm not hungry.'

He ignored the untruth. 'What did Vivian Durridge say to you?'

'He sacked me.'

'Yes, but what did he *say*?'

'He said I couldn't ride and that I sniffed glue and also cocaine.'

My father stared. 'He said *what*?'

'He said what you asked him to, didn't he? He said he had it on good authority that I took drugs.'

'Did you ask him who his "good authority" was?'

'No.' I hadn't thought of it until too late, in the car.

'You've a lot to learn,' my father said.

'It was no coincidence that you sent a car to wait for me.'

He smiled marginally, light gleaming in his eyes. He was taller than I, with wider shoulders, and in many ways inhabited an intenser, more powerful version of the body I had been growing into during the past five years. His hair was darker than mine, and curlier, a close rug on his Grecian-like head. The firmness in his face, now that he was approaching his late thirties, had already been apparent in his wedding photograph, when the gap in age had showed not at all, where the bridegroom had looked the dominant partner and the bride, smiling in her blue silk dress outside the registry office, had shone with youthful beauty.

'Why did you do it?' I asked, trying to sound more adult than bitter, and not managing it.

'Do what?'

'Get me kicked out.'

'Ah.'

He walked over to a pair of glass doors leading to a balcony and opened them, letting in the vivid coastal air and the high voices from the beach. He stood there silently for a while, breathing deeply, and then, as if making up his mind, he closed the windows purposefully and turned towards me.

'I have a proposition for you,' he said.

'What proposition?'

'It will take a good while to explain.' He lifted a telephone receiver and told the room service that whether or not breakfast had been officially over an hour ago, they were to send up immediately a tray of cereal, milk, hot toast, grilled bacon with tomatoes and mushrooms, an apple, a banana and a pot of tea. 'And don't argue,' he said to me, disconnecting, 'you look as if you haven't eaten for a week.'

I said, 'Did *you* tell Sir Vivian that I take drugs?'

'No, I didn't. Do you?'

'No.'

We looked at each other, virtual strangers though as closely tied as genetically possible. I had lived according to his edicts, had been to his choice of schools, had learned to ride, to ski and to shoot because he had distantly funded my preference for those pursuits, and I had not received tickets for Beyreuth, Covent Garden or La Scala because he didn't enthuse over time spent that way.

I was his product, as most teenage sons were of their fathers. I was also aware of his strict sense of honour, his clear vision of right and wrong and his insistence that shameful acts be acknowledged and paid for, not lied about and covered up. He was, as my four older cousins/brothers told me pityingly, a hard act to follow.

'Sit down,' he said.

The room was warm. I took off my jazzy zipped

jacket and laid it on the floor with my helmet and sat in a light armchair, where he pointed.

'I have been selected,' he said, 'as a candidate in the Hoopwestern by-election, in place of the sitting MP who has died.'

'Er . . .' I blinked, not quickly taking it in.

'Did you hear what I said?'

'Do you mean . . . you are running for office?'

'Your American friend Chuck would say I'm running for office, but as this is England, I am standing for Parliament.'

I didn't know what I should say. *Great? How awful? Why?* I said blunderingly, 'Will you get in?'

'It's a marginal seat. A toss up.'

I looked vaguely round the impersonal room. He waited with a shade of impatience.

'What is the proposition?' I asked.

'Well, now . . .' Somewhere within him he relaxed. 'Vivian Durridge treated you harshly.'

'Yes, he did.'

'Accusing you of taking drugs . . . That was his own invention.'

'But what *for*?' I asked, bewildered. 'If he didn't want me around, why didn't he just say so?'

'He told me you would never be more than an average-standard amateur. Never a top professional jockey. What you were doing was a waste of time.'

I didn't want to believe it. I couldn't face believing it. I protested vehemently, 'But I enjoy it.'

11

'Yes, and if you look honestly inside yourself, you'll admit that a pleasant waste of time isn't enough for you at this stage.'

'I'm not you,' I said. 'I don't have your . . . your . . .'

'Drive?' he suggested.

I thought it over weakly, and nodded.

'I am satisfied, though,' he said, 'that you have sufficient intelligence and . . . well . . . *courage* . . . for what I have in mind.'

If he intended to flatter me, of course he succeeded. Few young boys could throw overboard such an assessment.

'Father – ' I began.

'I thought we agreed you should call me Dad.'

He had insisted at parent-teacher-schoolboy meetings I should refer to him as 'Dad', and I had done so, but in my mind he was always Father, my formal and controlling authority.

'What do you want me to do?' I said.

He still wouldn't answer straightaway. He looked absent-mindedly out of the window and at my jacket on the floor. He fiddled with his fingers in a way that reminded me of Sir Vivian, and finally he said, 'I want you to take up the place you've been offered at Exeter University.'

'Oh.' I tried not to appear either astonished or annoyed, though I felt both. He went on, however, as if I'd launched into a long audible harangue.

'You've promised yourself a gap year, is that it?'

A gap year, so-called, was the currently fashionable pause between school and university, much praised and prized in terms of growing up in worldly experience before graduating academically. A lot to be said for it . . . little against.

'You agreed I should have a gap year,' I protested.

'I didn't prohibit it. That's different.'

'But . . . *can* you prohibit it? And why do you want to?'

'Until you are eighteen I can legally do almost anything that's for your own good or, rather, that I consider is for your own good. You're no fool, Ben. You know that's a fact. For the next three weeks, until your birthday on August thirty-first, I am still in charge of your life.'

I did know it. I also knew that though by right I would receive basic university tuition fees from the state, I would not qualify for living expenses or other grants because of my father's wealth. Working one's way through college, although just possible in some countries, was hardly an option in Britain. Realistically, if my father wouldn't pay for my keep, I wouldn't be going to university, whether Exeter or anywhere else.

I said neutrally, 'When I asked you, ages ago, you said you thought a gap year was a good idea.'

'I didn't know that you intended your gap year to be spent on a racecourse.'

'It's a growing-up experience!'

'It's a minefield of moral traps.'

13

'You don't trust me!' Even I could hear the out-raged self-regard in my voice. Too near a whine. I said more frostily, 'Because of your example, I would keep out of trouble.'

'No bribes, do you mean?' He was unimpressed by my own shot at flattery. 'You'd throw no races? Everyone would believe in your incorruptibility? Is that it? What about a rumour that you take drugs? Rumours destroy reputations quicker than truth.'

I was silenced. An unproven accusation had that morning rent apart my comfortable illusion that inno-cence could shield one from defamation. My father would no doubt categorise the revelation as 'growing up'.

A knock on the door punctuated my bitter thoughts with the arrival of a breakfast designed to give me a practically guilt-free release from chronic hunger. The necessity of keeping down to a low racing weight had occasionally made me giddy from deprivation. Even as I fell on the food ravenously I marvelled at my father's understanding of what I would actually eat and what I would reject.

'While you eat, you can listen,' he said. 'If you were going to be the world's greatest steeplechase jockey, I wouldn't ask . . . what I'm going to ask of you. If you were going to be, say, Isaac Newton, or Mozart, or some other genius, it would be pointless to ask that you should give it up. And I'm not asking you to give up riding altogether, just to give up trying to make it your life.'

Cornflakes and milk were wonderful.

'I have a suspicion,' he said, 'that you intended your gap year to go on for ever.'

I paused in mid munch. Couldn't deny he was right.

'So go to Exeter, Ben. Do your growing up *there*. I don't expect you to get a First. A Second would be fine; a Third is OK, though I guess you'll manage good results, as you always have done, in spite of the disadvantage of your birth date.'

I zoomed through the bacon, tomatoes and mushrooms and accompanied them with toast. Because of the rigid education system that graded schoolchildren by age and not ability, and because I'd been born on the last day of the age-grading year (September 1$^{st}$ would have given me an extra twelve months), I had always been the youngest in the class, always faced with the task of keeping up. A gap year would have levelled things nicely. And he was telling me, of course, that he understood all that, and was forgiving a poor outcome in the degree stakes before I'd even started.

'Before Exeter,' he said, 'I'd like you to work for *me*. I'd like you to come with me to Hoopwestern and help me get elected.'

I stared at him, chewing slowly but no longer tasting the mouthful.

'But,' I said, swallowing, 'I don't know anything about politics.'

'You don't have to. I don't want you to make speeches or any policy statements. I just want you to be with me, to be part of my scene.'

'I don't . . . I mean,' I more or less stuttered, 'I don't understand what I could do.'

'Eat your apple,' he said calmly, 'and I'll explain.'

He sat in one of the armchairs and crossed his legs with deliberation, as if he had rehearsed the next bit, and I thought that probably he had indeed gone over it repeatedly in his mind.

'The selection committee who chose me as their candidate,' he said, 'would frankly have preferred me to be married. They said so. They saw my bachelor state as a drawback. I told them therefore that I *had* been married, that my wife had died, and that I had a son. That cheered them up no end. What I'm asking you to do is to be a sort of substitute wife. To come with me in public. To be terribly *nice* to people.'

I said absentmindedly, 'To kiss babies?'

'*I*'ll kiss the babies.' He was amused. '*You* can chat up the old ladies, and talk football, cricket and racing to the men.'

I thought of the wild thrill of riding in races. I thought of the intoxication of risking my neck, of pitting such skill as I had against fate and disaster, of completing the bucketing journeys without disgrace. A far cry from chatting up babies.

I yearned for the simple life of carefree reckless speed; the gift given by horses, the gift of skis; and I

16

was beginning to learn, as everyone has to in the end, that all of life's pleasures have strings attached.

I said, 'How could anyone think I would bother with drugs when race-riding itself gives you the biggest high on earth?'

My father said, 'If Vivian said he would take you back, would you go?'

'No.' My answer came instinctively, without thought. Things couldn't be the same. I had gone a long way down reality's road in those few hours of an August Wednesday. I could acknowledge grimly that I would never be my dream jockey. I would never win my Grand National. But patting babies instead? Good grief!

'Polling day,' he said, 'is more than three weeks before term starts at Exeter. You will be eighteen by then . . .'

'And,' I said, without either joy or regret, 'I wrote to Exeter to say I wouldn't be taking up the place they'd offered me. Even if you instruct me to go, I can't.'

'I overruled your decision,' he told me flatly. 'I thought you might do that. I've observed you, you know, throughout your young life, even if we've never been particularly close. I got in touch with Exeter and reversed your cancellation. They are now expecting your registration. They have arranged lodging for you on campus. Unless you totally rebel and run away, you'll go ahead with your degree.'

I felt a lurching and familiar recognition of this man's power as a force that far outweighed any ordinary family relationship. Even Exeter University had done his bidding.

'But, Father . . .' I said feebly.

'Dad.'

'Dad . . .' The word was wholly inappropriate both for the image of him as the conventionally supportive parent of a schoolboy and for my perception of him as something far different from an average man in a business suit.

The Grand National, for him, I saw, was the road to Downing Street. Winning the race was the Prime Ministership in Number Ten. He was asking me to abandon my own unobtainable dream to help him have a chance of achieving his own.

I looked at the untouched apple and banana and had no more appetite.

I said, 'You don't need me.'

'I need to win votes. You can help with that. If I weren't totally convinced of your value as a constituent-pleaser you wouldn't be sitting here now.'

'Well . . .' I hesitated, 'to be honest, I wish I wasn't.'

I would have been pottering about happily in Vivian Durridge's stable yard, untroubled in my illusions. And I would have been drifting towards a less abrupt, less brutal awakening. I would also, I supposed, have been going to be cumulatively depressed. The alternative

18

future thrust at me now was at least challenging, not a slow slide to nowhere.

'Ben,' he said briskly, almost as if he could read my thoughts, 'give it a try. Enjoy it.'

He gave me an envelope full of money and told me to go out and buy clothes. 'Get anything you need. We're going to Hoopwestern from here.'

'But my stuff – ' I began.

'Your stuff, as you call it, is being packed into a box by Mrs Wells.' Mrs Wells had rented me a room in her house along the road from the Durridge stable. 'I'm paying her until the end of the month,' my father said. 'She's quite pleased about that, though she said, you'd like to know, that you were a nice quiet boy, a pleasure to have around.' He smiled. 'I've arranged for your things to be collected. You'll be reunited with them soon, perhaps tomorrow.'

It was a bit, I thought, like being hit by a tidal wave, and it wasn't the first time he had yanked me out of one easy way of life and set me down on a different path. My dead mother's sister, Aunt Susan (and her husband Harry) who had reluctantly agreed to bring me up, had felt affronted, and said so bitterly and often, when my father plucked me out of the comprehensive school that had been 'good enough' for her four sons, and insisted that I take diction lessons and extra tuition in maths, my best subject, and had by one way or another seen to it that I spent five years of intensive learning in a top fee-paying school, Malvern College.

My cousins/brothers had both envied and sneered, so that effectively I had become the 'only' child that I actually was, not the petted last addition to a big family.

The father who had planned my life to the point of my unsought arrival in Brighton took it for granted that in the last three weeks of his legal guardianship I would still act as he directed.

I suppose, looking back, that many boys of seventeen would have complained and rebelled. All I can say is that they weren't dealing with a trusted and proven benevolent tyranny: and since I knew he meant me the opposite of harm, I took the envelope of money and spent it in the Brighton shops on clothes I thought his constituents would have voted for if they'd been judging a candidate by his teenage son's appearance.

We left Brighton soon after three in the afternoon, and not in the morning's overpowering black car with the unnervingly silent chauffeur (obeying my father's 'no explanation' instructions, it seemed) but in a cheerful metallic coffee-coloured Range Rover with silver and gold garlands of daisy-like flowers in metal paint shining along the sides.

'I'm new in the constituency,' my father said, grinning. 'I need to get myself noticed and recognised.'

He could hardly be missed, I thought. Heads turned

to watch us all along the south coast. Even so, I was unprepared for Hoopwestern (in Dorset), where it seemed that every suitable pole and tree bore a placard saying simply 'VOTE JULIARD'. No one in the town could avoid the message.

He had driven the advertisement-on-wheels from Brighton, with me sitting beside him on the front seat, and on the way he gave me non-stop instruction on what I should say and not say, do and not do, in my new role.

'Politicians,' he said, 'should seldom tell the whole truth.'

'But – '

'And politicians,' he went on, 'should *never* lie.'

'But you told me always to tell the truth.'

He smiled sideways at my simplicity. 'You better damn well tell *me* the truth. But people as a rule believe only what they *want* to believe, and if you tell them anything else they'll call you a trouble-maker and get rid of you and never give you your job back, even if what you said is proved spot on right by time.'

I said slowly, 'I suppose I do know that.'

'On the other hand, to be caught out in a lie is political death, so I don't do it.'

'But what do you say if you're asked a direct question and you can't tell the truth and you can't tell a lie?'

'You say "how very interesting" and change the subject.'

21

He drove the Range Rover with both speed and caution, the way he lived his whole life.

'During the next weeks,' he said, 'people will ask you what I think about this and that. Always say you don't know, they'd better ask me themselves. *Never* repeat to anyone anything I've said, even if I've said it in public. OK?'

'If you say so.'

'Remember this election is a contest. I have political enemies. Not every smiling face is a friend.'

'Do you mean ... don't trust anyone?'

'That's exactly what I mean. People always kill Caesar. Don't trust *anyone*.'

'But that's cynical!'

'It's the first law of self-preservation.'

I said, 'I'd rather be a jockey.'

He shook his head in sorrow. 'I'm afraid you'll find that every world has its share of villains and cheats, jockeys not excepted.'

He drove into the centre of Hoopwestern, which proved to be one of those old indigenous market towns whose ancient heart had been petrified into a quaint cobbled pedestrian precinct, with the raw pulse of modern commerce springing up in huge office buildings and shopping malls on three sides around a ring road.

'This used to be a farming community,' my father said neutrally. 'Farming is now an industry like the

22

factory here that makes light bulbs and employs more people. I need the light-bulb votes.'

His campaign headquarters, I found, were in a remarkable back-to-back hybrid house with an old bay-windowed frontage facing the cobbled square and a box-like featureless shop behind, one of a row looking out over a half-acre of car park. The house, with basic living accommodation for him (and me) upstairs, had once been a shoe store (now bankrupt because of an aggressive local mall) and was the twin of the place next door to it, a charity gift shop.

The political headquarters bustled with earnest endeavour, brightly coloured telephones, a click-clacking floor-standing photocopier, constant cups of tea, desks, computers, maps on the walls with coloured pins in, directories in heaps, envelopes by the carton-load and three middle-aged women enjoying the fuss.

We had parked in the car park and walked to the unmistakable glass-fronted premises where it not only said VOTE JULIARD in huge letters but displayed three large pictures of my father, all of them projecting a good-natured, intelligent, forward-looking person who would do an excellent job at Westminster.

The three women greeted him with merry cries of pleasure and a stack of problems.

'This is my son,' he said.

The merry smiles were bent my way. They looked me up and down. Three witches, I thought.

'Come in, dear,' one of them said. 'Cup of tea?'

# CHAPTER TWO

The double shop, I found, was the regular constituency office of the party to which my father belonged. It was where Dennis Nagle, the previous Member, had lately held his Saturday 'surgeries', being present himself to listen to local problems and do his best to sort them out. Still in his fifties, he had died, poor fellow, of pancreatic cancer. His ambitious wife, Orinda, was reportedly steaming with vitriolic anger since the selection committee had passed her over in favour of my parent to fight to retain the vacant seat at the behest of the central party.

I learned about Orinda by sitting on an inconspicuous stool in a corner and listening to the three helpers describe to my father a visit the dispossessed lady had paid that day to the office.

The thinnest, least motherly help, who was also the most malicious, said with lip-curling glee, 'You'd think she'd be grieving for Dennis, but she just seems furious with him for dying. She talks about "*our* constituents", like she always did. She says she wrote his speeches and formed his opinions. She said it was understood from when Dennis was first ill that she would take his place. She says we three are traitors to be working for you, George. She was absolutely stuttering with rage. She says if you think she'll meekly go away, you have another think coming. And she says she is going to tonight's dinner!'

My father grimaced.

I thought that the selection committee had probably acted with good sense.

From my stool I also learned that the main opposition party was fielding 'a fat slob with zero sex appeal' against my father. His – Paul Bethune's – party had recently picked up a couple of marginal seats in by-elections and were confident of taking Hoopwestern since 'the need for change' was in the air.

In the days that followed I saw his picture everywhere: a grin above the slogan *'Bethune is better. Give him your X.'*

It made me laugh. Was he collecting divorcées?

On that first evening, though, all I learned of him was that he was a local councillor and losing his hair. Incipient baldness might in fact lose him the election, it seemed (never mind his mental suitability). America hadn't elected a bald president since the soldier-hero Eisenhower, and few people nowadays named their babies Dwight.

I learned that votes were won by laughter and lost by dogma. I learned that the virility of George Juliard acted like a friction rub on the pink faces of his helpers.

'My son will come with me to the dinner tonight,' he said. 'He can have Mervyn's place.' Mervyn Teck, he explained was the agent, his chief of staff, who was unavoidably detained in the Midlands.

The three aroused ladies looked me over again, nodding.

'The dinner,' he explained to me briefly, 'is being held at the Sleeping Dragon, the hotel straight across the square from here.' He pointed through the bow-fronted windows, showing me a multi-gabled façade, adorned with endless geraniums in hanging baskets, barely a hundred yards away. 'We'll walk over there at seven-thirty. Short reception. Dinner. Public meeting in the hall to the rear of the hotel. If we get some good hecklers, it may last until midnight.'

'You *want* hecklers?' I said, surprised.

'Of course. They set fire to things. Very dull otherwise.'

I asked weakly, 'What do I wear?'

'Just look tidy. There's a Front Bench bigwig coming. They wheel out the big guns to support a by-election as marginal as this. I'll wear a dinner jacket to start with, but I'll strip off my black tie later. Maybe unbutton my shirt a bit. See how it goes.' He smiled almost calmly, but I could sense excitement running in him deeply. He's a *fighter*, I thought. He's my father, this extraordinary man. He's kicked my dreams away and shown me a different world that I don't like very much, but I'll go with him, as he wants, for a month, and I'll do my best for him, and then we'll see. See how it goes . . . as he'd said.

We walked across the square at seven-thirty, I in grey trousers and navy blazer (new from the Brighton shops), he in black tailoring that was in itself a step forward in my education.

He was received with acclaim and clapping. I smiled and smiled at his shoulder and was terribly *nice* to everyone, and shook hand after hand as required. No babies in sight.

'My son,' he gestured. 'This is my son.'

Some of the perhaps eighty people at the reception and dinner were dressed formally like my father, others made political-equality statements like open-necked shirts and gingham with studs.

The Front Bench bigwig came with black bow sharply tied, his wife discreetly diamonded. I watched her being unpretentiously and endlessly charming to strangers, and when I in my turn was introduced to her she clasped my hand warmly and grinned into my eyes as if meeting me was a highlight of her evening. I had a long way to go, I thought, before I could put that amount of genuine and spontaneous friendliness into every greeting. I saw also that Mrs Bigwig's smile was worth a ballot-box full of Xs.

I realised slowly, as the room filled up, that the dinner was a ticket affair; that, except for the Bigwigs and my father, everyone had paid for their presence. My father, it appeared, had paid for me. One of the evening's organising committee was telling him he didn't have to.

'Never accept gifts,' he had warned me on the drive from Brighton. 'Gifts may look harmless, but they can come back to haunt you. Say no. Pay for yourself, understand?'

'Yes, I think so.'

'Never put yourself into the position of having to return a heavy favour when you know what you're being asked to do is wrong.'

'Don't take sweets from strangers?'

'Exactly so.'

The organising lady informed my father that if he had had a wife, her ticket would have been free.

He said with gentle, smiling finality, 'I will pay for my son. Dearest Polly, don't argue.'

Dearest Polly turned to me with mock exasperation. 'Your father. What a man!' Her gaze slid past me and her face and voice changed from blue skies to storm. '*Bugger*,' she said.

I looked, of course, to see the cause of the almost comic disapproval and found it was an earnest-eyed thin woman of forty or so sun-baked summers, whose tan glowed spectacularly against a sleeveless white dress. Blonde streaked hair. Vitality plus.

Dearest Polly said, 'Orinda!' under her breath.

Orinda, the passed-over candidate, was doing her

best to eclipse the chosen rival by wafting round the room embracing everyone extravagantly while saying loudly, 'Daaarling, we must all do our best for the party even if the selectors have made this *ghastly* mistake . . .'

'Damn her,' said Dearest Polly who had been, she told me, a selector herself.

Everyone knew Orinda, of course. She managed to get the cameraman from the local television company to follow her around, so that her white slenderness would hog whatever footage reached the screen.

Dearest Polly quietly fumed, throwing out sizzling news snippets my way as if she would explode if she kept them in.

'Dennis was a cuddly precious, you know. Can't think why he married that *harpy*.'

Dearest Polly, herself on the angular side of cuddly, had one of those long-jawed faces from which condensed kindness and goodwill flowed forth unmistakably. She wore dark red lipstick as if she didn't usually: it was the wrong colour for her yellowish skin.

'Dennis told us he wanted us to select Orinda. She *made* him say it. He knew he was dying.'

Orinda flashed her white teeth at a second cameraman.

'That man's from the *Hoopwestern Gazette*,' Dearest Polly said disgustedly. 'She'll make the front page.'

'But she won't get to Parliament,' I said.

Polly's eyes focused on me with awakening

amusement. 'Your father's son, aren't you, then! It was George's ability to identify the essential points that swayed us in his favour. There were seventeen of us on the selection panel, and to begin with most people thought Orinda the obvious choice. I know she took it for granted . . .'

And she'd reckoned without Dearest Polly, I thought. Polly and others of like mind.

Polly said, 'I don't know how she has the nerve to bring her lover!'

'Er . . .' I said. 'What?'

'That man just behind her. He was Dennis's best friend.'

I didn't see how being Dennis's best friend made anyone automatically Orinda's lover, but before I could ask, Polly was claimed away. Dennis's best friend, a person who managed to look unremarkable even in a dinner jacket, seemed abstracted more than attentive, but he did stick faithfully to Orinda's back: rather like a bodyguard, I thought.

I realised in consequence that Mr Bigwig himself had a genuinely serious bodyguard, a young muscular-looking shadow whose attention was directed to the crowd, not his master.

I wondered if my father accepted that bodyguards would be the price of success as he went up his chosen ladder.

He began circling the room and gestured for me to

join him, and I practised being Mrs Bigwig but fell far short of her standard. I could act, but she was real.

There was a general movement into the dining-room next door, where too many tables laid for ten people each were crowded into too small a space. Places were allocated to everyone by name and, my father and I entering almost last, I found that not only were we not expected at the same table – he was put naturally with the Bigwigs and the Constituency Association's chairman – but I was squeezed against a distant wall between a Mrs Leonard Kitchens and Orinda herself.

When she discovered her ignominious location Orinda flamed with fury like a white-hot torch. She stood and quivered and tried to get general attention by tapping a glass with a knife, but the noise was lost in the general bustle of eighty people chattering and clattering into their places. Orinda's angry outburst barely reached further than her knives and forks.

'This is an insult! I always sit at the top table! I *demand* . . .'

No one listened.

Through the throng I saw Dearest Polly busily set-tling my father into a place of honour and guessed with irony that Orinda's quandary was Polly's mischief.

Orinda glared at me as I hovered politely waiting for her to sit. She had green eyes, black lashed. Stage grease-paint skin.

'And who are *you*?' she demanded; then bent down

31

and snatched up the name card in front of my place. My identity left her speechless with her red mouth open.

'I'm his son,' I said lamely. 'Can I help you with your chair?'

She turned her back on me and spoke to her bodyguard (lover?) best friend of her dead husband, a characterless-seeming entity with a passive face.

'Do something!' Orinda instructed him.

He glanced past her in my direction and with flat expressionless eyes dismissed me as of no consequence. He silently held Orinda's chair for her to sit down and to my surprise she folded away most of her aggression and sat stonily and with a stiff back, enduring what she couldn't get changed.

At school one learned a good deal about power: who had it and who didn't. (I didn't.) Orinda's understated companion had power that easily eclipsed her own, all the more effective for being quiet.

Mrs Leonard Kitchens, on my right, patted my chair with invitation and told me to occupy it. Mrs Leonard Kitchens, large, comfortable in a loose floral dress and with the lilt of a Dorset accent on her tongue, told me that my father looked too young to have a son my size.

'Yes, doesn't he,' I said.

Leonard himself, on her other side, bristled with a bad-tempered moustache and tried unsuccessfully to

talk to Orinda across his wife and me. I offered
to change places with him: his wife said sharply, 'No.'

Mrs Leonard Kitchens' gift for small talk took us
cosily through dinner (egg salad, chicken, strawberries), and I learned that 'my Leonard', her husband,
was a nurseryman by trade with fanatical political
beliefs and a loathing for Manchester United.

With the chicken Mrs Kitchens, to my surprise, mentioned that Dennis Nagle had been an Under-Secretary
of State in the Department of Trade and Industry, not
a simple backbencher, as I had somehow surmised. If
my father won the seat, he would be a long way behind
Dennis in career terms.

Mrs Leonard Kitchens spoke conspiratorily into my
right ear. 'Perhaps I shouldn't tell you, dear, but Polly
very naughtily changed the name cards over, so as to
put Orinda next to you. I saw her. She just laughed.
She's never *liked* Orinda.' The semi-whispering voice
grew even quieter, so as not to reach the ears on my
left. 'Orinda made a great constituency wife, very good
at opening fêtes and that sort of thing, but one has to
admit she did tend to boss Dennis sometimes. My
Leonard was on the selection panel and he voted for
her, of course. Men always fall for her, you know.' She
drew back and looked at me with her big head on one
side. 'You're too young, of course.'

To my dismay I could feel myself going red. Mrs
Kitchens laughed her worldly laugh and shovelled her
strawberries. Orinda Nagle ignored me throughout,

while pouring out non-stop complaints to her companion, who mostly replied with grunts. I thought I would rather be almost anywhere else.

Dinner finally over, the talkative throng rose to its collective feet and transferred down a passage into the large room lit by chandeliers which made the Sleeping Dragon the area's popular magnet for dances, weddings and – as now – political free-for-alls.

Orinda's companion left his name card on the table, and out of not-very-strong curiosity I picked it up.

Mr A.L. Wyvern, it said.

I let 'Mr A.L. Wyvern' fall back among the debris of napkins and coffee cups and, without enthusiasm, drifted along with everyone else to the rows of folding chairs set up for the meeting. I'd read somewhere that affairs like this could draw tiny crowds unworthy of the name, but perhaps because my father was new to the district, almost double the number of the diners had turned up, and the whole place buzzed with the expectation of enjoyment.

It was the first political meeting I'd attended and at that point I would have been happy if it had been my last.

There were speeches from the small row of people up on a platform. The chairman of the Constituency Association rambled on a bit. Mr Bigwig was on his feet for twenty minutes. Mrs Bigwig smiled approvingly throughout.

My father stood up and lightened the proceedings

by making everyone laugh. I could feel my face arranging itself into Mrs Bigwig-type soppiness and knew that in my case anyway it had a lot to do with relief. I had been anxious that he wouldn't grab his audience, that he would embarrass me into squirming agony by being boring.

I suppose I should have known better. He told them what was right with the country, and why. He told them what was wrong with the country, and how to fix it. He gave them a palatable recipe. He told them what they wanted to believe, and he had them stamping their feet and roaring their applause.

The local TV station cameraman filmed the cheers.

Predictably, Orinda hated it. She sat rigidly, her neck as stiff as if she had an unbending rod there instead of vertebrae. I could see the sharp line of her jaw and the grim tight muscles round her mouth. She shouldn't have come, I thought: but perhaps she truly had believed that the selectors had made a ghastly mistake.

Dearest Polly, chief de-selector of Dennis's widow, regarded my father euphorically, as if she had invented him herself; and, indeed, without her he might not have been there to seize the first rung of his destiny.

Eyes alight with the triumph of his reception he asked for questions and, true to his intention, he stripped off his tie. He flung it on the table in front of him, and then he rounded the table so that there was nothing between him on the platform and the crowd below. He opened his arms wide, embracing them. He invited them to join him in a political adventure, to build for a better world and in particular for a better world for the constituents of Hoopwestern.

He held them in his hands. He had them laughing. His timing could have been learned from stand-up comics. He generated excitement, belief, purpose; and I, in my inconspicuous end-of-row seat, I swelled with a mixture of amazement, understanding and finally pride that my parent was publicly delivering the goods.

'I'm here for you,' he said. 'Come to my office across the square. Tell me your concerns, tell me what's troubling you here in Hoopwestern. Tell me who to see, who to listen to. Tell me your history . . . and I'll tell you your future. If you elect me I'll work for you, I'll take your wishes to Westminster, I'll be your voice where it matters. I'll light a bulb or two in the House of Commons . . .'

Laughter drowned him. The light-bulb factory fuelled the town's economy, and he wanted the light-bulb votes.

To do good one needed power, he said. Light bulbs were so much wire and glass without power. In humans, power came from inside, not delivered and metered. Power gave light and warmth. 'If you give me power, I'll light your lamps.'

My father's own electricity galvanised the crowd. They shouted questions, he shouted answers. He was serious where it mattered and funny everywhere else.

He had horror for genocide and sympathy for cats. He dodged cornering demands and promised never to put his name to anything whose consequences he didn't understand.

'Legislation,' he said jokingly, 'often achieves exactly what it is designed to avoid. We all know it. We moan about the results. I promise not to jump into emotional deep ends on your behalf. I beg the brains and common sense of Hoopwesterners to foresee disaster and warn me. I'll raise your voices in whispers, not shouts, because shouts annoy but whispers go round persuasively and travel sweetly to the heart of things, and lead to sensible action.'

Whether they understood him or not, they loved him.

The most dedicated hecklers of the evening proved not to be the Paul Bethune opposition supporters, several of whom had bought tickets to the dinner and who had afterwards formed an aggressive bunch on the flip-up chairs, but my father's presumed political allies (but in fact personal enemies), Orinda Nagle and Leonard Kitchens.

Both of them demanded firm commitments to policies they both approved. Both shouted and pointed fingers. My father answered with unfailing good humour and stuck to the party's overall stated position: he needed also to keep the die-hard backbone votes safely in his bag.

Orinda was professional enough to see she was

outgunned, but she didn't give up trying. Mr A.L. Wyvern narrowed his eyes and sank his ears down into his collar. Mr A.L. Wyvern's influence over Dennis and Orinda waned before my eyes.

My father paid tribute to Dennis Nagle. Orinda, far from placated, said that no way could an inexperienced novice like George Juliard replace her husband, however Hollywood-handsome he might be, however manly his hairy chest, however witty, quick-tongued, charismatic. None of that made up for political know-how.

Someone at the back of the hall booed. There was general laughter, a nervous release of the tension Orinda had begun to build up. The impetus swung back to my father, who sincerely thanked Orinda for her years of service to the party cause and deftly led an appreciation to her by clapping in her direction and encouraging everyone else to copy him. The clapping grew. The crowd gave generous but unaffectionate acclaim.

Orinda, to her impotent fury, was silenced and defeated by this vote of thanks. Leonard Kitchens bounced to his feet to defend her, but was shouted down. Leonard's moustache quivered with frustration, his thick glasses flashing in the light as he swung from side to side like a wounded bull. His cosy wife looked as if she would deliver the *coup de grâce* when she got him home.

My father courteously admired Leonard for his

faithfulness and told him and everyone that if elected he would aim always for Dennis Nagle's high and honest standard. Nothing less was worthy of the people of Hoopwestern.

He had them cheering. He exhorted them again to talk to him personally and the crowd stood and surged forward round the seats to take him at his word.

Dearest Polly chatted happily with the Bigwigs and beckoned me up onto the platform, and Mr Bigwig, regarding the clamorous excited throng, told me that my father already had all the skills that would propel him into high office. 'All he needs is luck – and to keep out of trouble,' he said.

'Trouble like Paul Bethune,' Polly said, nodding.

'What trouble?' asked Bigwig.

'Oh dear!' Polly looked flustered. 'George forbids us to attack Paul Bethune's character. George says negative campaigning can rebound on you. Paul Bethune has a mistress with an illegitimate daughter by him which he's tried hard to hush up and George won't attack him for it.'

Mrs Bigwig looked at me assessingly. 'I suppose there's no shadow over *your* birth, is there, young Ben?'

Polly assured her vehemently. 'No, of course not,' and I wondered if my father, all those years ago, could possibly have reckoned that my legitimacy would one day be important to him. After what I'd learned of him that day I saw that anything was possible, but in fact I stayed as convinced as I'd always been that his marriage to my mother had been an act of natural characteristic honour. I still believed, as I always had, that he would never shirk responsibility for his actions. I knew my birth had been a mistake and, as I'd often said, I had no quarrel at all with the quality of life he'd given me since.

It was indeed midnight by the time most of the crowd left to go home. Mr and Mrs Bigwig had long gone, with chauffeur and bodyguard in attendance. Polly yawned with well-earned fatigue. Orinda and Mr A.L. Wyvern were nowhere to be seen and Mrs Leonard Kitchens had hauled her Leonard away with the rough edge of her energetic tongue.

I waited for my father to the end, not only because I had no key to get into my bedroom above the campaign headquarters but also because he would need someone to unwind on after the cheers had died away. Even at not quite eighteen I knew that triumph needed human company afterwards. I'd gone back to an empty room in Mrs Wells's house after three (infrequent) wins in steeplechases and had had no one to bounce round the place with, no one to hug and yell with, no one to share the uncontainable joy. That night my father needed me. A wife would have been better; but he certainly would need *someone*. So I stayed.

He put his arm round my shoulders.

'*God*,' he said.

'You'll be Prime Minister,' I told him. 'Mr Bigwig fears it.'

He looked at me vaguely, his eyes shining. 'Why should he or anyone fear it?'

'They always kill Caesar. You said so.'

'What?'

'You were brilliant.'

'I can do without your sarcasm, Ben.'

'No, seriously, Father . . .'

'Dad.'

'Dad . . .' I was tongue-tied. I couldn't talk to him as Dad. Dads were people who drove you to school and threw snowballs and ticked you off for coming home late. Dads didn't send you a ticket to ski school in a Christmas card. Dads didn't send an impersonal fax to a hotel saying 'well done' when one won a teenage downhill ski race. Dads were there to watch. Fathers weren't.

Remnants of the meeting came up with shining faces to add congratulations. He took his arm off my shoulder and shook their hands, friendly and positive to all; and I had a vision of them going around for the next four weeks saying, 'Juliard, a very good man, just what we need . . . Vote Juliard, couldn't do better.' The ripple from that night would reach the Hoopwestern boundaries and eddy along its roads.

My father slowly came down a little from his high and decided he'd done enough for one day. We left the hall, returned to the hotel and eventually through a harmony of 'Good Nights' made our way out into the warm August night to walk across to the dimly lit bow-front opposite.

There were street lights round the square and the hotel lights at our back, but underfoot the decorative cobbles were dark and lumpy. In icy winters, I learned later, elderly people tended to skid on them and fall and crunch their bones; and on that euphoric night my father tripped on the uneven surface and went down forward on one knee, trying not to topple entirely and not managing it.

At exactly the same moment there was a loud bang and a sharp zzing and a scrunch of glass breaking.

I bent down over my father and saw in the light that his eyes were stretched wide with anxiety and his mouth grim and urgent with pain.

'Run,' he said. 'Run for cover. God dammit, *run*.'

I stayed where I was, however.

'Ben,' he said, 'for God's sake. That was a gunshot.'

'Yes, I know.'

We were halfway across the square, easy immobile targets. He struggled to get to his feet and told me again to run: and for once in my life I made a judgement and disobeyed him.

He couldn't put his weight on his left ankle. He half rose and fell down again and beseeched me to run.

'Stay down,' I told him.

'You don't understand . . .' His voice was anguished. 'Are you bleeding?'

42

'What? I don't think so. I twisted my ankle.'

People ran out of the hotel, drawn by the bang that had re-echoed round the buildings fringing the square. People came over to my father and me and stood around us, curious and unsettled, noncomprehension wrinkling their foreheads.

There was confusion and people saying, 'What happened, what happened?' and hands stretching down to my father to help him up, cushioning him with a lot of well-meaning concern and kindness.

When he was well surrounded he did finally take my arm and lean on other people and pull himself to his feet: or rather, to his right foot, because putting his left foot down caused him to exclaim with strong discomfort. He began to be embarrassed rather than frightened and told the crowding well-wishers that he felt stupid, losing his footing so carelessly. He apologised. He said he was fine. He smiled to prove it. He cursed mildly, to crowd approval.

'But that *noise*,' a woman said.

Heads nodded. 'It sounded like . . .'

'Not here in Hoopwestern . . .'

'Was it . . . a *gun*?'

An important-looking man said impatiently, 'A rifle shot. I'd know it anywhere. Some madman . . .'

'But where? There's no one here with a gun.'

Everyone looked round, but it was far too late to see the rifle, let alone the person taking pot-shots.

My father put his arm round my shoulders again,

but this time for a different, more practical sort of support, and cheerfully indicated to everyone that we should set off again to finish the crossing of the square.

The important-looking man literally shoved me out of the way, taking my place as crutch and saying in his loud authoritative way, 'Let me do this. I'm stronger than the lad. I'll have you over to your office in a jiffy, Mr Juliard. You just lean on *me*.'

My father looked over his shoulder to where I now stood behind him and would have protested on my behalf, I could see, but the change suited me fine and I simply waved for him to go on. The important-looking man efficiently half-carried my hopping father over the remaining stretch of square, the bunch of onlookers crowding round with murmurs of sympathy and helpful suggestions.

I walked behind my father. It came naturally, to do that. There was a high voice calling then, and I turned to find Polly running towards us, stumbling on the cobbles in strappy sandals and sounding very distressed.

'Ben . . . Ben . . . has George been shot?'

'No, Polly.' I tried to reassure her. 'No.'

'Someone said George had been shot.' She was out of breath and full of disbelief.

'Look, there he is.' I took her arm and pointed. 'There. Hopping. And hopping mad with himself for twisting his ankle and needing someone to help him along.'

Polly's arm was vibrating with the inner shakes, which only slowly abated when she could see that indeed George was alive and healthily swearing.

'But . . . the shot . . .'

I said, 'It seems someone did fire a gun at the same moment that he tripped on the cobbles, but I promise you he wasn't hit. No blood.'

'But you're so young, Ben.' Her doubts still showed.

'Even a tiny kid could tell you there's no blood.' I said it teasingly, but I guess it was my own relief that finally convinced her. She walked beside me and followed the pied-piper-like procession to the head-quarters' door, where my father produced a key and let everyone in.

He hopped across to his swivel chair behind his accustomed desk and, consulting a list, telephoned the local police.

'They've had several complaints already,' he told everyone, putting down the receiver. 'They're on their way here. Letting off a firearm . . . disturbing the peace . . . that sort of thing.'

Someone said, 'What you need is a doctor . . .' and someone else arranged for one to come.

'So kind. You're all so bloody kind,' my father said.

I left the hubbub and went to the open door, looking across the square to the Sleeping Dragon, who perversely had every eye wide open, with people leaning out of upstairs windows and people standing in brightly lit doorways below.

I remembered the '*zzing*' of the passing bullet and thought of ricochets. My father and I had been steering a straight line from hotel to headquarters; and *if* the bullet had been aimed at *him*, and *if* he'd stumbled at the exact second that the trigger was squeezed, and *if* the bullet's trajectory had been from upstairs somewhere in the Sleeping Dragon (and not from downstairs because there were still too many people about), and *if* the bullet had smashed some glass so that I heard the tinkle, then why was every pane of the window in the bow-fronted headquarters intact?

Because, I told myself, the whole thing had been a coincidence. The bullet had not been intended to stop George Juliard's political career before it started. Of course not. Dramatics were childish.

I turned to go back inside, and saw for an instant a flash of light on broken glass down on the ground.

It was a window of the charity shop next door that had been hit.

*Zzing. Ricochet. Smash.* The straight trajectory could have been deflected by the curve of a cobble. A rifle bullet travelling straight and true would very likely have gone right through glass without breaking it, but a wobbling bullet ... that might set up glass-smashing vibrations.

The police arrived at the car-park side of the head-quarters, and the doctor also. Everyone talked at once.

The doctor, bandaging, said he thought the injury a strain, not a break. Ice and elevation, he prescribed.

The police listened to the self-important man's view on gunshots.

I stood to one side and at one point found my father looking at me through the throng, his expression both surprised and questioning. I smiled at him a bit, and the window of line of sight closed again as people moved.

I did tell a junior-looking uniformed policeman that the glass of the charity shop's bow-front was broken, and he did come outside to look. But when I tentatively mentioned ricochets he looked quizzical and asked how old I was. I had done a bit of rifle shooting at school, I said. He nodded, unimpressed, and made a note. I followed when he returned to join his colleagues.

Dearest Polly stood at my father's side and listened to everything worriedly. A man with a camera flashed several pictures. Considering that no one had actually been shot the fuss went on for a long time and it was nearly two o'clock when I finally closed and bolted the doors, front and back, and switched off a few of the lights.

My father decided to go upstairs backwards, sitting down. He would accept only minimal help and winced himself in and out of the bathroom and into one of the single beds in the bedroom. I was to sleep on the pull-out sofa-bed in the small sitting-room, but I ended up lying on the second single bed, next to my father, half dressed and not at all sleepy.

I had in the past twenty hours hummed along from Mrs Wells's house on my bicycle and ridden a canter on grassy sunlit Downs. I'd had my life torn apart and entered a new world, and for long minutes I'd wondered if I would collect a bullet in the back. How could I sleep?

I switched off the bedside light.

In the dark, my father said, 'Ben, why didn't you run?'

After a pause I answered. 'Why did you tell me to?'

'I didn't want you to get shot.'

'Mm. Well, that's why I didn't run. I didn't want you to get shot.'

'So you stood in the way . . .?'

'More fun than patting babies.'

'*Ben!*'

After a while, I said, 'I'd say it was a .22 rifle, the sort used for target shooting. I'd say it was a high-velocity bullet. I know that noise well. If a .22 bullet hits you in the body, it quite likely won't kill you. You need to hit the head or the neck to be most probably lethal. All I did was shield your head.'

There was a silence from the other bed. Then he said, 'I'd forgotten you could shoot.'

'I was in the school team. We were taught by one of the country's best marksmen.' I smiled in the dark. 'You paid for it, you know.'

# CHAPTER THREE

Before nine the next morning I went downstairs and unbolted the door to the car park at the shrill summons of a man who was standing there with his finger on the bell button. He was short, black-haired, softly plump, held a bunch of keys in his hand and was very annoyed.

'Who are *you*?' he demanded. 'What are you doing in here? Why is the door bolted?'

'Benedict – ' I began.

'What?'

'Juliard.'

He stared at me for a moment, then brushed past and began bad-temperedly setting to rights the untidiness left all over both front and back offices by the events of the night.

'You're the son, I suppose,' he said, picking up scattered envelopes. 'George wasted all of yesterday going to collect you. As you're here, do something useful.' He gestured to the mess. 'Where is George, anyway? The radio is red hot. What did happen last night?'

49

'Upstairs. He sprained his ankle. And . . . er . . . who are *you*?'

'Mervyn Teck, of course.' He looked impatiently at my blank face. 'I'm the agent. Don't you know *anything*?'

'Not much.'

'I'm running this election. I'm here to get George Juliard into Parliament. The radio says someone shot at him. Is that true?' He seemed unconcerned and went on straightening papers.

'Possibly,' I said.

'Good.'

I said, 'Er . . .?'

'Free publicity. We can't afford to buy air time.'

'Oh.'

'It will get rid of Titmuss and Whistle.'

'Who are they?' I asked.

'Fringe candidates. We don't need to worry about them.'

My father hobbled downstairs saying, 'Morning, Mervyn. I see you've met my son.'

Mervyn gave me an unenthusiastic glance.

'Lucky he's here,' my father said. 'He can drive me around.'

I'd told him on the way from Brighton that I'd done errands to earn money for driving lessons and had held a full licence by then for nearly five weeks.

'Good,' he'd said.

'But I haven't driven since the test.'

'All in good time.' His bland expression now forbade me to reveal my inexperience. There was tolerance between the candidate and the agent, I saw, but no warmth.

A sharp-boned young woman arrived with disciplined hair and a power-dressing grey suit with a bright 'Juliard' rosette pinned to one shoulder. She was introduced as Crystal Harley, Mervyn Teck's secretary, and, as I learned during the morning, she was the only person, besides Mervyn himself, who received pay for running the by-election. Everyone else was a volunteer.

The three volunteer witches from the day before arrived one by one and smothered my father with cooing solicitude and endless coffee.

I had forgotten their names: Faith, Marge and Lavender, Faith chided me gently.

'Sorry.'

'A good politician remembers names,' Lavender told me severely. 'You won't be much use to your father if you forget who people are.' The thin lady with the sweet-smelling name was the one who had disapproved of Orinda Nagle. Difficult to please her, I thought.

Mervyn Teck and my father discussed streets and leaflet distributions. Crystal Harley entered endless details into a computer. Motherly Faith went round with a duster and Marge set the photocopier humming.

I sat on my stool and simply listened, and learned many surprising (to me) facts of electoral life, chief among which was the tiny amount of money allowed to be spent. No one could buy themselves into Parliament: every candidate had to rely on an army of unpaid helpers for door-to-door persuasions and the nailing of 'Vote for Me' posters to suitable trees.

There were Representation of the People Acts, Crystal told me crisply, her fingers busy on the keyboard, her eyes unwaveringly turned to the screen. The Acts severely limited what one could spend.

'There are about seventy thousand voters in this constituency,' she said. 'You couldn't buy seventy thousand half-pints of beer with what we're allowed to spend. It's impossible to *bribe* the British voters. You have to *persuade* them. That's your father's job.'

'Don't buy a stamp, dear, for a local letter,' Faith said, smiling. 'Get on a bicycle and deliver it by hand.'

'Do you mean you can't buy *stamps*?'

'You have to write down every cent you spend,' Crystal nodded. 'You have to make an itemised return after the election to show where the money went, and you can bet your sweet life Paul Bethune's people will be hoping like hell they'll find we've gone over the limit, just like we'll be scrutinising his return with a magnifying glass looking for any twopenny wickedness.'

'Then last night's dinner . . .' I began.

'Last night's dinner was paid for by the people who ate it, and cost the local Constituency Association nothing,' Crystal said. She paused, then went on with my education. 'Mervyn and I are employed by the local Constituency Association of this party, not directly by Westminster. The local association pays for these offices here, and the whole caboodle relies on gifts and fundraising.'

She approved of the way things were set up, and I wondered vaguely why, with everything carefully regulated to ensure the election of the fittest, there were still so many nutcases in the House.

The relative peace of just seven bodies in the offices lasted only until an influx of the previous night's social mix trooped in through both doors and asked endless questions to which there seemed no answers.

Mervyn Teck loved it. The police, the media people, the party enthusiasts and the merely curious, he expansively welcomed them all. His candidate was not only alive but being perfectly charming to every enquirer. The TV cameraman shone his bright spotlight on my father's face and taped the sincerity of his smile. Local newspapermen had been augmented by several from the major dailies. Cameras flashed. Microphones were offered to catch anything worth saying, and I, doing my bit, simply smiled and smiled and was terribly nice to everyone and referred every question to my parent.

Crystal, trying to continue working but having to cling physically to her desk to avoid being swept round the place like flotsam, remarked to me tartly that there would hardly have been more fuss if George Juliard had been killed.

'Lucky he wasn't,' I said, wedging my stool next to her to keep us both anchored.

'Did the noise of the gunshot make him trip?' she asked.

'No. He tripped first.'

'Why are you so sure?'

'Because the bang of a high-velocity bullet reaches you after the bullet itself.'

She looked disbelieving.

'I learned it in physics lessons,' I said.

She glanced at my beardless face. 'How old are you?' she asked.

'Seventeen.'

'You can't even vote!'

'I don't actually want to.'

She looked across to where my father was winning media allies with modesty and grace.

'I've met a fair number of politicians,' she said. 'Your father's different.'

'In what way?'

'Can't you feel his power? Perhaps you can't, as you're his son. You're too close to him.'

'I do sometimes feel it.' It stunned me, I should have said.

'Look at last night,' Crystal went on without pausing. 'I was there in the hall, sitting at the back. He set that place alight. He's a natural speaker. I mean, I *work* here, and he had my pulse racing. Poor old Dennis Nagle, he was a nice worthy man, pretty capable in a quiet way, but he could never have got a crowd cheering and stamping their feet like last night.'

'Could Orinda?' I asked.

Crystal was startled. 'No, she can't make people laugh. But don't judge her by last night. She's done devoted work in the constituency. She was always at Dennis's side. She's feeling very hurt that she wasn't selected to follow Dennis, because until your father galvanised the selection panel she was unopposed.'

'In fact,' I said, 'if *anyone* had a motive for bumping off my father, it would be her.'

'Oh, but she wouldn't!' Crystal was honestly dismayed. 'She can sometimes be a darling, you know. Mervyn *loves* her. He's quite put out that he's not working to get *her* elected. He was looking forward to it.'

My first impression of Crystal's sharp spikiness had been right only as regarded her outward appearance. She was kinder and more patient than she looked. I wondered if at one time she had been anorexic: I had known anorexic girls at school. The teeth of one of them had fallen out.

Crystal's teeth were straight and white, though seldom visible, owing to an overall serious view of life. I thought she was probably twenty-five or -six and hadn't had enough in life to smile about.

Mervyn Teck zig-zagged to my elbow through the busy crowd and said it was time to think about driving my father to his day's engagements in the outlying town of Quindle. The constituency was large in area with separate pockets of concentrated inhabitation: Mervyn gave me a map with roads and destinations marked, but looked at me doubtfully.

'Are you sure you're competent enough?'

I said, 'Yes,' with more confidence than I felt.

'One incident like last night's is a godsend,' he said. 'A car crash on top would be too much. We don't want any whiff of accident-prone.'

'No,' I said.

Across the room my father was dangling the Range Rover's keys in my direction. I went over to him and took them and he, with the help of a walking stick, detached himself from the chattering well-wishers (the police and media had long gone) and limped through the office and out to the car park.

Crowds beget crowds. There was a bunch of people outside the rear door who clapped and smiled at my father and gave him thumbs-up signs. I looked across the car park to where we had left the Range Rover on our arrival from Brighton the previous afternoon and my father asked me to fetch it over so that he wouldn't need to hobble that far.

I walked across to the conspicuous vehicle and stopped beside it, the keys in my hand. The sun shone again that day, gleaming on the gold-and-silver-painted garlands; and after a moment I turned away and went back to my father.

'What's the matter?' he said, half annoyed. 'Can't you drive it?'

'Is it insured for someone my age?'

'Yes, of course. I wouldn't suggest it otherwise. Go and fetch it, Ben.'

I frowned and went back into the offices, ignoring his displeasure.

'It's time you went,' Mervyn said, equally impatient. 'You said you could drive George's car.'

I nodded. 'But I'd be better in a smaller car. Like you said, we don't want an accident. Do you have a smaller one? Could I borrow yours?'

Mervyn said with obvious aggravation, 'My car isn't insured for drivers under twenty-one.'

'Mine is, though,' Crystal said. 'My nineteen-year-old brother drives it. But it's not very glamorous. Not like the Range Rover.'

She dug the keys out of her handbag and said that Mervyn (to his impatience) would give her a lift home if we were not back by five-thirty, and would pick her up again in the morning. I thanked her with an awkward kiss on the cheek, and with Mervyn Teck repeating his disapproval, went out to rejoin my father.

'I'm disappointed in you, Ben,' he said, when Mervyn Teck explained. 'You'd better practise in the Range Rover tomorrow.'

'OK. But today, now, before we go, would you arrange for some mechanics to come here and make sure there's nothing wrong with it?'

'Of course there's nothing wrong with it. I drove it to Brighton and back yesterday and it was running perfectly.'

'Yes, but it's been standing out in the car park all night. Last night it's possible someone tried to shoot you. Suppose someone's hammered a nail or two into the Range Rover's tyres? Or anything.' I finished self-deprecatingly, as if I thought sabotage a childish fantasy; but after a brief thoughtful silence my father said to Mervyn, 'I'll go in Crystal's car. Ben can practise on the Range Rover tomorrow. Meanwhile, Mervyn, get the Range Rover overhauled, would you?'

Mervyn gave me a sour look, but it was he, after all, who had most wanted to avoid the accident-prone label: or so he'd said.

In Crystal's small work-a-day box on wheels I therefore drove the candidate safely to his far-flung appointments, and again I saw and heard him shake awake the apathetic voting public, progressively attracting more and more people as his voice raised laughter and applause. His audience approved with their eyes and shouted questions, some friendly, some hostile, all of them getting thoughtful answers, lightly phrased.

I didn't know how much of the day's flashing enthusiasm would actually carry the feet to the polling booths, but it was enough, my father assured me, if they didn't walk into the opposition camp and write their X for Bethune.

We had squeezed into Crystal's car an invention of my father's that was basically two wooden boxes, each a foot high, one larger than the other, that would bolt together, one on top of the other, to form an impromptu stepped platform to raise a speaker above his listeners: just enough for him to be comfortably heard, not high enough to be psychologically threatening. 'My soapbox' my father called it, though it was many years since such crowd-pulling structures had contained soap.

I assembled the 'soapbox' in three places in the town's scattered focal points, and at each place a crowd gathered, curious, or anti, or uncommitted, and at each place, as I unbolted, or assembled or packed away the stepped platform, people would crowd round me with (mostly) friendly enquiries.

'Are you his chauffeur?'

'Yes.'

'Is he as knowledgeable as he seems?'

'More so.'

'What does he think about education?'

I smiled. 'He's in favour of it.'

'Yes, but – '

'I can't answer for him. Please ask him yourself.'

They turned away and asked him, and got politically correct and truthful answers that would never be implemented without a huge increase in taxes: I was learning the economic facts as rapidly as I'd ever assimilated quadratic equations.

My father's appearance in Quindle had been well publicised in advance by posters all over the town. Volunteers had distributed them and volunteers met and escorted us everywhere, their faces shining with commitment. My own commitment, I had already found, was to my father himself, not to his party nor his beliefs. My private views, if I had any, were that good ideas were scattered around, not solely the property of any shade of rosette: and of course what were to me good ideas were hateful errors to others. I didn't embrace any single whole agenda package, and it was always those who didn't care passionately, those who changed their minds and swung with the wind, those who felt vaguely dissatisfied, they it was who swayed one side in or another side out. The 'floating voters', who washed back and forth with the tide, those were my father's target.

Quindle, like Hoopwestern, had grown in response to industries planted in the surrounding fields; not light bulbs this time, but furniture and paint. There had then been a long policy of 'infilling' – the building of large numbers of small houses on every patch of vacant grass. The resulting town strained against its green belt and suffered from interior traffic snarl-ups on a standstill scale. It worked well for soapbox orators: in the summer heat cars crept past with their windows down, getting the message.

Among the blizzard of VOTE JULIARD posters there were some for TITMUSS and WHISTLE and, of course, many for BETHUNE IS BETTER. GIVE HIM YOUR X. Bethune's notices on the whole looked tattered, and I found it wasn't merely because it was three days since he'd stomped inner Quindle on his own soapbox tour, but because the local weekly paper, the *Quindle Diary*, had hit the newsagents with 'Bethune for Sleaze' as its headline.

One of the volunteers having tucked the *Quindle Diary* under my elbow, I read the front page, as who wouldn't.

*'As our representative in Westminster, do we want an adulterer who says he upholds the family values to which this newspaper in this young town is dedicated? Do we believe the promises of one who can't keep a solemn vow?'*

I read to the end and thought the whole tone insufferably pompous, but I didn't suppose it would do the Bethune camp much good.

At each of his three ascents of the soapbox, my father was bombarded with demands that he should at least deplore the Bethune hypocrisy, and at each place, carefully side-stepping the loaded come-ons, he attacked Bethune and his party only for their political aims and methods.

His restraint didn't altogether please his own army of volunteers.

'George could *demolish* Bethune if he would only take a hatchet to his character,' one of them complained. 'Why won't he do it?'

'He doesn't believe in it,' I said.

'You have to play the aces you're given.'

'Not five aces,' I said.

'What?'

'He would think it cheating.'

The volunteer raised his eyes to heaven but changed his approach. 'You see that thin man standing near your father, writing in a notebook?'

'Do you mean the one in a pink jogging suit and a baseball hat on backwards?'

'I do indeed. He's called Usher Rudd. He writes for the *Hoopwestern Gazette* and his column is also syndicated to the *Quindle Diary*. It's he who wrote the personal attacks on Paul Bethune. He's been following Bethune around ever since his party chose him as their candidate. Rudd's a highly professional siever of mud. Never, *never* trust him.'

I said in apprehension, 'Does my father know who he is?'

'I told George that Usher Rudd would be bound to turn up again, but he doesn't always look the same. The pink overalls and baseball cap are new.'

'Usher Rudd's an unusual name.'

The volunteer laughed. 'He's really young Bobby Rudd, always a menace. His mother was Gracie Usher before she married a Rudd. The Rudd family have a string of repair garages, for anything from bicycles to combine harvesters, but fixing cars isn't to young

Bobby's taste. He calls himself an investigative journalist. More like a muck-raker, I'd say.'

I said tentatively, 'Was he at the dinner last night?'

'That big do at the Sleeping Dragon? He would have been for a certainty. He'll be furious that the gunshot and all that happened was too late for today's *Gazette*. The *Gazette* is only twenty-four pages long, mostly advertisements, sports results, local news and re-hashed world events. Everyone buys it for the dirt Rudd digs up. He was a rotten peeping tom as a little boy, always had his snotty nose glued to people's windows, and he hasn't got better with time. If you want to have sex with the vicar, don't do it in Quindle.'

I said dryly, 'Thanks for the advice.'

He laughed. 'Beware of Bobby Rudd, that's all.'

With the present crowd listening to my galvanic father with devouring eyes as much as persuadable ears, I slowly strolled round to guard his back; I was some poor sort of guardian to my parent, I thought with self-condemnation, if I left him wide open to repeat bullets or other jokers.

I did my best to look purposeless, but clearly failed with that message as Usher Rudd, also as if guileless, came to stand casually beside me. His baseball cap advertised vigorous sports goods, as did his footwear, and he wore between, from neck to ankle, a soft rose-pink loose exercise suit of nylon-like fabric which, instead of hiding the thinness of his body inside, gave an impression that the arms and legs functioned on a system of articulated rods. I, in my jeans and T-shirt, looked almost invisibly ordinary.

'Hello,' he said. 'Where is the Juliard battle-wagon?'

Puzzled, I answered, 'We came in a different car.'

'I'm Usher Rudd.'

His accent was unreconstructed Dorset, his manner confident to arrogant. He had unexcited blue eyes, sandy lashes and dry freckled skin: the small-boy menace who had peeped through windows still lived close to the surface and made me for once feel older than my years.

'What's your name?' he demanded, as I made no response.

'Benedict,' I said.

'Ben,' he asserted, nodding his recognition, 'Ben Juliard.'

'That's right.'

'How old are you?' He was abrupt, as if he had a right to the information.

'Seventeen,' I said without offence. 'How old are *you*?'

'That's none of your business.'

I gazed at him with a perplexity that was at least half genuine. Why should he think he could ask questions that he himself would not answer? I had a lot to learn, as my father had said; but I instinctively didn't like him.

Close behind my back my father was answering the sort of questions it was proper he should be asked:

where did he stand on education, foreign policy, taxes, the dis-united kingdom and the inability of bishops to uphold the ten commandments? 'Shouldn't sins be modernised?' someone shouted. Moses was out of date.

My father, who certainly lived by 'thou shalt not' rather than by 'what can I get away with?' replied with humour, 'By all means pension off Moses if you would like your neighbour to covet your ox and your ass and carry off your wife and your lawn mower . . .'

The end of his sentence drowned in laughter and cheers, and for fifteen more minutes he had them spellbound, feeding them political nuggets in nourishing soup, producing a performance without microphone or footlights that they would never forget. All my life people would say to me, 'I heard your father speak in Quindle,' as if it had been a revelation in their existence: and it wasn't altogether *what* he said that mattered, I reckoned, but his whole, honest, joyous, vigorous presentation.

Against the final applause, Usher Rudd said to me, 'Birthday?'

'What?'

'Your birthday?'

'Yes,' I said.

'Yes, what?'

'Yes, I do have a birthday.'

He thought me dim. 'What's your mother's name?' he said.

'Sarah.'

'Her last name?'

'Yes. She's dead.'

His expression changed. His gaze grew thoughtful and flicked downward to the *Quindle Diary* that I held rolled in my hand. I saw him understand the obtuseness of my answers.

'Bethune deserves it,' he said sharply.

'I don't know anything about him,' I said.

'Then read my column.'

'Even then . . .'

'Everyone has secrets,' he declared with relish. 'I just find them out. I enjoy doing it. They deserve it.'

'The public has a right to know?' I asked.

'Of course they do. If someone is setting themselves up to make our laws and rule our lives they shouldn't sleaze it off with dirty sex on the side, should they?'

'I haven't thought about it.'

'If old George is hiding dirty secrets, I'll find them out. What's your mother's name?'

'Sarah. She's dead.'

He gave me a bitter antagonistic glare.

'I'm sure you do a good detective job,' I said mildly. 'My mother's name was Sarah Juliard. Married. Dead. Sorry about that.'

'I'll find out,' he threatened.

'Be my guest.'

My father disengaged himself from eager clutching

voters and turned to say he was ready for his lunch engagement: a volunteers' gathering in a pub.

'This,' I said, indicating the inhabitant of the pink tracksuit and the energetic shoes and baseball hat, 'is Usher Rudd.'

'Nice to know you,' my father said, automatically ready to shake hands. 'Do you work for the party, er . . . Usher?'

'He writes for newspapers,' I said. I unrolled the *Quindle Diary* so he could see the front page. 'He wrote this. He wants me to tell him my mother's name.'

I was getting to know my father. Twenty-four hours earlier I wouldn't have been aware that a tiny tensing of muscles and a beat of silence meant a fizzingly fast assessment of unwelcome facts. Not only powerful but dauntingly rapid: not only analytical but an instant calculator of down-the-line consequences. Some brain.

He smiled politely at Usher Rudd. 'My wife's name was Sarah. Unfortunately she died.'

'What of?' Usher Rudd, disconcerted by my father's pleasant frankness, sounded aggressively rude.

'It was a long time ago.' My father remained civil. 'Come on, Ben, or we'll be late.'

We turned away and walked three paces; and Bobby Usher Rudd, darting round and wheeling in the running shoes, came to a halt facing us, standing in our way.

His voice was thin, malicious and triumphant. 'I'll get you de-selected. Orinda Nagle will have her rights.'

'Ah.' My father packed all the understanding in the world into one syllable. 'So you rubbished Paul Bethune to give her a clear run, is that it?'

Usher Rudd was furious. 'She's worth ten of you.'

'She's a lucky woman to have so many fans.'

'You'll lose.' Usher Rudd almost danced with rage. 'She would have won.'

'Well . . .' My father detoured past him with me at his heels, and Usher Rudd behind us yelled the question I would never have asked but wanted like crazy to know the answer to. 'If your wife died long ago, what do you do for sex?'

My father certainly heard but there wasn't a falter in his step. I risked a flick of a glance at his face but learned nothing: he showed no embarrassment or anxiety, only, if anything, *amusement*.

The lunch in the pub was up-beat, the volunteers all intoxicated with the speech stops of the morning. In the afternoon we toured a furniture factory and then a paint factory, where the candidate (leaning on his walking stick) listened intently to local problems and promised remedies if he were elected. He shook countless hands and signed countless autographs, and left behind an atmosphere of hope.

When Mervyn Teck had made his plans he had expected it to be Orinda who charmed the woodworkers and the colour mixers, and there had been resistance in parts of the factories to the one seen as a usurper. My father defused criticism by praising

Orinda steadfastly without apologising for having been
chosen to take her place.

'A natural-born politician,' one of the lady volunteers said in my ear. 'The way the country's leaning,
we'd lose this marginal seat with Orinda, though she
doesn't believe that, of course. With your father we've
a better chance, but voters are unpredictable and can
often be downright vindictive, and they mostly vote
for party, not for individuals, and the sleaze accusations
won't hurt Paul Bethune much, especially with male
voters who privately don't think a spot of adultery too
much of a big deal, and will think "good luck to him".
And you'd fancy women wouldn't vote for adulterers,
but they do.'

'Doesn't Usher Rudd shift the Xs from one slot to
another?'

'Not as much as he believes, the little weasel. It's
not the locals that pay attention to him as much as
the big noises in Westminster. They're all shit-scared
of him digging into their pasts, and the higher they
climb the more they hate him. Haven't you noticed
that when an MP screws up his or her reputation, it's
their own party that dumps them quickest?'

The correct answer was no, I hadn't noticed,
because I hadn't been looking.

On our way back to Hoopwestern I asked my father
what he thought of Usher Rudd but he yawned, said
he was flaked out and his ankle hurt, and promptly
went to sleep. I drove carefully, still not instinctive in

traffic, and woke the candidate by a jerking halt at a red light at a crossroads.

'Usher Rudd,' he said without preamble, as if twenty minutes hadn't passed between question and answer, 'will burn his fingers on privacy laws.'

I said, 'I didn't know there were any privacy laws.'

'There will be.'

'Oh.'

'Usher Rudd has red hair under that baseball cap.'

'How do you know?'

'He came to the meeting after last night's dinner. Polly pointed him out to me. He wore a black tracksuit and black trainers. Didn't you see him?'

'I don't remember him.'

'Find out if he can shoot.'

I opened my mouth to say 'Wow' or 'How?' and thought better of both. My father glanced at me sideways, and I felt him smile.

'I don't think it was him,' I said.

'Why not?'

'His bullets of choice are acid ink.'

'Are you sure you want to be a mathematician? Why don't you try writing?'

'I want to be a jockey.' Might as well walk on the moon.

'Exeter University required to know where you would spend your gap year before they offered you a deferred entry: that is to say, you're going there not this October, but next year. They weren't enthusiastic about racecourses.'

'There's an Exeter racecourse.'

'You know damned well what they mean.'

'I don't like politics.' Change the subject.

'Politics are the oil of the world.'

'You mean . . . the world doesn't run without oil?'

He nodded. 'When politics jam solid, you get wars.'

'Father – ' I said.

'Dad.'

'No. Father. Why do you want to be a politician?'

After a pause he said, 'I am one. I can't help it.'

'But you've never . . . I mean . . .'

'I've never made a move before? Don't think I haven't considered it. I've known since I was your age or younger that one day I would try for Parliament. But I needed a solid base. I needed to prove to myself that I could make money. I needed to understand economics. And then there came a time not long ago when I said to myself "now or never". So it's now.'

It was the longest statement about himself that he'd ever made in my hearing; and he had simplified for my sake, I thought, an urge that had taken time to ripen and had burst out fully grown at the Sleeping Dragon. The Juliard dragon was awake now and roaring and prowling up broad Whitehall towards Number 10.

Thinking about him, I lost the way home. He made no sarcastic comment when I stopped, consulted the

map, worked out where I'd gone wrong and finally
arrived in the car park from an unexpected direction;
and for that forbearance alone I would have served
him as an esquire to a knight. How old-fashioned could
one get?

It was well after six o'clock when we reached the
car park which, in consequence, was almost empty. All
the bordering shops had closed for the day. The late
afternoon sunshine weakened to soft gold as I pulled
up and applied Crystal's brakes.

There were dim lights in the office, but no people.
I unlocked the door and we found a large note laid
out prominently on Mervyn Teck's desk.

'The Range Rover is in Rudd's Repair Garage.
They thoroughly overhauled it, and found nothing
wrong.'

# CHAPTER FOUR

I would have expected the nervous energy of the day-
long performance in Quindle to have earned my father
an evening's rest, but I had barely begun to wake up
to the stamina demanded of would-be public servants.
It seemed that far from a quiet top-up of batteries, he
was committed to another marathon shake-hands-and-
smile, not this time in the chandeliered magnificence
of the Sleeping Dragon's all-purpose hall, but in much
more basic space normally used as a schooling ground
for five-year-olds in Hoopwestern's outer regions.

There were kids' attempts at pictures pinned to cork
boards all round the walls, mostly thin figures with big
heads and spiky hair sticking straight out like Medusa's
snakes. There were simple notices – 'do not run' and
'raise your hand' – all written in self-conscious lower
case letters.

Primary colours everywhere bombarded the eyesight to saturation point, and I couldn't believe that
this sort of thing had been my own educational spring-
board; but it had. Another world, long left behind.

There were several rows of the temporary flip-up seats that grew more and more familiar to me as the days passed, and a makeshift speaker's platform, this time with a microphone that squeaked whenever tested, and on several other occasions when switched on or off.

The lighting was of unflattering greenish-white fluorescent strips, and there weren't enough of them to raise spirits above depression. Limbo must look like this, I thought: and the unenticing room had in fact drawn the sort of audience you could count on fingers and toes and still have enough left over for an abacus.

Mervyn Teck met us on the doorstep looking at his watch and checking, but by good luck and asking the way (less pride on my part than shame of arriving late) we had turned up at the exact minute advertised by a scatter of leaflets.

On the table on the platform, beside the temperamental microphone, there was a gavel for calling the meeting to order and two large plates of sandwiches secured by cling film.

Two or three earnest lady volunteers crowded round the candidate with goodwill, but it was plain, ten minutes after start time, that apathy, and not enthusiasm, had won the evening.

I expected my father to be embarrassed by the small turn-out and to hurry through the unsatisfactory proceedings, but he made a joke of it, abandoning the microphone and sitting on the edge of the platform, beckoning the sparse and scattered congregation to come forward into the first few rows, to make the meeting more coherent.

His magic worked. Everyone moved forward. He spoke to them familiarly, as if addressing a roomful of friends, and I watched him turn a disaster into a useful exercise in public relations. By the time the sandwiches had been liberated from the cling film even the few who had come to heckle had been tamed to silence.

Mervyn Teck looked both thoughtful and displeased.

'Something the matter?' I asked.

He said sourly, 'Orinda would have drawn a much better house. She'd have packed the hall. They love her here: she presents prizes to the children here every term. She buys them herself.'

'I'm sure she'll go on doing it.'

I meant it without irony, but Mervyn Teck gave me a glance of dislike and moved away. One of the lady volunteers sweetly told me that the time of the meeting had clashed with the current rave series on the television, and that even the pubs were suffering from it on Thursday nights. Tomorrow would be different, she said. Tomorrow the Town Hall would be packed.

'Er . . .' I said, 'what's happening in the Town Hall?'

'But you're his son, aren't you?'

'Yes, but . . .'

'But you don't know that tomorrow night your

father goes face to face in a debate with Paul Bethune?'

I shook my head.

'Fireworks,' she said happily. 'I wouldn't miss it for the world.'

My father, when I asked him about it on the short drive back to the centre of Hoopwestern, seemed full of equal relish.

'I suppose,' I said, 'there'll be more point to it than the sort of fiasco tonight could have been.'

'Every vote counts,' he corrected me. 'If I won only a few tonight, that's fine. You have to win the floaters over to your side, and they have to be persuaded one by one.'

'I'm hungry,' I said as we passed a brightly lit take-away, so we backtracked and bought chicken wings with banana and bacon, and even there my father, recognised, fell into political chat with the man deep-frying chips.

In the morning early I went out and bought a copy of the *Gazette*. Sleaze and Paul Bethune filled pages four and five (with photographs) but the front-page topic of concern was headlined 'JULIARD SHOT?'

Columns underneath said Yes (eyewitnesses) and No (he wasn't hurt). Statements from the police said nothing much (they couldn't find a gun). Statements from onlookers, like the self-important gunshot expert, said Juliard had definitely been the object of an assassination attempt. He thought so and he was always right.

The consensus theory of the reporters (including Usher Rudd) was that resentment against Juliard was running high in the Orinda Nagle camp. The editor's leader column didn't believe that political assassination ever took place at so low a level. World leaders, perhaps. Unelected local candidates, never.

I walked through the town to the ring road looking for Rudd's Repair Garage and found the staff unlocking their premises for the day. They had a large covered workshop and an even larger wire-fenced compound where jobs done or waiting stood in haphazard rows. The Range Rover was parked in that compound, sunlight already gleaming on its metallic paint.

I asked for, and reached, the manager, whose name was Basil Rudd. Thin, red-haired, freckled and energetic, his likeness to Usher Rudd made twins a possibility.

'Don't ask,' he said, eyeing my newspaper. 'He's my cousin. I disown him, and if you're out to be busy with your fists, you've reached the wrong man.'

'Well, I really came to collect that Range Rover. It's my father's.'

'Oh?' He blinked. 'I'll need proof of identity.'

I showed him a letter of authorisation signed by my parent and also my driving licence.

'Fair enough.' He opened a drawer, picked out a labelled ring bearing two keys and held them out for me to take. 'Don't forget to switch off the alarms. I'll send the bill to Mr Juliard's party headquarters. OK?'

'Yes. Thank you. Was there anything wrong?'

He shrugged. 'If there was, there isn't now.' He consulted a spiked worksheet. 'Oil change. General check. That's all.'

'Do you think I could talk to whoever did the job?'

'Whatever for?'

'Er ... I've got to drive my father round in that vehicle and I've never driven it before ... and I thought I might get some tips about engine management ... so I don't overheat it by crawling along the roads canvassing door to door.'

Basil Rudd shrugged. 'Ask for Terry. He did the work.'

I thanked him and sought out Terry who gave three instant physical impressions: big; bald; belly. Brown overalls, grease-stained from his job.

He too eyed my newspaper. He spoke with venom in a powerful Dorset voice.

'Don't mention Bobby bloody Rudd round here.'

I hadn't been going to, but I said, 'Why not?'

'He'll listen to you and your missus in bed with one of them window-vibrating bugging contraptions and before you know it, never mind the sex, he'll be printing what you said about the boss having his hand up a customer's skirt when she brings her car in for the twentieth time to be overhauled, though there's bugger all wrong with it in the first place. Got me sacked, Bobby did.'

'But,' I suggested, 'you're still here.'

'Yeah, see, Basil took me on because he loathes Bobby, who's his cousin, see. It was over in Quindle I got sacked by Bobby's dad, that's Basil's uncle, drunk half the time . . .' He broke off. 'If it's not to complain about Bobby Usher bleeding Rudd, what is it you want, lad?'

'I . . . er . . . you serviced my father's Range Rover. What was wrong with it?'

'Apart from the fancy paintwork?' He scratched his shiny head. 'Foreign body in the oil sump. I suppose you might say that. Nothing else. I gave it a good clean-out.'

'What sort of foreign body?'

He looked at me dubiously. 'I don't rightly know.'

'Well, um . . . how do you know it was there?'

He took his time in answering by starting at the beginning of his involvement. 'A man in your party's headquarters – said his name was Teck or some such – he phones Basil saying there might be something dicey about a fancy Range Rover they'd got there and to send someone over pronto to take a decko, so I went over there and this Mr Teck gave me the keys and the Range Rover started at first touch, sweet as anything.'

I looked at him without comment.

'Yeah, well,' he said, scratching his bald head again. 'This Teck guy said something about maybe someone took a pot shot at your old man and to check that the Range Rover's brakes hadn't been mucked about with or anything, so I looked it all over and could see nothing wrong. No bombs, nothing like that, but anyway this Teck guy said to bring it here and do a thorough service, so I did.'

He stopped for effect. I said obligingly, 'What did you find?'

'See, it was what I *didn't* find.'

'I wish you'd explain.'

'No plug on the sump.'

'What?'

'Oil change. Routine service. I run the Range Rover over the inspection pit and I take a spanner to unscrew the sump-plug to drain out the old oil, and there you are, no plug. *No plug*, I ask you. But there's oil there, according to the dipstick. Normal. Full. So I run the engine a bit and the oil pressure gauge reads normal, like it did on my way round here, so there has to be oil circulating round the engine, see, so why, if the sump-plug is missing, why hasn't the oil all emptied out?'

'Well, why?'

'Because there's something else plugging up the hole, that's why.'

'A rag?' I suggested. 'A wad of tissues?'

'Nothing like that, I don't think. Something harder.

Anyway, I poked a bit of wire into the hole and freed whatever was there and the oil poured out like it always does. Not filthy oil, mind you. It hadn't been long since the last oil change.'

'So the plug, whatever it is, is still in the sump?'

He shrugged. 'I dare say so. It won't do much harm there. The sump drain-hole's not much bigger than a little finger.' He held up his own grimy hand. 'It wasn't a *big* plug, see.'

'Mm.' I hesitated. 'Did you tell Basil Rudd about it?'

He shook his big head. 'He'd gone home for the day when I put the work-done sheets in his office, and I didn't think much of it. I found a new plug that fits the Range Rover and screwed it up tight. Then I filled up with clean oil, same as usual, and put the Range Rover out in the yard, where it is now. It's all hunky-dory. You'll have no trouble with it.'

'I'll take it in a minute,' I said. 'I'll just go back into the office to see about settling up.'

I went into the office and asked Basil Rudd if I could telephone my father in the party headquarters and he obligingly held out the receiver to me with a be-my-guest invitation.

I said to my father, 'Please could you ask whoever it was who worked on your Range Rover last if there was a normal plug on the oil-sump drain.' I relayed Terry's finding and his solution to the problem.

Basil Rudd looked up sharply from a sheet of paper

he was writing on and began to protest, but I smiled, said it was an unimportant enquiry, and waited for my father's answer. He told me to stay right where I was and five minutes later was back on the line.

'My mechanic is very annoyed at any suggestion that there was any irregularity at all with any part of the Range Rover. He did a complete overhaul on Monday. So what is going on?'

'I don't exactly know. It's probably nothing.'

'Bring the Range Rover back. We need it today.'

'Yes,' I said.

I gave the receiver back to Basil Rudd and thanked him for the call.

'Just what is this all about?' he said.

'I don't know enough,' I replied. 'I haven't been driving long. But I am concerned with keeping my father safe since the episode with the gun . . .' I waved the newspaper, 'so I'm probably being fussy over nothing. But on its last overhaul there was an ordinary plug screwed into the sump drain, and yesterday there wasn't.'

Basil Rudd showed first of all impatience and then anxiety, and finally stood up and came with me back to talk to Terry.

Terry, for a change, was scratching his brown-overalled belly.

I said, 'I'm not complaining about anything here, and please don't think I am. I do want to know what was plugging the sump, though, because I'm frankly scared of mysteries concerning anything to do with my father. So, please, how would you put a substitute plug in the drain-hole, and most of all, why?'

The two motor men stood in silence, not knowing the answers.

'The oil was quite clean,' Terry said.

Another silence.

Basil Rudd said, 'If you drain the new oil out again, and take the engine apart, you'll find whatever the stopper was that Terry pushed through the sump, but that's a very expensive procedure and not justified, I don't think.'

Another silence.

'I'll ask my father,' I said.

We trooped back to the office and I reported the last-resort expensive solution of dismantling the engine.

'Do nothing. Stay where you are,' my father commanded. 'Just do nothing, and wait. Let me speak to Basil Rudd.'

The chit-chat went on for several minutes. Basil Rudd said he thought the boy – meaning me – was making a hullabaloo over nothing much, but in the end he shrugged and said, 'Yes, yes, all right.' He put down the receiver and said to me, 'Your father is sending someone for the Range Rover. He wants you to stay here for now.'

Terry muttered that he had done a proper service on the Range Rover and no one could tell him different. Basil Rudd gave me a look of disfavour and said he couldn't waste any more time, he had mountains of paperwork to see to. I didn't exactly apologise, but I said I would wait outside in the Range Rover and walked peacefully across to where it stood in the wire-fenced compound. I disarmed the alarms, opened the door and sat behind the driving wheel, going through the systems and reading the instruction book.

I waited for over an hour until Basil Rudd appeared at the window beside me. I opened the door, stepped down to the ground and met the man accompanying the garage owner, who announced with a glint of irony that he had come to solve the mystery of the missing sump-plug. His name, he said, was Foster Fordham. He looked more like a lawyer than a mechanic: no blue collar to his grey and white pinstriped shirt or his neat dark suit. He had straight, dark, well-brushed hair, light-framed glasses and polished black shoes.

Basil Rudd, turning away, asked Foster Fordham to report to him in the office before leaving and, watching Rudd's departing back, Fordham, apparently bored to inertia, informed me that he was here to do my father a big favour, as normally he was a consultant engineer, not a hands-on minion.

I began to explain about the gunshot, but he interrupted that he knew all about it, and all about the missing plug.

'I work in car-racing circles,' he said. 'My field is sabotage.'

I no doubt looked as inadequate as I felt in the face of his quiet assurance.

He said, 'I understand that yesterday you were going to drive this vehicle from here to Quindle. How far is that?'

'About twelve miles.'

'Dual carriageway? Flat straight roads?'

'Mostly single lane, a lot of sharp corners, and some of it uphill.'

He nodded. He said we would now take the road to Quindle and he would drive.

Perplexed but trusting I climbed into the passenger seat beside him and listened to the healthy purr of the engine as he started up and drove off out of the garage compound onto the ring road round Hoopwestern, bound for Quindle. He drove fast in silence, watching the instrument panel as intently as the road, and said nothing until we had reached the top of the long steep incline halfway to what I thought was our destination. He stopped up there, however, and, still without explaining, did a U-turn and drove straight back to Rudd's garage.

Cars flashed past, appearing fast towards us from blind corners, as they had the day before. Fordham drove faster than I'd felt safe doing in Crystal's car, but if his field was racing, that was hardly surprising.

At the garage he told Terry to drain the engine oil into a clean container. Terry said the oil was too hot

85

to handle. Fordham agreed to wait a little, but insisted that the oil should still be hot when it was drained.

'Why?' Terry asked. 'It's clean. I did the oil change yesterday.'

Fordham didn't answer. Eventually, wearing heavy gloves, Terry unscrewed the sump-plug and let the hot oil drain out as requested into a clean plastic five-gallon container. Fordham had him put the container into the luggage space at the back of the Range Rover and then suggested he should screw the sump-plug back into place and refill the engine with fresh cool oil.

Terry signalled exasperation with his eyebrows but did as he was asked. Mr Fordham, calm throughout, then told me that he had finished his investigation and suggested we say farewell to Basil Rudd and return in the Range Rover to my father's headquarters. Basil Rudd, of course, wanted to know reasons. Fordham told him with great politeness that he would receive a written report, and meanwhile not to worry, all was well.

Fordham drove composedly to the car park outside my father's headquarters and, with me faithfully following, walked into the offices where my father was sitting with Mervyn Teck discussing tactics.

My father stood at the sight of us and limped outside with Fordham to the Range Rover. Through the window I watched them talking earnestly, then Fordham took the plastic container of oil out of the

Range Rover, put it into the boot of a Mercedes standing nearby, climbed into the driver's seat, and neatly departed.

My father, returning, told Mervyn cheerfully that there was now nothing wrong with the Range Rover and it could safely be driven all round the town.

We finally set off. I drove, feeling my way cautiously through the gears, learning the positive message of the four-wheel drive. My father sat beside me, accompanied by his walking stick. Mervyn Teck, carrying a megaphone, sat in the rear seat, squeezing his lumpy knees together to allow more space for two volunteer helpers, thin bittersweet Lavender and motherly Faith.

The rear-seaters knew their drill from much past practice, and I with eye-opening wonderment became acquainted with the hardest graft in politics, the door-to-door begging for a 'yes' vote.

The first chosen residential street consisted of identical semi-detached houses with clipped garden-defining hedges and short concrete drives up to firmly closed garage doors. Some of the front windows were adorned with stickers simply announcing 'BETHUNE': he had worked this land before us.

'This road is awash with floaters,' Mervyn said with rare amusement. 'Let's see what we can do about turning the tide our way.'

Directing me to stop the vehicle, he untucked himself from his seatbelt and, standing in the open air, began to exhort the invisible residents through the reverberating megaphone, to vote JULIARD, JULIARD, JULIARD.

I found it odd to have my name bouncing off the house fronts, but the candidate himself nodded with smiling approval.

Lavender and Faith followed Mervyn out of the car, each of them carrying a bundle of stickers printed JULIARD in slightly larger letters than BETHUNE. Taking one side of the road each they began ringing front door bells and knocking knockers and, where they got no response, tucking a sticker through the letter-box.

If a door was opened to them they smiled and pointed to the Range Rover from where my father would limp bravely up the garden path to put on his act, at which he was clearly terrific. I crawled up the road in low gear, my father limped uncomplainingly, Mervyn activated his megaphone and Lavender and Faith wasted not a leaflet. In our slow wake we left friendly waves and a few JULIARDs in windows. By the end of the street I was bored to death, but it seemed Lavender and Faith both revelled in persuasion tactics and were counting the road a victory for their side.

After two more long sweeps through suburbia (in which at least one baby got kissed) we respited for a late sandwich lunch in a pub.

'If ever you get invited into someone's home,' my father said (as he had been invited five or six times that morning), 'you go into the sitting-room and you say, "Oh, what an attractive room!" even if you think it's hideous.'

Lavender, Faith and Mervyn all nodded, and I said, 'That's cynical.'

'You've a lot to learn.'

We were sitting by a window. I looked through it to the Range Rover parked outside in plain view and reckoned that one way or another I actually had learned a lot that morning, and that what I'd learned had probably saved a good many votes.

My father, as if following my thoughts, said lightly, 'We'll talk about it later,' but it wasn't until we were changing before going to the Town Hall debate that he would discuss Foster Fordham.

By then I'd persuaded Mervyn to arrange a securely locked overnight garage for the Range Rover, backed by my casual parent who said mildly, 'The boy's got a point, Mervyn. It might be more satisfactory for us all. No harm, anyway, in keeping it safe from thieves,' and as the car belonged to my father himself and not to the party, he had his way.

'Foster Fordham wasn't sure how much you understood,' he said, combing through his tightly curled dark hair and leaving it much as it had been before. 'He was surprised you didn't ask him questions.'

'Terry – the mechanic – did ask. Fordham wouldn't answer.'

'So what do you conclude it was all about?'

'Well . . . if you or I or anyone else had driven the

Range Rover yesterday towards Quindle, it would quite likely have crashed. Or, at least, I think so.'

My father put down his comb and with stillness said, 'Go on.'

I said, 'I do think the bullet that came so near us was deliberately aimed at you, and even if it hadn't killed you, it would have stopped your campaign if you'd been badly injured. But all the town could see that all you'd done was twist your ankle. So if anyone was looking around for another way to put a stopper on you, there was the Range Rover, just standing there unguarded all night in the car park, conspicuously yours and painted with silver and gold to attract attention.'

'Yes.'

'When I was taking driving lessons, which was mostly in the Easter holidays, I read a lot of motoring magazines – '

'I thought you were supposed to be revising for your A levels, your university entrance exams.'

'Um... I was riding for Sir Vivian, too. I mean, I can *think* in algebra. I just had to make sure I understood all the exam questions that have been set before, set in the past. I don't mean to sound big-headed, really I don't, but I had sort of a lot of spare mental time, so I read the motor magazines. I didn't know you had a Range Rover – but I read about them. I read about their anti-thief devices. So when your Range Rover had stood quiet in the car park all night, and you had the only keys to disarm the screech alarms, then if anyone had done any harm it had to have been from outside . . . or underneath . . .' I tapered off, feeling silly, but he waved for me to go on.

'I thought the brake fluid might have been drained so that the brakes wouldn't work,' I said. 'I thought the tyres might have been slashed so that you'd have a blow-out when you were going fast. Things come whizzing round corners on that road to Quindle . . . you wouldn't have much chance in a car out of control, but a Range Rover is pretty well built like a tank – so *you* might be unhurt in a crash, but you might kill the people you crashed *into* . . . or at least injure them badly . . . and that would stop you being elected, wouldn't it?'

My father took his time in moving, and in answering. 'It wasn't the brakes or the tyres,' he said.

'It was the engine oil.'

He nodded. 'Tell me what you think.'

I said, 'I think Fordham knew what was wrong before he came. He said he was an expert in sabotage in motor racing, and nothing about the Range Rover surprised him. It must have seemed pretty elementary to him.'

My father, smiling, said, 'I've known him a long time. So, what did he tell me?'

This is some sort of test, I thought. I could only guess at answers; but anyhow, I guessed. 'Someone unscrewed the sump-plug and removed it, and stuffed up the hole so that the oil couldn't all run out.'

'Go on.'

'The stopper was something that would fall out later, so the oil would all drain out of the engine when it was going along, and the engine would seize up solid, and as it's a four-wheel drive you wouldn't be able to steer and you would be like a block of stone in the middle of the road.'

'Not bad.'

'But Terry – the mechanic – pushed the substitute plug right through into the sump like a cork in a bottle, which I honestly don't think he should have done, and screwed in a new plug before he refilled with clean oil . . . like I told you on the phone.'

'Mm. So what was the substitute plug made of?'

I'd been thinking about it while we drove round the suburbs. I said hesitantly, 'To begin with I thought it would be something chemical that could react with the oil and make it like jelly, or something, so that it couldn't be pumped round the pistons and they would seize up in the cylinders, but that can't have been right as the plug was in the sump when Foster Fordham drove fast towards Quindle and deliberately made the engine very hot, and he insisted on Terry draining out the clean oil again when it was still hot, so I thought that perhaps the temporary stopper had *melted*, and Fordham has taken the oil away to see what was in it.'

'Yes,' my father said.

'Because if it had melted away in the sump drain-hole when we were on our way to Quindle yesterday, it would have taken only about a minute for all the oil to drain out and ruin the engine. When the oil was hot this morning, when Terry drained it, it ran out as thin as water.'

'Fordham says it's an old trick. So old, it's never attempted now in motor racing.'

'Well . . . what was the plug made of?'

'What would you think?'

I hesitated. 'It had to be pretty simple. I mean, almost spur-of-the-moment, after the bullet had missed.'

'So?'

'So how about shoving a candle up the spout, and cutting it off? How about *wax*?'

My father peacefully tied his unexuberantly striped tie. 'Foster Fordham,' he said, 'will let us know.'

It was extraordinary, I thought, as we entered the Town Hall for the Bethune face-to-face confrontation, how many people I'd come to recognise in only two days.

Orinda was there, torturing herself, wearing a very short gold dress with a black feather boa that twisted round her neck and arms like the snake it was named for, and demanded admiring attention. Her green eyes flashed. An emerald and diamond bracelet sparkled on her wrist. No one could be unaware of her vibrant attendance.

A pace behind her, as ever, stood her shadow, whose name I remembered with an effort was A.L. Wyvern. 'A.L.', I thought, 'Anonymous Lover' Wyvern. He had looked uninteresting in a dinner jacket at the Sleeping Dragon dinner: in the Town Hall, in a grey suit and a blue shirt, he filled space without making an impression.

Large Mrs Kitchens, eagle-eyed, in navy blue with purple frills, held tight to 'my Leonard's' arm and succeeded in preventing him from beaming his sickly moustache into Orinda's airspace. Mrs Kitchens gave me a cheery wave and a leer – and I would *not* let her embarrass me.

Mervyn, of course, had arrived with Crystal at his side to take notes. The three witches were helping to seat people, and Dearest Polly, at the sight of us, made an enthusiastic little run in our direction, and bore off my father like a trophy to show him the lectern behind which he was to stand on the platform. Dearest Polly, it seemed, was stage-managing the evening.

As if with a flourish of trumpets the Bethune camp arrived. There was a stir and a rustle in the hall and a sprinkle of clapping. Hooray for adultery, I thought.

Paul Bethune, seen for the first time, was a portly and portentous-looking fifty or so with a double chin and the thinning hair that might in the end confound his chances more thoroughly than a love-child. He was accompanied by a busy Mervyn Teck lookalike, who was indeed his agent, and by a nervous woman who looked at the world in general in upward glances from under her eyebrows. She was shown to a seat in the front row of spectators and Dearest Polly, beckoning to me strongly, introduced me to Paul Bethune's wife, Isobel.

Isobel emitted severe discomfort at having me to sit beside her, but I gave her my best harmless grin and told her she couldn't want to avoid being there more than I did myself.

'I've only just left school,' I said. 'I don't know anything about politics. I understand this is the third campaign for you and Mr Bethune, so you probably don't find it as confusing as I do.'

'Oh dear,' she said. 'You're such a child, you can't possibly know . . .'

'I'm nearly eighteen.'

She smiled weakly, then suddenly stiffened to immobility, her face pale with a worse disaster than my proximity.

I said, 'What's the matter, Mrs Bethune?'

'That man,' she murmured. 'Oh God.'

I looked where she was looking, and saw Basil Rudd.

'That's not Usher Rudd, the newspaperman,' I said, understanding. 'That's his cousin. That's Basil Rudd. He mends cars.'

'It's *him*. That beastly writer.'

'No, Mrs Bethune. It's his cousin. They look alike, but that's Basil.'

To my absolute horror, she began to cry. I looked around urgently for help but Polly was elbow-deep in wires to microphones and television cameras, and Paul Bethune, eyeing his wife's distress, turned away deliberately with a sharply displeased grimace.

Unkind bastard, I thought. Stupid, too. A show of fondness might have earned him votes.

Isobel Bethune stumbled to her feet, searching unsuccessfully in her well-worn black handbag for something to mop up tears, and I, clumsily but with pity, offered her an arm to hold on to while I cleared a path towards the door.

She talked all the way in broken half-intelligible explanations. 'Paul insisted I came . . . I didn't want to, but he said I might as well stab him in the back if I didn't . . . and now he'll be so *furious*, but what does he expect me to do after all those pictures in the paper of him and that girl . . . and she had nothing on, well, next to nothing. He wants me to smile and pretend I don't mind, but he makes me look a fool and I suppose I am, but I didn't know about that girl until it was in the paper, and he doesn't deny it. He says what did I expect . . .'

We went through the entrance hall and out into the fresh air with everyone arriving and staring at Isobel's tears with hungry curiosity. At seven-thirty in the evening merciful dusk was still some time ahead, so I veered away from the entrance and she, wholly without resistance, came with me round the nearest corner.

The Town Hall formed one of the sides of the cobbled square. The Sleeping Dragon took up an adjoining side, with shops (and party headquarters) along the other two. Wide alleyways, that once had been open roads, led away from every corner, and on one of them lay the main Town Hall entrance doors. Along the side of the Town Hall that faced onto the square, there was a sort of cloister – a covered walkway with pillars and benches giving shelter and rest. Isobel Bethune crumpled onto one of the benches and, after a craven moment of wanting to ditch her, I sat beside her and wondered what to say.

I needn't have worried. She compulsively went on sobbing and pouring out her unhappiness and resentment at the unfairness of things. I half listened, watching the wretchedness that twisted her lipsticked mouth, and seeing in her swelling eyes and grey-flecked hair that not long ago she'd been quite pretty, before Usher Rudd had taken a photographic sledge-hammer to her complacent world.

Her sons were just as bad, she sobbed. Fifteen, seventeen, they sulked and argued with everything she said and complained non-stop. If Paul got elected it would at least take him away from home more, and, oh dear, she didn't mean to say that, but it was either him or her – and where would she go? She was at her wit's end, she said.

She was on the point of a full breakdown, I thought. I had been only about twelve when my Aunt Susan had screamed and yelled and slammed doors, had driven the family car across the lawn into a hedge and been taken to hospital, and had then got worse when her second son left to join a rap group and grew a beard and got AIDS. My Uncle Harry had gone to my father for help, and somehow or other my parent had restored general order and put some balance back in Susan; and if it was never a rapturously happy household after that, there was no actual abuse.

I asked Isobel Bethune, 'Do your sons want Mr Bethune to be elected?'

'They just grunt. You can't get a word out of them.' She sniffed, wiping her eyes with her fingers. 'Paul thinks he would have beaten Orinda easily, but he says George Juliard is different. Oh! I'd forgotten, you're his son! I shouldn't talk to you like this. Paul will be so cross.'

'Don't tell him.'

'No . . . would you like a drink?' She looked across at the Sleeping Dragon. 'Brandy?'

I shook my head but she said she badly needed a nerve-steadier and she wouldn't drink alone, so I went across the square with her and drank Coke while she dealt with a double Rémy Martin on ice. We sat at a small table in the bar, which was Friday-night busy with couples.

Both of Isobel's hands were shaking.

She left me to go and 'tidy up', returning with combed hair, freshened lipstick and powdered eyelids, still clutching a tissue but much more in control.

She ordered more brandy. I said no to Coke.

'I'm not going back to the Town Hall,' she said. 'I'll walk home from here. It's not all that far.'

When she picked up her refilled glass, the ice still clattered and shook in her grasp.

'Could I get you a taxi?' I asked.

She leaned across the table and put her hand on mine. 'You're a nice boy,' she said, 'whoever your father is.'

There was a familiar bright flash and the whine of a film winding on and there, a few feet away, stood the other Rudd, Bobby Usher himself, grinning triumphantly and radiating ill nature in megawatts.

Isobel Bethune lunged furiously to her feet but Usher Rudd, quick at getaways, was out of the door before she could draw breath to shout. 'I *hate* him,' she said, again near to tears. 'I'll kill him.'

I asked the barman to phone for a taxi.

'Mrs Bethune still owes for the drinks.'

'Oh.'

'I haven't any money,' she said. 'Pay for me, there's a dear.'

I salvaged from my pockets the remains of the

money my father had given me in Brighton and handed her all of it.

'You pay the man for the drinks. I'm not old enough yet to buy alcohol and I'm not getting into that sort of trouble.'

Both the barman and Isobel, open-mouthed, completed the sale.

# CHAPTER FIVE

Back at the Town Hall the debate had passed through lukewarm and was heating towards chopping motions with the hands of the two protagonists.

A local chess champion, brought in as referee, had come to the fray with a pinging time clock and, making his own set of rules, he had decreed that each candidate would in turn answer specific questions, the answers to last a maximum of five minutes before being silenced by the time clock's arbitration.

The format seemed to be working quite well, chiefly because both candidates knew how to speak. I was no longer surprised by my father's ability to rouse, amuse and convince, but somehow I'd expected Paul Bethune to be as bombastic and unkind as he'd seemed to his wife. Instead he delivered dryly witty and well-prepared responses to the questions and it was only afterwards that I wondered if he'd learned his best phrases by heart and had used them before.

The Town Hall was full. The seats given by Polly to me and Isobel Bethune now held the Mayor and his missus and, glad to be less exposed, I stood by the door and watched the waves of animation and agreement and fury roll in turn across the faces of the audience, and thought that at least they were *listening*, and obviously cared.

There could be no winner that night. They both won. Everyone applauded and went away talking.

Orinda had several times clapped Bethune. Leonard Kitchens kept his hands for ever in his pockets. Dearest Polly's long face glowed with goodness and pleasure, and freckly Basil Rudd looked even more like his obnoxious cousin when he smiled.

No one produced a gun.

My father and Paul Bethune shook hands.

Like star actors they left the stage last, each surrounded at once by chattering satellites, all with something to say, questions to ask, points to make. My father genuinely enjoyed it, and again his spirits were helium-ballooning as we headed back to our base.

'It's quicker if we walk straight across the square,' my parent objected as I tried to persuade him to take to the cloister. 'Why do you want to walk two sides of a triangle, not one, and you a mathematician?'

'Bullets,' I said.

'My God.' He stopped dead. 'But no one would try again!'

'You'd have said no one would try the first time, but they did.'

'We don't know for sure.'

'And the sump-plug?'

He shook his head as if in general disbelief, but he made no further objection to the cloister route, and seemed not to notice that I walked between him and the well-lit open square.

He wanted to talk about the debate. He also wanted to know why I'd missed half of it and where I'd been. I told him all of Isobel's troubles but I could feel he was barely attending: his mind and his tongue were still busy with points made and lost against the lady's unfaithful man.

'He's dedicated, you know. I can't stand his politics.'

I said, 'I hate what you say, but I'll defend to the death your right to say it.'

'Bull's eye. Don't tell me all those school fees weren't wasted.'

'Come down,' I begged. 'You're too high in the sky.'

Again he stopped walking. We had by then left the cloister and were passing dimly lit shop fronts on the way to the bay windows of first the charity gift shop and, next door, the party headquarters.

'You have no idea what it's like to hold an audience in your hand.'

'No.' Winners at long odds got little praise, and I'd never won on a favourite.

We walked on to the doorway.

Dearest Polly waited there, puzzled. 'Where have you been? You left ahead of me.'

'The boy,' my father said, pointing at me though

there were precious few other boys in sight. 'Benedict, my son, has this fixed idea that someone is violently seeking to put paid to my campaign, if not to my life. Dearest Polly, tell him I'll take my chances and I don't want him ever again to risk his own neck to preserve mine.'

'Dearest Polly,' I said – and she smiled vividly with sweetness – 'this is the only father I'm ever likely to have. Persuade him to give me a real job in this election. Persuade him he needs a full-time bodyguard. Persuade him to let me try to keep him safe.'

'I don't need a bodyguard,' he insisted. 'I need you to be a social asset. Isobel Bethune is useless to Paul, but you have this extraordinary gift – which I admit I didn't expect – of getting people to talk to you. Look at Isobel Bethune! Look at Crystal Harley! I haven't got a word out of her and she chatters away to you. Look at Mrs Kitchens, pouring information into your ears.'

Polly nodded, smiling. 'You're so young, you're no threat to anyone. They all need to talk, and you're safe.'

I said pensively, 'How about Orinda? She turned her back on me at the dinner and wouldn't say a word.'

Polly clapped her hands together with laughter. 'I'll give you Orinda. I'll manage it again.'

'But alone,' I said. 'I could talk to her if she was

alone, but the Anonymous Lover never leaves her side.'

'Who?'

'A.L. Wyvern.'

'Anonymous Lover!' Polly exclaimed. 'Enchanting. His name's really Alderney, I think. He plays golf. He used to play golf with Dennis.'

She moved around smoothly, at home in the office, sorting out mugs and making coffee. I couldn't guess her age nearer than ten years: somewhere between forty or fifty, I thought, but knew I could be wrong. She was again wearing the inappropriate crimson lipstick, this time with a green jacket over a long skirt of brownish tweed: heavy for August. Somehow, with the opaque stockings and 'sensible' shoes, one would have expected her to be clumsy, but she was paradoxically graceful, as if she had once been a dancer. She had no rings on her long capable fingers and for jewellery relied on a single strand of maidenly pearls.

One could have felt sorry for Polly at first sight, I thought, but that would have been a great mistake. She had an inner certainty to go with the goodness. She carried the fuddy-duddy clothes without self-consciousness. She was – I fished for the word – serene.

She said, pouring hot water onto instant coffee granules, 'I don't see any harm in Benedict appointing himself officially to look after you. After all, he hasn't done a bad job so far. Mervyn grumbled all over the Town Hall tonight about having to find a lock-up garage because Benedict wanted one. He says he doesn't like Benedict giving him orders.'

'It was a suggestion, not an order,' my father said.

'It felt like an order to Mervyn, therefore to him it *was* an order. Mervyn resents Benedict's influence over you. Mervyn likes to be in charge.'

'Ben's only been here two days,' my father protested.

Polly smiled. 'Ten minutes was probably enough. You're a brilliant politician on a grand scale, George, but it's your son who sees into individual minds.'

My father looked at me thoughtfully.

'He's good at it now,' Polly said, 'and he's not yet eighteen. Just wait ten years or so. You brought him here to give yourself social credibility, proving you had a son, you weren't a bachelor, confirmed or otherwise, and you've found an asset you didn't expect, so use him, George.'

She stirred the mugs of coffee and distributed it black. My father absentmindedly fished a small container out of a pocket and tapped a sweetener into his drink.

'George?' Polly prompted.

He opened his mouth to answer but before he could speak the telephone rang, and as I was nearest I picked up the receiver.

'Juliard?' a voice said.

'Benedict. Do you want my father? He's here.'

106

'No. You'll do. Do you know who you're talking to?'

'Foster Fordham,' I said.

'Right. And have you worked out what was plugging your sump?'

'Something that would melt when the oil got really hot.'

He laughed. 'I refrigerated the oil and filtered it. There were enough wax globules to make a good thick plug. There are also cotton fibres which may have been from the wick of a candle. Now let me talk to your father.'

I handed over the receiver and listened to half of a long discussion that was apparently about whether or not to report the sabotage to the police. There had been no further action that my father knew of over the rifle shot but, he thought, and his opinion persuaded, that his friend Foster should write an account of what he'd done and what he'd found, and that my father should give a copy of it to the boys in blue as a precaution.

Polly and I listened to snatches. 'They don't have the manpower for surveillance . . . they won't do it . . . you can't guard against a determined assassin . . . yes . . .' my father's gaze slid my way, ' . . . but he's too young . . . all right, then . . . we're agreed.' He put down the receiver carefully and with deliberation and a sigh said, 'Foster Fordham will write a report for the police. Ben will nanny me to the best of his ability and Mervyn will have to put up with it. And now, dearest Polly, I'm going to abandon tomorrow's canvassing and go where I'm not expected.'

Hanging from a hook on one wall was a large appointments calendar with an extensive square allocated to each day. Crystal had entered the basics of my father's advance plans in the squares so that one could see at a glance what he would be doing on each day.

The programme had started the previous Tuesday with 'Candidate arrives. Office familiarisation.' Wednesday's schedule of 'Drive round constituency' had been crossed off, and 'Fetch son from Brighton' inserted instead and, underneath that, 'Dinner at Sleeping Dragon'. Nothing about being shot at on the way home.

The Quindle engagements and the infant school evening were listed for Thursday, and door-to-door canvassing and the Town Hall debate for Friday.

More of the same stretched ahead. If I hadn't had the interest of attempting to foil seriously dangerous attacks on said candidate I would have suffered severe strain of the smiling muscles long before polling day.

How could he face it? I wondered. How could he *enjoy* it, as he clearly did?

'Tomorrow,' he said, pleased with his inspiration, 'tomorrow we'll go to Dorset County racecourse. Tomorrow will be for Ben. We'll go to the races.'

My first reaction was joy, which he noted. Fast on

joy's heels came a sort of devastation that I couldn't hope to be riding there, that I would spend the afternoon as an exile, envying my neighbour his ox and his ass and his saddle in the amateurs' steeplechase; but I let only the joy show, I think.

'We'll go in the Range Rover,' my father said decisively, pleased with his plan. 'And Polly will come with us, won't you, Poll?'

Polly said she would love to.

Did Polly ever lie?

We drank the coffee without stress, my father finally as calm as he'd achieved during this whole strange week. Polly went out through the back office to retrieve her car and drive home, which I understood was a house in a wood outside the town, and my father and I, bolting everything securely, climbed the steep little staircase and slept undisturbed until Saturday morning.

Mervyn leaned in heavy annoyance on the bell at breakfast time and of course frowned heavily over the change of destination. How did George ever hope to be successful in a marginal seat if he neglected the door-to-door persuasion routine, which was of *paramount* importance? The Dorset County racecourse, sin of sins, was outside the Hoopwestern catchment area.

Never mind, my father soothed him, the many

Hoopwestern voters who went to the races might approve.

Mervyn, unconvinced, shut his mouth grimly for half an hour, but as the day expanded decided to salvage at least crumbs from what he considered the ruins of canvassing's best weekend opportunity and got busy on the telephone, with the result that we were invited to lunch with the racecourse Stewards and were otherwise showered with useful tickets. Mervyn, from long experience, knew everyone of influence in the county.

He blamed me, of course, for the switch, and perhaps with reason. If he'd had his way he would have been dancing happy attendance on Orinda, walking backwards in her presence. What he would have done with A.L. Wyvern I couldn't guess, but presumably he was used to the enigmatic shadow, as the Anonymous Lover had been deceased Dennis Nagle's best friend also. They played golf.

Mervyn's disappointments, I thought, shrugging off his ill will, were just too bad. In his life's terms, success lay in getting his candidate elected, or, if not elected, a close runner-up. Mervyn was not about to ruin his own reputation as agent out of tetchiness with Juliards, father or son.

The chilly atmosphere in the offices was lightened by an unexpected visit from the woman who ran the charity shop next door. She and Mervyn knew each other well, but she was fascinated to meet the new candidate, she said; she had seen us come and go, she wanted to shake hands with George, she'd heard his son was a doll, she wondered if we would like a home-made apple pie.

She put her offering on my father's desk.

'Kind of you, Amy,' Mervyn said, and in his manner I read that not only had he known his neighbour a long time but he'd undervalued her for probably the whole period.

Amy was one of those people easy to undervalue; an apologetic unassuming middle-aged widow (Polly said) who received gifts of unwanted junk, spruced them up a bit to sell, and would never have dipped into the till before passing on the proceeds to the charity that maintained her. Amy was fluffy, honest and halfway to stupid: also kind and talkative. One day of unadulterated Amy, I thought, would last a lifetime.

It was easy not to listen to every word in the flow, but she did grab our attention at one point.

'Someone broke a pane of glass in our window on Wednesday night and I've had a terrible job getting it mended.' She told us at far too much length how she'd managed it. 'A policeman called, you know, and asked if the window had been broken by a rifle bullet but I said, of course not, I clean the floor first thing when I arrive every morning because, of course, I don't live upstairs like you can here. There's only a bath-room and one small room I use for storage, though sometimes I do let a homeless person sleep there in an emergency. Anyway, of course I didn't find a bullet. I told the policeman, Joe it was, whose mother drives a school bus, and he came in for a look round and made a note or two. I saw it in the paper about the gun going off and maybe someone was shooting at Mr Juliard, you never feel safe these days, do you? And then, just now when I was dusting an old what-not that I can't seem to sell to anybody, I came to this *bump*, and I pulled it out, and I wonder if this was what Joe was looking for, so do you think I should tell him?'

She plunged a hand into a pocket in her drab droopy cardigan and put down on the desk, beside the apple pie, a squashed-looking piece of metal that had certainly flown at high speed from a .22 rifle.

'I do think,' my father said carefully, 'that you should tell your friend Joe, whose mother drives a school bus, that you've found the little lump of metal stuck in a what-not.'

'Do you really?'

'Yes, I do.'

Amy picked up the bullet, squinted at it, and polished it a bit on her cardigan. So much for residual fingerprints, I thought.

'All right, then,' Amy said cheerfully, putting the prize back in her pocket. 'I was sure you would know what I should do.'

She invited him to look around her shop, but he

cravenly sent me instead, and so I found myself staring at an ugly six-foot-high cane and wicker what-not that had stood near the window and had stopped the slug.

'I call it an *étagère* these days,' Amy said sadly. 'But still nobody wants it. I don't suppose *you* . . .?'

'No,' I said. And nor did I want any of the silver spoons or children's toys or second-hand clothes neatly and cleanly arranged to do good.

I retrieved the Range Rover from its safe haven, picked up my father and (following Mervyn's ungracious directions) found Polly's unexpectedly grand house in the woods. She sat on the rear seat for our journey to the races and, with a touch of glee, detailed a few telephone calls she had made; a touch of persuasion here, a dangle of carrot there.

'Mr Anonymous Lover Wyvern,' she said, 'received a lovely last-minute invitation to play golf in the county's top pro-am event of the year, an offer he'd have to have been ice to refuse. So off he was due to go with his precious clubs, and that was *him* out of the way.'

'How did you manage it?' my father asked admiringly.

'Inducements,' she said darkly. 'And, shortly afterwards, Orinda got invited to the Stewards' box at the races . . .'

'That's where we're going to!' exclaimed my father.

'You don't say!' Polly teased him. 'Benedict,' she

admonished me, 'I'm giving you Orinda without the lover, so don't waste the day.'

'But what can he do?' my father protested.

'He knows,' Polly said. 'How he'll do it, I can't tell, but trust your son.' She switched her attention back to me. 'Orinda knows bugger all about racing. She's going today for the snob value of a Duke, who's one of the Stewards. You'll have to contend with that. Think you can do it?'

I said a bit helplessly, 'I don't know.' Polly's forthright language always disconcerted me, although everyday lurid stable-talk passed my ears unnoticed.

'Go for shit,' she said.

Orinda was already into lobster mousse with diced cucumber when we reached the Stewards' luncheon room and although she looked outraged at our arrival she could do little but choke and recover with sips of wine, patted delicately on the back by the Duke at her side.

The Duke rose and gave Polly a conspiratorial kiss on the cheek, and I saw how Orinda had been hooked and reeled in.

Orinda wore a white linen suit with a green silk scarf tied and floating from a black lizard handbag that swung from the back of her chair. Sleek, matt-skinned, her presence easily eclipsed every other woman in the room, especially Polly who had dressed as usual as if not sure of the event or the season.

My father shook hands all round, his innate unmistakable power turning every head his way even in a roomful of powerful men. Orinda hated him.

'My son Benedict,' he said, introducing me: but it was he who claimed their eyes.

The Duke, hesitantly, said to me, 'Haven't I met you before? Haven't you ridden against my son Edward?'

'Yes, sir. At Towcester last Easter. He won.'

The Duke had a remembering smile. 'You finished third! It was Eddie's birthday. We had an impromptu party to celebrate. You were there.'

'Yes, sir.'

'Nothing like racing, is there? Best thing on earth, Eddie says.'

My father looked sharply at my face.

'Best thing,' I said.

'Mind you,' the Duke said to my father, 'for all these young men, it's only a hobby. Amateurs can't make a living at it. The best amateurs used to be able to turn pro but for some reason it's hardly ever done these days. Eddie needs a job. Amateurs can't ride for ever. I expect your Benedict knows all that. A good fellow, your Benedict, Eddie says. Sit down, Mr Juliard. It's an excellent lunch.'

He seated my father on the other side of him from Orinda, whose enjoyment of the day had waned to twilight even though the sun outside shone brightly.

She pushed away her unfinished mousse as if she could no longer taste it and had difficulty, with rigid facial muscles, in smiling at her host.

A stocky man of perhaps sixty, the Duke looked less patrician than industrious, a worldly-wise business-man, a managing director more than a figurehead chairman. His son, Eddie, a good fellow himself, had once said he envied the time I could give to racing: his own father insisted he work for his living. Well, I thought ruefully, Vivian Durridge and my own father had more than evened us up. Eddie's father owned horses which the son could ride in races, and mine didn't.

Polly and I were seated several places down the lengthy white-clothed dining table on the other side from the uncomfortable Orinda, and placidly ate our mousse and cucumber which was, as the Duke said, excellent, even though, now I'd been let off near-starvation, I would have preferred a large salami pizza.

There was some sort of curried chicken next. As time ran out towards the first race, the Duke, looking at his watch, told my father that as Chief Steward for the day he (the Duke) would have to leave the party now in order to carry out his duties. As if by accident he saw the near panic on Orinda's face at being left without a buffer zone between herself and her beastly usurper, and found an irresistible and apparently spur-of-the-moment solution.

With a flick of a glance at Polly, who was looking

particularly bland, the Duke said to Orinda kindly, 'Now, Mrs Nagle, I am truly concerned that you should enjoy and understand our splendid sport of steeple-chasing, and as I'll be busily occupied I can think of no one better to entrust you to than young Benedict there. He knows all about racing, in spite of his age, and he will take you round and show you everything, and we will all meet up here again after, say, the second race. So, Benedict,' he spoke to me loudly down the table, 'be a good fellow and take Mrs Nagle down to see the horses walk round the parade ring. Watch the race with her. Answer her questions, right?'

I said, 'Yes, sir,' faintly, and the Duke, nodding benignly, more or less pushed Orinda into my arms. I sensed her begin to stiffen and refuse but the Duke made urging motions towards the door as if there were no possibility of a change of his plans, and over my shoulder, as I followed the white linen suit into the passage outside, I caught glimpses of astonishment on my father's face and a wide grin on Polly's.

Orinda marched along the passage and down the stairs at the end into the open air; and there she stopped dead and said, 'This is ridiculous.'

'Yes,' I said.

'What do you mean, yes?'

'I mean, you're not going to listen to me because you hate my father, which is pretty unreasonable when you look at it, but I'd probably feel the same

117

way, so if you like I'll just leave you here and go and look at the horses which is actually what I want to do anyhow.'

She said irritably, inconsequentially, 'I'm old enough to be your mother.'

'Easily,' I said. Hardly tactful.

In spite of her fury she almost laughed. 'You're supposed to say I couldn't be.'

'Sorry.'

'Mervyn says you're only seventeen.'

'I'll be eighteen in two weeks.'

'What will I do, if you just dump me here?'

'Well,' I said, 'I won't dump you. But if you want me to vanish, well, round that corner you'll find the parade ring where the horses walk round before the race so that everyone can see what they're putting their money on.'

'What if I want to bet?'

'Bookmakers or the Tote?'

'What's going to win?'

I smiled at her with real goodwill. 'If I knew, if anyone knew, I'd be rich.'

'And if you were rich?'

'I'd buy a string of racehorses, and ride them.'

I hadn't expected the question, and the answer I'd given her came straight from the honesty of childhood. I wasn't yet used to being adult. My mind, and also my voice and physical co-ordination, could switch disconcertingly sometimes back to fifteen, even in dreams to thirteen. Some days I could ski downhill with sharp turning certainty: other days I'd crash out on the first bend. Some days I'd move in total harmony with a horse's gallop: other days I'd have gawky arms and legs. Always, so far always, I could shoot and hit the inner or the bull, a two-inch spot at a hundred yards.

Orinda said formally, 'I'd be grateful if you'd accompany me to the parade ring.'

I nodded as if she were conceding nothing, and with minute body signs steered her to where the horses plodded round the ring, the sun shining on their coats, the smell and sound of them piercing my senses, the last four days setting up in me such an acute sense of loss that I wished myself anywhere on earth but on a racecourse.

'What's the matter?' Orinda said.

'Nothing.'

'That's not true.'

'It doesn't matter.'

She had given me a perfect opening for what I wanted to say to her, but I miserably shrank from it. I hadn't expected to feel so grindingly forlorn: an exile looking through a glass barrier at a life denied him.

I found a place for us to stand against the rails of the parade ring, and I gave her my racecard, as she had left her own upstairs. She needed spectacles from her handbag to see small print with, and help in identifying the runners from their number cloths.

'What do all these figures mean?' she asked, scratchily pointing to the card. 'It's double Dutch to me.'

'They tell you the horse's age and how much weight he's carrying in the race. Those very small figures tell you his results in the last races he's run in.' I pointed. 'F means fell, and P means he pulled up and didn't finish.'

'Oh.' She studied the card and read aloud the conditions of entry to the first race, a two-and-a-half-mile hurdle race for novices.

'A race for four-year-olds and upwards, which at the start of the season have not won a hurdle race . . . but if they *have* won a hurdle race since the start of the season, they are to carry a 7-lb penalty.' She looked up, disliking me. 'What's a 7-lb penalty?'

'Extra weight. Most often flat thin sheets of lead carried in pockets in the weight cloth which lies over the horse's back under the number cloth and saddle.' I explained that a jockey had to carry the weight allotted to his horse. 'You get weighed before and after a race . . .'

'Yes, yes, I'm not totally ignorant.'

'Sorry.'

She studied the racecard. 'There's only one horse in this race carrying a 7-lb penalty,' she announced. 'Will he win?'

'He might if he's very good.'

She turned the pages of the card, looking forward.

'In almost every race a horse carries a penalty if it's won recently.'

'Mm.'

'What's the heaviest penalty you can get?'

I said, 'I don't think there's any set limit, but in practice a 10-lb penalty is the most a horse will be faced with. If he had to carry more than ten pounds extra in a handicap he almost certainly wouldn't win, so the trainer wouldn't run him.'

'But you *could* win with a 10-lb penalty?'

'Yes, just about.'

'A lot to ask?'

'It depends how strong the horse is.'

She put her glasses away and wanted me to go with her to the Tote, where she backed the horse that had won on the first day of the season and earned himself an extra seven pounds of lead. 'He must be the best,' she said.

Almost as tall as I was, Orinda walked always a pace ah_____ _e as if it were natural to her to have he_____ er rear. She was used to being looked _____ see that her clothes drew admiratio_____ geared to Ascot than a country meetin_____ :ks of rural far-from-all-crowds Dorset.

We stood on the steps of the grandstand to watch the race. Orinda's choice finished fourth.

'Now what?' she said.

'Same thing all over again.'

121

'Don't you get bored with it?'

'No.'

She tore her Tote ticket across and let the pieces flutter to the ground like a seasoned loser.

'I don't see much fun in this.' She looked around at a host of people studying racecards. 'What do you do if it rains?'

The simple answer was 'get wet', but it would hardly have pleased her.

'People come to see the horses as much as to gamble,' I said. 'I mean, horses are marvellous.'

She gave me a pitying stare and said that after the following races she would return to the Stewards' room to thank the Duke for his hospitality, and then she would leave. She couldn't see the fascination that jump racing held for everyone.

I said, 'I can't see what fascination politics has for my father, but for him now it's his whole life.'

We were walking back towards the parade ring where the horses were beginning to appear for the second race. She stopped abruptly from one stride to the next and faced me with frank hostility.

'Your father,' she said acidly, biting off each word as if she could crunch them to splinters of glass, 'has stolen my purpose in life. It is *I* who should represent Hoopwestern in Parliament. It was *I* who was supposed to be fighting this election, and I'd have won it too, which is more than your precious father will do for all his machismo.'

'He didn't know you existed,' I said. 'He was sent by the central party in Westminster to fight the by-election, if he could get selected. He didn't set out to replace you personally.'

She demanded, 'How do you know?'

'He told me. He's been giving me a condensed course in politics since last Wednesday, when he brought me here as window dressing. He respects the way you feel. And actually, if he had you on his side, and if because of that he did get elected, then maybe you could be as good a team with him as you were with Mr Nagle.'

'You're a *child*,' she said.

'Yes . . . sorry. But everyone here says how outstanding you are at work in the constituency.'

She made no comment, angry or otherwise, but began as before to study her racecard, leaning on the parade ring rails as if at home.

After a bit she said, 'What your father wants is power.'

'Yes.' I paused. 'Do you?'

'Of course.'

Power stalked past us in the muscular rumps of fully grown steeplechasers, animals capable of covering ground at thirty miles an hour or more for distances of from four and a half miles: the length and speed of the Grand National. No animal on earth could better a racehorse for stamina and speed. That power . . . *that* was power for me. To share it, guide it, jump with it. Oh, dear God, give me that power.

'Usher Rudd,' Orinda said, 'do you know who I mean?'

'Yes.'

'Usher Rudd told my friend Alderney Wyvern – um, do you know who I mean by Alderney Wyvern?'

'Yes again.'

'Usher Rudd says George Juliard is not only lying about you being his legitimate son but maintains you are his catamite.'

'His what?' If I sounded bewildered, it was because I was. 'What's a . . . a cat of mice?'

'You don't know what he means?'

'No.'

'A catamite is a boy . . . a prostitute boy lover.'

I wasn't so much outraged as astonished. In fact, I laughed.

'Usher Rudd,' Orinda said warningly, 'is a tireless researcher. Don't take him lightly.'

'But I thought Paul Bethune was his sleaze target.'

'Anyone is,' Orinda said. 'He makes up lies. He likes to destroy people. He'll do it for money if he can, but if there's no money in it he'll do it for pleasure. He's a butterfly-wing puller. Are you George Juliard's legitimate son?'

'I look like him, a bit.'

She nodded.

'And he did marry my mother – in front of a lot

of witnesses.' (Disapproving witnesses, but never mind.)

The news seemed not to please her.

'I suppose,' I said, 'that you would prefer Usher Rudd to be right? Then you could have got rid of my father?'

'Alderney Wyvern says it will take more than an Usher Rudd fabrication. It's a matter of finding a strong lever.'

She sounded fiercely bitter. Whatever Polly thought of my ability to understand unhappiness and release it, I felt lost in the maze of Orinda's implacable grievances against my father.

'Someone took a shot at him,' I said.

Orinda shook her head. 'Another lie.'

'I was there,' I protested.

'So was Alderney,' she said. 'He saw what happened. George Juliard tripped on the cobbles and someone loosed a single shot out of high spirits and Juliard claimed it had been aimed at him! Utter *rubbish*. He'll do anything for publicity.'

I thought: Orinda herself would never get under a car and unscrew a sump-plug. However careful one might be, oil would run out before one could thrust a candle into the drain. Even if she knew how and where to unscrew the plug, engine oil and Orinda's clothes couldn't be thought of together in a month of canvassing.

Orinda needed glasses to read a racecard: I couldn't envisage her aiming and firing a target rifle.

Orinda might wish my father dead, but couldn't kill him herself, and didn't believe that anyone else had tried.

Orinda, I thought, hadn't asked or paid anyone to get rid of her rival physically. There were limits to her hate.

I took her across the course to watch the second race from near one of the fences, to give her at least some sensation of the speed involved. Her narrow high heels tended to dig into the turf and stick, making walking difficult, which didn't please her. I was not, I acknowledged to myself in depression, making a great success of the afternoon.

She was, though, impressed by the noise and energy of the half-ton horses soaring or crashing through the tops of the big black birch fence, and she could hear the jockeys shouting to each other and to their mounts; could see the straining legs in white breeches and the brilliant colours of the silks in the August sun. And whether she wanted me to know it or not, she did quite suddenly understand why this sort of racing fascinated the Duke and everyone else who had made the effort and the journey to the racecourse.

When the horses had surged past us again and were striving their way to the winning post, while the very air still vibrated with their passage, I said, 'I do understand what you feel about having been passed over by the selectors.'

Orinda said unkindly, 'You can't possibly. You're far too young.'

Almost in desperation I said, 'You've lost what you most wanted, and it's near to unbearable. You were looking forward to a sort of life that would be a joy every day, that would fulfil you and give you inner power to achieve your best dreams, and it's been snatched away. You've been told you can't have it. The pain of it's brutal. Believe me, I do know.'

She stared, the green eyes wide.

'You don't have to be old,' I said. 'You can feel it if you're only six and you passionately want a pony and you've nowhere to keep it and it's not sensible to start with. And I...' I swallowed. I wanted to stop again, but this time found the grit for the words. 'I wanted *this*.' I swept an arm to the black fence, to the whole wide racecourse. 'I wanted all of *this*. I've wanted to be a jockey for as long as I can remember. I've grown up in the belief that this would be my life. I've grown up feeling warm and certain of my future, and... well... this week it's been snatched away from me. This week I've been told I can't live this life, I'm not a good enough rider, I haven't the spark to be the jockey I want to be. The trainer I was riding for told me to leave. My father says he'll pay for me to go to university, but not for me to waste my time riding in races when I'm not going to be brilliant.

It didn't really sink in . . . I didn't know how absolutely *awful* it would be until I came here today . . . but I'd like to scream, actually, and roll on the ground, and if you think you have to be old enough to be my mother to feel as you do, well, you're wrong.'

# CHAPTER SIX

At the end of the afternoon I glumly drove the Range Rover back to Polly's house in the woods, feeling that I'd wasted all her planning and not only failed to profit from an unrepeatable opportunity but had positively made things worse.

By the time Orinda and I had recrossed the course (her heels were sticking worse than ever) and regained the Stewards' room, the Duke had disappeared again towards his duties. Orinda watched the third race from the viewing balcony leading out of the luncheon room, her back relentlessly turned towards me, her manner forbidding conversation.

A horse carrying a 7-lb penalty won the race. Orinda hadn't backed it.

When the Duke returned, all smiles at the sight of her, she thanked him charmingly for his hospitality and left. She said nothing to my father or to Polly or to myself, ignoring our existence, and I survived the last three races wishing I were smaller, richer, and at the very least a genius. Settling for the obvious privileges I had seemed dreary compared with the fairy-tale lost.

When Polly invited us into her house my father accepted at once.

'Cheer up,' he commanded to my silent reluctance. 'No one wins all the time. Say something. You haven't said anything for hours.'

'All right... Orinda said Usher Rudd wants to know if I'm your catamite.'

My father spluttered into the gin that Polly had poured him.

Polly said, 'What's a catamite?', but my father knew.

I said, 'Usher Rudd's trying to prove I'm not your son. If you have a marriage certificate, put it in a bank vault.'

'And your birth certificate, where's that?'

'With my stuff at Mrs Wells.'

He frowned. My things hadn't followed me so far. He borrowed Polly's phone and called my ex-landlady forthwith. 'She's packed everything,' he reported, 'but the carriers I ordered haven't turned up. I'll see to it again on Monday.'

'My bicycle is at the stables.'

He caught some sense of the wreck he'd made of my aspirations, but I also saw quite clearly that he still expected me to face reality thoroughly and grow up.

'Tough it out,' he said.

'Yes.'

Polly looked from one of us to the other and said, 'The boy's doing his best for you, George.'

Leaving her in her house I drove the Range Rover back to Hoopwestern, familiar at last with the four-wheel drive and the weight and size. I disembarked my parent at a church hall (directions from Mervyn) where he was due to meet and thank the small army of volunteers working for him and the party's sake throughout the whole scattered area of the constituency. The volunteers had brought their families and their neighbours, and also tea, beer, wine and cake to sustain them and my father's inexhaustible enthusiasm to energise them for the next three weeks.

'My son . . . this is my son.' He presented me over and over again, and I shook hands and smiled and smiled and chatted up old ladies and talked football with shaky knowledge and racing with piercing regret.

Mervyn moved from group to group with plans and lists. This ward would be canvassed tomorrow, that ward on Monday: leaflets . . . posters . . . visits . . . leave not one of seventy thousand voters unaware of JULIARD.

Three more weeks of it . . . Even with the spice of looking out for stray attacks, the campaign at that point seemed more like purgatory than appealing.

But I'd said I would do it . . . and I would.

I ate chocolate cake. Still no pizza.

At goodbye time I collected the Range Rover from where I'd parked it in a nearby road and was as sure as possible that no one had tampered with it that evening.

Foster Fordham had given me simple instructions on the telephone. 'Always take with you a carton of dishwasher powder in a box with a spout. When you park the vehicle, sprinkle a thin line of powder on the ground from behind each front wheel back to the rear wheel on the same side. If anyone has moved the vehicle or wriggled under it in your absence, the powder will tell you. Understand?'

'Yes. Thank you.'

'Always set the alarms carefully, and disable them and start the vehicle from a distance, however short a time you've been away.'

I'd followed his instructions faithfully, but our sump-plug merchant had tried no other tricks. I ferried my father safely from the church hall back to the bow-fronted head-quarters and left him there with Mervyn, the two of them endlessly discussing tactics, while I housed the Range Rover in its lock-up and finally ran a pizza to earth in the local take-away.

Mervyn and my father absentmindedly ate half of it. Mervyn laid out dozens of stickers and leaflets in piles, ready for distribution. Yes, he said when I asked him, *of course* by-elections were wildly exciting, they were the peaks of an agent's busy life. And there were the final touches to be arranged for the fund-raising fête organised for next week – such a pity Orinda wasn't in charge of it this time...

I yawned and climbed the narrow stairs, leaving my two elders to lock up: and I woke in the night to a strong smell of smoke.

*Smoke.*

I sat bolt upright in bed.

Without much more than instinct I disentangled my legs from the sheets and violently shook the unconscious lump on the neighbouring mattress, yelling at him, 'We're on fire!' as I leapt to the half-open door to see if what I said was actually, devastatingly true.

It was.

Down the stairs there were fierce yellow leaping flames, devouring and roaring. Smoke funnelled up in growing billows. Ahead of me the sitting-room blazed yellow with flames from the rear-office underneath.

Gasping at once for breath in the smoke, I swivelled fast on one foot and jumped into the bathroom. If I switched on the taps, I thought, the bath and the wash-basin would overflow and help to drown the flames: I pushed the stoppers into the plug-holes and opened all the taps to maximum: and I swept a large bath towel into the toilet bowl and pulled the flush. Whisking the sopping towel into the bedroom, I closed the door against the smoke and laid the wet towel along the bottom of the door with a sort of speed near to frenzy.

'The window,' I yelled. 'The bloody window's stuck.'

The window was stuck shut with layers of paint and had been annoying my father for days. We were both wearing only underpants, and the air was growing hot. 'We can't go down the stairs.' Doesn't he understand? I thought. He smoothly picked up the single bedroom chair and smashed it against the window. Glass broke, but the panes were small and the wooden frames barely cracked. We were above the bow windows facing the square. A second smash with the chair burst through the sticky layers of old paint and swung open both sides of the window – but underneath the fire had already eaten through the bay window's roof and was shooting up the wall.

The bay window of the charity shop next door blazed also with manic energy. If anything the fire next door was hotter and older and had reached the roof, with scarlet and gold sparks shooting into the sky above our heads.

I scrambled over to the door, thinking the stairs the only way out after all, but even if the wet towel was still holding back the worst of the smoke it was useless against flame. The door knob was now too hot to touch. The whole door had fire on the far side.

I shouted with fierceness, 'We're burning. The door's on fire.'

My father stared at me briefly across the room.

'We'll have to take our chances and jump. You first.'

He put the damaged chair against the window wall

and motioned me to climb up and leap out as far as I could.

'You go,' I said.

There were people now in the square and voices yelling, and the raucous siren of the fire engine coming nearer.

'Hurry,' my father said. 'Don't bloody argue. Jump.'

I stood on the chair and held onto the window frame. The paint on it scorched my hands.

'*Jump!*'

I couldn't believe it – he was struggling into shirt and trousers and zipping up his fly.

'Go on. *Jump!*'

I put a bare foot on the frame, pulled myself up and leapt out with every scrap of muscle power ... with strong legs and desperation: and I sailed through the flames from the bay window and missed the front burning edge of it by terrifying inches and crashed down onto the dark cobbled ground with a head-stunning disorientating impact. I heard people yelling and felt hands grabbing me to pull me away from the fire and I was choking with smoke and winded by hitting the unyielding ground and rolling, and also fighting to free myself from the firmly clutching hands to help to cushion my father's fall when he jumped down after me. I had no strength. Sat on the ground. Couldn't even speak.

Incredibly there were camera flashes. People were *recording* our extreme danger, our closeness to dying.

135

I felt helplessly angry. Outraged. Near to sobbing. Illogical, I dare say.

Voices were screaming to my father to jump and voices were screaming to my father *not* to jump, to wait for the bellowing fire engine now charging across the square, scattering onlookers and spilling people in yellow helmets.

'Wait, wait,' people screamed as firemen released their swivelling ladder to extend it to my father, but he was standing up silhouetted in the window with a reddish glow behind him. He was standing on the chair – and the door behind him was burning.

Before the ladder reached him there was an outburst of bright sunlike flame in the room at his back and he stood on the window frame and threw himself out as I had done, flung himself through the climbing fire of the bow windows below into the darkness beyond, knowing he might break his neck and smash his skull, knowing the ground was there but unable to judge how far away: but too near. Break-your-bones near.

A camera flashed.

Two men in yellow suits like moonsuits were sprinting, heavy-gloved hands outstretched, dragging as they went a circular trampoline thing for catching jumpers. No time to position it. They simply ran, and my father crashed down into them, all the figures sprawling, arms and legs flying. People crowded to help them and hid the tangle from my sight but my father's legs had been moving with life, and he had *shoes* on, which he hadn't had upstairs.

I was covered in smoky dirt and bleeding from a few cobble-induced scrapes and grazes, and I had tears running down my face, although I didn't know I was crying: and I was dazed still and was coughing and had blisters forming on my fingers and feet, but none of it mattered. Noise and confusion filled my head. I'd aimed to keep my father safe from danger and I hadn't even *contemplated* a smoke alarm.

His voice said, 'Ben?'

I looked up woozily. He was standing above me; he was *smiling*. How could he?

Men in yellow suits unrolled hoses and poured gallons from the tanker onto the killing bow-fronts. There was steam and smoke and unquenched flame: and there were people putting a red blanket round my bare shoulders and telling me not to worry. I wasn't sure where they had come from, or what I didn't have to worry about.

I wasn't actually *sure* of anything.

'Ben,' my father said in my ear, 'you're concussed.'

'Mm?'

'They say your head hit the ground. Can you hear me?'

'No smoke alarm. My fault . . .'

*Ben*!' He shook me. People told him not to.

'I'll get you elected,' I said.

'Christ.'

People's familiar faces loomed into my orbit and went away again. I thought it extraordinary that they were walking around fully dressed in the middle of the night but at one point learned that it was barely twenty minutes past eleven, not five to four. I'd gone early to bed and jumped out of the window wearing only my watch and my underpants and got the time wrong.

Amy was there, wringing her hands and weeping. Amy crying for the charity gifts lost to ashes, the ugly what-not gone for ever, still unsold. What's a what-not, Amy? An *étagère*, you know, an upright set of little shelves for filling an odd corner, bearing plates and photographs and what not.

And bullets?

'Oh dear,' she said. 'I left the bullet in my awful cardigan in the shop, and now I've lost it, but never mind, it was only a lump of old lead.'

Mrs Leonard Kitchens patted my shoulder reassuringly. 'Don't you worry, boy, there was nothing in those old shops but junk and paper. Leaflets. Nothing! My Leonard's here somewhere. Have you seen him? Likes a good fire, does my Leonard, but the fun's all over now. I want to go home.'

Usher Rudd stalked his prey backwards, framing his picture, stepping back and clicking. He grinned over my blanket, took time to focus, aimed his lens.

Flash.

The cameraman from the local TV station arrived with his brighter light that was still out-watted by fire.

Mervyn wrung his hands over the lost heaps of JULIARDS. He'd barely been home half an hour before someone had phoned to warn him the charity shop was on fire.

Crystal Harley knelt beside me, dabbing bloody trickles with tissues and said worriedly, 'Do you think I'd better come into work tomorrow?'

Paul and Isobel Bethune illicitly drove into the pedestrian-only precinct. Emergencies made new rules, the local councillor said, bustling towards my father, presenting a surface of urgent concern, all camaraderie for him and with hail-fellow greetings individually for the firemen.

Isobel asked me weakly if I were all right.

'Of course he's not,' Crystal snapped. 'He jumped through fire and hit the ground. What do you expect?'

'And ... er ... his father?'

'His father will win the seat,' Crystal said.

God bless politics, I thought.

'Paul was out at a meeting,' Isobel said. 'He came home to collect me when he heard about the fire, to see if there was anything I could do to help. It always looks better if I'm with him, he says.'

Water plumed out of the huge appliance and sizzled on the flames and ran out of the building again, soaking the cobbles. I and my red blanket dripped and chilled.

Another vast tanker in the car park at the rear raised soaring fountains above the roof so that the two arcs of glittering Niagara met and married and fell together as monstrous rain. Leaflets and junk a fiery furnace; two vulnerable organisms shivering outside.

The yellow-helmets prodigally aimed their hoses at the still dark buildings next to the blazing shops and, in time, inevitably, the ravaging tongues of fire ran out of fuel and began to diminish, to whisper instead of roar, to give up the struggle and leave the battlefield so that what fell from the sky into the square was no longer sparks but hot clinging ash, and what assaulted the senses wasn't heat but the acrid after-smell of burning.

Someone fetched the doctor who had seen to my father's ankle three days earlier; he peered into my eyes with bright lights and into my ears and felt the bump on my head and bound up blisters in huge padded dressings so that they wouldn't burst and get infected, and he agreed with my father that all a healthy boy needed was to see him in the morning.

My father solved the interim by enlisting the sympathy of the manager of the Sleeping Dragon, who gave us a bedroom and whose wife found me some clothes.

'You poor dears ... you poor dears ...' She mothered us, kind, but enjoying it, and both she and her husband happily welcomed the reporters from the

London dailies who thronged through the doors the next day.

Usher Rudd's admittedly brilliant photograph of my father in mid-leap with the flaming window behind him made the front pages, not only of the *Hoopwestern Gazette* and the next edition of the *Quindle Diary* (JULIARD JINX) but of every major paper in the land (JULIARD JUMPS) and hot on the heels of the factual news came endless comment and criticism and picking-to-pieces.

People will always tell you what you should have done. People will tell you what *they* would have done if they had woken in the night with fire underneath them. People will say that absolutely the first thing to do was call the fire brigade, and no one could be bothered to say how do I call the brigade when the only telephone is downstairs surrounded by flames? How do you call a fire brigade when the telephone line has melted?

Everyone can think logically afterwards, but in the heat and the smell and the noise and the danger, analytical reasoning is more or less out of the question.

People tend to think that wildly unreasonable behaviour in terrifying circumstances can be called 'panic', and forgiven, but it's not so much panic, a form of ultimate illogical fear, but a lack of time to think things through.

Perhaps my father and I would have done differently if we had been presented with the situation as a theoretical exercise with a correct and an incorrect solution.

Perhaps we should have thrown the mattresses out of the window as a possible way of breaking our fall. Perhaps, if we could have got them through the window. As it was, we both nearly died and, as it was, we both lived, but more by luck than reason.

Don't waste time with clothes, they'll tell you. Better go naked into this world than clothed into the next. But they – 'they', whoever they are – haven't jumped in front of the media's sharpened lenses.

I thought afterwards that I should at least have dashed into the burning sitting-room for my jacket and jockey's helmet, instead of bothering with the taps. Also I should have wrapped towels round my hands and feet before grasping the window frame.

But I don't think my father ever regretted the near-to-lethal seconds he spent in putting on his shirt and trousers. He knew in some way, even in that life-or-death split second, that a photograph of him jumping half naked from the flames would haunt his whole career. He knew, even in that fraught moment, that an orderly presentation was everything. Not even the worst that Usher Rudd could dredge up in the future ever showed George Juliard as anything but a fast-thinking headliner who was at his very best – *who put his shoes on* – in a crisis.

\*

The police investigation sauntered upwards from Joe, whose mother drove a school bus, to higher ranks at county level, but the firefighters couldn't swear the two bow-fronts had been torched and no one found a .22 rifle to match the lost-again bullet, and Foster Fordham's report on wax in the Range Rover's sump was judged inconclusive.

George Juliard *might* have been the target of three attempts on his candidature, if not on his life, but again he might not. There were no obvious suspects.

In the August doldrums for news, London editors gave the puzzle two full days of wide coverage. George Juliard shone on television nationwide. Every single voter in the Hoopwestern constituency knew who JULIARD was.

While my father dealt with publicity people and Mervyn Teck drove around like an agitated bluebottle searching for inexpensive substitute headquarters, I spent most of the Sunday sitting in an armchair by the window of our Sleeping Dragon room, letting bruises and grazes heal themselves, and looking across the square at the burnt-out building opposite.

From somewhere up here, I thought, from somewhere here among the many hanging baskets of geraniums (her Leonard, the nurseryman, had designed them, Mrs Kitchens had told me with pride), from among all these big clusters of scarlet pompoms and little blue flowers whose name I didn't know, and from among the fluffy white flowers that filled and rounded the bright living displays decorating the whole long frontage of the Sleeping Dragon, from somewhere up here someone had aimed a .22 rifle at my father.

The marksman probably hadn't been in this room given to us in the night, which was much further along towards the Town Hall than the main door of the hotel from which we'd walked. A shot from where I sat would have had to take into account that the target wasn't walking straight ahead but moving sideways. A stalker's shot; but not a stalker's gun.

A ricochet could, of course, take a bullet anywhere, but I thought it unlikely that a ricochet from where I sat would have turned and hit the charity shop.

At one point, shuffling on the padded blisters, I explored the length of the hotel's first floor, glimpsing the square through an open doorway or two and coming to a little lounge area furnished with armchairs and small tables that I reckoned lay directly above the front hall and main door, accessible to the world. Straight ahead through the window from there was the unmarked path I'd taken with my father across the cobbles.

Anyone ... *anyone* ... if they had the nerve, could have stood among the floor-length curtains, opened the window, rested the barrel of a .22 on the windowsill and shot through the geraniums and the warm night.

My father, interested, asked the manager for the names of the people sleeping in the bedrooms on

Wednesday night, but although the register was freely opened, no one familiar appeared.

'Nice try, Ben,' my father sighed; and the police had the same nice try in due course, with similar results.

By Monday morning Mervyn had rented an empty shop in a side street and borrowed a desk for Crystal and some flip-up chairs. The campaign hiccupped for two days while he cajoled his friendly neighbourhood printer into replacement leaflet and poster production at grand-prix speed and near-to-cost prices, but by late Tuesday afternoon the indefatigable witches, Faith, Marge and Lavender, had turned the empty shop into a fully working office complete with teapot and mobile phone.

On Monday and Tuesday George Juliard filled the newspapers, and enlivened some chat shows, and on Wednesday morning a miracle happened.

Mervyn had sticky-taped a new large-scale map onto the wall and was pointing out to me the roads I should drive along (feet OK by now) for Faith and Lavender to ring as yet untroubled door-bells. In the absence of a megaphone (burned) I would please occasionally toot the horn, just enough to announce our presence but *not enough*, he lectured me, to anger anyone trying to get a baby to sleep. The mothers of babies (he wagged a finger at me) swayed Xs in the polls like pendulums. Kiss a baby: win a vote. A hundred thousand politicians couldn't all be historically wrong.

'I'll kiss every baby in sight,' I promised recklessly.

He frowned at me, never one to take a joke. I was reminded of my father's most recent lesson: '*Never ever* make a joke to the police, they have *no* sense of humour. *Never* make a political joke, it will always be considered an insult. Always remember that umbrage can be taken by the lift of an eyebrow. Remember that if offence can possibly be taken, it will be.'

I'd gazed at my father. 'Are people that silly?'

'Silly,' he said with mock severity, 'isn't a word you should ever apply to people. They may be totally stupid, in fact, but if you call them silly you've lost their vote.'

'And you want silly people to vote for you?'

He laughed. 'Don't make jokes.'

He had gone to London on Wednesday morning when the miracle happened. There were just Mervyn, Crystal, Faith, Marge, Lavender and me in the makeshift office, just the bunch of us putting the best face possible on the lack of computer (for the totals spent on tea-bags), copier (schedules for volunteers) and fax (reports from distant galaxies like Quindle).

Orinda walked in.

All business stopped.

She wore pale citrus green: trousers, jacket and headband. Gold chains. She carried, beside the black lizard handbag, a substantial roll of papers.

She looked around the bare room, smiled faintly at Marge and fixed her gaze on me.

'I want to talk to you,' she said calmly. 'Outside.'

I followed where she led. We stood on the pavement in the sun, with shoppers passing by.

'Since Saturday,' she announced, 'I have been considering things. On Sunday morning, at half past eight or so, a newspaperman appeared at my house in an invasive procedure I believe is called "door stepping".'

She paused. I nodded faintly.

'He asked if I was glad or sorry that you hadn't been burned to death. You and your father, that is.'

'Oh.'

'It was the first I'd heard about the fire.'

'I'm surprised no one had phoned you.'

'I unplug the telephone when I sleep. I find it hard to sleep in any case.'

I said, 'Oh,' again, vaguely.

'The journalist wanted to know my opinion of the information he'd been given that close-to-death attacks had been made on George Juliard so that he would have to retire from the candidacy, clearing the way for my return.'

She paused, studying my face, and continued: 'I see that that thought isn't new to you.'

'No, but I don't think you did it.'

'Why not?'

'You're hurt. You're furious. But you wouldn't murder.'

'When will you be eighteen?'

'In ten days.'

'Then consider this a coming-of-age present.' She thrust the roll of papers into my hands. 'This is for you. It is because of you . . .' She stopped abruptly, swallowing. 'Use it in any way you like.'

With curiosity I unrolled the stiff sheets, having to hold them wide to prevent them rolling up again. The top one, in very large capital letters, read:

ORINDA NAGLE SAYS VOTE FOR JULIARD

My mouth, I know, fell open.

'There are ten of them,' she said simply. 'They're all the same. I had them printed this morning. They'll print dozens, if you like.'

'Orinda . . .' I was all but speechless.

'You showed me . . . at the races . . .' she began, and stopped again. 'You're so very *young*, but you showed me it's possible to bear an unbearable disappointment. You made me look into myself. Anyway, I will *not* have people thinking I would set fire to our old head-quarters in order to get rid of your father, so I'll *join* him. I'll support him from now on in every way. I should never have listened to all those people who told me he had robbed me. I don't know, to be really truthful, and the truth is awful . . . I don't know that I wasn't *relieved* not to be forced to go to Westminster, but I do like working in the constituency and that's what hurts most... that the people I've worked so hard for passed me over for some stranger from outside.'

She stopped talking and looked at me in a sort of desperation to see if I could possibly understand, and I understood so well that I leaned forward impulsively and kissed her on the cheek.

A camera flashed.

'I can't *believe* it,' Orinda screeched. 'He follows me round.'

Usher Rudd, with the advantage of surprise, was already scuttling away down the street to get lost in bunches of shoppers.

'He follows me, too,' I said, putting a hand on Orinda's arm, to deter her trying to catch him. 'You warned me and I told my father... but unless Usher Rudd breaks the law it seems he can't be stopped, and the law is still on the side of copy-cat Rudds.'

'But my private life is my own affair!' She glanced at me as if it were my fault that it wasn't.

I said, 'Drug dealers would be out of business if people didn't want drugs.'

'What?'

'The so-called war on drugs is fought against the wrong people. Lock up the users. Lock up the demand. Lock up human nature.'

She looked bewildered. 'What have drugs to do with Usher Rudd?'

'If people didn't flock to buy his sleaze, he wouldn't push it.'

'And you mean ... they always will?'

She needed no answer. She followed me into the shop/office and, after delivering her news, enjoyed a hugging session with Mervyn (no photo) and an ambiguous welcome from the three witches, who had with pink arousal transferred their effective allegiance to the new order.

'Where are you canvassing today, Mervyn?' Orinda asked, and he showed her on the map, with the unexpected result that when I drove the Range Rover round Hoopwestern that morning I had on board Mervyn, Orinda, Faith and Lavender, and all of Orinda's roll of commitment flattened out as placards.

As Mervyn had telephoned the editor of the *Gazette* – gasps of shock at having to U-turn his anti-all-politicians spin – we were greeted in the car park behind the burned shop by a hastily assembled crowd, by the leader-writer of the *Gazette* (the paper was short of news) and by the cameraman who had besottedly followed Orinda with his loving lens round the reception before the dinner a week earlier at the Sleeping Dragon.

Orinda flirted again with his lens (or with him – much the same thing) and told everyone prettily through a non-squeaking microphone that George Juliard, undoubtedly on the brink of becoming a nationally acclaimed politician, was the best possible substitute for her beloved husband Dennis, who had dedicated his life to the good citizens of this glorious part of Dorset.

Applause, applause. She appeared in the sitting-rooms of Hoopwestern on the lunchtime television news against the only slightly orchestrated cheers.

By the time my father returned on the train from London he'd heard of Orinda's media conference with mixed feelings – she might be stealing his limelight or she might just be saving his life – but at another church hall meeting of the faithful that evening he embraced her in a warm hug (reciprocated) that would have been unthinkable a day earlier.

Not everyone was pleased.

Orinda's shadow, Anonymous Lover Wyvern, followed her around like thunder. She, dressed in blackberry-coloured satin and glowing with a sense of generosity and virtue, kept giving him enquiring looks as if unsure of the source of his dudgeon. In her inner release she didn't seem to realise, as I did, albeit only slowly through the evening, that in dumping her anger at not being selected she had in some way lessened his status. He had been Dennis Nagle's best friend, but Orinda was leaving her Dennis behind.

Dearest Polly, to my surprise, positively scowled, even though she had herself delivered Orinda to her change of heart.

'I didn't count on such a radical about-face,' Polly complained. 'She's cast herself in the ongoing role of constituency wife! There's no doubt she was good at it, but she *isn't* George's wife and she can't surely imagine she can go on opening fêtes and things, and I bet that's what she's got in mind. Whatever did you say to her at the races?'

I said, 'I thought you wanted her on my father's side.'

'Well, yes, I do. But I don't want her going around saying all the time that *she* was the one we should have picked.'

'Get him into Parliament, Polly,' I said. 'Put him on the escalator, then he'll deal with Orinda and everything else.'

'*How* old did you say you are?'

'Eighteen at the end of next week. And it was you, dearest Polly, who said I look into people's minds.'

She asked in some alarm, 'Do you see into mine?'

'Sort of.'

She laughed uneasily; but I saw nothing but good.

One could say the opposite about Leonard Kitchens. I had come to notice that the tilt of his prominent moustache acted like a weather-vane, signalling the direction of his feelings. The upward thrust that evening was combative and self-important, a combination looking for a fight. Bulky Mrs Kitchens (in large pink flowers printed on dark blue) followed her Leonard's progress round the meeting with anxiety for a while and then made a straight line to my side.

'Do something,' she hissed into my ear. 'Tell Orinda to leave my Leonard alone.'

It seemed to me that it was the other way round, as Leonard's moustache vibrated by Orinda's neck, but at Mrs Kitchens' urgent and continuous prompting I went over to hear Leonard's agitated and whining drift.

'I would do *anything* for you, Orinda, you know I would, but you're joining the *enemy* and I can't bear to see him slobbering all over you, it's disgusting . . .'

'Wake up, Leonard,' Orinda said lightly, not seeing the seething lava below the faintly ridiculous exterior, 'it's a new world.'

The undercurrents might tug and eddy, but Orinda had definitely unified the party behind JULIARD; yet in our room that night my father would literally not hear a word said about her. In fact, he put a finger decisively against his lips and drew me out into the passage, closing our door behind us.

'What's up?' I asked, mystified.

'Tonight the editor of the *Gazette* asked me if I thought people who voted for me were silly.'

'But that's nonsense. That's – ' I stopped.

'Yes. Think back. When we joked about silly voters we were alone in this bedroom here. Did you repeat what we said?'

'Of course not.'

'Then how did the *Gazette* know?'

I stared at him, and said slowly, 'Usher Rudd.'

He nodded. 'Didn't you tell me that that mechanic – Terry, isn't that what his name is? – got sacked because Usher Rudd had listened to his pillow talk using one of those gadgets that pick up voice waves from the faint vibrations in the windows?'

'Usher Rudd,' I said furiously, 'is trying to prove I'm not your son.'

'Never mind, he's on a loser.'

'He's following Orinda too, not to mention the Bethunes.'

'He thinks if he flings enough mud, some will stick. Don't give him any target.'

As the days went by one could see that Orinda's flip-flop had most impact in Hoopwestern itself, less in Quindle, and not very much in the villages dotting the maps with a church spire, a couple of pubs and a telephone box. Cheers and clapping greeted her near home but news of her arrival to canvass in, say, Middle Lampfield (pop. 637) was more likely to be greeted with a polite 'Oo? Aah' and a swift return to 'Zoo-merzet' cider.

More local draught cider flowed down the constituency throats than babies' formula, and my father's head for the frothy fruit of the apple earned him approval. We rolled every day at lunchtime from pub to pub to pub (I drove) and I got used to hearing the verdict. 'A good chap, your father, he understands what we need in the countryside. Reckon I'll vote for him. That Bethune, that they say is a certainty, he's a *town* councillor, and you know what we think of them lot, thumbs down.'

My father made them laugh. He knew the price of hay. They would have followed him to the South Pole.

Orinda thought the villages a waste of time, and so did Mervyn.

'The bulk of the votes is in the towns,' they lectured. Dennis Nagle had been the star of the businessman circle.

'You vote for a man you play darts with,' my father said, missing double top. 'I buy my own drinks, they buy theirs. Neither of us is beholden.'

Orinda didn't like cider, and she didn't like pubs. Lavender, surprisingly, liked both: my father, Lavender and I therefore spent several days soap-boxing the outskirts in the silver and gold Range Rover, seeing to it (as my father said) that not a voter was left unturned.

The following week it was Orinda who nearly died.

# CHAPTER SEVEN

On the Tuesday of the last full week of canvassing, my box of possessions, and my bicycle, finally arrived by carrier from Mrs Wells.

Up in our room, my father picked with interest and curiosity through the meagre debris of my life: two trophies for winning amateur 'chases the previous Easter, several photographs of me on horses and skis, and other photos from school with me sitting in one of those frozen team line-ups (this one for target shooting), with the captain hugging a cup. There were books on mathematics, and racing biographies. Also clothes, but not many as, to my dismay, I was still growing.

My father extracted my passport, my birth certificate and the framed photograph of his wedding to my mother. He took the picture out of its frame and after looking at it for several long minutes he ran his finger over her face and sighed deeply, and it was the only time I'd known him show any emotion at all about his loss.

I said incautiously, 'Do you remember her? If she walked into the room now, would you know her?'

He gave me a look of such bleakness that I realised I'd asked a question of unforgivable intrusion, but after a pause all he said was, 'You never forget your first.'

I swallowed.

He said, 'Have you had your first?'

I felt numb, embarrassed almost beyond speech, but in the end I said truthfully, 'No.'

He nodded. It was a moment of almost unbearable intimacy, the first ever between us, but he remained totally calm and matter-of-fact, and let me recover.

He sorted through some papers he had brought in a briefcase from a recent trip to London, put my own identifications in the case, snapped shut the locks and announced that we were going to call on the *Hoopwestern Gazette*.

We called, in fact, on the editor, who was also the publisher and proprietor of the only local daily. He was a man in shirt-sleeves, harassed, middle-aged, and from the tone of his front pages, censorious. He stood up from his desk as we approached.

'Mr Samson Frazer,' my father said, calling him by name, 'when we met the other evening, you asked if I thought people who vote for me are silly.'

Samson Frazer, for all his importance in Hoopwestern, was no match in power against my parent. Interesting, I thought.

'Er . . .' he said.

'We'll return to that in a minute,' my father told him. 'First, I have some things for you to see.'

He unclipped the briefcase and opened it.

'I have brought the following items,' he said, taking out each paper and putting it down in front of the editor. 'My marriage certificate. My son's birth certificate. Both of our passports. This photograph of my wife and myself taken outside the registry office after our wedding. On the back – ' he turned the picture over, 'you will see the professional photographer's name and copyright, and the date. Here also is my wife's death certificate. She died of complications after the birth of our son. This son, Benedict, my only child, who has been at my side during this by-election.'

The editor gave me a swift glance as if he hadn't until that point taken note of my existence.

'You employ a person called Usher Rudd,' my father said. 'I think you should be careful. He seems to be trying to cast doubt on my son's identity and legitimacy. I'm told he has made scurrilous insinuations.'

He asked the editor just how he'd come to hear of 'silly' votes when he, my father, had only used the word – and in a joke – in the privacy of his own room.

Samson Frazer froze like a dazzled rabbit.

'If I have to,' my father said, 'I will send hair samples for DNA testing. My own hair, my son's hair, and some hair from my wife that she gave me in a locket. I hope you will carefully consider what I've said and what I've shown you.' He began methodically replacing the certificates in the briefcase. 'Because, I assure you,' he went on pleasantly, 'if the *Hoopwestern Gazette* should be so unwise as to cast doubt on my son's origins, I will sue the paper and you personally for defamation and libel, and you might quite likely wish you hadn't done it.' He snapped the locks shut so vigorously that they sounded in themselves like a threat.

'You understand?' he asked.

The editor plainly did.

'Good,' my father said. 'If you catch me in sleaze, that will be fair enough. If you try to manufacture it, I'll hang you out by the toes.'

Samson Frazer found nothing to say.

'Good day to you, sir,' my father said.

He was in high good humour all the way back to the hotel and went upstairs humming.

'What would you say,' he suggested, 'to a pact between us?'

'What sort of pact?'

He put the briefcase down on the table and drew out two sheets of plain paper.

'I've been thinking,' he said, 'of making you a promise, and I want you to make the same promise in return. We both know how vulnerable one is to people like Usher Rudd.'

'And it's not impossible,' I interrupted, 'that he's

listening to us at this moment, particularly if he knows where we've just been.'

My father looked briefly startled, but then grinned. 'The red-haired dung-beetle can listen all he likes. The promise I'll make to you is not to give him, or anyone like him, any grounds ever for messy publicity. I'll be dead boring. There will be no kiss-and-tell bimbos and no illicit payment for favours and no cheating on tax and no nasty pastimes like drugs or kinky sex . . .'

I smiled easily, amused.

'Yes,' he said, 'but I want *you* to make the same promise to *me*. I want you to promise me that if I get elected you'll do nothing throughout my political career that can get me discredited or sacked or disgraced in any way.'

'But I wouldn't,' I protested.

'It's easy for you to say that now while you're young, but you'll find life's full of terrible temptations.'

'I promise,' I said.

He shook his head. 'That's not enough. I want us both to write it down. I want you to be able to see and remember what you promised. Of course, it's in no way a legal document or anything pretentious like that, it's just an affirmation of intent.' He paused, clicking a ball-point pen while he thought, then he wrote very quickly and simply on one sheet of paper, and signed his name, and pushed the paper over for me to read.

It said: 'I will cause no scandal, nor will I perform any shameful or illegal act.'

Wow, I thought. I said, not wanting this to get too serious, 'It's a bit comprehensive, isn't it?'

'It's not worth doing otherwise. But you can write your own version. Write what you're comfortable with.'

I had no sense of binding myself irrevocably to sainthood.

I wrote: 'I'll do nothing that could embarrass my father's political career or drag his name in the dust. I'll do my best to keep him safe from any sort of attack.'

I signed my name lightheartedly and gave him the page. 'Will that do?'

He read it, smiling. 'It'll do.'

He folded both pages together, then picked up the wedding photograph and positioned it face down on the glass in its frame. He then put both of the signed pacts on the photo and replaced the back part of the frame, fastening it with its clips.

'There you are,' he said, turning the frame face up. 'Every time you look at your mother and me, you'll remember the promises behind the photo, inside the frame. Couldn't be simpler.'

He stood the picture on the table and without fuss gave me back my birth certificate and passport.

'Keep them safe.'

'Yes.'

'Right. Then let's get on with this election.'

Stopping only briefly to leave my identity in an envelope in the manager's safe, we went to the new headquarters to collect Mervyn, pamphlets, Faith and Lavender, and start a door-to-door morning round three Hoopwestern housing estates. Light-bulb workers, they said.

Mervyn, proud of himself, had found a replacement megaphone. His friendly printer continued to furnish a torrent of JULIARDS. Mervyn for once seemed content in his world, but his day shone even brighter when Orinda arrived, declaring her readiness for the fray.

With Faith and Lavender cool and Mervyn hot, therefore, six of us squeezed into the Range Rover, leaving behind Crystal (chronically anxious) and Marge (dusting and sweeping).

Only eight days after this one, I thought, and it will be over. And what will I do, I wondered, after that? There would be three or four weeks to fill before the Exeter term started. I mentally shrugged. I would be eighteen. I had a bicycle . . . might get to France . . .

I drove mechanically, stopping wherever Mervyn dictated.

Orinda had come in neat trousers and jacket, light orange-scarlet in colour. As usual, gold chains. Smooth, perfect make-up.

Babies got kissed. My father came across a clutch of child-minding house-husbands, factory shift workers, and learned about tungsten filaments. I chatted up a coffee-morning of old ladies who weren't satisfied until my parent shook their hands. (Pink smiles. A blossoming of votes.) Orinda met old friends. Mervyn alerted the streets to our presence like a musically tinkling fish-and-chip van, and Faith and Lavender left no door-bell un-rung.

When we drove out of the last of the estates we'd seen one or two TITMUSSES, no WHISTLE, not a BETHUNE to speak of, but many a window now proclaimed JULIARD. One could not but hope.

Mervyn and my father decided on one more long street, this time of varied and slightly more prosperous-looking houses. I, by this time, had had enough of door-to-dooring to last me several lifetimes, but as always the others seemed to have an indefatigable appetite. My father's eyes still shone with enthusiasm and people who disagreed with his political theories left him not downcast but stimulated. He never tired, it seemed to me, of trying to convert the heathen.

Without much hope I asked Faith and Lavender if they wouldn't prefer to say they'd done enough; how about lunch? 'No, no,' they insisted with fervour, 'every vote counts.'

Orinda alone seemed uneasy and withdrawn and not her usual positive and extravagant self, and in the end, while she and I waited together on the pavement beside the Range Rover for the others to finish galvanising an old people's home, I asked her what was the matter.

'Nothing,' she said, and I didn't press it, but after a moment or two she said, 'Do you see that white BMW there, along the road?'

'Yes.' I frowned. 'I saw it earlier, in one of the housing estates.'

'He's following us.'

'Who's following us? Is it Usher Rudd?'

'Oh, no.' She found the idea a surprise, which in itself surprised me. 'No, not Usher Rudd. It's Alderney Wyvern.'

It was I, then, who was surprised, and I asked, sounding astonished, 'Why on earth should he follow us?'

Orinda frowned. 'He's still furious with me for supporting your father.'

'Well . . . I'd noticed. But why, exactly?'

'You're too young to understand.'

'I could try.'

'Dennis used to do everything Alderney said. I mean, Alderney actually was how Dennis got advancement. Alderney would tell him what to say. Alderney is very clever, politically.'

'Why doesn't he find a parliamentary seat for himself?'

'He says he doesn't want to.' She paused. 'To be frank, he isn't easy to understand. But I know he expected me to be selected and to retain the seat as

Dennis' widow, and he worked on people like that creepy Leonard Kitchens, with that shudder-making moustache, to make sure I was selected. And then out of the blue the central party in Westminster decided they wanted George Juliard in Parliament, so he came and dazzled the selectors, who always listen to Polly, as a matter of course, and she fell for him like a ton of bricks . . . Anyway, Alderney got nowhere with your father. I sometimes think that that's the sort of power Alderney really wants, to be able to pull the levers behind the scenes.'

It seemed to me at that moment a wacky notion. (I still had a lot to learn.)

'So now that I've joined your father,' Orinda said, 'I'm not listening to Alderney as much. I used to do everything he suggested. We always did, Dennis and I, because Alderney would tell us such and such a thing would happen on the political scene and mostly he was right, and now I'm out with you and your father so much of the time . . . You'll laugh, but I almost think he's *jealous*!'

I didn't laugh. I'd seen my father's powerful effect on every female in Hoopwestern, from acid-tongued Lavender onwards. It wouldn't have surprised me if he'd left a comet-tail of jealousy through the constituency, except that he needed the men to vote for him as well as the women, and I'd watched him keep a tactical distance from their wives.

Alderney Wyvern, along the road, got out of his

car and stood aggressively on the pavement, hands on hips, staring at Orinda.

'I'd better go and talk to him,' Orinda said.

I said instinctively, 'No, don't.'

She caught the alarm in my voice and smiled. 'I've known him for years.'

I hadn't yet come across the adult grossly matured variety of jealousy, only the impotent rage of adolescence, but I felt intuitively that a great – and disturbing – change had taken place in A.L. Wyvern.

He had been by his own choice self-effacing on every occasion I'd seen him: quiet in manner, self-contained, behaving as if he didn't want to be noticed. All that had now gone. The stocky figure seemed heavier, the shoulders hunched, the face, even from a distance, visibly tense with menace. He had the out-of-control anger of a rioter, or of a militant striker.

I said to Orinda, 'Stay here.'

'Don't be silly.'

She walked confidently towards him in her brave orange-red clothes.

I could hear his voice, low and growling, but not what he said. Her reply was light and teasing. She put out a hand as if to stroke his arm affectionately, and he hit her very hard in the face.

She cried out with shock as much as pain. I ran towards her, and although Wyvern saw me coming he hit her again, back-handed, across her nose and mouth.

She squealed, raising her hands to shield her face,

trying at the same time to escape from him, but he clutched the shoulder of her jacket to prevent her running, and drew back his fist for a third blow.

She wrenched herself free. She half-overbalanced. She stumbled off the pavement into the roadway.

The prosperous residential street that had been so peaceful and empty suddenly seemed filled with a heavy lorry that bore down towards Orinda, brakes shrieking, horn blowing in banshee bursts.

Orinda tottered blindly as if disoriented, and I sprinted towards her without calculating speed or distance but simply impelled by the need of the moment.

The lorry driver was swerving about, trying to miss her and actually making things worse because his direction was unpredictable. I might easily have shoved her into his path rather than out of it, but I threw myself at Orinda in a sort of twisting rugby-football tackle so that she fell half under me onto the hard surface and rolled, and the screaming black tyres made skid marks an inch from our feet.

Orinda's nose was bleeding and her eyes were overflowing with pain-induced tears, and beyond that she was dazed and bewildered. I knelt beside her, winded myself and fearful that I'd hurt her unnecessarily when the lorry driver might have avoided her anyway.

The lorry had stopped not far beyond us and the driver, jumping down from his cab and running towards us, was already rehearsing aggrieved innocence.

'She ran out straight in front of me, I didn't have a chance. It isn't my fault . . . I couldn't help it . . . it isn't my fault she's bleeding all down her front.'

Neither Orinda nor I made any reply. It was irrelevant. It hadn't been his fault, and no one would say it had been. The person at fault stood in shocked rage on the pavement directly across the road from us, glaring and rigid and not coming to our aid.

With breath returning I asked Orinda if she was all right. Silly question, really, when her nose was bleeding and there were other marks of Wyvern's dangerous hands on her face. Her jacket was torn. One black shoe was off. The careful make-up was smeared and there was a slack weakness through all her body. The Orinda lying in the road looked far from the assured sophisticated flirter with cameras that I was used to; she looked a shattered, ordinary, middle-aged and rather nice woman trying to gather her wits and understand what had happened.

I leaned forward and slid an arm under her neck to see if she could sit up, and to my relief she let me help her to do that, until she was sitting in the road with her knees bent and her head and her hands on her knees.

She'd broken no bones, I thought gratefully. The fractures were internal and mental and couldn't be mended.

She said tearfully, trying to wipe blood with her fingers, 'Have you got a tissue?'

I hadn't.

'There's one in my bag.'

Her handbag, I knew, was in the Range Rover.

'I'll get it,' I said.

'No . . . Benedict . . . don't leave me!'

'Call an ambulance,' the lorry driver advised bull-ishly. 'I missed her, I know I did. It's not my fault she's bleeding.'

'No, it's not,' I agreed, standing up. 'But you're a big strong guy and you can help by picking up the lady and carrying her to that goldish Range Rover over there.'

'No fear,' he interrupted. 'I'm not getting her blood on me, it's not my sodding fault, she ran straight out in front of me.'

'Yes. OK,' I said. 'It wasn't your fault. But you did at least stop, so if you'd help and take her along to that vehicle, and if I just jot down your name and the firm you work for, that owns the lorry, then I'm sure you can carry on with whatever you were doing.'

'No police,' he said.

'You don't have to call the police to an accident unless someone's been injured, and you didn't injure this lady, as you said.'

'Straight up? How do you know that? You're only a boy.'

I'd learned it in the course of reading for my driving licence, but I couldn't be bothered to explain. I bent down and tried to get Orinda to her feet, and she

169

stood up shakily, clutching me to stop herself from falling.

I put my arms round her awkwardly. She was trembling all over. My father would simply have scooped her up and carried her to the Range Rover, but apart from my doubt of having adequate strength, I was embarrassed by the difference in our ages. Ridiculous, really. I felt protective, but unsure.

A couple of cars went by, the passengers craning their necks with curiosity.

'Oh, come on, missus,' the driver said suddenly, picking up her scattered shoe and putting it on for her, 'hold onto my arm.'

He offered her a rock-like support, and between the two of us Orinda walked unsteadily, setting her feet down gingerly as if not sure where the ground lay. In that fashion we reached the Range Rover and installed Orinda in the front passenger seat, where she relaxed weakly and thanked the driver.

'Hey!' he said suddenly, surveying the highly noticeable vehicle. 'Doesn't this motor belong to that politician? Some funny name?'

'Juliard.'

'Yeah.'

'I'm his son,' I said. 'This lady, that you cleverly missed hitting, and that you've helped just now, is a Mrs Orinda Nagle, whose husband was the MP here before he died.'

'Cor!' Surprise at least stopped the whine of self-justification. I reckoned he was already rehearsing a revised tale to his masters. 'I live in Quindle,' he said. 'They say your father's got no chance, the way things are, but maybe I'll vote for him now anyway. Can't say fairer than that!'

I wrote down his name, which he gave willingly, and the name of the furniture firm he worked for, and the telephone number, and he positively beamed at Orinda and told her not to worry, and drove off in his lorry giving us a smile – a *smile* – and a wave.

Alderney Wyvern, all this time, had remained as if the soles of his shoes were glued to the ground.

A few people had come out of the houses because of the noise of horn and brakes, but as there'd been no actual crash, and as Orinda had stood up and walked away, their curiosity had died quickly.

For once, with a real story to record, Usher Rudd and his lens had been missing.

My father, Mervyn, Faith and Lavender came out from a triumphant conversion of the old people's home and exclaimed in horror at Orinda's blood and distress. The tissue from her handbag had proved inadequate. Her tears by now were of uncomplicated misery, rolling half-mopped down her cheeks.

'What happened?' my father demanded of me fiercely. 'What have you done?'

'Nothing!' I said. 'I mean . . . nothing.'

Orinda came to my defence. 'George, Benedict

*helped* me . . . I can't believe it . . .' Her voice wailed. 'Alderney . . . *Alderney* . . . h-h-hit me.'

'He *what*?'

We all looked along the road to where Wyvern still pugnaciously stood his ground, and if I had needed an explanation of the emotions involved, my father didn't. He strode off with purposeful anger towards the visibly unrepentant ex-best friend and challenged him loudly, though we couldn't hear the actual words. Wyvern answered with equal vigour, arms waving.

'Benedict . . .' Orinda begged me, increasingly upset, 'go and stop them.'

It was easy enough for her to say it, but they were both grown men whereas I . . . Well, I went along there fast and caught my father's arm as he drew back his fist for an infuriated swipe at Wyvern who was, incredibly, sneering.

My father swung round and shouted at me, raging, 'Get out of my bloody way.'

'The pact,' I yelled at him. 'Remember the pact.'

'*What*?'

'The *pact*,' I insisted. 'Don't hit him. Father . . . Dad . . . don't hit him.'

The scorching fury went out of his eyes as suddenly as if he were waking up.

'He *wants* you to hit him,' I said. I didn't know how I knew or why I was so certain. It had something to do with the fact that Wyvern had remained on the spot instead of driving off, but it was mostly intuition derived from his body language. He was looking for trouble. He meant all sorts of harm to my father, not least adverse publicity before polling day.

My father gave me a blank look, then walked past me to go back to the Range Rover. I half turned to follow him but was grabbed and spun round by Wyvern, whose always unsmiling face was now set fast with brutal malice. If he couldn't get what he wanted from the father, he would take it out on the son.

I hadn't learned boxing or karate, but I did have naturally fast reflexes and, thanks to riding and skiing, an instinctive command of balance. Wyvern might have had weight in his fists, but I ducked and dodged two sizzling punches to the face that would have laid me out flat if they'd connected, and concentrated solely on staying on my feet.

He drove me back against the shoulder-height rough stone wall that divided a garden from the pavement, but I squirmed out of his grasp and simply ran, intent on escape and containment, not on winning any battles.

I could hear Wyvern coming after me, and saw my father with renewed fury turning back to my aid.

I yelled at him in frenzy, 'Get in the Range Rover. *Get in the vehicle*,' and he wavered and turned again and marvellously did as I said.

Three steps from the Range Rover I stopped running and swung round fast to face Wyvern, in whom calculation had never been wholly overwhelmed by emotion: he sized up the gallery he was playing to – Orinda, my father, Mervyn, Faith and Lavender – and under the glare of all those sets of eyes he abruptly conceded that further attack would have legal consequences he wouldn't relish and stopped a bare six paces from where I stood.

The venom in his expression shrivelled the saliva in my mouth.

'One day,' he said, 'I'll get you one day.'

But not today, I thought; and today was all that mattered.

He took a few steps backwards, his face smoothing out to its customary flatness, then he turned and walked towards his car as if nothing had happened. Easing into the driver's seat he started the engine and drove collectedly away with no burning of tyres or other histrionics.

He left a lot of speechlessness in and around the Range Rover.

In the end Mervyn, clearing his throat, said, 'Orinda needs a doctor.'

Orinda disagreed. 'I need a tissue.'

Faith and Lavender between them produced some crumpled white squares. Orinda wiped her face, looked in a small mirror and moaned at the wreck it revealed. 'I'm not going anywhere like this.'

'The police . . .?' suggested Faith.

'*No*,' Orinda said, and no one argued.

With everyone subdued I drove the Range Rover

back to the headquarters where my father transferred himself and Orinda into her nearby parked car and set off to her home, with me following to bring him back.

He was silent for the whole of the return journey, but as I braked to a halt at the end of it he said, finally, 'Orinda thinks you saved her from being run over by the lorry.'

'Oh.'

'Did you?'

'The lorry driver missed us.'

He insisted I tell him what had happened.

'Her eyes were watering,' I explained. 'She couldn't see where she was going.'

I made as if to get out of the vehicle, but he stopped me.

'Wait.' He seemed to be searching for words and not finding them.

I waited.

He said in the end, 'I'm afraid I've let you in for more than I expected.'

I half laughed. 'It hasn't been boring.'


He went to Quindle with Mervyn early on the following Saturday to undertake an all-embracing round of the town's suburbs and, because of a dinner that evening and yet more commitments on the Sunday morning, he stayed in Quindle overnight.

That Sunday was my eighteenth birthday. My father had told me he would leave me a birthday card with Crystal, and I was to go along at nine in the morning to collect it. He would return that afternoon, he said, and we would dine together that evening to celebrate. No more political meetings, he said. Just the two of us, with champagne.

When I arrived at the party office at nine the door was locked and fifteen minutes passed before Crystal arrived and made her way inside. Yes, she agreed, my father had left me a card: and many happy returns and all that.

She took an envelope out of the desk and gave it to me, and inside I found a card with a joke on it about growing old, and nothing else. 'Yours, Dad,' he'd written.

'George said,' Crystal told me, 'that you are to go out into the street and find a black car with a chauffeur in it. And don't ask me what it's about, George wouldn't tell me, but he was smiling fit to crack his cheeks. So off you go, then, and find the car.'

'Thanks, Crystal.'

She nodded and waved me off, and I went outside and found the black car and the chauffeur a hundred yards away, patiently parked.

The chauffeur without speaking handed me a white envelope, unaddressed.

The card inside read '*Get in the car.*'

And underneath, '*Please.*'

With a gleam and a breath of good spirits I obeyed the instructions.

It wasn't much of a surprise when the chauffeur (not the same man as before, nor the same car) refused to tell me where we were going. It was, however, clear shortly that the direction was westwards and that many signposts distantly promised Exeter.

The chauffeur aimed at the heart of that city and pulled up outside the main doors of its grandest hotel. As before, the car's rear door was ceremoniously opened for me to step out and again, smiling broadly (not in the script), he pointed silently towards the interior and left me to the uniformed porters enquiring sniffily about my luggage.

My luggage this time again consisted of what I wore: a white long-sleeved sweatshirt, new blue jeans, and well-tried running shoes. With undoubtedly more self-confidence than at Brighton I walked into the grand lobby and asked at the reception desk for George Juliard.

The receptionist pressed buttons on a computer.

'Sorry, no one called Juliard staying at the hotel.'

'Please check again.'

She checked. Gave me a professional smile. Still no one called Juliard, past, present or future.

I was definitely not this time in sawn-off shorts and message-laden T-shirt land. Even on the last summer Sunday of August, business suits here prevailed. Ladies were fifty. In a cathedral city, people had been to church. The chauffeur, I gloomily concluded, had taken me to the wrong place.

The hotel's entrance lobby bulged at one side into a glass-roofed conservatory section with armchairs and green plants, and I sat there for a while considering what I should do next. Had my father intended me to get to know Exeter before I went to its university?

Or what?

After about half an hour a man dressed much as I was myself, though a good ten years older, appeared in the lobby. He looked around and drifted unhurriedly in my direction.

'Juliard?' he said. 'Benedict?'

'Yes.' I stood up, taller than he by an inch or two, which seemed to surprise him. He had yellow-blond hair, white eyelashes and outdoor skin. A man of strong muscles, self-confident, at home in his world.

'I'm Jim,' he said. 'I've come to collect you.'

'Who are you?' I asked. 'Where are we going?'

He smiled and said merely, 'Come on.'

He led the way out of the hotel and round a few corners, fetching up beside a dusty dented red car that contained torn magazines, screwed-up sandwich papers, coffee-stained polystyrene cups and a mixed-parentage dog introduced as Bert.

'Disregard the mess,' Jim said cheerfully, sweeping crumpled newspapers off the front passenger seat onto the floor. 'Happy birthday, by the way.'

'Uh . . . thanks.'

He drove the way I'd been taught not to; jerking acceleration and sudden brakes. Start and stop. Impulse and caution. I would have gone a long way with Jim.

It turned out to be only eight miles westward, as far as I could judge. Out of the city, past a signpost to Exeter University's Streatham Campus (home among much else of the department of mathematics), deep into rural Devon, with heavy thatched roofs frowning over tiny-windowed cottages.

Jim jerked to a halt in front of a larger example of the basic pattern and pointed to a heavy wooden front door.

'Go in there,' he instructed. 'Down the passage, last room on the left.' He grinned. 'And good luck.'

I was quite glad to be getting out of his car, even if only to stop the polymorphous Bert from licking my neck.

'Who lives here?' I asked.

'You'll find out.'

He left me with a simple choice: to do as I'd been told or find a way of returning to Exeter. Alice down the bleeding rabbit hole, I thought.

I opened the heavy door and went along the passage to the last room on the left.

# CHAPTER EIGHT

In the last room on the left a man sat behind a large desk, and at first I thought with an unwelcome skipped heart-beat that he was Vivian Durridge, intent on sacking me all over again.

He looked up from his paperwork as I went in and I saw that though he wasn't Vivian Durridge himself he was of the same generation and of the same severe cast of mind.

He gave me no warm greeting, but looked me slowly up and down.

'Your father has gone to a great deal of trouble for you,' he said. 'I hope you're worth it.'

No reply seemed suitable, so I didn't make one.

'Do you know who I am?' he demanded.

'I'm afraid not . . . sir.'

'Stallworthy.'

He waited for the name to trickle through my brain, which it did pretty fast. It was the implication of his name that slowed my reply. Too much hope was bad for the pulse.

'Er . . . do you mean Spencer Stallworthy, the race-horse trainer?'

'I do.' He paused. 'Your father telephoned me. He wants to buy a horse and put it in training here with me, so that you can bicycle over from the university to ride it out at exercise. He asked me to enter it in amateur events so that you can ride it in races.'

He studied my face. I must have looked pretty ecstatic because a slow wintry smile lightened his heavy expression.

'I just hope,' he said, 'that you can ride well enough not to disgrace my stable.'

I just hoped he hadn't been talking to Vivian Durridge.

'Your father asked me to find a suitable horse. We discussed price, of course. I told him I train forty or so horses and one or two of them are always for sale. I have two here at present which might fit the bill. Your father and I agreed that you should come here today and have a ride on both. You are to choose which of them you prefer. He wanted it to be a surprise for your birthday – and I see it is.'

I breathlessly nodded.

'Right. Then go out of the back door. My assistant, Jim – he was the one who brought you here – he'll drive you along to the stables where the horses are ready for you. So off you go, then.'

'Er . . .' I said. 'Thank you . . . very much.'

He nodded and bent his head to his paperwork;

and Jim, grinning widely, drove half a mile to the stable yard that was old, needed paint and had sent out winners by the dozen over the years to small races on West Country courses. Stallworthy didn't aim for Cheltenham, Sandown or Aintree. He trained for local farmers and businessmen and ran their horses near home.

Jim stood in the yard and laconically pointed. 'Tack-room there.' He half turned. 'Horse in number twenty-seven. OK?'

'OK.'

I took a look at the occupant of box 27 and found a heavily muscled chestnut gelding standing there, anxious, it seemed, to be out on the gallops. He had nice short legs, with hocks not too angular, and a broad chest capable of pushing his way over or through any obstacle which came his way. More the type of a tough hardy steeplechaser than an ex-flat racer graduating to jumps.

I guessed at stamina and an unexcitability that might take a tiring amateur steadfastly towards the finish line, and if there were anything against him at first sight it was, perhaps, that he was a bit short in the neck.

Jim whistled up a lad to saddle and bridle the chestnut, though I had the impression that he had at first intended that I should do it myself.

Jim had considered me a sort of a joke. Perhaps my actual presence in the yard had converted me from joke to customer. In any case, neither Jim nor the lad saw anything but ordinary sense when I asked if I could see the chestnut being led round the yard at a walk. Somewhere along the way in my scrappy racing education I'd been told and shown by an avuncular old pro jockey that a horse that walked well galloped well. A long slow stride boded well for long-distance 'chases. A tittupping scratchy little walker meant a nervous scratchy little galloper.

The stride of the chestnut's walk was long enough and slow enough to suggest a temperament that would plod for ever. When he and his lad had completed two circuits of the yard I stopped him and felt his legs (no bumps from past tendon trouble) and looked in his mouth (which perhaps one shouldn't do to a gift horse) and estimated him to be about seven years old, a good solid age for a steeplechaser.

'Where do I ride him?' I asked Jim, and he pointed to a way out of the yard which led to a gate into a vast field that proved to be the chief training ground for the whole stable. There were no wide open down-land gallops, it seemed, in that cosy part of Devon.

'You can trot or canter down to the far end,' Jim said, 'and come back at a half-speed gallop. He . . . the chestnut . . . knows the way.'

I swung onto the chestnut's back and put the toes of my unsuitable running shoes into the stirrups, lengthening the leathers while getting to know the 'feel' of the big creature who would give me half speed and at least an illusion of being where I belonged.

I might never be a great jockey, and I might at times be clumsy and uncoordinated owing to growing in spurts and changing shape myself, but I'd ridden a great many different horses in my school holidays by working for people who wanted a few horses cared for while they went away on trips. I'd begged racehorse experience from trainers, and for the past two years had ridden in any race offered: I had had twenty-six outings to date, with three wins, two thirds and three falls.

The Stallworthy chestnut was in a good mood and let me know it by standing still patiently through the stirrup-leather lengthening and the pause while Jim sorted out a helmet in the tack-room, insisting that I wear it even though it was a size too small.

The chestnut's back was broad with muscles and I hadn't sat on a horse for three and a half weeks; and if he'd been mean-spirited that morning he could have run away with me and made a fool of my deficient strength, but in fact he went out onto the exercise ground as quietly as an old hack.

I didn't enjoy his trot, which was lumpy and threw me about, but his canter was like an armchair. We went in harmony down to the far end of the exercise field where the land dropped away a bit, so that the first part of the gallop home was uphill, good for strengthening legs.

At a half-speed gallop, riding the chestnut was a bit like sitting astride a launched rocket: powerful, purposeful, difficult to deflect. I reined to a slightly breathless walk and went over to where Jim waited beside the gate. 'Right,' he said noncommittally, 'now try the other one.'

The other horse – a bay gelding with a black mane – was of a leaner type and struck me as being more of a speed merchant than the one I'd just ridden. He carried his head higher and was more frisky and eager to set off and get into his stride. Whether that stride would last out over a distance of ground was, perhaps, doubtful.

I stood with my toes in the irons all the way down the field, letting the trot and canter flow beneath me. This was not a horse schooled to give his rider a peaceful look at the countryside; this was a fellow bred to race, for whom nothing else was of interest. At the far end of the field, instead of turning quietly, he did one of those swerving pirouettes with a dropped shoulder, a manoeuvre guaranteed to fling an unwary jockey off sideways. I'd seen many horses do that. I'd been flung off myself. But I was ready for Stallworthy's bay to try it; on his part more from eagerness to gallop than from spite.

His half-speed gallop home was a battle against my arms all the way: he wanted to go much faster. Thoughtfully I slid off his back and led him to Jim at the gate.

'Right,' Jim said. 'Which do you want?'

'Er . . .' I patted the bay's neck. He shook his handsome head vigorously, not in disapproval, I gathered, but in satisfaction.

'How about,' I suggested, 'a look at the form books and the breeding over a sandwich in a pub?'

I was quite good at pub life after three and a half weeks with my father.

Jim briefly laughed. 'I was told I was to fetch a school kid. You're some school kid.'

'I left school last month.'

'Yeah. Makes a difference!'

With good-natured irony he collected the necessary records from inside Stallworthy's house and drove us to a local pub where he was greeted as a friendly regular. We sat on a high-backed wooden settle and he put the form books on the table beside the beer (him) and the diet Coke (me).

In steeplechase breeding it's the dams that matter. A dam who breeds one winner will most likely breed others. The chestnut's dam had never herself won, though two of her progeny had. The chestnut so far hadn't finished nearer than second.

The bay's dam had never even raced, but all of her progeny, except the first foal, had won. The bay had won twice.

Both horses were eight.

'Tell me about them,' I said to Jim. 'What ought I to know?'

There was no way he was going to tell me the absolute truth if he had any commission coming from the sale. Horse traders were as notorious as car salesmen for filling the gear box with chaff.

'Why are they for sale?' I asked.

'Their owners are short of money.'

'My father would need a vet's certificate.'

'I'll see to it. Which horse do you want?'

'I'll talk to my father and let you know.'

Jim gave me a twisted smile. He had white eyebrows as well as white lashes. I needed to make a friend of him if I were to come often to ride exercise, so regrettably, with all my father's wily political sense, I deliberately set about canvassing Jim's pro-Ben vote, and thought that maybe I'd learned a few reprehensible techniques, while being willing to listen to people's troubles and desires.

Jim told me, laughing, that he'd hitched himself to Stallworthy because he hadn't been able to find a comparable trainer with a marriageable daughter. A good job I wasn't Usher Rudd, I thought.

Spencer Stallworthy apparently slept on Sunday afternoons, so I didn't see him again that day. Jim (and Bert) drove me back to Exeter by three o'clock and with a grin and a warm slap on the back he handed me over to the black car with the silent chauffeur.

'See you, then,' Jim said.

'I can hardly wait.'

The future had spectacularly clarified. My father,

instead of giving me a monthly allowance, had through my teens sent me one lump sum at Christmas to last me for the year: consequently I had enough saved away both to find myself a temporary lodging within cycling distance of Spencer Stallworthy and to immerse my brain in the racing press.

The chauffeur took me not to the headquarters from where he'd collected me, but to a playing field on the edge of Hoopwestern where, it appeared, an afternoon amalgam of fête and political rally was drawing to a close. Balloons, bouncy castle, bright plastic chutes and roundabouts had drawn children (and therefore voting parents) and car-boot-type stalls seemed to have sold out of all but hideous vases.

Painted banners promised 'GRAND OPENING BY MRS ORINDA NAGLE AT 3.00' and 'GEORGE JULIARD, 3.15.' Both of them were still present at 5.30, shaking hands all round.

Dearest Polly saw the black car stop at the gate and hurried across dry dusty grass to greet me.

'Happy birthday, Benedict. Did you choose a horse?'

'So he told you?' I looked across the field to where he stood on the soapbox surrounded by autograph books.

'He's been high as a kite all day.' Polly's own smile stretched inches. 'He told me he'd brought you here to Hoopwestern originally as window-dressing for the campaign, and he'd got to know you for the first time ever, and he'd wanted to give you something you would like, to thank you for all you've done here . . .'

'Polly!'

'He told me he hadn't realised how much he'd asked you to give up, with going to university instead of racing, and that you hadn't rebelled or walked out or cursed him. He wanted to give you the best he could.'

I swallowed.

He saw me from across the field and waved, and Polly and I walked over and stopped just outside the hedge of autograph seekers.

'Well?' he said over their heads. 'Did you like one?'

I couldn't think of adequate words. He looked, however, at my face, and smiled at what he saw there, and seemed content with my speechlessness. He stepped off the soapbox and made his way through the offered books, signing left and right, until he was within touching distance, and there he stopped.

We looked at each other in great accord.

'Well, go on,' Polly said to me impatiently, 'hug him.'

But my father shook his head and I didn't touch him, and I realised we had no tradition between us of how to express greeting or emotion, and that until that moment there had never been much intense mutual emotion to express. Far from hugging, we had never shaken hands.

'Thanks,' I said to him.

189

It sounded inadequate, but he nodded: it was enough.

'I want to tell you about it,' I said.

'Did you choose one?'

'More or less, but I want to talk to you first.'

'At dinner, then.'

'Perfect.'

Orinda was smiling warmly at me, fully recovered, make-up hiding any residual marks, all traces of the shaking, frightened woman in blood-spattered clothes overlaid by Constituency Wife, Mark I, the opener of fêtes and natural hogger of cameras.

'Benedict, daaahling!' She at least had no inhibitions about hugging, and embraced me soundly for public consumption. She smelled sweetly of scent. She wore a copper-coloured dress with green embroidery to match her eyes, and Polly beside me stiffened with the prehistoric reaction of Martha to butterfly.

Dearest Polly. *Dearest* Polly. I was far too young externally to show I understood her, let alone insult her by offering comforts. Dearest Polly wore remnants of the awful lipstick, a chunky necklace of amber beads and heavily strapped sandals below a muddy-green dress. I liked both women, but on the evidence of their clothes, they would never equally like each other.

Instinctively I looked over Orinda's shoulder, expecting the everlasting Anonymous Lover to be back at his post, but Wyvern had once and for all abandoned Hoopwestern as his path to influence. In his place behind Orinda loomed Leonard Kitchens with a soppy grin below his out-of-control moustache. Close on his heels came Mrs Kitchens, looking grim.

Usher Rudd was wandering about with his intrusive malice trying to catch people photographically at a disadvantage but, interestingly, when he caught my eye he pretended he hadn't, and veered away. I had no illusions that he wished me well.

Mervyn Teck and a retinue of dedicated volunteers, stoutly declaring the afternoon a success, drove my father and me back to the Sleeping Dragon. Four days to polling day, I thought; eternity.

Over a good dinner in the hotel dining-room I told my father about the two Stallworthy horses. A phlegmatic chestnut stayer and a sprinting excitable bay with a black mane.

'Well . . .' he said, frowning, 'you love speed. You'll take the bay. What makes you hesitate?'

'The horse I want has a name that might disturb you. I can't change his name: one isn't allowed to, after a thorough-bred has raced. I won't have that horse unless it's OK with you.'

He stared. 'What name could possibly disturb me so much?'

After a pause I said flatly, 'Sarah's Future.'

'Ben!'

'His dam was Sarah Jones; his sire, Bright Future. It's good breeding for a jumper.'

'The bay – ?'

191

'No,' I said. 'The chestnut. He's the one I want. He's never won yet, though he's been second. A novice has a wider – a better – choice of a race. Apart from that, he felt right. He'd look after me.'

My father absentmindedly crumbled a bread roll to pieces.

'*You*,' he said eventually, '*you* are literally Sarah's future. Let's say she would be pleased. I'll phone Stallworthy in the morning.'

Far from slackening off during the run-up to polling day, the Juliard camp spent the last three days in a non-stop whirl.

I drove the Range Rover from breakfast to bedtime. I drove to Quindle three times, and all around the villages. I screwed together and unclipped the soapbox until I could do it in my sleep. I loaded and unloaded boxes of leaflets. I made cooing noises at babies and played ball games with kids and shook uncountable hands and smiled and smiled and smiled.

I thought of Sarah's Future, and was content.

On the last evening, Wednesday, my father invited all his helpers and volunteers to the Sleeping Dragon for a thank-you supper. Along in a room off the Town Hall, Paul Bethune was doing the same.

The Bethune cavalcade had several times crossed our path, their megaphone louder, their travelling circus larger, their campaign vehicle not a painted

Range Rover but a roofless double-decker bus borrowed from his party headquarters. Bethune's message
followed him everywhere: 'Dennis Nagle was out of
touch, old-fashioned. Elect Bethune, a local man, who
knows the score.'

A recent opinion poll in the constituency had put
Bethune a few points ahead. Titmuss and Whistle were
nowhere.

The *Gazette* had trumpeted merely 'An End to
Sleaze' and waffled on about 'the new morality'
without defining it. Though by instinct a Bethune man,
the editor had let Usher Rudd loose and thereby both
increased his sales and scored an own-goal. The editor,
I thought in amusement, had dug his own dilemma.

My father thanked his faithful workers.

'Whatever happens tomorrow,' he said, 'I want you
to know how much I appreciate all you've done ... all
the time you've given ... your tireless energy ... your
friendly good nature. I thank our agent, Mervyn, for
his excellent planning. We've all done our best to get
the party's message across. Now it's up to the voters
to decide.'

He thanked Orinda for rallying to his side. ' ... All
the difference in the world to have her support ...
immensely generous ... reassuring to the faithful ...'

Orinda, splendid in gold chains and emerald green,
looked modest and loved it.

Polly, beside me, made a noise near to a retch.

I stifled a quivering giggle.

'Don't think I've forgotten,' she said to me severely, 'that it was you who changed Orinda from foe to angel. I bear it only because the central party wants to use your father's talents. Get him *in*, they said. Just like you, they more or less told me to put his feet on the escalator, and he would rise all the way.'

But someone, I thought, had tried to prevent that first step onto the escalator. Had *perhaps* tried. A bullet, a wax plug, an unexplained fire. If someone had tried to halt him by those means and hadn't left it to the ballot-box . . . then *who*? No one had seriously tried to find out.

The speeches done, my father came over to Polly and me, his eyes gleaming with excitement, his whole body alive with purpose. His strong facial bones shouted intelligence. His dark hair curled with healthy animal vigour.

'I'm going to win this by-election,' he said, broadly smiling. 'I'm going to win. I can feel it.'

His euphoria fired everyone in the place to believe him, and lasted in himself through breakfast the next morning. The glooms crowded in with his second cup of coffee and he wasted an hour in doubt and tension, worrying that he hadn't worked hard enough, that there was more he could have done.

'You'll win,' I said.

'But the opinion polls . . .'

'The people who compile the opinion polls don't go round the village pubs at lunchtime.'

'The tide is flowing the wrong way . . .'

'Then go back to the City and make another fortune.'

He stared and then laughed, and we set out on a tour of the polling stations, where the volunteers taking exit polls told him they were pretty even, but not to lose hope.

Here and there we came across Paul Bethune on a similar mission with similar doubts. He and my father were unfailingly polite to each other.

The anxiety went on all day and all evening. After weeks of fine weather it rained hard that afternoon. Both sides thought it might be a disaster. Both sides thought it might be to their advantage. The rain stopped when the light-bulb workers poured out of the day shift and detoured to the polling booths on their way home.

The polls closed at ten o'clock and the counting began.

My father stood at our bedroom window staring out across the cobbled square to the burned-out shell of the bow-fronted shops.

'Stop worrying,' I said. As if he could.

'I was head-hunted, you know,' he said. 'The party leaders came to me and said they wanted to harness my economic skills for the good of the country. What if I've let them down?'

'You won't have,' I assured him.

He smiled twistedly. 'They offered me a marginal

seat to see what I was made of. I was *flattered*. Serves me right.'

'Father . . .'

'Dad.'

'OK, Dad. Good men do lose.'

'Thanks a lot.'

We went in time along the square to the Town Hall where, far from offering peace, the atmosphere was electric with hope and despair. Paul Bethune, surrounded by hugely rosetted supporters, was trying hard to smile. Isobel Bethune, in dark brown, tried to merge into the woodwork.

Mervyn talked to Paul Bethune's agent absentmindedly and I would have bet neither of them heard what the other was saying.

Usher Rudd took merciless photographs.

There was a smattering of applause at my father's entrance and both Polly (in pinkish grey) and Orinda (in dramatic glittering white) sailed across the floor to greet him personally.

'George, daaahling,' Orinda crowed, offering her smooth cheek for a kiss. 'Dennis is with us, you know.'

George daaahling looked embarrassed.

'It's going quite well, George,' Polly said, giving succour. 'First reports say the town votes are fairly even.'

The counting was going on under all sorts of rigorous supervision. Even those counting the Xs weren't sure who had won.

My father and Paul Bethune looked as calm as neither was feeling.

The hall gradually filled with supporters of both sides. After midnight, getting on for one o'clock, the four candidates and their close supporters appeared on the platform, shuffling about with false smiles. Paul Bethune looked around irritably for his wife, but she'd hidden herself successfully in the crowd. Orinda stood on the platform close beside my father as of right and no one questioned it, though Polly, beside me on the floor, fumed that it should be me up there, not that . . . that . . .

Words failed her.

My father told me afterwards that the result had been whispered to the candidates before they faced the world, presumably so no one would burst into tears, but one couldn't have guessed it from their faces.

Finally the returning officer (whose function was to announce the result) fussed his way onto the centre stage, tapped the microphone to make sure it was working (it was), grinned at the television cameras, and rather unnecessarily asked for silence.

He strung out his moment of importance by looking around as if to make sure everyone was there on the platform who should be and, finally, slowly, in a silence broken only by a throng of heartbeats, read the result.

Alphabetically.

Bethune . . . thousands.

Juliard . . . thousands.

Titmuss . . . hundreds.

Whistle . . . 69.

It took a moment to sink in. Staring down a preliminary cheer from the floor, the returning officer completed his task.

George Juliard is therefore elected . . .

The rest was drowned in cheers.

Polly worked it out. 'He won by just under two thousand. Bloody well done.'

Polly kissed me.

Up on the stage Orinda was loudly kissing the new MP.

It was too much for Dearest Polly, who left my side to go to his.

I found poor sad Isobel Bethune at my elbow instead.

'Look at that *harridan* with your father, pretending it was *she* who won the votes.'

'She did help, to be fair.'

'She would never have won on her own. It was your *father* who won the election. And my Paul lost. He positively *lost*. Your father never mentioned that bimbo of his, not once, though he could have done, but the public never forget those things. Sleaze sticks, you know.'

'Mrs Bethune . . .'

'This is the third time Paul's contested the seat,' she told me hopelessly. 'We knew he would lose to Dennis Nagle the last two times, but this time the party said he was bound to win, with the way the recent by-elections have been swinging in our favour, and with the other party ignoring Orinda and bringing in a stranger, and they'll never let Paul stand again. He's lost worse than ever this time with everything on his side, and it's that *horrid* Usher Rudd's fault and I could *kill* him...' She smothered her face in a handkerchief as if to shut out the world and, stroking my arm, mumbled, 'I'll never forget your kindness.'

Up on the stage her stupid husband still looked self-satisfied.

A month ago, I thought, I hadn't known the Bethunes existed.

Dearest Polly had bloomed unseen.

I hadn't heard of Orinda, or of Alderney Wyvern.

I hadn't met Mrs Kitchens nor her fanatical unlovable Leonard, and I hadn't known plump efficient Mervyn or worried Crystal. I never did know the last names of Faith or Marge or Lavender, but I was certain even then that I would never forget the mean-spirited red-haired terror whose delight in life was to find out people's hidden pleasures in order to destroy them. Bobby Usher bleeding Rudd.

# CHAPTER NINE

So my father went to Westminster and I to Exeter, and the intense month we had spent in getting to know each other receded from a vivid present experience into a calmer, picture-filled memory.

I might not see him for weeks at a time but we talked now often on the telephone. Parliament was still in its summer recess. He would go back as a new boy, as I would, when my first term began.

Meantime, I rode Sarah's Future every morning under Stallworthy's critical eye and can't have done as badly as for Vivian Durridge because when I asked if he would enter the chestnut in a race for me – any race would do – he chose a novice 'chase at Wincanton on an inconspicuous Thursday and told me he hoped I'd be worth it as it was costing my father extras in the way of horse transport and shoeing with racing plates, not to mention the entry fee.

Laden thus half with glee and half with guilt I went with Jim in his car to Wincanton, where Jim declared and saddled the horse and then watched him win with as much disbelief as I felt when I sailed past the post first.

'He *flew*!' I said, thrilled and astonished, as I unbuckled the saddle in the winner's enclosure. 'He was brilliant.'

'So I saw.'

Jim's lack of much enthusiasm, I discovered, was rooted in his not having had the faith for a bet. Neither was Stallworthy overjoyed. All he said the next morning was, 'You wasted the horse's best win. You haven't any sense. If I'd thought for a moment you would go to the front when the favourite fell, I'd have told you to keep the chestnut on a tight rein so we could have put the stable money on him next time out. What your father will say, I can't imagine.'

What my father said was, 'Very well done.'

'But nobody backed it . . .'

'Don't you listen to Stallworthy. You listen to *me*. That horse is for you to do your best on. To win whenever you can. And don't think I didn't back it. I have an arrangement with a bookmaker that wherever – *whenever* – you ride in a race, I am betting on you at starting price. I won on you at twenties yesterday . . . I'm even learning racing jargon! *Always* try to win. Understand?'

I said, 'Yes,' weakly.

'And I don't care if you lose because some other horse is faster. Just keep to the rules and don't break your neck.'

'OK.'

'Is there anything else you want?'

'Er . . .'

'You'll get nowhere if you're afraid to tell me.'

'I'm not exactly afraid,' I said.

'Well, then?'

'Well . . . will you telephone Stallworthy? Will you ask him to run your horse in the novice 'chase at Newton Abbot a week tomorrow? He's entered him but now he won't want to run him. He'll say it's too soon. He'll say the horse will have to carry a 5-lb penalty because I won on him yesterday.'

'And will he?'

'Yes, but there aren't many more races – suitable races, that is – that I can ride him in before term starts. Stallworthy wants to win but I just want to *race*.'

'Yes, I know.' He paused. 'I'll fix it for Newton Abbot. Anything else?'

'Only . . . thanks.'

His laugh came down the wire. 'Give my regards to Sarah's Future.'

Feeling a bit foolish I passed on the message to the chestnut, though in fact I had fallen into a habit of talking to him, sometimes aloud if we were alone, and sometimes in my mind. Although I had ridden a good many horses, he was the first I had known consistently from day to day. He fitted my body-size and my level of skill. He undoubtedly recognised me and seemed almost to breathe a sigh of relief when I appeared every morning for exercise. We had won the race at Wincanton because we knew and trusted each other, and when I'd asked him for maximum speed at the end he'd understood from past experience what was needed, and had seemed positively to exult in having at last finished first.

Jim forgave the success and grew interested. Jim was by nature in tune with horses and, as I gradually realised, did most of the actual training. Stallworthy, although he watched the gallops most mornings, won his races with pen and entry forms, totting up times and weights and statistical probabilities.

Up the centre of the long exercise field there were two rows of schooling fences, one of three flights of hurdles, and one of birch fences. Jim patiently spent some mornings teaching both me and the chestnut to go up over the birch with increasing precision, measuring our stride for take-off from further and further back before the actual jump.

The riding I'd learned to that date had been from watching other people. Jim taught me, as it were, from inside, so that in that first month with Sarah's Future I began to develop from an uncoordinated windmill with a head full of unrealistic dreams into a reasonably competent amateur rider.

Grumbling at great length about owners who knew nothing at all about racing and should leave all decisions to their trainer, Stallworthy complainingly sent the chestnut to carry his 5-lb penalty at Newton Abbot.

I'd never before ridden on the course and at first sight of it felt foolish not to have listened to Stallworthy's judgment. The steeplechase track was an almost one-and-a-half-mile flat circuit with sharpish turns, and the short grass gave little purchase on rock-hard ground, baked by the sun of August.

Stallworthy, with several other runners from his yard, had brought his critical eye to the course. Jim, saddling Sarah's Future, told me the chestnut knew the course better than I did (I'd walked round it a couple of hours earlier to see the jumps, and the approaches to them, at close quarters) and to remember what I'd learned from him at home, and not to expect too much because of the weight disadvantage and because the other jockeys were all professionals, and this was not an amateur race.

As usual, it was the speed that seduced me and fulfilled, and the fact that we finished third was enough to make my day worthwhile, though Stallworthy, who had incidentally also trained the winner, announced to me several times, 'I told you so. I told your father it was too much to expect. Perhaps you'll listen to me next time.'

'Never mind,' Jim consoled. 'If you'd won today you'd have to have carried a 10-lb penalty at Exeter races next Saturday, always supposing you can persuade the old man to let him run there after this. He'll say it's too soon, which it probably *is*.'

The old man (Stallworthy) conducted a running battle over the telephone with my father.

My father won.

So, blisteringly, by six lengths, did Sarah's Future, because the much longer galloping track, up on Haldon Moor above Exeter, suited him better. He carried a 5-lb penalty, not 10, and made light of it. The starting price, my father assured me later, would pay the training fees until Christmas.

Two days after that, in cooler blood, I went to learn mathematics.

My father learned back-bench tactics, but that wasn't what the party had sent him to Hoopwestern for. He tried to explain to me that the path upward led through the Whips' office, which sounded nastily about flagellation to me, though he laughed.

'The Whips' office is what gives you the thumbs up for advancement towards the ministerial level.'

'And their thumbs are up for you?'

'Well ... so far ... yes.'

'Minister of what?' I asked, disbelievingly. 'Surely you're too young?'

'The really forward boys are on their way by twenty-two. At thirty-eight, I'm old.'

'I don't like politics.'

'I can't ride races,' he said.

To have the Whip withdrawn, he explained, meant the virtual end to a political career. If getting elected was the first giant step, then winning the Whips' approval was the second. When the newly elected member for Hoopwestern was shortly appointed as Under-Secretary of State in the Department of Trade and Industry, it was apparently a signal to the whole fabric of government that a bright fast-moving comet had risen over the horizon.

I went to listen to his maiden speech, sitting inconspicuously in the gallery. He spoke about light bulbs and had the whole House laughing; and Hoopwestern's share of the illumination market soared.

I met him for dinner after his speech, when he was again in the high exaltation of post-performance spirits.

'I suppose you haven't been back to Hoopwestern?' he said.

'Well, no.'

'I have, of course. Leonard Kitchens is in trouble.'

'Who?'

'Leonard . . .'

'Oh, yes. Yes, the unbalanced moustache. What sort of trouble?'

'The police now have a rifle which may be the one fired at us that evening.'

'By the police,' I asked as he paused, 'do you mean Joe the policeman whose mother drives a school bus?'

'Joe whose mother drives a school bus is actually Detective Sergeant Joe Duke, and, yes, he's now received from the Sleeping Dragon a very badly rusted .22 rifle. It seems that after the trees shed their leaves the guttering round the roof of the hotel got choked with them, as happens most years, and rainwater overflowed instead of draining down the pipes as it should, so they sent a man up a ladder to clear out the leaves, and they found it wasn't just leaves clogging the guttering, it was the .22 rifle.'

'But what's that got to do with Leonard Kitchens?'

My father ate peppered steak, rare, with spinach.

'Leonard Kitchens is the nurseryman who festoons the Sleeping Dragon with all those baskets of geraniums.'

'But – ' I objected.

'Apparently in a broom cupboard on that bedroom level he keeps a sort of trolley with things for looking after the baskets. Clippers, a long-spouted watering can, fertiliser. They think he could have hidden the gun in the trolley. If you stand on a chair by the window you can reach up far enough outside to put a rifle up in the gutter. And someone *did* put a gun up there.'

I frowned over my food.

'You know what people are like,' my father said. 'Someone says, "I *suppose* Leonard Kitchens could have put the rifle in the gutter, he's always in and out of the hotel," and the next person drops the "I suppose" and repeats the rest as a fact.'

'What does Leonard Kitchens himself say?'

'Of course, he says it wasn't his gun and he didn't put it in the gutter, and he says no one can prove he did.'

'That's what guilty people always say,' I observed.

'Yes, but it's true, no one can prove he ever had the gun. No one has come forward to connect him to rifles in any way.'

'What does Mrs Kitchens say?'

'Leonard's wife is doing him no good at all. She goes around saying her husband was so besotted with Orinda Nagle that he would do anything, including shooting me in the back, to get me out of Orinda's way. Joe Duke asked her if she had ever seen a rifle in her husband's possession, and instead of saying no, as any sensible woman would, she said he had a garden shed full of junk, and it was possible he had *anything* lying around in there.'

'Did Joe by any chance search the shed? I mean, did he have a look round to see if Leonard had any bullets?'

'Joe couldn't get a warrant to search, as there were no real grounds for suspicion. Also, as I suppose you know, it's quite easy to buy high-velocity bullets, and even easier to throw them away. There's no chance of telling that it was indeed that rifle that was used because, even if you could remove all the rust, there is no bullet to match it to, as the one from the what-not finally got lost altogether in the fire. No one ever found any cartridge cases in the hotel either.'

My father continued with his steak. Putting down his knife and fork he said, 'I took the Range Rover to Basil Rudd's garage and had him dismantle the engine for a thorough check of the oil system. There was nothing in the sump except oil. It was actually extremely unprofessional for that mechanic – Terry, I think he is – to push the substitute plug up into the sump, but Basil Rudd won't hear a word against him, and I suppose there was no harm done.'

'There might have been,' I said. I thought for a moment and asked, 'I suppose Leonard Kitchens isn't accused of being in possession of candles?'

'You may laugh,' my father said, 'but in the shop at his garden centre, where they sell plastic gnomes and things, they do have table centre-pieces with candles and ribboned bows and stuff.'

'You can buy candles anywhere,' I said. 'And what about the fire? Was that Leonard Kitchens, too?'

'He was there,' my father reminded me, and I remembered Mrs Kitchens saying her Leonard liked a good fire.

'Did the firemen ever find out how that fire started?'

My father shook his head. 'They didn't at the time. Some of them are now saying unofficially that it could have been started with candles. Leonard Kitchens fiercely denies he had anything to do with it.'

'What do you think, yourself?'

My father drank some wine. He was trying to indoctrinate me into liking burgundy but, to his disgust, I still liked diet Coke better.

He said, 'I think Leonard Kitchens is fanatical enough to do almost anything. It's easy enough to think of him as a bit of a silly ass, with that out-of-proportion moustache, but it's people with obsessions who do the real harm in the world, and if he still has a grudge against me, I want him where I can see him.'

I did my best with the wine, but I didn't really like it.

'There's no point in his arranging accidents for you any more, now that you're elected.'

My father sighed. 'With people like Kitchens you can't be sure that good sense will be in control.'

I stayed with him that night in his Canary Wharf apartment by the Thames. His big windows looked down the wide river where once a flourish of cranes had been busy with shipping, though he himself couldn't remember 'the Docks' except as a long-ago political lever. His old office (he ran his investment-consultant business from home) gave him a two-mile walk along the Embankment to his new office in Whitehall, a leg-stretching that was clearly keeping him muscularly fit. He blazed with vigour and excitement. Even though he was my father I felt both energised and overwhelmed by his vitality.

In a way, I deeply loved him.

In a way I felt wholly incapable of ever equalling

his mental force or his determination. It took me years to realise that I didn't have to.

On the morning after his maiden speech I caught the early train from Paddington to Exeter, clicketing along the rails from reflected fame to anonymity.

In Exeter, one of eight thousand residential students, I coasted through university life without attracting much attention, and absorbed reams of calculus, linear algebra, actuarial science and distribution theory towards a Bachelor of Science degree in Mathematics with Accounting: and as a short language course came with the package I also learned French, increasing my vocabulary from *piste* and *écurie* (track and stable) to law and order.

As often as possible I cycled to Stallworthy's stable to ride Sarah's Future, and on several Saturdays set off from starting gates. After the first flourish as a novice, finding winning races for a steady but unspectacular jumper proved difficult, but also-ran was fine by me: fourth, fifth, sixth, one easy fall and no tailed-offs.

On one very cold December Saturday towards the end of my first term I was standing on the stands at Taunton watching one of Stallworthy's string scud first towards the last flight of hurdles when it crashed and fell in a cascading cartwheel of legs, and snapped its neck.

211

They put screens round the disaster and winched the body away, and within ten minutes I came across Stallworthy trying to comfort the female owner. Crying ladies were not Stallworthy's speciality. He first asked me to find Jim and then cancelled that instruction and simply passed the weeping woman into my arms, and told me to take her for a drink.

Many trainers went white and shook with emotion when their horses died. Stallworthy shrugged and drew a line across a page.

Mrs Courtney Young, the bereaved owner, wiped away her tears and tried to apologise, while a large bracer of gin took its effect.

'It's all right,' I assured her. 'If my horse died, I'd be devastated.'

'But you're so young. You'd get over it.'

'I'm sure you will too, in time.'

'You don't understand.' Fresh tears rolled. 'I let the horse's insurance lapse because I couldn't afford the premium, and I owe Mr Stallworthy a lot of training fees, and I was sure my horse would win today so I could pay off my debts, and I backed it with a bookie I have an account with, and I haven't any money to pay him. I was going to have to sell my horse anyway if he didn't win, but now I can't do even that . . .'

Poor Mrs Courtney Young.

'She's mad,' Jim told me later, saddling Sarah's Future. 'She bets too much.'

'What will she do?'

'Do?' he exclaimed. 'She'll sell a few more heir-looms. She'll buy another horse. One day she'll lose the lot.'

I grieved very briefly for Mrs Courtney Young, but that evening I telephoned my father and suggested he insure Sarah's Future.

'How did you get on today?' he asked. 'I heard the results and you weren't in the first three.'

'Fourth. What about insurance?'

'Who arranges horse insurance?'

'Weatherbys.'

'Do you want to?'

'For your sake,' I said.

'Then send me the paperwork.'

Weatherbys, the firm that arranged insurance for horses, were the administrators for the whole of racing. It was Weatherbys who kept the records, who registered horses' names and ownership details including colours; Weatherbys to whom trainers sent entries for races; Weatherbys who confirmed a horse was running and sent details of racing programmes to the press; Weatherbys who printed racecards in colour by night and despatched them to racecourses by morning.

Weatherbys published the fixture list, kept the thorough-bred Stud Book and acted as a bank for the transfer of fees to jockeys, prize money to owners, anything to anyone. Weatherbys ran a safe computer database.

There wasn't much in racing, in fact, that Weatherbys didn't do.

It was because of mad, tearful, silly Mrs Courtney Young that I began to think that one distant day I might apply to Weatherbys for a job.

In the spring of my third year of study my father came to Exeter to see me (he had been a couple of times before) and to my surprise brought with him Dearest Polly.

I had spent a week of each Christmas holidays skiing (practising my French!) and I'd been riding and racing in every spare minute, but I also played fair and passed all my exams and assessments with reasonable grades if not with distinction, so when I saw him arrive a quick canter round the guilt reflexes raised no wincing spectres, and I shook his hand (we had at least advanced that far) with uncomplicated pleasure.

'I don't know if you realise,' my father said, 'that we are fast approaching a General Election.'

My immediate reaction was 'Oh, God. No.' I managed not to say it aloud, but it must have been plain on my face.

Dearest Polly laughed and my father said, 'This time I'm not asking you to canvass door to door.'

'But you need a bodyguard . . .'

'I've engaged a professional.'

I felt instantly jealous: ridiculous. It took me a good

ten seconds to say sincerely, 'I hope he'll mind your back.'

'He's a she. All sorts of belts in martial arts.'

'Oh.' I glanced at Polly, who looked merely benign.

'Polly and I,' my father said, 'propose to marry. We came to hear if you had any objections.'

'Polly!'

'Dear Benedict. Your father is so abrupt. I would have asked you more gently.'

'I've no objections,' I said. 'Very much the opposite.' I kissed her cheek.

'Goodness!' she exclaimed. 'You've grown.'

'Have you?' my father enquired with interest. 'I hadn't noticed.'

'I've stopped at last,' I sighed. 'I'm over an inch taller and fifteen pounds heavier than I was at Hoop-western.' Too big, I might have added, for much scope as a professional jockey, but an excellent size for an amateur.

Polly herself hadn't changed, except that I saw with interest that the hard crimson lipstick had been jetti-soned for an equally inappropriate scarlet. Her clothes still looked unfashionable even by charity shop stan-dards, and no one had taken recent scissors to her hair. With her long face and thin stringy body, she looked a total physical mismatch for my increasingly powerful father, but positive goodness shone out of her as always, and her sincerity, it seemed to me, was now tinged with amusement. There had never been anything gauche or self-conscious in her manner, but only the strength to be her own intelligent, uncompromising self.

More than a marriage of true minds, I thought. A marriage of true morality.

I said sincerely to my father, 'Congratulations,' and he looked pleased.

'What are you doing next Saturday?' he asked.

'Racing at Chepstow.'

He was shaking his head. 'I want you to stand beside me.'

'Do you mean...' I hesitated, 'that you are marrying... next Saturday?'

'That's right,' he agreed. 'Now that we've decided, and since you seem quite pleased, there's no point in delaying. I'm going to live with Polly in her house in the woods, and I'll also find a larger flat in London.'

Polly, I learned by instalments through that afternoon, had inherited the house in the woods from her parents, along with a fortune that set her financially free to work unpaid wherever she saw the need.

She was two years older than my father. She had never been married: a mischievous glint in her eye both forbade and answered the more intimate question.

She didn't intend, she said, to make a wasteland of Orinda Nagle's life. Orinda and Mervyn Teck had been running the constituency day to day and making a success of it. Polly didn't hunger to open fêtes or flirt with cameras. She would organise, as always, from behind the scenes. And she would be listened to, I thought, where influence mattered.

Six days later she and my father married in the ultimate of quiet weddings. I stood by my father and Polly was supported by the Duke who'd lured Orinda to the races, and all of us signed the certificates.

The bride wore brown with a gold and amber necklet given by my father, and looked distinguished. A photographer, at my request, recorded the event. A discreet paragraph appeared in *The Times*. The *Hoopwestern Gazette* caught up with the story later. Mr and Mrs George Juliard, after a week in Paris, returned to Hoopwestern to keep the light-bulb workers faithful.

I still disliked politics and I was extremely grateful that the approach of my final exams made it impossible for me to repeat my by-election stint.

There were many politically active students at Exeter, but I kept my head down with them too and led a double life only on Stallworthy's gallops and various racetracks. I won no races that spring, but the sensation of speed was all that mattered: and, in an oddity of brain activity, the oftener I raced the more clearly I understood second-order differential equations.

The General Election swelled and broke under me like a Pacific surf, and my father, along with his party, were returned to power. A small majority, but enough.

No one shot at him, no one plugged his sump-drain

with wax, no one set fire to Polly's house, and no one let the martial arts expert earn her fee.

Suspicion of shooting and arson still lay heavily on Leonard Kitchens, but no one could accuse him of anything this time as his formidable and unforgiving wife insisted on his taking her on a double Mediterranean cruise. They were in Athens on polling day.

Poor Isobel Bethune had been right: Paul Bethune's party dumped him as a candidate in favour of a worthy woman magistrate. Though it was no longer hotly scandalous news, Paul Bethune's roving eye had settled again outside his home, and Isobel, at last fed up with it, had shed her marriage and her sullen sons and gone to live with her sister in Wales.

Polly kept me informed, her humour dry. My father couldn't have married anyone better.

I told him to beware of bikini-clad bimbos falling artistically into his lap with Usher Rudd in attendance for accusations of sleaze. Hadn't I heard, he asked, that Usher Rudd had been sacked by the *Gazette* for manufacturing sleaze where it didn't exist? Usher Rudd, my father cheerfully said, was now telephoto-lens-stalking a promiscuous front-bencher of the Opposition.

When the party in power reassembled after the whole country had voted, there was a major reshuffle of jobs. To no one's surprise at Westminster, my father's career skipped upwards like helium and he became a Minister of State in the Ministry of Transport, one step down from a seat in the Cabinet.

I had the best photograph of his wedding to Polly framed and stood it beside the one of him and my mother. I took the pacts we'd signed out of my mother's frame and read them thoughtfully, and put them back. They seemed to belong to a different life. I had indeed grown up at Exeter, and I'd had 'the first' that I would never forget: but the basic promises of those pacts had so far been kept, and although now it might seem a melodramatic statement, I knew that if it ever became necessary, I would indeed defend my father against any form of attack.

I took my final exams and, seeing that I'd probably done enough to gain a Bachelor of Science degree of a reasonable standard, I wrote to Weatherbys and asked for a job.

They replied, what job?

Any, I wrote. I could add, subtract and work computers, and I had ridden in races.

Ah, *that* Juliard. Come for an interview, they said.

Weatherbys, a family business started in 1770 and currently servicing racing in increasingly inventive and efficient ways, stood quietly in red brick surrounded by fields, trees and peaceful countryside near the small ancient town of Wellingborough, some sixty miles north-west of London in Northamptonshire.

Inside, the atmosphere of the furiously busy secretariat was notably calm and quiet also. Knowing the vast scope and daily pressure of the work being done there, I suppose I'd expected something like the clattering frenzy of an old-fashioned newspaper office, but what I walked into was near to silence, with rows of heads bent over computer monitors and people walking among them with thoughtfulness, not scurrying, carrying papers and boxes of disks.

I was handed from department to department and shown around, and in an undemanding interview at the end was asked for my age and references. I went away in disappointment: they had been polite and kind but had asked none of the piercing questions I would have expected if they'd had a job to offer.

Back at Exeter, living in rooms halfway between the university and Stallworthy's yard, I began dispiritedly to send job applications to a list of industries. Weatherbys had seemed my natural home: too bad they didn't see me as their child.

They did, however, follow up on the references I'd given them: my tutor at the university and Stallworthy himself.

The gruff old trainer told me he'd said my character and behaviour were satisfactory. Thanks a lot, I thought. Jim laughed. 'He doesn't want you to leave and take Sarah's Future with you. It's a wonder he didn't call you a loud-mouthed trouble-maker!'

There was a letter from my tutor:

Dear Benedict,

I enclose a photocopy of a reference I have sent to an institution called Weatherbys, that has something to do with horse racing, I believe.

His testimonial in full read:

'Benedict Juliard is likely to have gained a creditable degree in Mathematics with Accounting, though not a brilliant one. He took very little part in student activities during his three years at University, as it seems he was exclusively interested in horses. There are no adverse reports of his character and behaviour.'

Shit, I thought. Oh, well.

Much to my astonishment, I also received a letter from Sir Vivian Durridge:

My dear Benedict,

I am delighted to have seen over the past three years that you have had the opportunity to ride successfully as an amateur on your father's horse, Sarah's Future. I am sure that he has told you he enlisted my help in making you face the fact that you were not cut out for rising to the top three in the steeplechase jockeys' list. Looking back, I see that I was unnecessarily brutal in accusing you of drug-taking, as I knew perfectly well at the time that with your sort of character you did not, but on that particular morning it seemed to me – and I regret it – that it was the only thing that would disturb you so badly that you would do as your father wanted, which was to go to university.

I have now heard from a friend of mine at Weatherbys that you have applied to them for a job. I enclose a photocopy of a letter I have written to them, and I hope that some way this may straighten things between us.

Yours sincerely,
Vivian Durridge

His enclosure read:

To whom it may concern:
Benedict Juliard rode my horses as a sixteen- and seventeen-year-old amateur jockey. I found him completely trustworthy in every respect and would give him my unqualified endorsement in any position he applied for.

I sat down, the pages shaking in my hands. Vivian Durridge was about the last person I would ever have applied to for a thumbs up.

I had vaguely been looking for a safe place to keep my birth certificate, so as not to lose it while I moved from lodgings to lodgings. I knew I wouldn't lose the marriage photographs so I decided to put my birth certificate behind my father and Polly, and as I'd been doing that when Vivian Durridge's remarkable letter arrived, I folded his pages into the frame too.

Three days later the mail brought an envelope bearing the Weatherbys logo, a miniature representation of a stallion standing under an oak tree, from a painting by George Stubbs.

I was cravenly afraid of opening it. It would begin '*We regret . . .*'

Well, it had to be faced.

I opened the envelope, and the letter began '*We are pleased . . .*'

*Pleased.*

That evening my father telephoned. 'Is it true you've got yourself a job at Weatherbys?'

'Yes. How do you know?'

'Why didn't you ask for my help?'

'I didn't think of it.'

'I despair of you, Ben.' He didn't, though, sound particularly annoyed.

He had been talking to one of the Weatherby cousins at a dinner in the City, he said. The web of insider chat in the City far outdid the Internet.

I asked if I could move Sarah's Future from Devon.

'Find a trainer.'

'Thanks.'

Spencer Stallworthy grumbled. Jim shrugged: life always moved on. I parted from them with gratitude and boxed my chestnut pal to a new home.

Weatherbys took me into their Racing Operations department which handled entries, runners, weights, riders, the draw: all the details of every race run in Britain, amounting to about a thousand transactions most days and up to three thousand at busy times.

All this computer speed took place in airy light expanses of desks and floor space, and in the calm quietness so impressive on my first visit. I'd thought that at a couple of days over twenty-one I might be at a disadvantage from youth, but I found at once that the whole staff were young, and enjoyed what they were doing. Within a month I couldn't imagine working anywhere else.

Every so often my own name cropped up, both whenever I was actually racing, but also in the next door department of Racing Administration that dealt with records of owners. It became a sort of running joke – 'Hey, Juliard, if you race that nag again at Fontwell, he'll suffer a 7-lb penalty,' or 'Hey, Juliard, you carried overweight at Ludlow. Cut down on the plum duff!'

Sarah's Future, as far as I could tell, enjoyed the exchange of the soft air of Devon for the brisker winds of further north. He still acknowledged my morning arrivals with much head-nodding and blow-breathing down his wide black nostrils, and he seemed to think it normal that I should embrace his neck and tell him he was a great fella, and mean it.

Anyone who says there can be true fusing of animal/

human consciousness is probably deluding themselves, but after several intimate years of speed together, that chestnut and I were probably as near to brothers as interspecies relationships could get.

One Saturday, about a year after I'd started at Weatherbys, the horse and I lined up at Towcester for an uneventful three mile 'chase, my father's inconspicuous colours of gold and grey made even less discernible by a persistent drizzle.

No one on the stands seemed afterwards to be sharply clear what happened. From my point of view we were rising cleanly in a well-judged take-off to a big black open ditch fence coming up the hill towards the straight. Another horse tripped and crashed into us, knocking Sarah's Future completely off balance. He had jumped that fence expertly several times over the past years: neither he nor I was expecting disaster. His feet were knocked sideways. He landed in a heap, throwing me off forwards. I connected with the ground in one of those crunching collisions that tells you at once that you've broken a bone without being sure *which* bone. I heard it snap. I rolled, tucking my head in to save it from the hooves of the runners behind me. The remainder of the field of half-ton horses clattered over my head as I lay winded and anxious on the slippery grass with blades of it in my mouth and up my nose, and dislodging my goggles after an uncontrollable slide.

The clamour of the contest faded away towards the

next fence. Two horses and two jockeys weren't going to be worrying about that. The horse that had crashed into Sarah's Future scrambled to its unsteady feet and trotted off as if dazed, and his unseated rider bent over me with 'Are you all right, mate?' as his best effort at an apology.

I gripped his hand to haul myself to my feet and found that the bone I'd broken was somewhere in my left shoulder.

Sarah's Future, also on his feet, was trying to walk but succeeding only in hobbling around in a circle. He couldn't put any weight on one of his forelegs. A groundsman caught him by the bridle and held him.

In hopeless love for the horse I walked over to him and tried to will it not to be true, not to be possible that after so long this closest of companionships should have so suddenly come to the edge of a precipice.

I knew, as every rider of any experience knew, that there was nothing to be done. Sarah's Future, like Sarah herself, was going to eternity in my hands.

I wept. I couldn't help it. It looked like the rain. The horse had broken his near foreleg. His jockey, his left collar-bone.

The horse died.

The jockey lived.

# CHAPTER TEN

My father discontinued the insurance of Sarah's Future when I went to work for Weatherbys; partly, he'd said, because the horse was getting old and lessening in value and partly, punctiliously, so that if the horse were killed, Weatherbys would not have to pay up.

He would hear no apologies when I telephoned him. He briefly said, 'Bad luck.'

When I went back to work two days after Towcester, the man who had originally interviewed me drew up a chair at my desk and said, 'We used to insure that horse of yours, of course.'

I explained why my father had let the insurance lapse.

'I didn't come to talk to you about your loss,' the Weatherbys man said, 'though you do have all my sympathy. And is your arm all right? I came to ask you whether you would be interested in transferring yourself from here into our Insurance Services department, to work there from now on.'

The insurance department, mainly one long room

walled by books, more books and files and more files, was inhabited also by two men in their twenties. One was leaving the firm. Would I like his place?

Yes, I would.

Promotion struck the Juliards twice in one week. Another internal upheaval shuffled the cards in the government, and when the hurt feelings settled my father had moved upwards to the Cabinet as Minister of Agriculture, Fisheries and Food.

I congratulated him.

'I would have preferred Secretary of State for Defence.'

'Better luck next time,' I said flippantly.

My father's resigned sigh came down the wire. 'I suppose you've never heard of Hudson Hurst?'

'No.'

'If you think I'm going up fast, he's going up faster. He beat me to Defence. He's currently the can-do-nothing-wrong flavour-of-the-year with the Prime Minister.'

'How's Polly?' I asked.

'You're incorrigible.'

'I'm sure the jellied eels and the brontosaurus-burgers will be safe in your hands.'

There were for once no agricultural crises looming, and both he and I spent the autumn of that year rooting ourselves comfortably in new realms.

Not a great deal to my surprise, I took to insurance with energy: it not only satisfied my inclination to numbers and probabilities, but I got sent out fairly often on verification trips, to see, for instance, if the polo ponies I was asked to set a premium for actually existed.

As Evan, my co-worker and boss in the insurance department, preferred office work and computers, I did more and more of the leg work, and it seemed to be a useful arrangement all round, as I knew what good stables looked like and fast developed a nose and an instinct for the preparatory arrangements for a rip-off. Preventing insurance fraud at the planning stage became a game like chess: you could see the moves ahead and could put the knights where they would zig-zag sideways for the chop.

A great advantage, it transpired, was my youth. I might not look seventeen any more, but often at twenty-two I wasn't taken seriously enough. A mistake.

In the normal everyday honestly intentioned work of the department, Evan (twenty-nine) and I handled bona fide policies on every sort of horse and need, from the chance of infertility in a stallion to barrenness in a mare.

We also arranged cover for stable yards, all buildings, personal accident, public liability, fire, theft and measles. Anything for everyone. As agents, we kept underwriters busy.

I did abominably miss my early mornings on Sarah's Future, but as dawn grew later and colder towards winter, I would have found, as I had the previous year, that only weekends gave me much scope.

As for riding in races, I was lucky in that: the Northamptonshire trainer who'd taken the chestnut phoned me one day to say an owner of his, a farmer, wanted a free jockey – in other words, an amateur – for a runner he thought had no chance.

Why run it? I thought. I happily took the ride and plugged away, and the horse finished third. Delighted, the farmer put me up again, and although I never actually won for him, I got handed around to his friends like a box of chocolates, and cantered down to a start somewhere most Saturdays.

It wasn't the same without Sarah's Future, but I wasn't ready to try to replace him, even if I could have afforded it. One day, I thought. Perhaps. When I'd paid off the instalments on a car.

I had rationalised my liking for speed. Taking intoxicating risks was normal in growing up. Warrior genes were in-bred: it was necessary to fight the birch fences and the ski slopes, perhaps, in lieu of war.

Nearing Christmas my father said we'd been invited to a reception at No. 10 Downing Street – himself, Polly and I – for the customary jolly given by the current Prime Minister to the members of his Cabinet and their families.

Polly wore a reasonable dress and my father hired a chauffeur, and the Juliards in good formation walked through the famous front door. Staff greeted my father

as one who belonged there. Polly had been through
the portals before, but I couldn't help but feel awed
as I trod through the crimson-walled entrance hall
over the black-and-white squared floor and through
into the inner hall and up the historic staircase in a
river of other guests. The brilliant yellow staircase wall,
going up round a central wall, was hung with portraits
of all the past Prime Ministers; and I knew from the
friendly way he looked at them that my father would
try his best to join them, one of these days.

Never mind that there were about twenty other
Cabinet ministers with the same dream, let alone all
the 'shadow' ministers in the Opposition: one never
got to hang on that wall without ambition.

The reception was chattering away in the large
formal area upstairs known as the pillared drawing-
room. (It had pillars. Two.)

We were greeted sweetly by Mrs Prime Minister –
her husband was *bound* to arrive shortly – and were
wafted onwards to trays of filled glasses and tiny
Christmassy mince pies surrounded with holly.

I no longer asked annoyingly for diet Coke. I drank
the Prime Ministerial champagne and liked it.

I knew almost no one, of course, even by sight.
Polly kept me in tow for a while, though her husband
had drifted away as if on wheels, greeting and laughing
and making no enemies. Polly could identify all the
Cabinet after eighteen months with my father, but

knew none of them – as Orinda would have done – as 'daaahling'.

The Prime Minister did arrive (he was *bound* to, after all) and my father saw to it that the great man shook Polly's hand with warm recognition and mine with at least a show of interest.

'You win races, don't you?' he asked, brow furrowed.

'Er . . . sometimes,' I said weakly.

He nodded. 'Your father's proud of you.'

I did, I suppose, look astounded. The Prime Minister, a gently rounded man with a steel handshake, gave me an ironic smile as he passed to the next group, and my father didn't know whether or not to call him a liar.

Dearest Polly squeezed my arm. 'George doesn't *say* he's proud of you. He just certainly sounds it.'

'That makes us equal.'

'You really are a dear boy, Benedict.'

'And I love you too,' I said.

My father's attention had purposefully wandered. 'You see that man over there?'

There were about twenty men 'over there'.

Polly said, 'Do you mean that one with flat white hair and circular eyes? The Home Secretary?'

'Yes, dearest. But I meant the one he's talking to. The one who's looking presidential and suitable for high office. He's Hudson Hurst.'

Polly shook her head. 'Surely not. Hudson Hurst has

an oiled black pony-tail and one of those silly little black moustache and beard combinations that frame a man's mouth and distract you from what he's saying.'

'Not any more.' My father smiled, but not with joy. 'Someone must have persuaded Hudson Hurst that the topiary work was a political no-no. He's cut off the hair and shaved off the beard. What you see now are the unadorned petulant lips of the Defence Secretary, God help us all.'

Five minutes later my father was putting a seemingly affectionate hand on the Defence Secretary's shoulder and saying, 'My dear Hud, have you met my wife and my son?'

Love thine enemies . . .

I hated politics.

Hud had a damp cold handclasp that I supposed he couldn't help, and if he had lately had an oiled black pony-tail and a black moustache-beard mouth-circling combination, they had very likely been dyed. His present hair colour was the dark-lightly-flecked-with-grey that a passing girl-friend had told me couldn't be faked, and he'd had a cut in a swept-back and duck-tailed style straight from the films of James Bond. Distinguished. Impressive, one had to admit. It inspired trust.

My father's own mat of natural dark close curls was cut to display to advantage the handsome outline of his skull. Expert stuff. Ah, well.

Hudson Hurst was overpoweringly pleasant to Polly.

Smile and smile, I thought, remembering Hoop-western: smile and smile and shake the hands and win the votes. He flicked me a glance, but I wasn't important.

Sweet Mrs Prime Minister appeared at my elbow and asked if I was having a good time.

'Oh, yes. Splendid, thank you.'

'You look a bit lost. Come with me.' She led me across to the far side of the big room and stopped beside a sharply dressed woman who reminded me strongly of Orinda. 'Jill, dear, this is George Juliard's son. Do look after him.'

Jill gave me a comprehensive head-to-toe and stared at Mrs Prime Minister's retreating back without enthusiasm.

'I'm really sorry,' I said, 'I don't know your name.'

'Vinicheck. Education.'

'Minister of?'

Her grim lips twitched. 'Certainly.'

She was joined by another woman in the simplest and best of current fashion: another Orinda-clone. Secretary of State for Social Security.

She said bluntly, 'Where does your mother get her clothes?'

I followed her gaze across the room and saw Polly talking unself-consciously to the man with flat white hair and circular eyes: the Home Secretary. Polly's clothes, as always, had nothing to do with popular opinion but very clearly revealed her individual character.

Jill Vinicheck (Education) kindly said, 'Your father may have a bright career in front of him, but your mother will have to change the way she dresses or she'll be clawed to bits by those bitches who write about fashion in the newspapers.'

The Secretary of State for Social Security agreed. 'Every woman in politics gets the hate treatment. Haven't you noticed?'

'Oh, not really, no.'

'Your mother's skirt is the wrong length. You don't mind me telling you? I'm only being helpful. Frankly, it would be the wrong length whatever length it was, according to the fashion bitches. But you can pass on some tips to her from us, if you like.'

'Er . . .'

'Tell her,' Jill Vinicheck said, enjoying herself, 'never to buy clothes in shops.'

Social Security nodded. 'She must have them made.'

Jill Vinicheck: 'Always wool or silk or cotton. Never polyester, or tight.'

'There's a marvellous man who could make your mother really elegant, with her long thin figure. He totally changed the way the papers write about us now. They discuss our policies, not our clothes. And he doesn't do it only for women. Look at the change in Hudson Hurst! Hud frankly looked a bit of a gangster, but now he's a statesman.'

'No time like the present,' Jill Vinicheck said with the briskness that had no doubt propelled her up the ladder. 'Our wand-waving friend is here somewhere. Why don't we introduce him to your mother straight away?'

'Er . . .' I said. 'I don't think she – '

'Oh, *there* he is,' said Social Security, stepping sideways and pouncing. 'Let me introduce you . . .'

She had her hand on his arm and he turned towards her, and I came face to face with A.L. Wyvern.

Alderney Anonymous Lover Wyvern.

No wonder Education and Social Security had reminded me of Orinda. All those years ago his ideas had dressed her, too.

I knew him instantly, but it took him several seconds to add four years to my earlier appearance. Then his face hardened to ill-will and he looked disconcerted, even though with my father in the Cabinet he might have considered that he and I might both be asked to the families' Christmas reception. Maybe he hadn't given it a thought. In any case, my presence there was to him an unwelcome surprise.

So was his to me.

Education and Social Security were looking puzzled.

'Do you two know each other?' one of them asked.

'We've met,' Wyvern said shortly.

His own appearance, too, had changed. At Hoop-western he had made a point of looking inconspicuous, of being easily forgettable. Four years later he wasn't finding it so simple to fade into the wallpaper.

I had thought him then to be less than forty, but I now saw that to have been probably an underestimate. His skin had begun to show a few wrinkles and his hair to recede, and he was now wearing glasses with narrow dark frames. There was still about him, though, the strong secretive aura of introverted clout.

At the Downing Street Christmas party there was no overt sign of the sleeping anger that had blazed across Orinda's face and nearly killed her. He was not this time saying to me aloud in fury, 'One day I'll get you,' but I could see the intent rise again in his narrowed eyes as if no interval for second thoughts had existed.

The extraordinary response I felt was not fear but excitement. The adrenalin rush in my blood was for fight, not flight. And whether or not he saw my reaction to him as vividly as I felt it, he pulled down the shutters on the malice visible behind the dark-framed lenses and excused himself with the briefest of courtesies to Education and Social Security: when he moved slowly away it was as if every step were consciously controlled.

'Well!' exclaimed Jill Vinicheck. 'I know he's never talkative, but I'm afraid he was . . . impolite.'

Not impolite, I thought.

Murderous.

*

After the reception Polly, my father and I all ate in one of the few good restaurants in London that had taken the din out of dinner. One could mostly hear oneself speak.

My father had enjoyed a buddy-buddy session with the Prime Minister and Polly said she thought the circular eyes of the Home Secretary were not after all an indication of mania.

Didn't the Home Secretary, I asked, keep prisoners *in* and chuck illegal immigrants *out*?

More or less, my father agreed.

I said, 'Did you know there was a list on a sort of easel there detailing all the jobs in government?'

My father, ministerially busy with broccoli that he didn't actually like, nodded, but Polly said she hadn't seen it.

'There are weird jobs,' I said, 'like Minister for Former Countries and Under Secretary for Buses.' Polly looked mystified but my father nodded. 'Every Prime Minister invents titles to describe what he wants done.'

'So,' I said, 'theoretically you could have a minister in charge of banning yellow plastic ducks.'

'You do talk nonsense, Benedict dear,' Polly said.

'What he means,' my father said, 'is that the quickest way to make people want something is to ban it. People always fight to get what they are told they cannot have.'

'All the same,' I said mildly, 'I think the Prime

Minister should introduce a law banning Alderney Wyvern from drinking champagne at No. 10 Downing Street.' ·

Polly and my father sat with their mouths open.

'He was there,' I said. 'Didn't you see him?'

They shook their heads.

'He kept over the far side of the room, out of your way. He looks a bit different. He's older, balder. He wears spectacles. But he is revered by the Minister of Education, the Secretary of State for Social Security and the Secretary of State for Defence, to name those I am sure of. Orinda and Dennis Nagle were kindergarten stuff. Alderney Wyvern now has his hands on levers he can pull to affect whole sections of the nation.'

· 'I don't believe it,' my father said.

'The dear ladies of Education and Social Security told me they had a friend who would do wonders for my . . . er, mother's wardrobe. He had already, they said, turned Hudson Hurst from a quasi mobster into a polished gent. What do you think they give Alderney in return?'

'No,' my father said. 'Not classified information. They couldn't!'

He was scandalised. I shook my head.

'What then?' Polly asked. 'What do they give him?'

'I'd guess,' I said, 'that they give him attention. I'd guess they listen to him and act on his advice. Orinda said years ago that he had a terrific understanding of what would happen in politics. He would predict things and tell Dennis Nagle what to do about them and Orinda said he was nearly always right. Dennis Nagle had his feet on the upward path, and if he hadn't died I'd think he'd be in the Cabinet by now with Wyvern at his shoulder.'

My father pushed his broccoli aside. A good thing his broccoli farmers weren't watching. They were agitating for a broccoli awareness week to make the British eat their greens. A law to ban excess broccoli would have had healthier results.

'If he's so clever,' Polly asked, 'why isn't he in the Cabinet himself?'

'Orinda told me the sort of power Alderney really wants is to be able to pull the levers behind the scenes. I thought it a crazy idea. I've grown up since then.'

'Power without responsibility,' my father murmured.

'Allied,' I said ruefully, 'to a frighteningly violent temper which explodes when he's crossed.'

My father hadn't actually seen Wyvern hit Orinda. He hadn't seen the speed and the force and the heartlessness; but he had seen the blood and tears and they alone had driven him to try to retaliate. Wyvern had wanted to damage my father's reputation by provoking my father to hit him. I dimly understood, but still hadn't properly worked it out, that attacking Wyvern would, in the end, destroy the attacker.

My boss Evan agreeing, I'd tied in the No. 10 Thursday evening reception with a Friday morning trip to meet a claims inspector to see if a haybarn had burned by accident or design (accident) and was due to stay again on Friday night in London with Polly and my father, before going to ride at Stratford-upon-Avon on Saturday, but en route I got a message to return to meet my father in Downing Street by two that Friday afternoon.

'I thought you might like to see more of the house,' he said cheerfully. 'You can't see a thing at those receptions.'

He had arranged for one of the household staff – called a messenger – to accompany us and show us round officially, so we went up the yellow staircase again, spending longer over the pictures, and wandered round the three large drawing-rooms leading off the ante-room at the top of the stairs: the white drawing-room, the green drawing-room and the pillared drawing-room where they'd held the reception.

The messenger was proud of the house which he said looked better and was better looked after than at any time in its rickety history. It had once been two houses back to back (rather like the burnt shops of Hoopwestern): the small Downing Street house facing one way, and a mansion to the rear of it facing the other. The interior layout over two and a half centuries had been constantly redesigned, and a modern refurbishment had bestowed overall an eighteenth-century ambience that hadn't been there before.

'The green drawing-room used to be the blue

drawing-room,' the messenger said happily. 'All the beautiful plaster work on nearly all the ceilings is relatively new. So are the classical mantels over the doorways. It all looks now like it always should have done, and never did.'

We admired it all copiously, to his satisfaction.

'Through here,' he said, marching off into one corner of the pillared drawing-room, 'is the small dining-room.' (It seated twelve in comfort.) 'Beyond that is the State Dining-Room.' (Dark panelled walls, seats for twenty-four.)

He told us about all the paintings in every room. I thought of all the past prime ministers for whom this graceful splendour had not existed, who had used this building as an office. It seemed a shame and a waste, somehow.

Back in the ante-room to the drawing-rooms our guide told us, pointing, 'Up those stairs is the Prime Minister's private apartment, and behind that locked door is his own personal room where no one goes unless he invites them. And downstairs . . .' he led the way expertly, via a lift to the ground floor ' . . . along this passage, as of course you know well, sir, is the ante-room to the Cabinet Room itself, sir, and I'll leave you to show those yourself to your son, sir, and I'll see you again just on your way out.'

My father thanked him sincerely for his trouble, and I reflected, slightly overwhelmed, that I'd never before given much of a thought to the living legacy of history my father hoped to inhabit.

The ante-room was any ante-room: just a gathering place, but with brilliant red walls.

The Cabinet Room, at the rear of the old mansion section, was long, with tall windows down one side and across one end, facing out into a peaceful-looking walled garden.

Irish terrorists had lobbed a bomb into that garden while all the Cabinet ministers were in the building. The bomb had done little damage. The grass now looked undisturbed. Peace was relative. Guy Fawkes could rise again.

Extraordinarily, Sir Thomas Knyvet, the magistrate who arrested Guy Fawkes red-handed with his barrels of gun-powder, lived in a house on the exact spot where the developer George Downing later built No. 10.

'This is where I usually sit,' my father said, walking down the room and coming to rest behind one of the two dozen chairs. 'That chair with arms, halfway along the table, that is the Prime Minister's chair. It's the only one with arms.'

The long table down the centre of the room wasn't rectangular but a much elongated oval, in order, my father explained, for the Prime Minister to be able to see the various members more easily.

'Go on, then,' I teased him. 'Take the arms.'

He was half embarrassed, half shy, but he couldn't

resist it. There was only his son to see. He crabbed sideways round the table and sat in the chair with arms; he nestled into it, resting his wrists, living the dream.

Above and behind him on the wall hung the only picture in that room, a portrait of Sir Robert Walpole, the first to be given the title Prime Minister.

'It all suits you,' I said.

He stood up self-consciously and said, as if to take the emotion out of the moment, 'The chair opposite the Prime Minister is normally where the Chancellor of the Exchequer sits.'

'And how many of you put your feet up on the table?'

He gave me a disgusted look. 'You're not fit to be taken anywhere.'

We returned to the front hall, my father looking at his watch. The messenger appeared as if on cue to see us off the premises, and I wondered vaguely if there were interior monitoring video cameras – which would be merely normally prudent – to trace the comings and goings of visitors.

While we said lengthy farewells the front door opened and in walked the Prime Minister, followed by two alert young men: bodyguards.

The Prime Minister said, 'Hello, George,' without surprise and glanced at his own watch revealingly. 'Come this way. And you ... er ...'

My father said, 'Ben.'

'Ben, yes. The racerider. You come too.'

He led the way through the front hall and past the staircase into a crowded and busy office crammed with desks, office paraphernalia and people, who all stood up at his approach.

'Now, Ben, you stay here with these good people while I talk to your father.'

He went through the office, opened a door and gestured to my father to follow. The office staff gave me a chair and a friendly welcome and told me that I was in the room where all the real work got done; the running of the Prime Minister's life as opposed to his politics.

They told me that quiet though the house might seem on a Friday afternoon, almost two hundred people worked there in the buildings in connected offices and that someone had once counted how many times the front door of No. 10 had been opened and closed in twenty-four hours, and it was more than nine hundred.

At length, in response to one of the constant telephone calls, I was invited through the office and into the next room in the wake of my father, and found myself in a large quiet tidy place that was part office, part sitting-room.

My father and the Prime Minister sat in the two fattest armchairs, looking relaxed, and I was waved to join them.

'Your father and I,' the Prime Minister said, 'have

been discussing Alderney Wyvern. I've met him once or twice, but I've seen no harm in him. I know that Jill Vinicheck and other women in the Cabinet say they owe him a great deal, and Hudson Hurst, above all, has benefited from a change of presentation. I've seen nothing sinister or unacceptable in any of this. The man is quiet, tactful, and as far as I can see, he hasn't put a foot wrong politically. Jill Vinicheck, in particular, has once or twice found his considered advice helpful, and certainly the Press have stopped making frivolous comments on her clothes, and take her as the serious politician that she is.'

'Er . . .' I said. 'Yes, sir.'

'Your father says that he and you have seen a different side of Alderney Wyvern. A violent side. He says you believe this capacity for violence still exists. I have to tell you that I find this hard to believe, and until I see something of it myself I have to give Wyvern the benefit of the doubt. I am sure you have both acted with the best of intentions in drawing my attention to the influence Wyvern may have with my ministers but, George, if you'll excuse my saying so, your son is a very young man without much experience of the world, and he may be exaggerating trouble where little exists.'

My father looked non-committal. I wondered what the Prime Minister would have thought if he himself had seen Wyvern hit Orinda. Nothing less, it seemed, was going to convince him that the outer shell of the man he'd met hid a totally different creature inside, rather like a beautiful spiky and shiny conch-shell hiding the slippery slug-like mollusc inside, a gastropod inching along on its stomach.

The Prime Minister said, 'I will take note and remember what you have both said, but at the moment I don't see any real grounds for action.'

He stood up, indicating that the meeting was over, and shook hands with my father with unabated good nature; and I remembered my father's teaching on the very first day when I'd driven with him from Brighton to Hoopwestern, that people only believe what they want to believe. It applied, it seemed, even to prime ministers.

After we'd left No. 10 I said glumly to my father, 'I did you no good.'

'He had to be told. He had to be warned. Even if it does my career no good, it was the right thing to do.'

My father's strict sense of right and wrong might destroy him yet, I thought.

# CHAPTER ELEVEN

After Christmas that year several things happened that changed a lot of lives.

First of all, on New Year's Eve, a wide tongue of freezing air licked down from the Arctic Circle and froze solid all of Canada, all of northern Europe, and all of the British Isles. Weathermen stopped agitating about global warming and with equally long faces discussed permafrost. No one seemed to mention that when Stonehenge was built in around 3000 B.C. the prevailing climate was warm, and no one remembered that, in the nineteenth century, Britain was so cold in the winters that on the Thames in London, they skated, held fairs and roasted oxen.

In the houses of that time people huddled in wing chairs with their feet on footstools to avoid draughts, and women wore a dozen layers of petticoats.

In the winter when I was twenty-two it rained ice on top of snow. People skated on their lawns and built igloos for their children. Diesel oil congealed to jelly. All racing came to a halt, except on a few specially built all-weather tracks, but even they had to be swept clear of snow. Owners cursed as their training bills kept rolling in, professional jockeys bit their fingernails and amateurs were grounded.

Claims for frost damage avalanched into Weatherbys, and in the middle of all this Evan, my boss, announced that he was leaving the firm to join a growing insurance company as managing director. I expected Weatherbys to replace him, over my head, but instead they told him to spend his three months' notice teaching me his job. I thought I was too young, even by Weatherbys' standards, but they seemed oblivious to my date of birth and merely told me that in following Evan I had a great deal to live up to.

Evan, tall, thin and with a bird-like head on a long neck, had taken over a department that had formerly acted mainly as a convenience for racing's owners and trainers, and in five years had fertilised it with imagination and invention into an agency major by any standard.

In his last three months, in addition to our ordinary busy work, he took me to meet personally all the underwriters he fixed deals with on the telephone, so that in the end I could wander round the 'boxes' at Lloyds knowing and being known in the syndicates and speaking their language.

He taught me scams. 'Beware the friendship scam,' he said.

'What's that?'

'Two friends conspire,' he told me, amused. 'One friend has a horse with something fatally wrong, a kidney ailment, say. OK? Instead of calling in a vet, Friend A sends his sick fellow to the sales. Friend B buys the sick animal at auction, insuring his purchase onwards from the fall of the hammer. Fall-of-the-hammer insurance was introduced to cover accidents like a million-pound colt stumbling on its way out of the sale ring and breaking a leg. Fall-of-the-hammer insurance comes into effect *before* a vet's inspection, see? So Friend B buys and insures a dud horse from the fall-of-the-hammer. Friend A acts all innocent ... "would never have sold such a horse if I'd known ..." Friend B humanely kills his dud and collects the insurance. Friends A and B split the proceeds.' He laughed. 'You've a nose for crooks, Ben. You'll do all right.'

During that same three months my father became the front man in an ongoing fish war, discussing at international high level who could take how many fish of such and such a species of such and such a size out of any particular area of the world's oceans. With wit and understanding, and by going to sea himself in freezing salt-crusted net-festooned seasickness factories, he learned the gripes and the legitimate arguments of men who lived close to Davy Jones and his ever-ready locker.

The Press took notice. Headlines appeared: 'JULIARD HOOKS AGREEMENT' and 'JULIARD IN JAPAN'.

People in insurance began to say, 'This Juliard person – no relation of yours, I suppose?'

'My father.'

'Seems to be doing a good job for my fish and chips.'

Fish and chips – the potatoes in agriculture – put my father on the map.

A television station sent a cameraman to sea with him: the cameraman, though sick the whole time, shot fearsomely memorable footage of my father hanging half-overboard in oilskins above the breaking waves and *grinning*.

Schoolchildren recognised pictures of 'the Fish Minister' instantly: his Cabinet colleagues didn't like it.

One of the top tabloids dug up the five-year-old stunning photograph of my father in mid-jump from the burning constituency office and printed it big in a centre-page spread extolling virility and presence of mind and the 'hands-on' policy out on the deep blue sea.

Even the Prime Minister didn't much like *that*. George Juliard as a relative newcomer with a normally quiet department in his charge was fine. George Juliard on the fast track upwards in public acclaim was a threat.

'One mustn't make a Minister a *cult*,' the Prime Minister said in a television interview: but others talked of 'leadership qualities' and 'getting things done', and Polly advised Dearest George to damp it

down a bit and not let his success antagonise his colleagues.

My father therefore paid lavish tribute to the army
of civil servants behind his fish-war solutions. 'Without
their help . . .' and so on and so on. He did a lot of
modest grovelling in Cabinet.

Towards the end of the long winter freeze the racing
papers – frantic for something to fill their pages after
weeks of near stagnation – gave a lot of space to the
news that Sir Vivian Durridge, at seventy-four, had
decided to retire from training.

The article, full of sonorous clichés like 'long and
distinguished career', detailed his winners of the Derby
(four) and other great races ('too numerous to
mention') and listed both the chief owners he'd trained
for ('royalty downwards') and the chief jockeys he'd
employed ('champions all').

Tucked away near the end came the riveting information that, according to the form book, 'Benedict
Juliard had, for two years, ridden the Durridge horses
as an amateur.'

*'Benedict Juliard, as everyone in racing knows, is the
son of George Juliard, charismatic Minister of Agriculture, Fisheries and Food. Ben Juliard won three races
on horses trained by Sir Vivian, and then left.'*

End of Vivian Durridge. *A happy retirement, Sir
Vivian.*

It seemed the freezing temperatures had put a
brake even on adultery. Usher Rudd, still active with

his telephoto-lens and his mean spirit, had hit a dry patch in his relentless pursuit of the unfortunate Opposition front-bencher, whose progress from bimbo to spanked bimbo (with the odd choir-boy for variety) had either temporarily ceased or he had gone into hiding.

Usher Rudd, sacked by the *Hoopwestern Gazette* as a sleaze generator and definitely now *non grata* under many flags, had all the same as a freelance found a market in weekly sex magazines on the edge of perversion.

The motto he everlastingly lived by: SLEAZE SELLS. *And where it doesn't exist, invent it.*

The Opposition front-bencher killed himself.

Shock reverberated through Parliament, and shivered in many a conscience.

He had been the Shadow Chancellor, the one who would have written the country's budget if his party had been in power. Rudd, for all his digging, had found no cent out of place.

Leader writers, hands raised in semi-mock horror, pointed out that though adultery (like suicide) might be a sin, it was not, under British law, a crime. Hounding a man to despair – was that a sin? Was that a crime?

Usher Rudd, smirking and unrepentant, repeated his credo again and again: if people in the public eye chose to behave disgustingly in private, the public had a right to know.

Did they? What was disgusting? Who should judge? Chat shows discussed it endlessly.

Usher Rudd was either 'the watchdog of the people', or a dangerous voyeur.

My father, walking with me in the woods round Polly's house, believed Usher Rudd would now be looking for another target.

'Until he's safely locked on to some other poor bastard,' he said. 'Just you remember how he listened to us in the Sleeping Dragon, so be very careful. He had a go at us then, and we got him sacked.'

'Yes, but,' I said, 'I'm certain you've stuck to what you wrote that day in those pacts: "That you would do nothing shameful or unlawful and would cause no scandal." Usher Rudd can't therefore touch you.'

He smiled. 'Those pacts! Yes, I've kept my bargain. But a small thing like innocence wouldn't stop that red-haired shit. Have you found your side of the promise difficult to keep?'

I shook my head. 'I've kept it.'

It was undoubtedly true, though, that the pact I'd written myself had shaped and inhibited what one might call my sex life. More accurately, my lack of sex life. I'd had two brief but pretty satisfactory interludes, one at university, one in racing, but both times I'd drawn back from any deep involvement. As for promiscuity – Usher Rudd had proved a bigger threat than AIDS.

When the sun at last shone warmingly on the house

in outer Wellingborough where I lived in a 'granny flat' built for a dear-departed granny, the ceilings first drizzled rain from burst pipes in the attic and then fell down completely. As major replastering was obviously required, I packed my stuff again in nomadic boxes and drove them to the office, storing them in the leg-room under my desk.

Evan was stripping the office of the clutter of his five-year tenure. Pin-ups, long lusted over, disappeared. He arranged a thousand files in easy order and gave me an index. He bequeathed me three straggly green plants suffering from sunlight deficiency.

'I can't manage without you,' I said.

'You can always phone me.' His bird-like head inspected his non-personalised end of the room. 'You won't, though. You'll make your own decisions. If anyone thought you couldn't, you wouldn't be taking my place.'

He left in a flurry of farewell beers, and I spent the whole summer at first tiptoeing and then striding into new responsibilities, and in six swift months shed the last remnants of boy and grew in confidence and perhaps in ability until I had settled into the person I would be for the rest of my life.

When I mentioned how I felt to Polly, she said the change was obvious and that I was lucky: some people weren't sure who they were till the far side of thirty.

My father, who'd known who he was at nineteen, had during the early summer consolidated himself in

255

the Cabinet, and by conscientious work had converted his colleagues' jealousy into acceptance, if not admiration. George Juliard had arrived as a political fact.

I asked him about Alderney Wyvern.

My father frowned. 'I haven't seen Wyvern anywhere since Christmas, but he's somewhere about – though the Prime Minister still won't hear a word against him. I'd say both Hudson Hurst and Jill Vinicheck are voting to his tune. They're both apt to say on one day that they haven't made up their minds on a point of discussion, but a couple of days later their minds and opinions are firm, and they always agree with each other... and I think those opinions are Wyvern's, though I've no way of proving it.'

'And are they good opinions?'

'Sometimes *very* good, but that's not the point.'


Parliament went into summer recess. Polly and the member for Hoopwestern spent the first part of the break in the constituency, living in Polly's house and working with Mervyn and Orinda. The four of them had settled into an energetic and harmonious team to the great benefit of all the voters, floating or not.

My father then took Polly round the world with stopovers in capital cities to learn about famine and fertilisers and freaks of climate, and came back with a fair understanding of how a billion people fed themselves on the blue planet.

I, in my little world at Wellingborough, computed numbers and risks and moved back into my granny flat when the new ceilings were dry.

Usher Rudd began stalking a bishop. Everyone except His Reverence sighed with relief.

I rode a winner in August and another in September.

Beneath this surface, although none of us knew it, little upheavals were growing and coalescing like cumulonimbus. My father had once said that they always killed Caesar, and when Parliament reconvened the knives were ready to drive into the toga.

My father, worried, told Polly and me that Hudson Hurst intended to challenge the Prime Minister for the leadership of the party. Hudson Hurst was cosying up to each Cabinet member in turn to ask for support. With his now polished manner he was smoothly saying that the party needed a tougher, younger leader who would galvanise the nation to prepare for the big build-up towards the next General Election, three years ahead.

'Alderney Wyvern,' I said, 'is writing the script.'

Polly said, horrified, 'He couldn't.'

My father said, 'It's been Wyvern's aim all along to rule by stealth.'

'Then stop him!' Polly exclaimed.

But Hudson Hurst resigned from the Cabinet and announced to the world that a majority of the party in power was dissatisfied with the decisions being made in its name and that he could do better.

'Stop him,' Polly said again. 'Oppose him.'

The three of us, sitting round the kitchen table in Polly's house, were silenced by the suddenness and size of the task. Sure, my father had aimed if possible one day to be Prime Minister, but had thought of acceding peacefully after a resignation, not of being a contender for the Ides of March.

My father, considering loyalty to be a paramount virtue, went to Downing Street and declared himself the Prime Minister's man. The Prime Minister, however, seeing that the party wanted a change, decided it was time to go just as soon as a new leader was elected. The way was now clear for my father to declare himself as a candidate for the ultimate job. The battle was now joined.

On a harmless-looking Tuesday morning in October I went into Weatherbys as usual and found that no one would look at me. Puzzled but unalarmed I made my way into my office and found that someone had kindly – or unkindly – left on my desk a copy of *SHOUT!* open at the centre pages.

*SHOUT!* was the weekly magazine that regularly printed Usher Rudd's most virulent outbursts.

There was a photograph, not of my father, but of myself, dressed as a jockey.

The headline in huge letters read, 'DOPE!'

Underneath it said: *'Jockey son of George Juliard, self-aggrandising Minister of Agriculture, Fisheries and Food, was fired for snorting cocaine, says trainer.'*

In disbelief I read the trailing paragraphs.

*'I had to get rid of him,'* says Sir Vivian Durridge. *'I could not have a glue-sniffing, drug-taking bad apple, infecting my good stable's reputation. The boy is no good. I am sorry for his father.'*

His father, the magazine pointed out, had entered the ring in the power struggle currently rending apart the Party. How could George Juliard proclaim himself a paragon of all the virtues (including family values) when he had failed as a parent himself, as his only child was a drug addict?

I felt as I had in Vivian Durridge's study on that morning five years earlier; numb from the ankles down. It hadn't been true that I had ever sniffed glue or cocaine or anything else, and it still wasn't true, but I wasn't fool enough now to think that everyone would believe me.

I picked up the magazine and, with eyes speculatively following every step I took, went to see the chairman, the working boss of Weatherbys, in his office. He sat at his desk. I stood before him.

I needn't have taken the magazine with me. He had a copy of it already on his desk.

'It's not true,' I said flatly.

'If it's not true,' the chairman asked, 'why on earth

would Vivian Durridge say it is? Vivian Durridge is one of the most highly respected men in racing.'

'If you'll give me the day off, I'll go and ask him.'

He stared up at me, considering.

'I think,' I said, 'that this is an attack on my father more than on myself. This article was written by a journalist called Usher Rudd who tried to discredit my father once before, in fact five years ago, when he first stood for Parliament in a by-election. My father complained to the editor of the newspaper and Usher Rudd was sacked. This looks like revenge. You'll see that this article says my father is involved in a power struggle in the party and, well, he is. Whoever wins the struggle will be the next Prime Minister. Usher Rudd is determined it won't be George Juliard.'

The chairman still said nothing.

'When I applied here for a job,' I said, 'Sir Vivian sent you a reference about me, and, oh' – I remembered in a blinding flash of joy – 'he sent me a letter, which I'll show you . . .' I turned towards the door. 'It is actually here in this building, in the insurance office.'

I didn't wait for him to comment but hurried back to the long insurance office and retrieved the cardboard box full of my stuff from under my desk. I simply hadn't bothered to take it back to my reconstructed room and clutter the place up again with bits and pieces. Somewhere in that box were my father's wedding photos with wives one and two.

In the frame behind the picture of himself and Polly

the letter from Vivian Durridge was as clean and fresh as the day I received it.

As a precaution, I made several copies of the letter and put them in one file among hundreds, and took the original to the chairman.

He had already, fair man that he was, retrieved from his records the short 'To whom it may concern' reference that Sir Vivian had spontaneously sent. It was lying on his desk on top of the magazine.

I handed him the letter, which he read twice.

'Sit down,' he said, pointing to the chair opposite his desk. 'Tell me what happened the day Sir Vivian Durridge accused you of taking drugs.'

'Five years ago' – it seemed a lifetime – 'like it says in the letter, my father wanted to make me face the reality that I would never be a top jockey.'

I told the chairman about the car and the chauffeur, and the hotel in Brighton facing the sea. I told him that my father had asked me to give him family background to help with his by-election campaign.

The chairman listened and at the end asked, 'Who, besides you and your father, knew that Vivian Durridge had accused you of drug taking?'

'That's just it,' I said slowly. 'I certainly told no one, and I don't think my father did either. Will you let me go and find out?'

He looked at the letter again, and at the reference and at the magazine article with its malice and lies, and made up his mind.

'I'll give you a week,' he said. 'Ten days. Whatever it takes. Before you came, Evan was second in command to an insurance specialist who is now on our board of directors. He will do your job until you come back.'

I was grateful and speechless in the face of his generosity. He merely waved me away with a gesture towards the door and, looking back as I left, I saw him slide the magazine, the letter and the reference into a drawer in his desk and lock it.

Back in my own office the telephone was ringing. My father's voice said, 'What the hell's going on? What does Vivian Durridge think he's doing? I can't get any answer from his telephone.'

The reason he couldn't get any answer from Vivian Durridge's telephone, I discovered three hours later, was because he was not in his own home.

The gravel in the drive was tidily raked. The porticoed front of the near-mansion spoke as usual of effortless wealth, but no one answered the doorbell.

Along in his stable yard there were no horses, but the head lad, who lived in an adjoining cottage, was pottering aimlessly about.

He recognised me without hesitation, though it was over five years since I'd left.

'Well, Ben,' he said, scratching his head, 'I never knew you took drugs.'

He was old and small and bandy-legged and had loved and been loved by the great beasts in his care.

The life he'd lived in their service had pathetically gone, leaving him without anchor, without purpose, with only a fading mental scrap-book of victories past.

'I never did take drugs,' I said.

'No, I wouldn't have thought so, but if Sir Vivian says . . .'

'Where is he?' I asked. 'Do you know?'

'He's ill, of course.'

'Ill?'

'He's gone in the wits, poor old man. He was walking round the yard with me one day at evening stables, same as usual, when all of a sudden he clapped a hand to his head and fell down, and I got the vet to him – '

'The *vet*?'

'There's a telephone in the tack-room and I knew the vet's number.' The head lad shook his own old head. 'So, anyway, the vet came and he brought with him the doctor and they thought Sir Vivian had had a stroke or some such. So an ambulance came for him, and his family, they didn't want us to say he was ga-ga, but he couldn't go on training, poor old man, so they just told everybody he'd retired.'

I wandered round the yard with the once supreme head lad, stopping at each empty box for him to tell me what splendid winners had once stood in each.

All the owners, he said, had been asked to take their horses away and send them somewhere else temporarily, but the weeks had passed and the old man wasn't coming back; one could see that now, and nothing was ever going to be the same again.

'But where,' I asked gently, 'is Sir Vivian at this moment?'

'In the nursing home,' he simply said.

I found the nursing home. A board outside announced 'Haven House'. Sir Vivian sat in a wheelchair, smooth of skin, empty of eye, warmed by a rug over his knees.

'He's confused. He doesn't know anyone,' the nurses warned me; but even if he didn't recognise me, he garrulously talked.

'Oh dear, yes,' he said in a high voice, not like his own gruff tones. 'Of course, I remember Benedict Juliard. He wanted to be a jockey, but I couldn't have him, you know! I couldn't have anyone who sniffed glue.'

Sir Vivian's eyes were wide and guileless. I saw that he now did believe in the fiction he had invented for my father's sake. I understood that from now on he would repeat that version of my leaving him because he truly believed it.

I asked him, 'Did you yourself ever actually see Benedict Juliard sniffing glue, or cocaine, or anything else?'

'Had it on good authority,' he said.

Five years too late I asked him, 'Whose authority?'

'Eh? What? Whose authority? Mine, of course.'

I tried again. 'Did anyone tell you that Benedict

Juliard was addicted to drugs? If anyone told you, who was it?'

The intelligence that had once inhabited the Durridge brain, the worldly experience that had illuminated for so long the racing scene, the grandeur of thought and judgment, all had been wiped out by a devastating haemorrhage in some tiny recess of that splendid personality. Sir Vivian Durridge no longer existed. I spoke to the shell, the chaos. There was no hope that he would ever again remember anything in detail, but he would be for ever open to suggestion.

I sat with him for a while, as it seemed he liked company and, even if he didn't know who I was, he didn't want me to go.

The nurses said, 'It settles him to have people near him. He was a great man once, you know. And you're the second person, outside his family, who has been to see him recently. He is so pleased to have visitors.'

'Who else came?' I asked.

'Such a nice young man. Red hair. Freckles. So friendly, just like you. A journalist, he said. He was asking Sir Vivian about someone called Benedict Juliard, who had ridden his horses for him once. Oh, my goodness – ' the nurses said, clapping hands to surprised mouths. 'Benedict Juliard ... isn't that who you said you were?'

'That's right. What would Sir Vivian like that he hasn't got?'

The nurses giggled and said, 'Chocolate biscuits and gin, but he isn't supposed to have either.'

'Give him both.'

I handed them money. Vivian Durridge sat in his wheelchair and understood nothing.


I telephoned my father.

'People believe what they want to believe,' I said. 'Hudson Hurst will want to believe your son is a drug addict and he'll go around asserting to your colleagues that that makes you unfit to be Prime Minister. Well, you remember what I wrote that day when we made the pacts . . . that I would do my best to keep you safe from attack?'

'Of course I remember.'

'It's time to do it.'

'But Ben . . . how?'

'I'm going to sue him for libel.'

'Who? Hurst? Usher Rudd? Vivian Durridge?'

'No. The Editor of *SHOUT!*'

After a pause my father said, 'You need a lawyer.'

'Lawyers are expensive. I'll see what I can do myself.'

'Ben, I don't like it.'

'Nor do I. But if I can make a charge of libel stick to *SHOUT!*, Hudson Hurst will have to shut up. And there's no time to lose, is there, as didn't you say the first round of voting for the new leader is next week?'

'It is, yes. Monday.'

'Then you go back to your fish and chips, and I'll take a sword to Usher bleeding Rudd.'

From Durridge's place in Kent I drove across much of southern England to Exeter and round to the training stables that to me seemed like home, the domain of Spencer Stallworthy.

I arrived at about six-thirty, when he was just finishing his round of evening stables.

'Hello,' he said, surprised. 'I didn't know you were coming.'

'No . . .' I watched him feed carrots to the last couple of horses and wandered over to look into the box that had held Sarah's Future for three splendid years. It was inhabited now by a long-necked grey, and I grieved for the simple happiness of days gone.

Jim was still there, closing the boxes for the night, checking that the lads had filled the hay nets and positioned the water buckets: all so familiar, so much missed.

The evening routine finished, I asked if I could talk to them both for a while, which meant a short drive to Stallworthy's house and an issue of well-remembered sherry.

They knew my father was in the Cabinet and I explained about the power struggle. I showed them the centre pages of *SHOUT!*, which shocked them back to the bottle.

Jim blinked his white eyelashes rapidly, always a sign of disturbance, and Stallworthy said, 'But it's not true, is it? You never took drugs. I'd have known it.'

'That's right,' I said gratefully, 'and that's what I'd like you to write for me. A statement that I rode from your stables for three years and won races and showed no sign of ever being interested in drugs. I want as many affidavits as I can get to say that I am not a drug addict and never was as far as you can possibly tell. I'm going to sue this magazine for libel.'

Both Stallworthy and Jim were outraged on my behalf and wrote more fiercely in my defence than I could have asked for.

Stallworthy gave me a bed for the night and a horse to ride in the early morning, and I left after breakfast and drove along the familiar country roads back to the university.

The two years since I'd graduated seemed to vanish. I parked the car in the road outside the Streatham Campus and walked up the steep path to the Laver Building, home of the mathematics department. There, after a good deal of casting about, I found my tutor – the one who had written for me the reference sought by Weatherbys – and explained to him, as to Stallworthy and Jim, what I was asking of him.

'*Drugs*? Of course, a lot of the students experiment and, as you know, we try to get rid of the hard core,

268

but you were about the last student I would have suspected of getting hooked. For a start, drugs and mathematics don't mix, and your work was particularly clear-headed. This magazine article is all rubbish.'

I beseeched him to put those views in writing, which he did with emphasis.

'Good luck,' he said when I left. 'These journalists get away with murder.'

I hiked back to my car and drove across country to my old school at Malvern.

There on its hillside campus, steep like Exeter University, though not so big, I sought out the man who had taught me mathematics. He passed the buck to my one-time house-master, who listened and sent me to the Head.

The Headmaster walked with me down the broad familiar stone-floored passage in the Main Building and up the stone stairs to his study, where I showed him a copy of *SHOUT!* and also a copy of Vivian Durridge's letter.

'Of course I'll support you,' he said without hesitation and wrote, and handed me the handwritten page to read.

It said:

Benedict Juliard attended Malvern College for five years. During the last two, while he was successfully working towards his A levels and university entrance, he spent all breaks either riding racehorses

– he won three steeplechases – or skiing, in which sport he won a European under-18 downhill race.

In addition to those skills he was a considerable marksman with a rifle: he shot in the school team that won the prestigious Ashburton Shield.

In all these activities he showed clear-headedness, natural courage and a high degree of concentration. It is ludicrous to suggest that he was ever under the influence of hallucinatory drugs.

I looked up, not knowing quite what to say.

'I admire your father,' the Headmaster said. 'I'm not saying I agree with him all the time politically, but the country could certainly do worse.'

I said, 'Thank you,' rather feebly, and he shook hands with me on a smile.

Onwards I went to Wellingborough where I briefly called in to see the chairman to tell him what I'd been doing and what I proposed to do. Then, taking a couple of the photocopies of Vivian Durridge's letter and his reference from their folder, and making copies of all the letters I'd collected, I drove to Wellingborough station and, tired of the roads, I caught the train to London.

*SHOUT!* emanated, it transpired, from a small and grubby-looking building south of the Thames. The editor wouldn't in the least want to see me but, late in the afternoon, I marched straight into his office shedding secretaries like bow-waves. He was sitting in a sweatshirt behind a cluttered desk typing on the keyboard of a computer.

He didn't recognise me, of course. When I told him who I was he invited me to leave.

'I am going to sue you for libel,' I said, opening the copy of *SHOUT!* at the centre pages. 'I see from the small print at the beginning of this magazine that the name of the editor is Rufus Crossmead. If that's who you are, I'll be suing Rufus Crossmead personally.'

He was a small pugnacious man, sticking his chest out and tucking his chin in like a pugilist. I supposed briefly that dealing with wronged and furious victims of his destructive ethos was a regular part of his life.

I remembered how, five years earlier, my father had pulverised the editor of the *Hoopwestern Gazette*, but I couldn't reproduce exactly that quiet degree of menace. I didn't have the commanding strength of his vibrant physical presence. I left Rufus Crossmead, however, in no doubt as to my intentions.

I laid down in front of him copies of the strong letters from Spencer Stallworthy, Jim, my Exeter tutor and the Headmaster of Malvern College, and I gave him finally a copy of the letter Vivian Durridge had sent.

'The only good defence in a libel suit,' I said, 'is to prove that the allegations are true. You can't use that defence, because you've printed lies. It will be easy for me to establish that Sir Vivian Durridge is now hopelessly confused after a stroke and doesn't know

what he's saying. Usher Rudd must have been aware
of it. He was trying to revenge himself for my father
having got him sacked from the *Hoopwestern Gazette*.
No reputable paper has employed him since. He suits
your style, but he's dropped even you in the shit.'

Rufus Crossmead gloomily read the various papers.

'We'll settle out of court,' he said.

It sounded to me as if he'd said it often before, and
it wasn't at all what I'd expected. I wasn't sure it was
even what I wanted.

I said slowly, 'I'll tell you what I'll settle for . . .'

'It's up to the proprietors,' Crossmead interrupted.
'They'll make you an offer.'

'They always do?' I asked.

He didn't exactly nod, but it was in the air.

'Then you tell the proprietors,' I said, 'that I'll settle
for a retraction and a statement of sincere regret from
you that your magazine's accusations were based on
incorrect information. Tell your proprietors that I'll
settle for a statement appearing very visibly in next
Tuesday's issue of *SHOUT!* In addition, you will send
immediately – by registered post – a personally signed
copy of that retraction and statement of regret to each
of the 650 or so Members of Parliament.'

272

# CHAPTER TWELVE

It wasn't enough, I thought, to defend.

I should have written in that pact, 'I will attack my father's attackers.' I should have written that I'd go to war for him if I saw the need.

At almost eighteen, I'd written from easy sentiment. At twenty-three, I saw that, if the pact meant anything at all, it pledged an allegiance that could lead to death. And if that were so, I thought, it would be feeble just to sit around waiting for the axe.

It had been Tuesday when *SHOUT*! had hit the newsagents, and late afternoon on Wednesday when I'd crashed into Rufus Crossmead's editorial office. On Friday I drove from Wellingborough to Hoopwestern, and spent the journey looking back to the end of that confrontation and the answers I'd been given.

I'd asked *SHOUT*!'s editor why he had sent Usher Rudd to see Vivian Durridge, and he'd said he hadn't, it had been Usher Rudd's own idea.

'Usher – well, his name is Bobby – said he'd been asked to dig into everything you'd ever done, and come up with some dirt. He was getting ultra frustrated because he couldn't find any sludge. He went blasting on a bit that no one could be as careful to stay out of trouble as you had been, and then there was this announcement of Sir Vivian Durridge's retirement, which said you had ridden for his stable, so Bobby went off on the off-chance, and he came back laughing. Crowing. He said he'd got you at last. So he wrote the story and I printed it.'

'And you didn't check.'

'If I had to check every word I print,' the editor had said with world-weariness, 'our sales would plummet.'

On Wednesday, early evening, I'd phoned Samson Frazer, the editor of the *Hoopwestern Gazette*.

'If you're thinking of reprinting a story about me from *SHOUT!*,' I'd said, 'don't do it. Usher Rudd wrote it. It's not true and it'll get you into court for libel.'

Gloomy silence.

Then, 'I'll re-set the front page,' he'd said.

On Thursday, with prudent speed, *SHOUT!*'s proprietors had acted to avoid the heavy expenses of a libel action and had written and posted the retractions I'd asked for to the Members of Parliament.

My father, attending the House of Commons on Friday morning, found that several registered letters had already reached their targets. In addition, he gave everyone – from the Prime Minister downwards – a copy of Vivian Durridge's letter to me, along with a brief confirmation from himself that he'd asked Durridge to think of a way of persuading me to leave. Apparently the general reaction had been relief and relaxation, though Hudson Hurst had insisted there had to be some truth in the dope story somewhere.

'Why do you think so?' my father related that he'd asked, and the only reply had been stutter and dismay.

My father said, 'I asked Hudson Hurst if he himself had sent Usher Rudd to Vivian Durridge. He denied it. He looked bewildered. I don't think he did it.'

'No, I agree.'

I now negotiated a roundabout. Fourteen more miles to Hoopwestern.

I thought about Hudson Hurst, the ugly duckling converted to swan by scissors and razor. On television he was smooth, convincing and read his speeches from an auto-cue. No inner fire. A puppet.

Alderney Wyvern pulled his strings.

How to prove it? How to stop him?

Attacking Alderney Wyvern could destroy the attacker. I sensed it strongly. History was littered with the laments of failed invasions.

I arrived at Hoopwestern at noon and parked in the car park behind the old party headquarters. Polly had told me that the charity that had owned the whole of the burned double bow-fronted building had chosen to rebuild it much as before, with new bow windows fronting onto the cobbled square and new shops matching the row at the rear. When I walked in from the car park all that seemed different were heavy fire doors and a rash of big scarlet extinguishers.

Mervyn Teck was there, and greeted me with ambivalent open arms and wary eyes.

'Benedict!' He was plumper than ever. Rotund, nowadays.

'Hi, Mervyn.'

He shook hands awkwardly, and glanced past me to where, on his desk, lay two newspapers, both *SHOUT!* and the *Hoopwestern Gazette*.

'I didn't expect you,' Mervyn said.

'No, well, I'm sorry. I expect my father telephoned to say he couldn't get down this weekend for the surgery?' Most Saturday mornings the public came to headquarters with their complaints. 'I expect you'll do fine without him.'

My father, in fact, was busy in London with secretive little lunches and private dinners, with hurried hidden meetings and promises and bargains, all the undercover manoeuvring of shifts of power. I hoped and trusted that A.L. Wyvern was fully occupied in doing the same.

A young woman sitting behind a computer stood up with unaffected welcome.

'Benedict!'

I said, 'Crystal?' tentatively.

'I'm so glad to see you,' she said edging round her desk to give me a kiss. 'It's such ages since you were here.'

276

A great change here too had taken place. She was no longer thin and anxious, but rounded and secure; and she wore a wedding ring, I saw.

They gave me coffee and local news, and I read with interest what the *Gazette* had made of *SHOUT!*. 'An unfair attack on our MP through his son. No truth in this allegation ... shocking ... libellous ... retractions and regrets are in the pipeline.'

'The by-line in *SHOUT!* says Usher Rudd.' Mervyn pointed. 'Vicious little nerd.'

'Actually,' I said as their indignation boiled on, 'I came hoping to see Orinda, but she doesn't answer her phone.'

'Oh dear,' Crystal said, 'she isn't here. She went away for the weekend. She won't be back till Monday.'

They didn't know where she'd gone.

I'd made a short list of people I aimed to see. Mervyn, helpful with addresses, knew where to find Isobel Bethune at her sister's house in Wales, and as she – telephoned – was not only at home but would be glad to see me, I drove to Cardiff that afternoon and discovered Paul Bethune's rejuvenated wife in a pretty terraced house in the suburbs.

I'd never before seen her happy. She too was a different woman: the grey lines of worry had smoothed into peaches and cream.

It was she, however, who exclaimed, 'How you've changed. You've grown older.'

'It happens.'

Her sister had gone shopping. I sat with Isobel and listened to her remembering for my benefit how Usher Rudd had uncovered her husband's bimbo affair.

'Usher Rudd just dug away and wrote it up sensationally, but it was all Paul's fault. Men are such bloody fools. He confessed to me in snivelling tears in the end that he'd boasted – *boasted*, I ask you – to some stranger that he was playing golf with that he was having an affair his wife didn't know about. Snigger, snigger. Can you believe it? And that stranger turned out to be that weird nobody that was always hanging about round the Nagles. He used to play golf with Dennis.'

'His name's Wyvern.'

'Yes, I know that now. When Dennis died, that Wyvern person wanted to make sure Orinda got elected, so he arranged to play golf with Paul, to see where Paul was weakest . . . I hated Usher Rudd, but it wasn't until after your father got elected that Paul broke down and told me what had happened.' She sighed. 'I was shattered then, but I don't care now, isn't that odd?'

'How are your sons?'

She laughed. 'They've joined the army. Best place for them. They sometimes send postcards. You're the only one that was kind to me in those days.'

I left her with a kiss on the peaches-and-cream cheek and drove tiredly back to Hoopwestern for the night, staying in Polly's house in the woods and eating potted shrimps from her freezer.

On Saturday morning I went to the police station and asked to see Detective Sergeant Joe Duke, whose mother drove a school bus.

Joe Duke appeared questioningly.

'George Juliard's son? You look older.'

Joe Duke was still a detective sergeant, but his mother no longer drove a bus. 'She's into rabbits,' he said. He took me into a bare little interview room, explaining he was the senior officer on duty and couldn't leave the station.

He thoughtfully repeated my question. 'Do I know if that fire you could have died in was arson? It's all of five years ago.'

'A bit more. But you must have files,' I said.

'I don't need files. Mostly fires in the night are from cigarettes or electrical shorts, but none of you smoked and the place had been re-wired. Is this off the record?'

'On the moon.'

A dedicated policeman in his thirties, Joe had a broad face, a Dorset accent and a realistic attitude to human failings. 'Amy used to let tramps sleep above the charity shop sometimes, but not that night, she says, though that's the official and easy theory of the cause of fire. They say a vagrant was lighting candles downstairs and knocked them over, and then ran away. Nonsense, really. But the fire did start, the fire-fighters reckoned, in the charity shop, and the back door there wasn't bolted, and both shops of the old place were lined and partitioned with dry old wood, though they've rebuilt it with brick and concrete now, and it's awash with smoke alarms. Anyway, I suppose you heard the theory that crazy Leonard Kitchens set light to the place to frighten your father off so that Orinda Nagle could be our MP?'

'I've heard. What do you think?'

'It doesn't much matter now, does it?'

'But still . . .'

'I think he did it. I questioned him, see? But we hadn't a flicker of evidence.'

'And what about the gun in the Sleeping Dragon's gutter?'

'No one knows who put it there.'

'Leonard Kitchens?'

'He swears he didn't. And he's heavy and slow. It needed someone pretty agile to put that gun up high.'

'Did you ever find out where the rifle came from?'

'No, we didn't,' he said. 'They're so common. They've been used in the Olympics for donkey's years. They're licensed and locked away and accounted for these days, but in the past . . . and theft . . .' He shrugged. 'It isn't as if it had killed anyone.'

I said, 'What's the penalty for attempted murder?'

'Do you mean a deliberate attempt that didn't come off?'

'Mm.'

'Same as murder.'

'A 10-lb penalty?'

'Ten years,' he said.

From the police station I drove out to the ring road and stopped in the forecourt of Basil Rudd's car-repair outfit. I walked up the stairs into his glass-walled office that gave him a comprehensive view over his wide workshop below, only half busy on Saturday morning.

'Sorry,' he said, without looking up. 'We close at noon on Saturdays. Can't do anything for you till Monday.'

He was still disconcertingly like his cousin; red hair and freckles and a combative manner.

'I don't want my car fixed,' I said. 'I want to find Usher Rudd.'

It was as though I had jabbed him with a needle. He looked up, and said, 'Who are you? Why do you want him?'

I told him who and why. I asked him if he remembered the Range Rover's questionable sump-plug, but his recollection was hazy. He was quite sharply aware, though, of the political damage that could be done to a father by a son's disgrace. He had a copy of *SHOUT!* on his desk, inevitably open at the centre pages.

'That's me,' I said, pointing at the photograph of the jockey. 'Your cousin is lying. The *Gazette* sacked him for lying once before, and I'm doing my best to get him finally discredited – struck off, or whatever it's called in newspaper-speak – for what is called dishonourable conduct. So where is he?'

Basil Rudd looked helpless. 'How should I know?'

'Find out,' I said forcefully. 'You're a Rudd. Someone in the Rudd clan must know where to find its most notorious son.'

'He's brought us nothing but trouble . . .'

'Find him,' I said, 'and your troubles may end.'

He stretched out a hand to the telephone, saying, 'It may take ages. And it'll cost you.'

'I'll pay your phone bills,' I said. 'When you find him, leave a message on the answer-phone at my father's headquarters. Here's the number.' I gave him a card. 'Don't waste time. It's urgent.'

I went next to the Sleeping Dragon to see the manager. He had been newly installed there at the time of the by-election, but perhaps because of that he had a satisfactorily clear recollection of the night someone had fired a gun into the cobbled square. He was much honoured, he said, to be on first-name terms with my father.

'There were so many people coming and going on that night, and I was only beginning to know who was who. Someone left a set of golf clubs in my office and said they were Dennis Nagle's but, of course, the poor man was dead and I didn't know what to do with them, but I offered them to Mrs Nagle and she said she thought they belonged to her husband's friend, Mr

Wyvern, so I gave them to him.' He frowned. 'It was so long ago. I'm afraid I'm not being much help.'

I left him and walked upstairs and from the little lounge over the main lobby looked down again onto the cobbled square where, on that first night, my father and I had by good luck not been shot.

Golf clubs . . .

Mervyn Teck, at the end of a busy morning surgery, told me where to find Leonard and Mrs Kitchens, and on Saturday afternoon, without enthusiasm, I found their substantial semi-detached house on the outskirts of the town.

The house, its lack of imagination, and the disciplined front garden were all somehow typical of a heavy worthiness: no manic sign of an arsonist.

Mrs Kitchens opened the front door at my ring and, after a moment's hesitation for recognition, said, 'My Leonard isn't in, I'm afraid.'

She took me into a front sitting-room where the air smelled as if it had been undisturbed for weeks, and talked with bitterness and freedom about 'her Leonard's' infatuation for Orinda.

'My Leonard would have done *anything* for that woman. He still would.'

'Er . . .' I said, 'looking back to that fire at the party headquarters – '

'Leonard said,' Mrs Kitchens interrupted, 'that he didn't do it.'

'But *you* think – ?'

283

'The silly old fool did it,' she said. 'I know he did. But I'm not going to say it to anyone except you. It was that Wyvern who put him up to it, you know. And it was all pointless, as your father is much better for the country than Orinda would have been. Everyone knows that now.'

'People say,' I said gently, 'that Leonard shot a rifle at my father and then put the gun up into the gutter of the Sleeping Dragon.'

Clumsy, large, unhappy Mrs Kitchens wouldn't hear of it. 'My Leonard doesn't know one end of a gun from the other!'

'And does your Leonard change the oil in his own car?'

She looked utterly bewildered. 'He can make plants grow, but he's hopeless at anything else.'

I left poor Mrs Kitchens to her unsatisfactory marriage, and slept again in Polly's house.

For most of Sunday I sat alone in the party's headquarters, wishing and waiting for Basil Rudd to dislike his cousin enough to help me, but it wasn't until nearly six in the evening that the telephone rang.

I picked up the receiver. A voice that was not Basil Rudd's said, 'Is it you that wants to know where to find Bobby Usher Rudd?'

'Yes, it is,' I said. 'Who are you?'

'It doesn't matter a damn who I am. Because of his snooping, my wife left me and I lost my kids. If you want to fix that bastard Usher Rudd, at this very moment he is in the offices of the *Hoopwestern Gazette*.'

The informant at the other end disconnected abruptly.

Usher Rudd was on my doorstep.

I'd expected a longer chase, but the *Hoopwestern Gazette's* offices and printing presses were simply down the road. I locked the party headquarters, jumped in my car, and sped through the Sunday traffic with the devil on my tail, anxious not to lose Usher Rudd now that I'd found him.

He was still at the *Gazette*, though, in mid-furious row with Samson Frazer. When I walked into the editor's office it silenced them both with their hot words half spoken.

They both knew who I was.

Bobby Usher Rudd looked literally struck dumb. Samson Frazer's expression mingled pleasure, apprehension and relief.

He said, 'Bobby swears the dope story's true.'

'Bobby would swear his mother's a chimpanzee.'

Usher Rudd's quivering finger pointed at a copy of Thursday's *Gazette* that lay on Samson's desk, and he found his voice, hoarse with rage.

'You know what you've done?' He was asking me, not Samson Frazer. 'You've got me sacked from *SHOUT!*. You frightened Rufus Crossmead and the proprietors so badly that they won't risk my stuff any more, and I've increased their bloody sales for them

285

over the years . . . it's bloody *unfair*. So now they say they're the laughing stock of the whole industry, printing a false story about someone whose father might be the next Prime Minister. They say the story has backfired. They said it will *help* George Juliard, not finish him. And how was I to know? It's effing unfair.'

I said bitterly. 'You could have seen Vivian Durridge didn't know what he was saying.'

'People who don't know what they're saying are the ones you listen to.'

That confident statement, spoken in rage, popped a light bulb in my understanding of Usher Rudd's success.

I said, 'That day in Quindle, when I first met you, you were already trying to dig up scandal about my father.'

'Natch.'

'He tries to dig up dirt about anyone,' Samson put in.

I shook my head. 'Who,' I asked Usher Rudd, 'told you to attack my father?'

'I don't need to be told.'

Though I wasn't exactly shouting, my voice was loud and my accusation plain. 'As you've known all about cars for the whole of your life, did you stuff up my father's Range Rover's sump-plug drain with a candle?'

'*What?*'

286

'Did you? Who suggested you do it?'

'I'm not answering your bloody questions.'

The telephone rang on Samson Frazer's desk.

He picked up the receiver, listened briefly, said, 'OK,' and disconnected.

Usher Rudd, not a newspaperman for nothing, said suspiciously, 'Did you give them the OK to roll the presses?'

'Yes.'

Usher Rudd's rage increased to the point where his whole body shook. He shouted, 'You're printing without the change. I insist . . . I'll kill you . . . *stop the presses* . . . if you don't print what I told you to, I'll kill you.'

Samson Frazer didn't believe him, and nor, for all Rudd's passion, did I. Kill was a word used easily, but seldom meant.

'What change?' I demanded.

Samson's voice was high beyond normal. 'He wants me to print that you faked Sir Vivian's letter and forged his signature and that the story about sniffing glue is a hundred per cent sterling, a hundred per cent kosher, and you'll do *anything* . . . *anything* to deny it.'

He picked a typewritten page off his desk and waved it.

'It's Sunday, anyway,' he said. 'There's no one here but me and the print technicians. Tomorrow's paper is locked onto the presses, ready to roll.'

'You can do the changes yourself.' Usher Rudd fairly danced with fury.

'I'm not going to,' Samson said.

'Then don't print the paper.'

'Don't be ridiculous.'

Samson put the typewritten page into my hands.

I glanced down to read it and, as if all he'd been waiting for had been a flicker of inattention on my part, Bobby Rudd did one of his quickest getaways and was out through a door in a flash – not the door to the outside world, but the swinging door into the passage leading deeper into the building; the passage, it transpired, down to the presses.

'Stop him!' yelled Samson, aghast.

'It's only paper,' I said, though making for the door.

'No . . . sabotage . . . he can destroy . . . catch him.'

His agitation convinced me. I sprinted after Usher Rudd and ran down a passage with small empty individual offices to both sides and out through another door at the end and across an expanse inhabited only by huge white rolls of paper – newsprint, the raw material of newspapers – and through a small print-room beyond that with two or three men tending clattering machines turning out coloured pages, and finally through a last swinging door into the long high room containing the heart and muscle of the *Hoopwestern Gazette*, the monster printing presses that every day turned out twenty thousand twenty-four-page community enlightenments to most of Dorset.

The presses were humming quietly when I reached them. There were eight in a row with a tower in the centre. From each end of four, the presses put first a banner in colour – red, green, blue – on the sheets that would be the front and back pages, and then came the closely edited black and white pages set onto rollers in an age-old, but still perfectly functional, offset litho process.

I learned afterwards how the machines technically worked. On that fraught Sunday I saw only wide white paper looping from press to press and in and out of inked rollers as it collected the news page by page on its journey to the central tower, from where it went up in single sheets and came down folded into a publishable newspaper, cut and counted into bundles of fifty.

There were two men tending the presses, adjusting the ink flow and slowly increasing the speed of the paper over the rollers and through the mechanism. Warning bells were ringing. Noise was building.

When I ran into the long thundering area, Usher Rudd was shouting at one of the men to turn everything off. The technician blinked at him and paid no attention.

His colleague activated another alarm bell and switched the presses to a full floor-trembling roar. Monday's edition of the *Hoopwestern Gazette*, twenty thousand copies of it, flowed from press to press and up the tower and down at a speed that reduced each separate page to a blur.

Samson Frazer, catching up with me as I watched with awe, shouted in my ear, 'Don't go near the presses while they're running. If you get your little finger caught in any of the rollers it would pull your whole arm in – it would wrench your arm right out of your body. We can't stop the presses fast enough to save an arm. Do you understand?'

'Yes,' I yelled.

Usher Rudd was screaming at the technician.

Samson Frazer's warning was essential.

There was a space of three or four feet between each machine where one was wholly exposed to the revolving accelerating rollers. When the presses were at rest, the printers – the technicians – walked with safety into these spaces to fit the master sheets onto the cylinders and to check the state of the inking rollers. When the presses, switched on, ran even at minimum inch-by-inch speed, the danger began. An arm could be torn out, not in one jerking terror but worse, in inch by excruciating inevitable inch.

I asked later why no guarding gates kept people away. The machines were old, built before safety standards sky-rocketed, Samson Frazer said, but they did indeed now have gates. It was illegal in Britain to operate without them. These gates pulled across like trellises and locked into place, but they were fiddly, and an extra job. People who worked round these presses knew and respected the danger, and sometimes didn't bother with the gates. He didn't approve, but he'd had no tragedies. There were computerised programs and printers to be had, but the old technology worked perfectly, as it had for a hundred years, and he couldn't afford to scrap the old and to install the new, which often went wrong anyway, and one couldn't guard against maniacs like Usher Rudd. No one had to insure against lunatics.

I could have sold him a policy about that: but on that particular Sunday evening, what we needed for Usher Rudd was a straitjacket, not a premium.

He was still swearing at the technician who looked over the Rudd shoulder and saw Samson Frazer's arrival as deliverance.

Stopping the presses, I learned later, meant hitting one particular button on one of the control panels to be found on the end of each press that regulated the overall speed of the printing. The buttons weren't things the size of door-bells, but scarlet three-inch-diameter flat knobs on springs. Neither the technician nor Samson Frazer pushed the overall stop control, and neither Rudd himself nor I knew which of several scarlet buttons ruled the roost. The presses went on roaring and Bobby Usher Rudd completely lost control.

He knew the terrible danger of the presses. He'd worked for the *Hoopwestern Gazette*. He'd been in and out of newspapers all his adult life.

He grabbed the technician by his overalls and swung him towards unimaginable agony.

The technician, half in and half out of one of the lethal spaces, screamed.

Samson Frazer screamed at Usher Rudd.

The second technician sprinted for refuge in the smaller print-room next door.

I, from instinct, leapt at Usher Rudd and yanked him backwards. He too started screaming. Still clutched by the overalls, the technician stumbled out of the fearsome gap, ingrained awareness keeping his hands close to his body: better to fall on the floor than try to keep his balance by touching the death-dealing machinery.

Usher Rudd let go of the overalls and re-routed his uncontrolled frenzy onto me. He was no longer primarily trying to stop the print-run, but to avenge himself for the cataclysms he had brought on himself.

The glare in his eyes was madness. I saw the intention there of pushing me instead of the technician onto the rollers and had we been alone he might have managed it. But Samson Frazer jumped to grab him while the technician, saved from mutilation, gave a horror-struck final shout as he made his terrified stumbling run for the door, and by unplanned chance barged into Usher Rudd on the way, unbalancing him.

Rudd threw Samson off him like an irrelevance, but it gave me time to put space between me and the nearest press, and although Rudd grasped and lurched in an effort to get me back again into the danger zone, I was fighting more or less for my life and it was amazing how much strength ultimate fear generated.

Samson Frazer, to his supreme credit – and maybe calculating that any death on his premises would ruin him – helped me struggle with the demented kicking and punching and clutching red-haired tornado: and it was Samson who delivered a blow to Rudd's head with a bunched fist that half-dazed his target and knocked him to the ground face downwards. I sat on his squirming back while Samson found some of the wide brown sticky tape used for parcels and with my active help, circled one of Usher Rudd's wrists, and then the other, and fastened his arms behind his back in makeshift handcuffs. Samson tethered the wildly kicking legs in the same way and we rolled Rudd onto his back and stood over him panting.

Then with each of us looping an arm under Rudd's armpits we dragged him into the comparative quiet of the secondary print-room next door and propped him in a chair.

All of the technicians were in that room, wide-eyed and upset. Samson told them unemotionally to go back to work, there was a paper to be got out; and slowly, hesitantly, they obeyed him.

In his chair, Rudd began shouting, 'It's all his fault. Wyvern did it. Wyvern's the one you want, not me.'

'I don't believe it,' I contradicted, though I did.

Usher Rudd tried to convince me. 'Wyvern wanted your father out of the way. He wanted Orinda in Parliament. He wanted to get her promoted, like Dennis. He would have done anything to stop your father being elected.'

'Like sabotaging his car?'

'I didn't want to do it. I would write what he wanted. I trailed Paul Bethune for weeks to find his bimbo, to please Wyvern, so that people would vote for Orinda, but messing up a Range Rover, cutting the brake-lines like Wyvern wanted, that was too much. I didn't do it.'

'Yes, you did,' I told him conclusively.

'No, I didn't.'

'What did you do then?'

'I didn't do anything.'

'Your cousin, Basil, knows what you did.'

Usher Rudd cursed Basil with words I'd hardly ever heard even on a racecourse, and somewhere in the tirade came a description of how he'd wriggled under the Range Rover in the black tracksuit he'd worn to the meeting after the dinner in the Sleeping Dragon. The brilliant performance my father had given that evening had convinced Wyvern that he wouldn't get rid of my father without at least injuring him badly. Wyvern had been furious with Usher Rudd that his sabotage had been so useless.

Usher Rudd's rage slowly ran down and he began

first to whine and then deny that he had ever said what Samson and I had both just heard.

Samson phoned the police. Joe Duke was not on duty, but Samson knew all the force individually and put down the receiver, reporting a promise of immediate action.

Usher Rudd shouted, 'I want a lawyer.'

He got his lawyer, passed a night in the cells and on Monday morning collected a slap on the wrist from busy magistrates (for causing a disturbance indoors at the *Hoopwestern Gazette*) who had no real conception of the speed and noise and danger involved.

No actual damage had been done. The newspaper had appeared as usual. Usher Rudd, meek and respectful, walked out free.


I talked to Joe Duke.

I said, 'It was Usher Rudd who stuffed wax in the sump-drain of the Range Rover, and Leonard Kitchens who started the fire. Both of them were put up to it by Alderney Wyvern.'

Joe Duke slowly nodded. 'But they didn't stop your father, did they? And as for you' – he gave a half smile – 'I'll never forget you that night of the fire, sitting there half-naked on the cobbles with that red blanket over your shoulders and no sign of pain, though you'd burns on your hands and feet and you'd smashed down into the square. Don't you ever feel pain?'

'Of course, but there was so much happening – '

'And you're used to falling off horses?'

'Horses fall . . . Anyway, I suppose so. I've hit the ground quite a lot.'

The smile broadened. 'Then why do it?'

'Speed,' I told him. 'Nothing like it.' I paused. 'If you want something badly enough, you can risk your life for it and consider it normal behaviour.'

He pondered. 'If you want Orinda Nagle to be an MP enough, you'll risk . . .'

'Almost anything. I think it was Wyvern who shot at my father.'

'I'm not saying you're wrong. He could have carried a rifle in his golf bag, with one of those covers on it that they use for clubs.'

'Yes.'

'And he'd had to have had murder in his mind to do that.'

'Uh-huh. And when he heard and saw my father's success at that meeting, he judged he needed to get rid of him at once.'

'He was crazy.'

'He still is.'

Joe Duke knew my father was engaged in a power struggle but was dismayed when I explained about Hudson Hurst.

'You don't think,' Joe said, horrified, 'that Wyvern would try *again* to kill your father?'

'Wyvern's stakes are higher now, and my father still stands in his way. If my father is chosen to lead his party, I'm sure he'll be in appalling danger. It frightens me badly, to be honest.'

Joe said thoughtfully, 'You know what . . .?'

'What?'

'Just in case we're doing Wyvern a great injustice, thinking it was he that shot at you . . . I mean, so far we've only got theory to go on, really. Why don't you and I do an unofficial walk-through . . . a reconstruction? I'll use a walking stick for a gun. I'll transport it in a golf bag. And I'll carry it up into the little lounge, and aim it at you while you're crossing the square, like you did that night, and I'll see how difficult it will be to put the walking stick up in the gutter. What do you think?'

'Can't do any harm.'

'We might come across something we haven't thought of. It often works that way with reconstructions.'

'OK.'

'We'll have to do it at night,' Joe said.

'It was after midnight.'

'After midnight, then. I'll be off duty. It will just be the two of us.'

I agreed that we would meet that evening in the

Sleeping Dragon, and that Joe would tell the manager what we were doing.

I went to see Orinda who had finally returned from her weekend and answered the telephone.

Five years had been kind to her. She looked as striking as ever, the green eyes black-lashed, the greasepaint make-up smooth and blended. She was less brittle, less stressed, more fulfilled.

She called me darling with only two or three 'a's. 'Daaarling.'

'Orinda.' I hugged her.

'How you've grown,' she exclaimed. 'I mean, not just upwards, but older.'

She had made us a salad lunch with diet Coke and coffee after.

She knew about the power struggle going on in the party and mentioned that every time there was this sort of leadership contest, the politicians changed the rules.

'They invent whatever procedure they think will give a result that everyone thinks is fair, even if not everyone is happy with the eventual winner. It's now all up to the party's MPs.'

I had forgotten how much Orinda knew about government.

'I suppose Dennis told you how it all works.'

'No, it was Alderney Wyvern.' She frowned. 'I never want to see that man again.'

I said neutrally, 'Did you know that Wyvern now controls Hudson Hurst, like he used to control you and Dennis? Do you realise that if Hurst wins the ballot and becomes Prime Minister, it will be Alderney Wyvern who effectively governs this country?'

Orinda looked horrified but shook her head. 'Your father's more popular in the country.'

'Don't forget *Schadenfreude*.'

Orinda laughed. 'You mean the malicious enjoyment of someone else's misfortune?'

I nodded. 'Half the Cabinet would like to see my father come a cropper after his spectacular way of fighting the fish war.'

'It will be marvellous for this constituency if he wins.' She smiled widely. 'I never thought I would say that, but it's true.'

I told Orinda about the reconstruction that Joe Duke and I had planned.

I asked, 'Do you remember much about that evening?'

'Of course I do. I was *furious* at not being chosen as candidate.'

'How much were you with Alderney Wyvern after the political meeting?'

'I wasn't. I was angry and miserable and drove straight home.'

'Do you know if Alderney Wyvern had his golf clubs with him at the meeting in the hall?'

'What an extraordinary question! He always used to have them in the back of the car.'

Orinda might have hated my father that night, but not enough to do him harm. She had no wickedness in her nature.

I spent a comfortable hour or two longer with her and then drove to Polly's house to wait for my father to telephone from London with the result of the ballot.

He gave me news from his car. 'It was all indecisive,' he reported. 'It was basically a three-way split. All that's certain is that we have to vote again tomorrow.'

'Do explain,' I begged him.

He described a day that had been full of doubt and manoeuvring, but it seemed that what had finally happened was that neither my father nor Hudson Hurst had received enough votes in the first round to secure victory outright. Jill Vinicheck (Education), the third candidate, had received fewest votes and had been eliminated. The next ballot would be a straight fight between Hurst and Juliard, and no one was predicting who would win.

My father sounded tired. He said he and Polly were on their way to join me at the house for a quiet night. He had done all he could behind the scenes to sway the vote his way: now it was up to his colleagues to choose whom they wanted.

I explained about Joe Duke and the reconstruction and, after a brief discussion with Polly by his side, he said they would meet me in the Sleeping Dragon and we would eat together.

Any thought that we might have had about a peaceful evening disappeared between the soup and the apple pie.

While neither Joe Duke nor I had made any particular secret about our plan for the reconstruction, we had not expected the manager of the hotel to broadcast the scenario. He appeared to have told the whole town. The hotel was buzzing, as it had on the night of the dinner, and people came up to my father in droves to shake his hand and wish him well.

Samson Frazer came from the *Hoopwestern Gazette* with his cameraman and gave my horrified father extra details of how Usher Rudd had spent his Sunday.

Usher Rudd himself came – free, unrepentant, bitter-eyed and steaming with malice, glaring at my father and talking into a mobile phone.

When Joe Duke came, he looked at first aghast at the bustle and movement, but my father resignedly told him, as he joined us for coffee, that the hotel had been packed on the night we were reproducing, and the present crowd would make everything seem more real.

Moreover, my father said he would walk with me across the square as he had done before, and although I didn't like the idea, Joe Duke nodded enthusiastically.

Why wait for midnight? people asked. Everyone was ready *now*, and now was eleven-thirty.

Because Joe explained, half of the lights in the square switched off automatically at twelve o'clock, and if the reconstruction was to mean anything, the conditions had to be as near as possible what they had been before.

Joe Duke brought in a bag of golf clubs from his car and showed everyone the long walking stick with the tartan cover that disguised it.

The manager frowned in puzzlement, and I wanted to ask him if he had remembered something significant, but Joe and the crowd swept all before them, anxious to get started. I would ask him later, I thought.

Midnight came. Half the lights in the square faded to darkness. All that were left glowing threw shadows on the cobbles. Over the far side of the square a few lights showed dimly in the party headquarters and the charity shop.

When my father and I walked out into the square, the only lights blazing brightly were those of the Sleeping Dragon at our back.

It was planned that my father and I would walk halfway across the square and wait while Joe aimed his walking stick out of the window and BANG, and then reached or climbed up to put the stick in the gutter. People would hurry from the Sleeping Dragon towards my father, as they had done before.

It all felt alarmingly real to me, but everyone was smiling.

Joe, surrounded by encouraging crowds, turned to go towards the staircase while I and my father walked out across the cobbles. I stopped after a while to look back at the hotel but my father walked on, calling over his shoulder, 'Come on, Ben, we haven't reached the spot yet.'

I looked up at the hotel. Joe's walking stick was pointing out of one of the windows, half hidden by the seemingly perpetual geraniums.

Three thoughts jammed into my consciousness simultaneously.

First, Joe hadn't had time to get up the stairs and walk along to the lounge and hide behind the curtain.

Second, the stick was pointing out of the wrong window.

Third, there was a gleam on the stick and a hole, a black round hole, in the end of it.

*It wasn't a stick. It was a gun.*

My father was ten yards ahead of me across the square. I sprinted as I had for Orinda and for the technician in the presses, without pause, without thought, with raw intuition, and I jumped in a flying rugger tackle to knock my father down.

The bang was real enough. The bullet was real enough, but the happy crowd which poured out of the hotel still thought it was a game.

The bullet hit me while I was still in the air, jumping

and colliding with my father, and it would have gone into his back if I hadn't been there.

It entered high on my right thigh and travelled down inside my leg to the knee, the kinetic energy bursting apart all muscles and soft tissue in its path.

The force of it whirled me round so that when I crashed to the cobbles I was facing the Sleeping Dragon; half lying, propped on my left elbow, shuddering throughout all my body with my brain disoriented and protesting with universal outrage.

There was enough pain everywhere to satisfy Joe Duke. My eyes watered with it and my skin sweated. I'd been injured now and then in racing falls, and I'd felt shivery and sore the night of the fire, but nothing had even begun to warn me that there was an unimaginable dimension far beyond cuts and breaks.

It didn't really help that I knew the physics of high-velocity bullets and the damage they could do. I'd fired hundreds of them at targets. I shot in a world where all one hit was paper. I didn't know that I'd ever be able to fire a rifle again.

My father was on his knees beside me, his face screwed up with anxiety. My right trouser leg was dark and saturated with blood. The crowd from the Sleeping Dragon were running now, with Polly at their head. I could hear her agonised voice, 'George ... oh, George.'

It was all right, I thought. It wasn't George.

My father held my hand.

Besides the encompassing pain I felt remarkably ill. I wanted to lie down, to stand up, to move somehow, and I couldn't. I wanted someone to come along and shoot me again, but in the head; to give me oblivion, like they did with horses.

Time passed. Nothing got better.

Although ordinary traffic was banned from the square, police cars, ambulances and fire engines weren't. Two police cars and one ambulance arrived, roof lights flashing. People from the police cars went into the hotel. Someone from the ambulance came and, with large scissors, cut open my right trouser leg.

I went on wishing for oblivion.

My leg, exposed to the dim light in the square, looked literally a bloody mess. I gathered that the bullet hadn't severed the femoral artery, because if it had I would have already bled to death. There was, however, somewhere in my mangled muscles, a hard white finger-shaped length of what I understood with shock to be bone. Femur. Uncovered, but also unbroken.

The man from the ambulance hid the devastation with a large padded dressing and went back to the ambulance. He'd gone to summon a doctor, my father said: there were all sorts of rules and regulations about gun-shot wounds.

It didn't cross my mind that I might lose my leg and, in fact, I didn't. What I lost, once everything was stitched and repaired, was the strength to ride half-ton steeplechasers over the black birch. What I lost was speed.

People came out of the hotel and got into the police cars. One of them was Alderney Wyvern, in handcuffs.

When the cars had driven away, Joe Duke walked across the square and sat on his heels to talk to my father and me.

He said to me, 'Can you take in what I'm saying?'

'Yes.'

Joe said, 'When I went up the stairs to position the walking stick, the hotel manager hurried up after me and caught me before I reached the little lounge. He said he didn't know if it was just a coincidence, but not long before, in fact at about eleven o'clock, a man had booked in as a guest at the hotel and he too was carrying a bag of golf clubs. And what was slightly odd about him, the manager said, was that he was wearing *gloves*.'

Joe stood up to stretch his legs for a moment, and then sat back on his heels. 'Are you taking in what I'm saying?' he said.

'Yes,' I groggily replied.

'We heard that cracking bang of the gun going off and the manager used his pass-key to open a bedroom door, and inside we found Alderney Wyvern coming towards the door carrying his bag of golf clubs, but when the manager snatched it from him and emptied

306

them out onto the floor, all that was in it was golf clubs.'

Joe went on, 'He hadn't time to put the rifle up in the gutter, but it was there with him all right. He'd put the gun-butt in the hanging basket with the geraniums, with the barrel pointing skywards, among the chains hanging the basket. I then used the room telephone to bring my colleagues from the police station. While we waited for them to arrive I asked, out of curiosity, how Wyvern had known about the reconstruction. How had he known that he would have a chance to shoot George Juliard?'

Joe smiled lopsidedly. 'Wyvern said Usher Rudd had phoned him and told him.' He stood up again.

My father said, 'How did Wyvern think he would get away with it?'

Joe shrugged. 'He did last time. In the commotion, he simply walked away. If it hadn't been for the hotel manager, he quite likely would have done it again. But it was odd. He seemed just plain tired. There was no fight left in him. He could see he hadn't managed to finish either of you, and he simply gave up. We had no trouble arresting him.'

'And what are you charging him with?' my father asked.

'Attempted murder,' Joe said.

I faintly smiled. 'A 10-lb penalty.'

'Ten years,' Joe said.

*

The next Prime Minister held my hand.

I gripped his tight, as if he would give me comfort and security when I needed them badly.

I gripped his hand as if I'd been a little boy.